Negation and Utopia

Cover vignette of Mohonk mountain silhouette courtesy of the Publications Office, State University College, New Paltz, New York.

Studies in Modern German Literature

Peter D. G. Brown
General Editor

Vol. 56

PETER LANG
New York • San Francisco • Bern • Baltimore
Frankfurt am Main • Berlin • Wien • Paris

Calvin N. Jones

Negation and Utopia

The German Volksstück from Raimund to Kroetz

PETER LANG
New York • San Francisco • Bern • Baltimore
Frankfurt am Main • Berlin • Wien • Paris

Library of Congress Cataloging-in-Publication Data

Jones, Calvin N.
  Negation and utopia : the German Volksstück from Raimund to
Kroetz / Calvin N. Jones.
    p. cm.—(Studies in modern German literature ; Vol. 56)
    Includes bibliographical references and index.
    1. Folk drama, German—History and criticism.   2. Folk drama, Austrian
—History and criticism.   3. Negation (Logic) in literature.   4. Utopias in
literature.   I. Title.   II. Series.
PT701. J66   1993   832.009—dc20   93-20110
  ISBN 0-8204-2075-1
  ISSN 0888-3904

Die Deutsche Bibliothek-CIP-Einheitsaufnahme

Jones, Calvin N.:
Negation and utopia : The German Volksstück from Raimund to
Kroetz / Calvin N. Jones.—New York; Berlin; Bern; Frankfurt/M.;
Paris; Wien: Lang, 1993
    (Studies in modern German literature ; Vol. 56)
    ISBN 0-8204-2075-1
NE: GT

The paper in this book meets the guidelines for permanence and
durability of the Committee on Production Guidelines for
Book Longevity of the Council on Library Resources.

© Peter Lang Publishing, Inc., New York 1993

Printed in the United States of America.

für Christa

Acknowledgements

This book owes its existence to a large number of people and institutions to whom I would like to acknowledge my appreciation. In order to conduct the initial research for this project I received a Faculty Service and Development Award and a Research Committee Grant from the University of South Alabama. I am also grateful to my Department, to the College of Arts and Sciences, and to the Office of Research for publication assistance. Much of the work was done at the Universitätsbibliothek and the library of the Deutsches Seminar in Freiburg im Breisgau, and I also used resources of the University of South Alabama library, whose reference and interlibrary loan departments were most helpful. An article containing arguments from my Introduction and chapters on Raimund and Horváth was published in 1991 in *The German Quarterly*. To my chairman, Bernard Quinn, I owe a special debt of gratitude for his consistent encouragement and facilitation of research. Other colleagues in the Department of Foreign Languages and Literatures, including Heide Lomangino, Caryl Lloyd, Bonnie Marshall, and Joe Mozur read portions of the manuscript for a meeting of our departmental discussion group, where they offered helpful suggestions. Similarly, my brother Miller Jones provided useful comments on Ernst Bloch. I am especially grateful to Lawrence Schehr for his thorough reading of the entire manuscript and his valuable and insightful advice. Rick Daughenbaugh saved me countless hours with his computer assistance. The department secretary, Pat Dyess, was always helpful with correspondence and the many other tasks involved in such a project. I owe a special debt of gratitude to my parents, Jameson and Dorothy Jones, for their encouragement and inspiration throughout my career. And finally I would like to thank my wife Christa and my daughters Sara, Miriam, and Jessica for their patience, support, and companionship during the odysseys that this undertaking involved.

Contents

Chapter I

Introduction

Nur um der Hoffnungslosen willen ist uns die Hoffnung gegeben.
— Walter Benjamin[1]

THE TERM *VOLKSSTÜCK* DESCRIBES A type of drama that has existed in literary form in German-speaking countries since the end of the eighteenth century. Scholars have employed this designation with varying degrees of precision to plays they consider members of this category, whether or not the authors themselves applied this name to their texts. Estimation of the genre's literary merit has also varied greatly. In its early years this type of play was closely associated with the institution of the *Volkstheater*, where it was most frequently performed. Nowadays the *Volksstück* is less closely linked to a particular theater and audience, but there are a number of respected contemporary writers who, in designating their plays as *Volksstücke*, consciously evoke a comparison with earlier representatives of this genre. Yet the vast differences among the dramas that have borne this designation provide one of the greatest problems to be resolved in a study of this type of literature. There are several approaches that an investigation of the *Volksstück* could pursue, though many of them would restrict themselves to certain aspects while ignoring others that are essential to an understanding of the genre. For example, one approach could concentrate on defining the genre itself; a second might produce a literary history that attempts to trace a genealogy as it chronicles plays of this type. Yet a third could examine a series of separate plays as textual objects in themselves; a fourth possibility would be to view them as expressions of the social context in which they were created. I will begin by addressing these issues before developing a theoretical approach that will guide the discussions of individual plays in the following chapters.

The Problem of Genre

The *Volksstück* is a dramatic genre that a number of scholars and lexica have attempted to define quite precisely. However, the very notion of genre is problematic, and the lack of permanence in generic designations represents one of the central issues under consideration in this study.

Definitions of genre are rarely used prescriptively, unless they are limited, as in the requirement that a sonnet have fourteen lines. Descriptive designations have more use, yet they are difficult to achieve because of the difficulty of breaking into the hermeneutic circle: as Karl Viëtor has pointed out, we do not know what belongs to a genre without knowing what the characteristics of that genre are, and vice versa (441). More importantly, since individual representatives of a genre exist in specific historical situations (not simply because of differences in genius, talent, or peculiarity of individual authors) they could not possibly conform in content and form to their predecessors. Thus the limits of the genre have to expand constantly to include the new examples. To Viëtor, genre represents an "abstraction, i.e., a conceptual, schematic definition;" it is "a structure of both form and content that always provides a basis, but which never completes itself and never coincides with an individual literary work" (438). Walter Benjamin was also concerned with the problem of the inductive versus the deductive method of defining genre. The latter method would take the notion of genre as an ideal, but Benjamin feels that criticism should take an immanent approach. He reaches the conclusion that major works of art thus stand outside the limits of the genre, that they, paradoxically, either establish a genre or terminate it, and that perfect works do both.[2] The existence of such an ideal in the minds of many dramatists and spectators is of course what allows the horizon of literary expectations to be expanded when a new work "transgresses" against the previous confines.[3] This phenomenon points both to the impossibility of determining an unchanging ideal and to the possibility of using generic changes to convey a specific effect, as will become evident in the discussion of *Volksstücke* from different periods. The differences displayed by successive manifestations demonstrate the historical character of the concept of genre.

More recently, Jacques Derrida has called into question the possibility of generic precision, or of a "law of genre." He finds that a récit by Maurice Blanchot seems "to make light of all the tranquil categories of genre-theory and history in order to upset their taxonomic certainties, the distribution of their classes, and the presumed stability of their classical nomenclatures. It is a text destined, at the same time, to summon up these classes by conducting their proceeding, by proceeding from the proceeding to the law of genre" (63). Viëtor, Benjamin and Derrida correctly point out the impossibility of closure in reaching a definition. Difficulties such as those discussed above have caused some to question the value of genre distinctions altogether, since they find such categories meaningless.[4] Yet Viëtor perceives that these categories do have a function, and Derrida's essay, if not Blanchot's "account," would not exist without them.

Fredric Jameson, an exponent of a quite different theoretical perspective, is also aware of the falsity of assuming that genre designations can be fixed, although he too recognizes their usefulness. In a chapter entitled "Magical Narratives: On the Dialectical Use of Genre Criticism," which is a part of his study of *The Political Unconscious*, he comes to the conclusion that Manzoni's *I Promessi Sposi* can be read as a sort of Gothic novel in its inward and psychologizing Lucia narrative and as a social-historical novel because of the quite different narrative register that deals with Renzo's adventures. In displaying what Jameson calls "generic discontinuities" the novel is "not so much an organic unity as a symbolic act that must reunite or harmonize heterogeneous narrative paradigms which have their own specific and contradictory ideological meaning."[5] Finding similar inter-weavings of discontinuous narrative registers in Stendhal, he concludes that "all generic categories, even the most time-hallowed and traditional, are ultimately to be understood (or 'estranged') as mere ad hoc, experimental constructs, devised for a specific textual occasion and abandoned like so much scaffolding when the analysis has done its work" (PU 145).

This comparison to scaffolding goes even further than Viëtor's "struc-ture," which always serves as an ideal but with which no particular texts ever coincide, and it is similar to Derrida's in that it views particular texts as deconstructing (usually unconsciously) the generic form of which they are supposedly availing themselves. But this by no means makes the idea of genre useless or simply a form of "error" that is to be replaced by something "truer": on the contrary, the discontinuities that inevitably occur within a given text are formal attempts to resolve contradictions that exist on a social, historical level. Only by starting with the previous concept of genre can one begin to analyze the significance of such contradictions and the changing formal attempts to resolve them.

Authors choose certain genres in order to give their publics a certain expectation, even when they designate their texts ironically. Although no final, precise, closed definition can be attained, the notion of *Volksstück* does serve a useful and necessary purpose. The concept itself, to which no specific examples ever coincide, is formed over time through communication among texts, authors, the public, and scholars. An examination of the changes with respect to the form, content and intended audience of plays that have been considered *Volksstücke* will provide a better understanding of literature and its place in society through the example of one of its kinds at particular moments in history. This discussion will not focus on the various minor disagreements as to what does and does not ideally constitute a *Volksstück*, since there is no such thing as a final definition; however, the viewpoint adopted here for the analysis of individual texts provides an additional means of indicating how *Volksstücke* are to be understood.

The *Volksstück*: Attempts at Definition

Providing an English translation for the concept *Volksstück* is not easy, since the genre arose as a phenomenon peculiar to German-speaking stages during a specific period. Moreover, this word has come to be rather indiscriminately applied to quite a number of different subgenres that show varying degrees of relationship to one another and that range from improvised farces to sophisticated literary texts. The frequently encountered "popular comedy" can be misleading for a number of reasons: not all *Volksstücke* are comedies, and "popular," according to Webster, does not simply mean "of or carried on by the common people" or "suitable or intended for the people at large" but also "liked by most people." And even the term *Volk* is not so simple. It does not here imply "ethnic group" in the exalted sense employed during the period of romanticism and emerging national sentiment and found in compounds such as "Volksdichtung" or "Volkspoesie." Nor is it synonymous with the exaggerated use of the word employed by more recent racist ideologies. During the two centuries under discussion here it tends to refer to an undifferentiated broad public below the upper stratum of society, but a more precise description will have to be given for each of the authors or periods under discussion.[6]

At the time of Raimund "Volk" denoted the social class below the nobility and the bourgeoisie. This is not to say the proletariat, for in the early nineteenth century there was not yet a large class of industrial workers. Habermas indicates that absolutism on the continent perpetuated class differences for a longer period than was the case in England: a stricter distance was kept between nobility and bourgeoisie and between bourgeoisie and *Volk*. To the last category belong, "in addition to the population in the country (from farmhand to tenant farmer to yeoman) and the actual underclass (day laborers, soldiers and servants) the small shopkeepers, craftspeople and workers.... Those who were once burghers par excellence, the retail tradesmen and craftsmen, are no longer counted among the bourgeoisie by the 'Bürgerliche.' The criterion for the latter is education; the middle classes belong to the educated ranks— business people and academics (scholars, clerics, civil servants, physicians, lawyers, teachers etc.)" (92–93).

Even though members of other classes sometimes attended the *Volkstheater*, it was for the newly expanded group beneath the "Bürgerliche," a group that we would now consider comprising the lower and not so well-educated middle classes, that *Volksstücke* were originally written. Jürgen Hein basically concurs insofar as the theater is concerned, stating that "'Volk' is almost always an indiscriminate concept and means a public that does not go to the theater of the educated and ruling classes" ("Volksstück: Entwicklung" 10). It is important that "Volk" not be taken as a timeless, reified concept: it is a relational term that signifies varying class boundaries in different periods. From the servants, craftsmen, and tradesmen of the early part of the period under discussion the term came to be applied to the group that also encompassed the industrial proletariat and later to the petite-bourgeoisie in general. Some playwrights also addressed rural audiences of small farmers and day laborers, either specifically or as examples of any people in a subordinate station. Successive authors have had to take into account changes in the make-up of their public, but in any case the *Volk* addressed as audience and portrayed as subject matter is a group that is excluded from full participation in society.

Just as the category *Volk* has changed, so have definitions of the *Volksstück*. This term should not be considered timeless either, nor, as mentioned earlier, a fixed ideal. Differences in the concept can be observed, moreover, in the ways in which the general public, scholars, and playwrights have perceived it.[7] An examination of several definitions will reveal that they are seldom in complete agreement and best serve as indicators of a general direction rather than as fixed limits or categories. Two definitions from non-specialist reference works indicate what is often conventionally associated with this generic designation. In his *Sachwörterbuch der Literatur*, Gero von Wilpert calls the *Volksstück*:

a genre of stage plays for city *Volkstheater* and suburban stages with a plot taken from the life of the common people in a popular, unpretentious form that is easy to understand, yet which corresponds to the taste of the metropolitan public through the inclusion of music, song, and dance as well as through the use of effects, sentimentality, and other inferior elements without losing its often serious and at times even tragic tone. (837)

The definition in Arnold's *Grundzüge der Literaturwissenschaft* is similar: "The *Volksstück* corresponds to the public taste with transparent plots, simple language, calculated effects, and sentimentality; it usually relates to particular social classes or geographic areas. Its proximity to the regional play is unmistakable" (498–99). These definitions demonstrate the rather imprecise boundaries of the term and illustrate the pejorative connotations that it has tended to hold for many. Such views are not without some basis, since many of the plays grouped in this category are examples of trivial literature that is constructed according to predictable formulas and that panders to public tastes, or that is principally characterized by the inclusion of local elements. But other dramas and dramatists in this category have received literary as well as public acclaim: quite a few authors, critics, and scholars have come to feel that many *Volksstücke* demonstrate real accomplishment, rather than simply providing ephemeral farces.[8]

Not all of the authors associated with this type of literature used the term *Volksstück* or other genre designations with the prefix *Volk-*, and those who have employed it have either consciously or unnconsciously given it new meaning. Raimund is associated with this tradition because his plays were performed in the *Volkstheater*. Nestroy called most of his witty comedies *Possen*, and it was the later historian Otto Rommel who applied the term Volkstück to him, grouping a number of plays together under this heading in his collection of Nestroy's works. In Nestroy's day the word had a rather restricted use, applying to the more serious, edifying play with idealized characters that critics preferred over irreverent satires (Yates, "Idea"). Friedrich Kaiser was the chief exemplar of this type of play, with which he intended to provide a *Lebensbild*, or "faithful picture of life," that would enable the popular comedy to regain its "influence on the people" (qtd. in Yates, "Object" 464; cf. May 265–66). Anzengruber, the first of the authors discussed in this study to make consistent use of the term, employed it in a sense somewhat similar to Kaiser's for plays that had literary merit and a serious, didactic purpose, even when they employed comedy. But the term has not been restricted to this sense, nor does it need to be in this study.

Bertolt Brecht, for example, felt that the term and the type of play to which it should refer had value, though his call for renewal in 1940 shows that what he considers in need of change are the more trivial examples of the genre that had become dominant in the repertoires of many theaters. In issuing this appeal Brecht stresses the *Volksstück*'s bad reputation:

> The *Volksstück* is usually intended for crude and unpretentious theaters, and scholarly aesthetics hushes it up or treats it condescendingly.... It contains coarse jokes, mixed with sentimentality, it has preposterous morality and cheap

sexuality. The bad are punished, and the good are married off, the diligent receive an inheritance, and the lazy undertake their troubles in vain.[9]

Yet he felt that something called *Volksstück* was also capable of providing a useful dramatic medium and gave the following description of what it should be, as well as writing *Herr Puntila und sein Knecht Matti* in order to provide a concrete example: "Indeed one can admit the need for a theater that is naive, but not primitive, poetic, but not romantic, realistic, but not topical" (1163).

Brecht was not the only author to find this term a useful one with which to operate, as long as it was employed in a way that distinguishes what are considered adequate and inadequate manifestations. As will be observed below in greater detail, Anzengruber, Thoma, Horváth, and Kroetz have all used this genre designation for plays that differed from what had been written before. The repeated return to the concept *Volksstück* and the call for a change within the genre indicate that the form has not remained static throughout its history, and the fact that some authors refer to a "renewal" shows that it contained elements worth saving. In their study, Aust, Haida, and Hein agree that the history of the genre consists of its continual renewal (17). The first two definitions quoted above fail to take these factors sufficiently into account. More accurate is a description such as that of Jürgen Hein, who discusses the two main lines of development in the history of this genre, or family of genres: "the trivial regional play that is confined to its locality, closely linked to its dialect, unpretentious, (and) 'merely' entertaining" and, especially after its rediscovery and renewal in the twentieth century, "a form of critical-realistic (self-)representation of the *Volk* that nonetheless operates with entertaining means" ("Volksstück: Entwicklung" 9). Hein goes on to discuss various sub-genres of the *Volksstück* as well as the types of institutions at which they have been performed: in nineteenth-century Vienna and certain other cities this was mainly the theater in the districts just outside the city center, the *Vorstadt*, or "suburbs," where most of the *Volk* lived, but in other regions there were also village theaters for farm audiences.

All these remarks indicate that this genre is difficult to define precisely because of the variety of elements that it encompasses: the class that provides subject matter and audience, its thematics, its formal resources, and the theatrical institutions with which it has been associated. My investigation deals with all these aspects and the historical changes within them, rather than restricting itself to the thematics of *Volk*, which has often provided the most obvious focus of attention. The complex relationships among these components are, to varying extents, important for reaching an adequate understanding of any type of literature, but because they are so pronounced in the phenomenon *Volksstück*, a study of this genre can offer a particularly instructive model. Since the word *Volksstück* has been applied in so many different ways, it will be necessary to review briefly a history of the theaters and some of the authors with which it has been associated before I discuss the elements that I wish to stress in a working definition of my own.

The *Volksstück*: A Brief History

Plays that have been considered *Volksstücke* have varying degrees of connection to one another: in fact it may seem strange that authors so different as Raimund and Kroetz could possibly be included in the same literary category. In attempting to write a history, one runs into problems similar to those encountered when drawing up a definition. Although I will not attempt to trace a genealogy, I think it is important to review the important manifestations of the literary *Volksstück* in its broadest sense. The plays considered in this study all relate to one another, even if the later manifestations cannot be regarded as direct descendants of the earlier dramas. It should be emphasized that the history of the *Volksstück* was at the beginning simultaneously a history of the *Volkstheater*. Hein says that in the development of the *Volksstück* into a play "with a contemporary plot that is closely related to reality and to society, the public ... is a definite factor in the production" ("Volksstück: Entwicklung" 12; cf. also Baur 28; Hüttner, "Parodie" 133). Rarely in the history of the theater has there been such a close working together of author, actor, theater technician, and public.

Even though this study will emphasize the texts of the plays under consideration, it should not be forgotten that the history of the early Viennese *Volkskomödie* is not just a literary one: it is a history of the theater in the widest possible sense.[10] In early nineteenth-century Vienna there were two court theaters whose public came from the court, the diplomatic corps, the nobility, the officer corps, officials, foreign scholars, and capitalists; in addition, three *Vorstadttheater* served the lower classes.[11] Performances at these "suburban" theaters were also attended by members of the upper classes and foreign visitors, although the principal group of spectators came from the *Volk* as described by Habermas. Other cities in Germany had similar separations between court and popular theaters, but because of the strength of the *Volkstheater* as an institution in Vienna, it has received the greatest amount of attention, and the origins of the literary popular comedy are traced back to the theater of this city in the eighteenth century. One of the first and most thorough treatments of the subject is Otto Rommel's *Die Alt-Wiener Volkskomödie*, which covers the history of this dramatic institution "from the baroque theater of the world to the death of Nestroy." Rommel sees the forerunners of this genre in a synthesis of the visually spectacular and allegorical elements of baroque opera and Jesuit-drama with the folk-comic elements of traveling players and *commedia dell'arte* (24ff.). The combination of different elements from a variety of sources marked its beginnings and continued to inform it throughout the years.

The two most frequently emphasized components in the majority of the comedies of the early Viennese period through Nestroy are "entertaining dramatic form and critical, satirical commentary" (Hein, "Volksstück: Entwicklung" 14). Both aspects were already evident in the eighteenth century when authors such as Joseph Anton Stranitzky, Gottfried Prehauser, and Joseph Felix von Kurz struggled for the right to express themselves extemporaneously in the *Stegreiftheater* [improvisational theater], which was finally forbidden in 1752 because of its tendency to criticize social, political, and religious institutions. Some authors, such as Philipp Hafner, continued to make use of social themes, though the censorship of the period caused them to turn away from critical topics. Others turned to the old form of the musical *Zauberstück*, or magical play, which made use of phantastic and fairy tale elements; Schikaneder's libretto for Mozart's *Die Zauberflöte* is of course one of the best-known examples. Another variation, which continued the use of these magical elements and which also attempted to combine edification (more along the lines of personal betterment than social criticism) with entertainment has been referred to as the *Besserungsstück*; its main proponents in the early nineteenth century were Alois Gleich, Karl Meisl, and Adolf Bäuerle.

It is important to be aware of the characteristics of the *Volkstheater* up this point in order to understand the plays of Ferdinand Raimund (1790-1836), the first of the authors to be considered here in detail and one who is still performed today. Most of his plays combine various elements of the *Volkstheater* tradition, such as magic, impressive stage effects, songs, and Viennese dialect with a happily resolved plot in which the main characters usually learn some sort of lesson, which is taught in a world of phantasy and allegory. The next major author to be treated in this study is Johann Nestroy (1801–1862), who has attained the status of a "classic," as evidenced by the frequency with which he is still performed today and the amount of critical attention that has been devoted to him. His first works continued in the *Zauberstück* tradition, yet the prolific Nestroy preferred a form called the *Posse*, a kind of farce noted for its close relation to its own locality, its improvisational character, musical elements, and its relation to satire.

Following Rommel's view, the consensus used to hold that the period after Nestroy's death was one of decline. In fact, increased industrialization, migration to the city, and economic crises that led to more expensive theater tickets resulted in changes within the old *Volkstheater* audience. The idealized and edifying *Lebensbilder* [pictures of life], which represented the true *Volksstück* in most critics' eyes, proved increasingly less popular with the public, who tended to turn to more trivial farces or to the operetta for entertainment.[12] But the history of the *Volksstück* is also the history of altered dramatic responses to changes in audience, society, and literary possibilities and expectations: instead of a decline one might speak of a change, and changes are not unique to this period.

Ludwig Anzengruber (1839–1889), the next major playwright investigated in this study, sought a renewal in a type of dialect play that frequently mixed serious and comic elements and attempted to provide enlightenment. His use of elements of nineteenth-century realism and extra-theatrical models, such as the *Dorfgeschichte* or village tale, expands the boundaries of the genre, as does his decision to include tragedies as well as comedies among his *Volksstücke*. The use of outside influences does not hinder a consideration of his plays as *Volksstücke*, however: the *Volkstheater* had frequently availed itself of sources and styles from other traditions. Anzengruber is the last in the tradition that began with the founding of the Viennese *Volkstheater*: the close interrelationship between the play and a particular theatrical institution. After him the *Volksstück* begins to lead a more independent literary existence (Hein, "Volksstück: Entwicklung" 19).

Although the most renowned authors of *Volksstücke* in the nineteenth century were from Vienna, plays for the *Volk* featuring dialect, songs, and local milieu were popular in other German-speaking areas as well. David Kalisch and Adolf Glassbrenner in Berlin, Ernst Elias Niebergall in Darmstadt, and Franz Prüller in Munich are some of the authors who achieved success in other regions. Any of these authors could be fruitfully subjected to analysis; space limitations represent the principal reason for failing to include them in this study. In the twentieth century, the *Volksstück* has become less tied to one area and has become more diversified in its form. Karl Schönherr in Tirol continued to write plays with rural settings in the manner of Anzengruber, but more important is the journalist and author Ludwig Thoma (1867–1921). Some of his comedies are merely amusing farces, but others achieved greater depth through the use of satire, which had long been a part of plays addressed to the *Volk*. The play discussed here is his *Magdalena*, a rural tragedy that shows similarities to Anzengruber, although its depiction of the effects of social milieu on its characters link it more closely to Naturalism. The history of the performance of Thoma's plays also indicates an expansion of the confines of the genre: despite its use of dialect and portrayal of farmers among the principal figures, his satire *Die Medaille* was first staged at Munich's court theater before receiving equal acclaim when performed by folk troupes on rural stages. *Erster Klasse*, written for a friend's *Bauerntheater*, took the opposite route and ended up in city theaters. The process of dissociation of the *Volksstück* from the institution of the *Volkstheater* became more complete and the *Volksstück* no longer tended to be as restricted to a particular region, class of audience, or type of theater. Thoma's plays therefore represent a transition between the *Volksstücke* of the nineteenth century and those of the twentieth.

In 1925 Carl Zuckmayer's *Der fröhliche Weinberg* (*The Merry Vineyard*) made use of music, humor, dialect, and other local elements of the author's native region of Rhine-Hesse and showed how features of the *Volksstück* tradition could successfully be incorporated into more mainstream drama. For this work Zuckmayer won the prestigious Kleist prize and soon became the most frequently performed playwright in Germany. In the Austria of the 1930s the young Jura Soyfer combined *Volksstück*-elements with techniques of modernism in shorter satirical pieces for the cabaret. Marieluise Fleißer (1901–1974), from the Lower Bavarian city of Ingolstadt, was less acclaimed at the time than Zuckmayer, though she is more important to this investigation. Fleißer makes use of regional themes and dialect, yet her critical treatment of the banality of lower middle-class life prevented a positive reception in her home town. Ödön von Horváth (1901–1938) displays a similar choice of themes and treatments, and the plays of these two authors are more representative of the bleakness of modernism than of the lightness of the *Lokalposse*. As practiced by these authors, the *Volksstück* no longer has the same entertaining appeal to a mass audience. Like Brecht, Horváth called explicitly for a renewal of the genre: in his essay "Zur Erneuerung des Volksstückes" he says that his *Die Bergbahn* (The Mountain Railway) is a *Volksstück* not just because it is a dialect play dealing with workers, but because it is a play "in which problems are constructed and treated in a manner typical of the *Volk*, and concerns of the

people, their simple worries, are seen through the eyes of the people"
(*Gesammelte Werke* 4: 662).

In the 1960's and 1970's several young authors such as the Hessian
Wolfgang Deichsel, the Austrians Wolfgang Bauer, Harald Sommer, and
Peter Turrini, and the Bavarians Martin Sperr, Rainer Werner Faßbinder
and Franz Xaver Kroetz began writing plays that they linked to this genre
and that show certain similarities to the *Volksstücke* of Brecht, Horváth, and
Fleißer. Kroetz, born in 1946, is the best known and will receive closer
treatment in this study. His theoretical ideas have undergone a number of
metamorphoses: in his early period enlightenment meant political enlightenment. In order to accomplish the latter he included such subjects as abortion,
child abuse, and violence to show the extent of present-day alienation and
spiritual bankruptcy. He later changed his methods of depiction from direct,
uncommented portrayal to more experimental means.[13]

It is obvious from this brief overview that the spectrum of dramas
represented by the various authors from Raimund to Kroetz displays quite
a diversity of form and content, and that one definition would not be able
to encompass them all, nor could it, since a fixed description in words
would reify something that is constantly changing. A variety of influences
has played a role in shaping the genre: there is not just one tradition that
links all the authors directly to one another.[14] This diversity provides
evidence of generic discontinuities that result from changing historical
conditions and that need to be examined more closely in individual plays,
since each play interacts with those changing conditions.

Despite the many difficulties associated with the use of the term
Volksstück, it is my contention that there is good reason for applying it to
all of the authors discussed in this study. The starting point for a definition
lies in the *Volk*, which all of these playwrights address as audience, whether
or not they are successful in reaching it, and which they incorporate as
characters within the drama in a way that relates to the actual situation of
the *Volk* at a given moment in history, whether or not the means chosen
employ verisimilar realism. Their stance toward the *Volk* is one of respect,
and their attitude toward social conditions is one not merely of criticism, but
of opposition, since the *Volk* is always in a subordinate position and in some
way excluded from a full realization of its potential. Addressing this material
and this audience with this attitude allows, however, for quite a number of
formal approaches. Since *Volk* is basically a sociological category, and
Volksstück a literary form, it will first be necessary to investigate the

relation between these two areas before defining more precisely the method employed and the texts analyzed in this study.

Methods of Investigation: The Immanent and the Social Character of the Text

The sophistication of the texts under discussion here, their repeated performance, their influence, and the critical attention that has been devoted to them show that they do not fit the pejorative definition of *Volksstück* as trivial literature. In addition, they provide an important object of study in the attempt to reach a better understanding of the entire phenomenon of literature, not just in terms of the immanent workings of the text but also with regard to its role in society. Recent analyses of the relations between literature and society have often concentrated on the novel as the representative literary form of the bourgeoisie. Various reasons have been put forth, such as the novel's simultaneous development with the rise of capitalism and the increasing autonomy of the individual; moreover, the form of narrative parallels that of history itself. Yet the drama is also an important expression of the changing social conditions of the nineteenth and twentieth centuries. It too is closely connected with external reality, though that connection may take the form of an attempted reflection of reality, a diversion from it, or a transformation. And plays, in addition to their other materials, have also traditionally placed a strong emphasis on plot. Because of its necessary relationship with the institution of the theater, the drama is very obviously a social form of literature. It can portray both individuals and society, but in a medium that is less private than the novel.

The plays of Lessing serve as an example of expression of the emerging middle-class viewpoint of the Enlightenment within the public forum of the theater. As the middle classes successfully asserted themselves against the nobility and later attempted to consolidate their position in the face of opposition from below, literature also found its role modified. While most of the dramas in the traditionally accepted canon of nineteenth- and twentieth-century German drama are expressions of the upper- and middle-class theaters, it should not be forgotten that there was also a type of theatrical literature that was of and for the *Volk*. The *Volksstück* provides an additional, alternative voice in the literary and social dialogue of the period in question: this study examines how particular dramas at times affirm, and at times oppose the forces that attempt to maintain the status quo.

Mikhail Bakhtin, a theorist whose principal area of interest was the novel, introduced the valuable concept of dialogism into literary studies. Among his various theoretical contributions is a view of language as a contest between centripetal forces that attempt to hold things together and centrifugal forces that tend to pull them apart. He pointed out that a language is at any given moment "stratified not only into dialects in the strict sense of the word ..., but is ... stratified as well into languages that are socio-ideological: languages belonging to the professions, genres, languages peculiar to generations, etc."[15] The novel was the genre that was shaped by the centrifugal forces toward "heteroglossia." This was particularly evident in the lower genres, such as "the *fabliaux* and *Schwänke* of street songs, folksayings, anecdotes," whose language represented a "heteroglossia consciously opposed to this literary language.... It was heteroglossia that had been dialogized" (272–73). The novel tends to incorporate these new languages, whereas, according to Bakhtin, the drama "strives toward a unitary language, one that is individualized merely by the dramatic personae who speak it" (405). He makes a slight exception of comedy, however, and it will become evident from an examination of *Volksstücke* below that the latter incorporate the languages of the lower classes in order to inject them into dialogues within individual plays. These voices also enter into the dialogue taking place between classes in the institution of the theater and in society as a whole. The appearance of the *Volksstück* within the domain of literary drama resembles the entrance of dialects into literary language as Bakhtin describes it:

> Literary language is a highly distinctive phenomenon ...; within it, intentional diversity of speech (which is present in every living dialect as a closed system) is transformed into diversity of language; what results is not a single language but a dialogue of languages. (294)

Jameson says that the normal form of the dialogical between classes is an antagonistic one (PU 84). Even when a *Volksstück* does not overtly oppose the ruling political or literary establishment, its self-assertion through a previously excluded form provides an opposing voice. Providing a voice for the *Volk* had important implications for the theater's concept of its own function. Urbach contrasts the suburban Viennese *Volkstheater* with the court theater as follows: "The Theater in der Leopoldstadt met its public half-way. Here the theater was a forum. At the center of town, in the Hofburg, the theater had become a temple" (64).

It is therefore essential to investigate carefully the means of expression employed in these dramas. In what respects do the plays really represent a new self-assertion by the *Volk*, and when do they merely offer nostalgia for a situation that cannot be preserved or that never existed in the first place? Do they even represent expressions of the *Volk* itself (as a form of mass culture), or are they offered from above as the type of entertainment that their authors think the *Volk* would like to receive (in the manner of the products of the "culture industry," which often appropriates valid forms of popular expression to serve its own ends)? And in recent years, has the appropriation by mainstream theater of *Volksstück*- elements represented a triumph or a weakening of the message of the *Volksstück*? Answering such questions involves at least in part a sociological, historical method, an approach that has frequently been employed in the study of the *Volksstück*. There is a difference, of course, between using literature as a source of data for sociologists and studying it as art: I do not intend to make the texts secondary to extrinsic categories, to use their content as empirical data for already completed historical theories, or to confuse the plays with society itself. It is therefore necessary to examine more closely the relationships between the literary text and the external conditions of the social, the economic, and the historic.

A purely immanent approach, such as those represented by formalism or New Criticism, would view the work of art as autonomous in itself and capable of being understood internally in terms of its own norms, without recourse to the external situation in which it finds itself.[16] Formal methods of criticism have of course contributed immensely to the study of literature through their emphasis on a close reading of the text, yet their exclusion of the context in which literature is produced and read limits their effectiveness. However, if too great an emphasis is placed on external "reality", literature becomes secondary and a mere epiphenomenon: criticism that views literature as a reflection of the society in which it finds itself often produces little more than superficial typologizing.[17] To find a method that is better able to take these complexities into account, it will be necessary to proceed to a closer examination of the relation between art and external reality. This relationship has, of course, been the subject of a great deal of debate, and recent theorists have attempted to offer an alternative to the simplistic notion of a mechanistic base-superstructure causality. Even though this type of causality may be at work at times, such as in the changes within the nineteenth-century *Volkstheater* that resulted in altered economic conditions and rising ticket prices, it does not sufficiently explain the complexity of the "causes" at work in the formation of individual texts.

As an alternative to simplistic mechanical causality and to the expressive causality of Leibniz and Hegel, Louis Althusser proposed the notion of structural causality, which avoids the necessity for a cause that is external and transcendant by proposing that "the whole existence of the structure consists of its effects" (188–89).[18] Fredric Jameson carries this idea farther, and although he subscribes to many of the points in Althusser's argument, he is unwilling to deny completely the effects of history within written texts, because to do so would mean to deny the political unconscious whose expression in texts his book sets out to explore.[19] For Jameson, the interpretive task for the expressive causality associated with Hegel and Lukács would thus be to seek a unified meaning, whereas structural causality would "find its privileged content in rifts and discontinuities within the work ... the appropriate object of study emerges only when the formal unification is unmasked as a failure or as an ideological mirage."[20] He believes that the strength of his form of criticism is its ability to include other modes of criticism and maintain their positive findings while it historicizes them (PU 47).

This discussion of Jameson's ideas was necessary to give a notion of some of the basic assumptions from which this book proceeds, yet I should stress that Jameson's system will by no means be adopted wholesale as a scheme with which to decode the *Volksstücke* under consideration, for there are certain major problems contained in it. Its strengths have been explained or alluded to: it shows a thorough knowledge of and respect for other forms of criticism, such as immanent criticism, Freudian criticism, structuralism, and post-structuralism, and it makes fruitful use of their positive achievements. It respects the text on its own terms while at the same time attempting to open it up to new levels of meaning in its existence in society and history. In the process, it avoids the traditional weaknesses of typologizing and reduction. Yet even though history cannot and should not be denied as the ultimate ground against which literary texts are written and which is itself rewritten through them, Jameson's definition of history as the sequence of modes of production still resembles too closely a form of transcendent truth which determines everything else, and which he is at such great pains to avoid. He is forced to admit that he considers "History as ground and untranscendable horizon [that] needs no particular theoretical justification" (PU 102). This conclusion is less than satisfactory, and acceptance of this idea leads to all the dangers inherent in a totalizing system. Ideology can be demonstrated in most theories and practices, even in New Criticism, for example; yet what makes the ideology in Jameson's system more valid than the others? His explanation, that in the Marxian system it is a collective unity, rather than an individual subject that is able to see through the illusion of false consciousness, seems to be a further displacement and similarly fails to solve the problem completely (PU 283).

If Jameson's thought leads to a conclusion that this study is not prepared to adopt, why should it be considered at all in a discussion of the *Volksstück*? The plays that I examine in detail are, like their authors and spectators, objects of history, but in addition, they have a function as a form of expression for human beings, who are also the subjects of history. To a great extent these *Volksstücke* do indeed represent a political unconscious, since the rifts and discontinuities within them result from social insufficiencies which their creators did not see or were unable to articulate explicitly. But rather than using a specific concept of history as a pre-formed grid through which to interpret them, I will examine these dramas to see how they provide an opening to history, as opposed to viewing how a particular concept of history explains the plays. Similarly, a pre-determined notion of class may not necessarily be a completely accurate framework for understanding the *Volk* and the *Volksstück*: it is equally important to study this form of literary expression to arrive at an undertaning of class. To do so respects the dialectic of the plays' existence as texts within history and is more likely to lead to a better understanding of both areas. In any event, many of the elements of Jameson's methodology can prove useful in examining the subtle interrelationships and discontinuities between text and social ground in order to avoid the incompleteness of a purely immanent approach and the over-simplification of a historical approach that merely categorizes. Especially valuable are his comments on form.

Form will be important to this study for a number of reasons, the simplest of course being the attempt to avoid the reductiveness of discussing literary content as a reflection of social context. Georg Lukács pointed this out in 1912 in the foreword to his Hegelian *Entwicklungsgeschichte des modernen Dramas*:

> The greatest mistakes of the sociological method of viewing art lie in its seeking and investigating the content of artistic creations and attempting to draw a direct line between them and specific economic conditions. The truly social in literature, however, is form. Form is what makes the experience of the poet communicable to others ... and art becomes social in the first place by means of this formed

communication, through the possibility of effect and the effects that actually result. (*Literatursoziologie* 71–72)

He argues further that "the receiver of the artwork does not perceive that (in art) the Non-formed does not exist," and that content can have an effect only because it comes into being through form (72).

Jameson is aware of the importance of form on all three of the horizons against which he examines literature. On the political level, he considers form as a symbolic act and employs Kenneth Burke's alternation of emphases on the two words in the term "symbolic act": an artistic response is both a genuine act and a symbol that does not bring about any change in real conditions. Rather than a resolution, it provides a projection of social contradiction (PU 76–83). An aesthetic resolution within a *Volksstück* can thus represent a response to a social contradiction for which it provides no real external solution.

At the level of the second, or social, horizon Jameson says that texts function as *paroles* in the *langue* of class discourse, a discourse that is dialogical (in Bakhtin's sense) in its structure. Here the relation of popular culture to high art is important. Both cultures would take part in the same discourse, but would use each other's vocabulary in different ways, either for subversion or for co-optation and neutralization. The forms of the religion of black slaves, for example, do not necessarily represent a duplication of imposed beliefs and thus the acceptance of the hegemony of the slave owners, but rather a replacement of the content of that religion with quite different and often coded messages. The reverse occurs when high culture appropriates forms such as the folk dance into the minuet or the vernacular into its own speech patterns in order to revitalize itself and to extend its domination by implying that there is only one culture (PU 83–88). Both of these uses of another discourse, in which upper-class aesthetic forms are incorporated into the plays of the *Volk* and in which elements of popular theatrical styles are appropriated into the drama of high culture, are central to a discussion of the *Volksstück*.

On the third horizon, the level of history in the larger sense, form is perceived as content. As an example, Jameson gives genre, which can be appropriated or subverted to send a variety of messages. One does not have to accept his view that the modes of production represent the ultimate organizing factor of history (see PU 98–99 and "Cognitive Mapping" 356) to agree that the form employed by a text carries a message, or more precisely, a mixture of messages as a result of the form's development in history. The formal methods employed to deal with the contradictions and alienation within the society of the nineteenth and twentieth centuries will thus be central in all the discussions of *Volksstücke* that follow.

Negation and Utopia: Two Impulses Behind the *Volksstück*

Many scholars have considered the dual function of the *Volksstück* to be that of *prodesse et delectare*, to instruct and to entertain. Of the authors who tried to accomplish these two functions, many strove for a harmonious balance, but others tended to consider one more important than the other.[21] For plays in which the didactic purpose is paramount, the content is often viewed as the message that is made palatable by coating it in an entertaining form. Yet it is not easy to separate form and content so precisely, since content is transmitted through form, and since form carries a message of its own. The two exist in a dialectical relationship to one another, and even though *Volksstücke* may in fact instruct and entertain, the manner in which they do so is not necessarily so neatly divisible into two parts. Rommel recognized that the chief formal characteristic of the early period, the comic, was not simply a superficial ornament designed to attract the audience to a more important lesson; rather it was "precisely the creative element in the old Viennese *Volkstheater*" (*Alt-Wiener Volkskomödie* 22). Hein claims that literature for the *Volk* can lie anywhere between the poles of the didactic and the entertaining, and that the early *Volkstheater* lived in a state of tension between the two. When balanced, they turned the drama into a medium of critical self-representation, but when plays succumbed completely to the demands of the latter function, they deteriorated into trivial, uncritical farces ("Volksstück: Entwicklung" 9–10). The interplay between these two poles can thus impart creative life to the *Volksstück*. In another essay Hein says that the didactic represents a problematic constituent within the *Volksstück* which has caused literary scholars great difficulty in evaluating the genre ("Volksstück als didaktisches Drama" 97). Yet since the didactic can be either critical or edifying and can be put into comic or serious form, Hein considers this element to be the one that links the earlier *Posse* to the contemporary critical *Volksstück* and is what allows a history of the genre to be written: the purpose remains constant, even though the form undergoes a reversal (99).

While I would not deny the importance of the didactic to the genre or the strength imparted by its combination with the entertaining, I find that to describe the *Volksstück* as a composite of the two functions is not to reach a conclusion about it. Rather, it poses new sets of questions that have to be answered. First of all, what sort of instruction or didacticism is meant here? Literature aimed at the *Volk* could either be written from above, as a sort of edification produced by the educated classes, or it could be an expression of the *Volk* itself. And even if the latter is the case, the message could be of several different types. Authors could either encourage people to be satisfied with their lot and to submit to the existing order, or they could point to injustice and encourage opposition. But how effectively can the content of a work of art bring about change in society or consciousness? Even if plays seem to preach opposition, they could actually function as safety valves that release the public's demand for real change by serving as symbolic substitutes.[22] Raimund might seem to be an example of an author who encourages submission, and Brecht and Kroetz of ones who seek to effect change. But using these terms tends to confuse authorial intention with what was actually produced, and unless care is exercised, one overlooks the form and reduces the text to the "content" of its message.

Thus the form, and the relations and differences between form and content, as well as between the play and society, need to be examined closely. Then one will not be able to contrast Raimund and Brecht so neatly. Most of Raimund's characters were supposed to learn the lesson of integrating themselves into their environment in order to live a happy life, but if such integration is impossible in reality, how does Raimund achieve a harmonious closure within the text? Is this textual closure the result of a sort of "strategy of containment" that maintains the illusion that harmony has been achieved in the text and thus can be achieved in the real world? If so, rifts and discontinuities within the text should become obvious and lead to further investigations that provide a fuller understanding of the text and of the drama in its moment of social and historical existence. Although the *prodesse-delectare* formula retains a certain usefulness in the discussion of the *Volksstück*, it tends to perpetuate too strong a distinction between content and form and also runs the danger of stressing the author's intent over what is actually achieved within the play itself; as a result, it fails to go as far as it might in attempting to comprehend its object of investigation. And since the didactic can be of several types, it cannot by itself provide the constituent element that links *Volksstücke* of different periods. Therefore, I propose a different perspective, in which the *Volksstück* would be viewed as the expression of two impulses that at first seem quite contradictory: negation and utopia.

The importance of social criticism to the *Volksstück* has already been mentioned; as satire or outright condemnation of governmental policies the plays often exercised a negative function with respect to the ruling powers. This criticism was frequently disguised in order to slip past the censors, but whether open or hidden this type of criticism is negative on a purely local or topical level and exists mainly as content. In discussing the negative aspects of the *Volksstück*, it is necessary to go beyond a play's social criticism and investigate a number of different components, including the very institution of the *Volkstheater* itself. As a place separate from the theaters of the nobility and the educated bourgeoisie, the *Volkstheater* represented in effect an alternate establishment, a gathering place and center for maintaining the distinct identity of the people.[23]

The opportunity for self-expression was extremely important, even though constraints such as censorship and the economic need to appeal to a broader public kept that expression from being completely free. The *Volkstheater* was already providing the type of literature for the people advocated by the young Hegelians of the 1840's. Even though it did not utter appeals to rebellion, the function of opposition consisted, in Uwe Baur's words, of demonstrating "die Überlegenheit der Unterlegenen" (superiority of the underlings; 32). Even when the plays performed the function of bread and circuses in dissipating rather than channelling the dissatisfactions of the lower classes, and even when they carried overt calls for their audiences to remain content with the status quo, the institution where they were being performed was itself a statement of otherness, a sign that the ruling power was not the expression of a unified whole. Today the boundaries between classes have been obscured by greater mobility and access to education, and universal suffrage makes it seem as though the public and the ruling power are actually one. Yet the distinction in power between property owner and wage laborer still exists, and the continued existence and usefulness of the concept *Volksstück* gives evidence of rifts within the social whole. The institution, the genre, certain features of the content, and aspects of the form itself all reveal that the *Volksstück* serves as a negative phenomenon by its utter refusal to accept things as they are, either in society or in literature.

Yet negation as opposition to accepted aesthetic standards or social norms is not what usually comes first to mind when the *Volksstück* is mentioned. Comedy, songs, sentiment, amusing effects and pleasant portrayals of the local milieu are important elements in the standard definitions quoted above; if such is the case, the *Volksstück* offers a positive picture for the enjoyment

✓ of its audiences. The happy ending in most of the earlier plays would seem
to indicate that good fortune is possible, and the local elements appear to be
✓ an affirmation rather than a rejection of the public's environment. I would
contend that these positive features are indeed an essential part of the
Volksstück and are the result of a utopian impulse that is just as important
as the negative one. Even when utopia is not portrayed directly (if, in fact,
it is possible to portray the utopian directly), this impulse is a necessary
formative feature. In the earlier *Volksstücke* the negative was less visible,
but in the bleaker portrayals of texts from this century it is the utopian that
is less obvious, and the negative seems to come to the fore. Even in recent
comedies, the humor is blacker and illusory resolutions are more transparent. Yet refusal to accept what exists is coupled with a hope for what could
be, and throughout the history of the *Volksstück* both the negative and the
utopian have provided essential creative impulses, though they have had to
find changing formal expression in their relation to changing social and
historical conditions and literary expectations.

The manner in which these seeming opposites attempt to achieve a formal
resolution imparts a dialectical tension to the genre and constitutes the focus
of my investigation of each of the plays. In order to reach a better
understanding of these impulses within literature and society, I will examine
the crucial role that they play in the philosphical and aesthetic thought of
two major twentieth-century German philosophers: negation for Theodor W.
Adorno in *Negative Dialektik* [*Negative Dialectics*] and *Ästhetische Theorie*
[*Aesthetic Theory*], and the utopian for Ernst Bloch in *Das Prinzip Hoffnung*
[*The Principle of Hope*]. Although these are not the only theorists and
scholars whose thought plays a role in my investigation, their ideas are basic
to my approach and will set the direction for the analyses of individual
plays.

Theodor Wiesengrund Adorno (1903–1969) was for many years
associated with the interdisciplinary Institut für Sozialforschung [Institute for
Social Research] and helped develop its methodology of "critical theory" for
the investigation of contemporary social and cultural phenomena. Leo
Löwenthal has admitted to the difficulty of assigning a precise definition to
the term "critical theory," which he describes as "a perspective, a common
critical way of thinking with respect to all cultural phenomena, without ever
raising the claim to a system" (*Mitmachen* 77). He stresses the importance
of the negative moment in this type of thought: "Precisely the negative was
the positive, this consciousness of not participating, of refusing; the
relentless analysis of the existing as far as we were competent to do it, that

is really the essence of critical theory" (80). Adorno's *Negative Dialektik*, completed in 1966, represents the culmination of his philosophical thinking: it is a critique of philosophy that justifies his procedures and represents, according to him, an "Antisystem."[24]

Out of the very complex and involved thought of *Negative Dialektik*, I propose merely to look at those strands of thinking that are relevant to this study of the *Volksstück*. The roots of negative dialectics go back at least to *Dialektik der Aufklärung* [*Dialectic of Enlightenment*], which Adorno and Max Horkheimer wrote in New York in 1944 and which discusses the attempt of the Enlightenment to demythologize the world and to replace presumption (*Einbildung*) with knowledge (11). In this sense, its aim was positive, yet what it has achieved is quite different: Horkheimer and Adorno criticize the Enlightenment for having reduced reason (*Vernunft*), whose goal was the reconciliation of contradictions, to instrumental reason, which has served only to advance the cause of domination in an administered world.[25] In failing to go beyond non-dialectical immediacy, the type of thinking that Horkheimer and Adorno criticized retained the "static repetition of mythic time" and thwarted "the possibility of historical development" (Jay, *Dialectical Imagination* 261). Negative dialectics thus represented a counter to "identity thinking," which sets up false equivalencies and tries to subsume all particular objects under general concepts, thereby dissolving the particular into the universal (Held 203).

This might be illustrated in terms of the difficulties encountered in defining the *Volksstück*. Under identity thinking, individual *Volksstücke* would be understood in terms of the general definition, but, as we have seen, particular texts are not identical with the ideal, and in fact contradict it. Moreover, identity thinking would not allow for the possibility of development, which is by necessity historical and which implies the negation of a previous tradition in order to continue. In *Negative Dialektik* Adorno's concern is of course not so much definitions of this type as philosophy itself, and his critique is in a number of respects a reply to Hegel. Adorno tried to preserve certain aspects of Hegel's thought, such as his dialectical method, his emphasis on becoming (*Werden*), and his notion of determinate negation (*bestimmte Negation*).

However, he could not accept Hegel's system or his notions of the identity of subject and object and of the Absolute Idea (Held 203). Because of his unwillingness to identify the part with the whole, Adorno, unlike Hegel, finds philosophy's true interest in the individual and the particular.[26] Although he agrees that the dialectic serves reconciliation (ND 18), he disputes Hegel's belief that negation of the negative results in affirmation. Such an equation is the "quintessence of identity," with which the "anti-dialectical principle wins the upper hand." True negation, however, would remain negative, "its positive would remain determinate negation alone, critique, not a shifting result that happily held affirmation in its hands" (ND 161). Non-dialectical identity thinking is also criticized in the discussion of recent philosophy, which, according to Adorno, has made a mistake in de-historicizing thought, for there is no such thing as a pure form unaffected by time (ND 63–64). The telos of philosophy is open and anti-systematic, and dialectics tends toward the open as opposed to the mythical or the "always the same" (ND 63–66). Negative dialectics does not "come to rest in itself, as if it were total; that is its form of hope" (ND 398).

Adorno contributed not just to philosophy, but also to sociology and the criticism of music and literature. His last major work, published posthumously in 1970, was his *Ästhetische Theorie*, which has a direct bearing on the study of literature. In this discussion of aesthetics the negative plays an important role. Similar to the notion of the concept discussed above, art "determines itself in relation to that which it is not." It is to be explained only in terms of its law of motion, not through invariables.[27] Adorno thus rejects the reified and unhistorical aspects of identity thinking in his discussion of art; he does not set up absolute categories, but remains dialectical in his approach. "There is no truth in works of art without determinate negation; it is up to aesthetics to expound this" (AT 195). One sees more precisely how art is negative by examining its dual nature: it is both autonomous and social. It is obviously social because it is a product of the "social labor of the mind" and also because its content has a social origin.

But for Adorno these two reasons are less important than a third, which results, paradoxically, from the autonomous side of its nature: "Rather art becomes social through its position counter to society, and only when it is autonomous does it occupy this position. By crystallizing itself in itself as something all its own (*Eigenes*) instead of complying with social norms and qualifying itself as 'socially useful,' it criticizes society by its mere existence" (AT 335). Thus art that exemplifies the greatest oppositional power is art that has no function (*das Nutzlose*): "Works of art stand in for things that are no longer deformed by exchange, for that which is not preparatory to profit and the false needs of degraded humanity" (AT 337). Adorno says that Marx's scorn for the shamefully low price that Milton received for *Paradise Lost* is actually the strongest defense of art against middle class society's tendency to functionalize it, since it denounces the market's failure to regard it as socially useful work. "A liberated society would be beyond the irrationality of its *faux frais* and beyond the end-means-rationality of profitability. This encodes itself in art and is its social detonator" (AT 337–38). The relationship between art and society is thus to be found in the immanent problems of its form: "it is here that the unresolved antagonisms of reality appear" (AT 16). Two more comments by Adorno, typical of the dialectical, aphoristic style of his non-systematic philosophy, express further the social opposition of autonomous art: "For only that which does not fit into the world is true" (AT 93), and "The adequate attitude of art would be one of closed eyes and gritted teeth" (AT 475).

Adorno obviously does not reduce the critical power of art to its content. He finds that the material of art, the treatment of social objects, whether open or concealed, is among the "most superficial and most deceptive" mediations of art and society (AT 341). One of the most frequent mistakes of contemporary art criticism is to confuse the artist's intentions with the content of his work, with what he wants to say rather than how he says it. "What an artist can say, he says only through form, not by letting form communicate it" (AT 226). This confusion occurs for example in countries that have promoted socialist realism: thinking that a work of art that contains a proletarian hero is better than one that does not is encouraged only when art is subsumed under something else, such as an increase in industrial production (AT 341). To keep from confusing the work of art with empirical reality one needs to keep in mind a comment of Schönberg's, which Adorno quotes: "One paints a picture, not what it represents" (AT 14). To demonstrate that form is the "locus of social content" Adorno discusses Kafka, "who codifies more faithfully and more powerfully what happens to humans under total social constraints than do novels about corrupt industrial trusts." In Kafka's epic style, not in the material he writes about, is to be found the mimesis of the reification that assumes and further confirms the inevitability and unchangeability of that which is, and the "how" of his text, his language, makes the delusive coherence of society recognizable (AT 342).

Adorno had already developed similar ideas on autonomous art and its form in his well-known essay "Engagement" ["Commitment"]. He makes a distinction between commitment in a work of art and tendency, which merely aims at making particular, practical changes.[28] Jean-Paul Sartre's plays fall into the latter category, says Adorno, because instead of maintaining an objectivity through a dialectics of formation and expression they are simply subjective vehicles for the communication of the author's philosophy and therefore little more than content or material. Because their form is so conventional they have achieved great success and, despite Sartre's wishes, are also acceptable to the "culture industry" (En 115–16). Adorno is skeptical of the ability of works of art to intervene politically; their actual effect on society is highly mediated, a participator in the spirit [*Geist*] "that contributes in subterranean processes to changing society" (AT 359). More effective than either Sartre or the *Lehrstücke* of Brecht is Samuel Beckett, whose plays and novels accomplish what tendentious literature only talks about: they arouse fear. "As dismantlings of appearance they explode art from within, which self-proclaimed commitment subdues from without, and therefore only apparently" (En 129). This negative moment, which expresses the idea that "it must be otherwise" ["Es soll anders sein"] is mediated through the form of the work, "whose crystallization makes itself into a parable of that Other, which should be" (En 134). In other words, the meaning of art is not "pointedly to express alternatives, but to resist the course of the world with nothing other than its form" (En 114).

Adorno does not ignore content altogether of course: he agrees with Sartre that it would be impossible to write a good novel in praise of anti-Semitism, and, in reference to Brecht's *Die Maßnahme* [*The Measures Taken*], he says that it is impossible to write a good play justifying the Moscow show trials, because "political untruth contaminates aesthetic form" (En 122). Yet his emphasis on an immanent, dialectic attention to form and the negativity that results from its autonomy is what leads to a more productive investigation of the work of art and its relation to society. Adorno's wariness concerning didactic capabilities needs to be kept in mind when investigating a type of literature that has often been pointedly didactic. His theoretical remarks do not rule out the possibility of art to change consciousness, but demonstrate an awareness of the complexities involved. Expressions of negation in the various *Volksstücke* examined here will not be sought principally in the content of any message that may be offered, but in the form, or more precisely, in the relation between form and content. In authors as diverse as Raimund and Brecht it will become apparent that the form is what reinforces, or at times circumvents, the "message."

To examine the second of the two major impulses behind the creation of the *Volksstück*, the utopian, it is necessary to turn to the thought of Ernst Bloch. Bloch (1885-1977), whose unorthodox Marxism resulted in his departure from the German Democratic Republic in 1961 to a teaching position in Tübingen, was the philosopher of a secularized Messianism or a Marxian "metaphysics," of a redemption in this world rather than in an afterlife. His major text is *Das Prinzip Hoffnung* [*The Principle of Hope*, published in 1959], which finds its culmination in the future *Heimat* [home, homeland] that is the object of hope. Unlike most previous philosophers, Bloch focuses his attention on the future, since that is where man in his striving really lives: "The past does not come until later, and a genuine present has hardly come into existence at all."[29]

Even though longing, expectation, and hope direct us forward toward an unknown utopia, most knowledge has been oriented toward the past, toward that which has already occurred. Thinking that pursues this direction finds its most typical expression in the Platonic *anamnesis*, the teaching "that all knowledge is merely recollection" (PH 7; cf. also 17 and 158ff.). Thus what is to come is viewed as a reproduction of what has already existed. According to Fredric Jameson, nihilism is the reverse of hope, whereas anamnesis is its absolute inversion, in which everything that in reality belongs to the future is attributed to the past (*Marxism and Form* 128). For Bloch, only philosophy that directs its thought toward changing the world is relevant for the future. In the process of becoming and realizing the future through the past, that philosophy takes as its theme "the still undeveloped, unattained *Heimat* (PH 8).

Although the object of longing can take various forms, such as day-dreams, travel, art, or political models of utopias, true *Heimat* should not be confused with inadequate objects of desire. The emotions that affect our comprehension of a goal are divided by Bloch into two categories: fulfilled affects [*gefüllte Affekte*], such as envy, greed, and veneration, whose object is already present in the existing world, and expectation affects [*Erwartungs-affekte*], such as *Angst*, fear, and hope, whose object is not attainable in the world as it now exists. The future envisioned by the former is not genuine, since it offers nothing new, whereas the latter emotions offer a genuine future of that which has objectively not yet existed. Of the expectation affects only hope is positive; for Bloch it is the most human of emotions, and the one that is "directed toward the farthest and brightest horizon" (PH 82–84). Since utopia, the goal of hope, is something other than what already exists, Bloch's approach is dialectical and open-ended, as evidenced in his contrast between the utopias presented in *The Divine Comedy* and *Faust II* (PH 961–68). Although both pictures of paradise are symbolic and metaphorical, Bloch claims that Dante's utopia is actually achieved, whereas Goethe's remains a rich intimation to be reached after infinite striving. The attainment of the Dantean Rose tries to express directly the peace and repose that is utopia, whereas Goethe's symbol of the mountain represents the attempt to reach it. Yet Bloch realizes that the revelations of religious art contain their truth only as *representatives* of a utopian real content, not as their immediate depiction.

This open-ended vision is crucial to Bloch's view of utopia: its form is still to be attempted, rather than something that can already be fully described, even though artistic representations provide a glimpse of the goal. Art is an allegorical pre-appearance [*Vor-Schein*] consisting of "fragments, real fragments, through which the process streams unendingly and advances dialectically to further fragmented forms" (PH 255). Art is then much more than a reaction to its social context; for Bloch "the truth of art has an ontological, and not only a social dimension" (Hudson 175). Thus the objects of "gefüllte Affekte," such as daydreams, travel, and escapist films, are static, ahistorical reifications that are inadequate as fulfillments of the utopian vision. Process itself is an important part of Bloch's philosophy, which is in effect an "open system:" almost all his own books remain uncompleted by design. He rejects both the metaphysical and identity, "inasmuch as for him being is precisely incomplete, in process, not yet altogether there" (Jameson, *Marxism and Form* 123). Thus the goal cannot be delineated as an absolute present. Yet for Bloch the not-yet is not merely an anticipatory feature of human consciousness that permits the envisioning of future possiblities, but rather a property of reality as well (Hudson 95). The last sentences of *Das Prinzip Hoffnung* show explicitly that *Heimat* is something new that humans will create in the future as a fulfillment of the past:

> *The true genesis is not at the beginning, but at the end*, it only starts to begin when society and existence become radical, that is, when they grasp themselves by the root. The root of history, however, is the working, creating human being who transforms and surpasses actuality. If humans have comprehended themselves and established what belongs to them without deprivation and alienation in true democracy, then there arises in the world something that shines into the childhood of all and where no one has ever been: *Heimat*. (PH III, 1628; emphasis in the original)

The choice of the word "Heimat" is significant not only because Bloch uses it to refer to utopia, but also because of its basic meaning of "homeland" or "native region." This German word is, unfortunately, emotionally and ideologically charged because it was so easily appropriated into the blood-and-soil politics of the Nazis, and because even in the 1980's and 1990's the organizations of *Heimatvertriebene* (expellees from the homeland) have tried to perpetuate the belief that a true home can be achieved in a particular location by re-establishing earlier boundaries and political forms. Moreover, the term is closely associated with *Heimatliteratur*, a type of writing that has often tended toward triviality as a result of its sentimental and idealized depictions of a local region. Indeed, many *Volksstücke* that are closely associated with their native settings can be called *Heimatliteratur*: Anzengruber's dramas of Alpine villagers would be an example, though of course his plays are more interesting artistically than the maudlin works of a Ludwig Ganghofer.

Because of right-wing appropriations of the concept of *Heimat* and its association with so much inferior literature, it was regarded in the years following World War II with a great deal of skepticism by writers and critics alike, yet there have been recent calls for a reconsideration. Brigitte Wormbs, for example, seeks a reclamation of the landscape and the concept of *Heimat*, not as an anachronistic idyll but as a "changeable reality that must be changed" (110). Manfred Bosch criticizes the lack of a proper reception of "left *Heimatliteratur*, for which, to be sure, this term is not used," and calls for a better understanding of the tradition that links the dialect plays of Ludwig Thoma, Karl Valentin, and Marieluise Fleißer with those of recent authors such as Martin Sperr, Rainer Werner Faßbinder, and Franz Xaver Kroetz (98–99). The difference between sentimentalized versions of *Heimat* and the bleaker portrayals in the work of these latter playwrights and of novelists such as Franz Innerhofer cause them to be regarded by some as creators of *Anti-Heimatliteratur* (Koppensteiner 9–19). When *Heimat* is presented nostalgically as an actual *topos* that exists now or has already existed in the past, it is changeless and regressive, but when it reveals the gap between what is and what could be by means of images of the childhood home that give an intimation of a better world, it opens the possibility of movement towards a better future. This is the sense of the conclusion to Bloch's *Das Prinzip Hoffnung* that was quoted above, and it indicates his reason for calling utopia *Heimat*: it was what gleamed in our childhood, but which was not yet fulfilled there. The nostalgia that we feel towards it is not an end itself, but an impetus propelling us toward what can only be realized in the future.

The recent discussion of the concept *Heimat* and the rekindling of interest in dialect literature show that the concept remains of vital interest, just as the continued, though changing, role of the *Volksstück* indicates that this type of drama remains important in literature and society. The superficial sense of *Heimat*, as material from a particular local region that is depicted as content, has always played an important role in the development of *Volksstücke*. A transfiguration of the near and familiar provides a comforting reassurance to marginal groups whose existence is less than complete. The danger in such a presentation lies of course in duping such groups into believing that the best of all worlds is attainable for individuals within the world as it is. But the better *Volksstücke* ultimately avoid such a message and are instead governed by a more complex and higher sense of the concept: *Heimat* as a *Vor-Schein* of utopia, as the formal expression of the still unfulfilled, future goal of hope.

Bloch, through his emphasis on hope and utopia, thus seems a positive counter to the more pessimistic Adorno, who throughout his work laid such great stress on the negative. Yet it would be wrong to regard the presence of the dual impulses of negation and utopia as completely paradoxical: there is a dialectical relationship between them, as the thought of both Adorno and Bloch attests. Adorno states as one of the antinomies of present-day life "that art must be and wants to be utopia and all the more decidedly so the more actual functional relationships dismantle utopia, but, in order not to betray the appearance and consolation of utopia, art is not permitted to be utopia. If utopia fulfilled itself in art, that would be its temporal end" (AT 55–56). Hegel, according to Adorno, betrayed utopia by constructing the existing as if it were utopia, the Absolute Idea. Utopia can thus only be conceived negatively, whether by art or by theory: "only through its absolute negativity does art express the inexpressible, utopia" (AT 56).

Adorno's pessimism comes through quite strongly in sentences such as the following:

> Because, however, utopia, the not-yet-being, is draped in black for art, it remains through all its mediation a memory of the possible as opposed to the actual that suppressed the possible; something like the imaginary reparation of the catastrophe known as world history; freedom, which, under the curse of necessity, has not yet come into being, and, concerning which, it is not certain if it ever will.... Art is the promise of happiness, which is broken. (AT 204–05)

Yet the utopian is never absent from Adorno's thought: its promise is to be found in the non-identity of the particular, an idea that he took from Ernst Bloch. Bloch used the term *Spuren* [traces] for such non-identical moments of hope that are already contained in the present.[30] The hint of utopian promise is crucial for both thinkers, however unlikely Adorno may have considered the possibility of its fulfillment.

Although *Das Prinzip Hoffnung* emphasizes hope, Bloch also admits the possibility of the *Nichts* [nothing], rather than the *Heimat* or *Alles*: it, too, is a utopian category, albeit an anti-utopian one (PH 11). And as we have seen, he is as skeptical as Adorno concerning the ability of art to present the utopian fully-formed as such. In being something other than what is, it is necessarily negative. One of Bloch's literary essays, "Bittere Heimatkunst," praises the bitterness in Ernst Elias Niebergall's *Volksstück Datterich* (1841) as an element that criticizes rather than supports existing conditions. Although the work is an amusing comedy, Bloch stresses that this play about an amoral drunkard is a "bitter picture of contemporary petit-bourgeois hardships with Datterich in the middle, a shaky, but by no means weak, ray of freedom" (*Literarische Aufsätze* 171). Genuine pictures, according to Bloch, never lack a touch of this Datterich, who is actually an anti-hero. A work about the contemporary *Heimat* can only be bitter in order to remain true to the utopian. And for Adorno art both testifies to the unreconciled in life and anticipates the reconciliation of a not yet existing, unified society (AT 251).

Parallels to and differences with the thought of Bloch and Adorno can be found in the writings of Adorno's older colleague, Walter Benjamin, who also knew Bloch and who more closely resembled him in his attempts to find a critical method for transcending the inadequate status quo; for Benjamin, redemption played the role that utopia did for Bloch. Richard Wolin points out that "for both Bloch and Benjamin works of art represent alternative models of experience endowed with the capacity to break through the eternal recurrence of the 'always the same' (Benjamin) or the 'darkness of the lived moment' (Bloch). For Benjamin they are 'now-times' (*Jetztzeiten*); for Bloch they serve as anticipatory images of utopia ([das] *Vorscheinen*)" (25–26; also see p. 16). Although Wolin is, in my opinion, mistaken in his later claim that works of art are actually aesthetic incarnations of utopia for Bloch, he is correct in stressing the importance for Benjamin of the Judaeo-Marxian *Bilderverbot*, or prohibition against making images, which refuses to equate the present embodied in works of art with utopia itself (25–26). The negativity inherent in the *Bilderverbot*, which implicitly aims at exposing the delusions of reality, seems closer to Adorno.[31] Both Benjamin and Adorno criticize the positive, affirmative aspects of the "aura" in traditional art, but when Benjamin praises the possibilities of de-auraticized, mechanically reproduced artworks which are accessible to the masses, Adorno thinks that he has failed to take the negative into account, since forms such as film are easily co-opted into a support of the status quo.[32] Truly autonomous art is more radical in its omission of the positive.

The difference between these two thinkers is in many ways one of emphasis, a difference that Adorno would doubtless have criticized in Bloch as well: Benjamin's search for a means of redemption led him to place more stress on the "positive aspects of aesthetic rationalization ... insofar as they exhibited, however faintly, traces of the path to 'salvation'" (Wolin 193). Benjamin thought that a greater threat came from forgetting the possibility of utopia. This difference in emphasis, however, had significant implications for the interpretation of the ability of art to have an effect; for Adorno the paragon was the esoteric dissonance of Schönberg, whereas for Benjamin in "The Work of Art" essay it was exemplified by the mass appeal of Chaplin. Adorno was well aware of the danger of regression that lay in placing too much emphasis on the positive or in believing either that utopia once existed in the past or could exist as such in art. But if the artistic image is not identified with an always-the-same attainment of a mythical utopia, it can have the valid function of revealing the inadequacies of the present historical moment and furnish an impulse for a transformation.

One of the sources of Benjamin's utopian images was his childhood memory of Berlin; in Jameson's opinion, nostalgia need not be associated only with the regressive or fascist: "there is no reason why a nostalgia conscious of itself, a lucid and remorseless dissatisfaction with the present on the grounds of some remembered plenitude, cannot furnish as adequate a revolutionary stimulus as any other; the example of Benjamin is there to prove it" (*Marxism and Form* 82). Most of the *Volksstücke* investigated here do not express overt calls for revolution, and Adorno is no doubt justified in his skepticism concerning the ability of art to have a direct, political effect in social reality. Its effect is of a much more complex, formally negative sort. But when *Volksstücke* assume an adequate literary form, they both refuse to accept the current state of affairs and demand the radically new, even though these stances may not be expressed in a concretely political way. The *Volksstück* incorporates both utopian and negative impulses, and it will be the purpose of this study to investigate to what degree each plays a role, and what the complex and subtle relationships between them are.

The *Volksstück* may appear at first glance to have more in common with the products of the culture industry that Adorno condemned than with the starkly esoteric artists that he praised, such as Schönberg, Kafka, and

Beckett. The earlier *Volksstücke* did indeed achieve popular acclaim, and the concern for financial success at many of the theaters at which they were performed did affect their production, but the creation of works of art is not so deterministic that they can be totally reduced to mere products of these constraints. Moreover, a "culture industry" had not developed to the extent that it had under late capitalism, when it began to rationalize and standardize artistic commodities (Horkheimer and Adorno 108–09). Nonetheless, the extent to which some of the criticisms applicable to the culture industry are also valid for *Volksstücke* will also have to be investigated. Examples would be the repeated combination of new effects with old schemes in order to support the status quo by providing novelty in the place of something genuinely new, and the use of uncomplicated amusement that encourages spectators not to have to think their own thoughts (121–23). Recent *Volksstücke* that are also more complex works of literature have not always been as "popular," and their inability to find the same mass appeal is a sign of their negativity, and, to a certain extent, their autonomy. Thus they may be regarded as valid objects in terms of Adorno's theories, though they of course have also had to make some attempt to address the class of people with which they deal. *problematic*

In his discussion on the developing "New German Cinema" of the 1960's Adorno himself seemed to indicate that it was occasionally possible for expressions of opposition to be contained within the culture industry ("Transparencies"). And it is also my contention that a search for negation in the earlier plays is of equal interest. The avant-garde may seem to be a more obvious means of expressing negation, but a genre that takes as its starting point an excluded class and its culture can achieve this end as well, if it avoids succumbing to the temptation of providing entertainment alone. Although much of Adorno's thought serves as a basis for this study, I do not agree with him on all counts, and modifications will have to be made as the *Volksstücke* are examined.[33] What is useful in Adorno's critical method and aesthetics is his emphasis on the negative and his appreciation for the complexity of the relationships between the artwork and social and economic relations.

To employ the thought of Adorno, Bloch, or any of the other theorists mentioned in this study as schemata by which to measure the texts under investigation would result in a reification of their thought and a violation of the spirit of critical theory by putting an end to the dialectics of the investigation. It would also be inadequate to the object of study through its assumption of an identity between the object and the critical method. These theories serve as important starting points because of the insights they provide into the *Volksstück* as literature and its place in society. The relation of these thinkers to this study may be regarded as parts of a constellation in Benjamin's sense of the term: "a juxtaposed rather than integrated cluster of changing elements that resist reduction to a common denominator, essential core, or generative first principle" (Jay, *Adorno* 14). These theories would thus be dialectically related to one another and to the literary texts. For example, Adorno was overly exclusionary in many of his judgments, such as his criticisms of jazz, and here the thought of Bloch provides a necessary counter. Unlike some of the members of the Frankfurt School, Bloch provided "a positive hermeneutics of popular culture," often finding revolutionary rather than diversionary potential in forms such as advertisements, illustrated magazines, dance crazes and Hollywood films (Hudson 179–80). But his positive evaluation of such forms results from their negative counter-tendency to wretched existence ("das schlecht Vorhandene"); they become ideology when they embellish reality rather than oppose it (PH 167–71). Since the not-yet will come into being only through the efforts of an active subject, simply accepting what is and what will come represents "the false defeatist teaching of an objective automatism" (PH 168).

One cannot simply accept the existence of popular forms as evidence of opposition, however; they must be critically analyzed to see to what extent they pander to false affects, thus confirming existing ideologies, and to what extent they offer a glimpse of the completely new. But an otherness can exist in popular or folk art, as well as in the radically autonomous. In one of his literary essays Bloch defends the fairy tale, despite its close association with the mythical that had only recently been appropriated by the Nazis. He says that its origins among the people cause it to radiate a completely different message from the myth of the master [*Herrenmythos*] proclaimed by the genre of the saga. No matter how harmless or child-like fairy tales may seem they bear the inscription: "No one is a serf, no one is born into the estate dictated to him by a thousand myths of the master."[34]

The *Volksstück*, the object of this study, is a form of popular drama that begins in the *Volk*, a subordinate class whose precise composition varies over time. The *Volksstück* addresses this group as audience and incorporates its members as material. It has provided entertainment, but has also served the function of self-expression, providing a theatrical voice that was unavailable at the court theater. This expression became more refined and self-confident as the genre became more articulate and began to achieve literary sophistication. Since many of the plays traditionally classified under this heading pander to inferior tastes in the hope of achieving quick box-office success, and others attempt to edify the *Volk* from a perspective that the ruling classes consider appropriate to them, it is necessary to examine closely a number of the more highly regarded texts to see how they serve as suitable representations of the capabilities of the *Volksstück*.[35] Though the earlier and later plays emerge from different theatrical experiences, a common thread can be found in the authors' expressed use of the genre or need to address the people in a literary form that respects them, their inadequate present situation, and their hope for a radically different future. In their attempts to give the *Volk* a genuine form of expression, the dramas analyzed here stand as negation with relation to the status quo, while at the same time holding out the hope for a future utopia.

Chapter II

Reconciliation through Magic?
Ferdinand Raimund's *Der Alpenkönig und der Menschenfeind*

Er ist ein Dichter; er glaubt es zu sein und weiß nicht, wie
sehr er es ist. Vor allem ist er dies: ein Kind des Volkes.
Darum ist er Individuum und ist zugleich eine Welt.
　　　　—Hugo von Hofmannsthal, "Ferdinand Raimund" (472)[1]

THE "ZAUBERSPIELE," OR MAGIC PLAYS, of Ferdinand Raimund have long
presented a problem for scholars, critics, and the theater-going public: the
unusual mixture of serious and comic, fairy-tale and everyday, prose and
verse, and literary and theatrical elements found in these plays has been
difficult to analyze and classify. Audiences of Raimund's time did not
always know how to receive the new type of drama that he offered them,
and spectators of today are less prepared to accept the explicit messages
urging audiences to seek contentment in the world as it is. It would be
tempting to dismiss these plays as exaggerated spectacles, curious relics of
a by-gone era, but one cannot get around their persistent popular appeal and
aesthetic interest. The scholarly consensus affirms the literary value of these
dramas even as it stresses that they are firmly rooted in the Viennese
Volkstheater tradition.[2]

The three chief *Volkstheater* authors who immediately preceded Raimund
wrote from 78 to 230 plays apiece to satisfy audience demand, although the
size of this output was achieved at the expense of weaknesses within the
plays themselves.[3] Raimund, who began his career as an actor, was pushed
into writing his first play, *Der Barometermacher auf der Zauberinsel* [The
Barometer-maker on the Magic Island, 1823], to fill a gap in the theater's
schedule. This play, as well as his second, differed little from the standard
offerings of his predecessors. But Raimund was not content to mass-produce
theatrical spectacles according to successful formulas, and his last six plays
show considerable innovation. He used both traditional forms and his own
elements to turn the genre into a literary medium that combined mimic,
theatrical effects with verbal, dramatic ones (Hein, *Raimund*, 13). Though
Raimund's output of eight plays was considerably more meager than that of
his predecessors and his form more demanding, he too met with public
acclaim. Because of the changes he brought to the genre, however, his

contemporaries tended to regard his works (along with Nestroy's) as the endpoint of a tradition that they also destroyed, since subsequent authors were not able seriously to offer dramas of the type written by Gleich, Bäuerle, and Meisl.

On the other hand, more recent research views Raimund from a different perspective and sees signs of renewal and restoration of traditional elements (Hein, *Wiener Volkstheater* 87). In this respect, Raimund is like all of the *Volksstück*-authors who have attracted critical attention: Brecht and Horváth in the twentieth century were not the first to call for or bring about a "renewal" of the *Volksstück*. Raimund's more demanding plays provided an improvement over the previous offerings of the *Volkstheater*. Mere repetition of inherited forms counteracts the utopian, either by falsely implying that the best of worlds has already been attained or by fatalistically implying that such a state cannot come into being. Change, however, can impart a forward direction.

In order to understand the limits and possibilities of Raimund's art it is necessary to stress the role of the public in its creation. David says that in the history of German literature most comedies stand out like foundlings without any apparent relationship to other works because there was no strong comic theater tradition, and each author had to develop his or her own comic means. The Viennese popular theater represents an exception, however, and in providing an institution with a strong tradition of comic theater, resembles the situation in which, for example, Molière worked.[4] In writing plays for this type of theater Raimund had to keep his public in mind and create works that they would understand and find entertaining. He was thus limited to the comic and practically compelled to use expected elements such as music, magical effects, local color, and elaborate stage sets, often involving complicated machinery. The need to satisfy the public's "Schaulust" [desire for spectacle] had been a requirement of the Viennese stage ever since the Baroque, and one of Raimund's talents was creating effective pictorial settings.[5] Although the primary emphasis of this study is the literary text, the reader should not forget the importance of the theatricality of the performance to this Viennese institution. In his portrayal of the spirit world, Raimund's pictures often convey more than his words.

Comic and spectacular effects fulfilled the demand to be entertained, as did fireworks in the Prater, but for Raimund, providing diversion was not sufficient. Thus instead of simply employing the magic elements of the tradition as parody, he used them to help convey his more serious message. As Baroque writers had done, Raimund allegorized his mythical figures to make them representatives of a higher "truth." Aware of creating something new, he added the word "Original" to the genre designation in the subtitle to his third play, *Das Mädchen aus der Feenwelt, oder Der Bauer als Millionär* [The Girl from the Fairy World, or the Farmer as Millionaire, 1826]. Audiences responded favorably to his changes, and Raimund attempted to stress the message even more in his next two plays, *Moisasurs Zauberfluch* [Moisasur's Magic Curse, 1827] and *Die gefesselte Phantasie* [Phantasy in Chains, 1828], which are set almost entirely in a mythological, allegorical world.

But the public rejected these more personal visions with their loftier intentions about the limitations of the artist and the importance of virtue in the worldly struggle between good and evil, and Raimund returned to a more harmonious balance between originality and public expectations in *Der Alpenkönig und der Menschenfeind* [The King of the Alps and the Misanthrope, 1828]. In this and his final play, *Der Verschwender* [The Spendthrift, 1834], two of his finest works, the magic world recedes while contemporary, human figures occupy center stage. Spectators as well as critics of the time felt that he had restored the proper relationship between *Volkstheater* and public.[6] Despite his constant struggle to keep from succumbing to purely entertaining comedy, Raimund could not ignore public esteem. In fact, the last stanza of the play's concluding song states that art wishes to be recognized and courts public favor (II.xv, 411).[7] The form of the play was thus a compromise among the often conflicting demands of "adherence to tradition, censorship, the requirements of the theater business, and the expectations of the public" (Hein, *Raimund* 65). The text of *Der Alpenkönig und der Menschenfeind*, although written by Raimund, also serves as a form of public expression without simply repeating conventional expectations. It represented an important step in giving a more autonomous literary existence to the drama of the *Volkstheater*-tradition and therefore of giving more weight to the voice of the *Volk* in the public dialogue.

It is clear that *Der Alpenkönig und der Menschenfeind* is firmly rooted in a popular dramatic genre that it renews and changes, but what is the play's real significance? The traditional answer, that Raimund created an improved version of the drama of moral improvement, can hardly be disputed: "Raimund intended to have a pedagogical effect on his native city in the tradition of the drama of betterment by demonstrating how human changes toward evil are motivated and in what way changes back to the good can ensue. For him the art of the stage stood beneath the old double law *delectare et prodesse*" (Fülleborn 20). And the commonly accepted reason for Raimund's success was his ability to convincingly unify a loftier message with a mixture of established forms of popular entertainment. Grillparzer's praise of his formal unity (94) is echoed even today in Mühlher's claim that Raimund was unique in combining contradictory genres into an organic whole (24). Raimund's carefully constructed works are quite different from the hurriedly written pastiches of many of his contemporaries, yet the unity that he achieved still contains many rifts, and the question remains as to why this particular form was chosen to try to unite such seemingly irreconcilable parts. Similarly, agreeing that *delectare et prodesse* is the function of the *Der Alpenkönig und der Menschenfeind* is not sufficient, because such a stance tends to dismiss the comic and the magic elements as a sugar-coating for the more serious lesson. In addition, one should question whether the moral, which is rather obvious, can be so easily accepted in its explicitly stated form.

The relationship between form and content is more complex than this, and Raimund should not simply be described as a conservative apologist for his age who preached quietism and resignation to the public, nor should one attempt to read something into his plays that is not there with the purpose of reclaiming him as a secret opponent of the regime. Though his plays express in both form and content the dominant ideology of the restoration period, they also serve to reveal the limits of that ideology.[8] Recent scholarship has gone beyond the earlier positivist approaches that interpreted his plays as autobiographical expressions of his own hypochondriac depressions or as attempts to reach the higher audiences of the Burgtheater that were always denied him. Investigations of his dramatic and linguistic forms (Harding, Wiltschko), the function of his comedy (Hein, "Gefesselte Komik"), his relation to his public and to society (Klotz, Urbach, Sengle, Prohaska), and his use of myth (Schaumann) have proved to be more fruitful. My own treatment looks at *Der Alpenkönig und der Menschenfeind* from a perspective that takes these various interrelationships of the genre *Volksstück* into account and that does not subordinate form to content. More precisely, this study will explore the manner in which Raimund's plays simultaneously function as the expression of a negation of the current state of affairs and of a utopian longing. But before pursuing this further, we should briefly review the play itself and how it functions as a *Besserungsstück*.[9]

Der Alpenkönig und der Menschenfeind opens with a pleasant overture and a majestic Alpine setting. Astragalus, the king of the Alps, comments in his opening monologue that both spirits and humans are often divided by discord and that he sometimes intervenes sympathetically in the affairs of the world to lead straying mortals to the "Tempel der Erkenntnis" [Temple of Recognition, or Understanding] (I.iv, 331–32). The human problem is soon revealed by Malchen, a young woman prevented from marrying August by her father Rappelkopf, whose misanthropy is so extreme that he cannot even get along with his loving, idealized Biedermeier family. The first act displays his increasing attacks of anger in which he progressively destroys his relations with his servants, his family, and even himself until he withdraws into the forest, and Astragalus intervenes to attempt a "Besserung," or moral improvement. When reason does not succeed, he employs his magic powers to force Rappelkopf into conceding that he must change his ways. But it is in the second act that the actual betterment takes place, and the means employed are designed to bring about a new perception rather than change through force: Rappelkopf is given the identity of his absent brother-in-law Silberkern so that he can observe his own behavior in the form of Astragalus, disguised as Rappelkopf. Astragalus is even more consistent than Rappelkopf in his misanthropy, and so angers Rappelkopf-Silberkern that he demands the satisfaction of a duel, although the latter realizes just in time that in killing Astragalus he would kill himself. In the final scene, in the *Tempel der Erkenntnis*, Rappelkopf states that he has retired from his misanthropy and become reconciled with the world: he now gives his daughter permission to marry.

The fact and manner of this moral improvement distinguish Raimund's play from most previous plays about misanthropy or other *Besserungsstücke* in the *Volksstück*-tradition. Neither Shakespeare's Timon nor Molière's Alceste is cured, and neither returns to the fold of humanity. In earlier *Besserungsstücke* such as Gleich's *Der Berggeist, oder die drei Wünsche* (1819) and *Ydor, der Wanderer aus dem Wasserreich* (1820), a change is effected, but through magic powers alone. Schmidt-Dengler points out that the *deus ex machina* who turns loose the powers of nature at the end of Raimund's first act would have formed the conclusion of a conventional *Besserungsstück*. Yet Raimund did not want to produce an external change only, but an inner, psychological transformation resulting from an experience that causes the character to recognize his own shortcomings (165). Rappelkopf's problem appears to be a personal one: rather than criticizing a corrupt society, the play attempts to demonstrate how an individual is cured and finds his way back into an intact society.[10] This play contains the message, then, that a harmonious reintegration into society is possible once an individual has achieved the proper self-recognition, and the play seems to express that harmony in both form and content. It therefore does not appear to convey negation, since the form is basically accessible to the public and its content acceptable to the existing ruling powers. Nor does it seem very utopian either, since it appears to demonstrate the possibility of inner, individual betterment and acceptance of the status quo in the present.

Yet there are quite a number of opposing elements in the play that Raimund is able to reconcile only with difficulty, if at all. These opposites in fact give life and strength to the drama because their relationship is complex and dynamic; they refrain from presenting an oversimplified duality of black and white. The play's title names two such opposites, and even though the human problem is paramount, the King of the Alps is no less important, because the cure would never have taken place without his intervention.[11] Even in *Der Verschwender*, where the appearance of spirits is kept to a minimum, a solution cannot be reached without their aid (see Crockett). But it would be wrong to think of Astragalus either as a *deus ex machina* who achieves his will through the force of magic or as the incarnation of a precise Raimundian *Weltanschauung* that conceives of a divine harmony behind quotidian appearances. Raimund's public did not subscribe to a concrete belief in these imaginary mythical figures as did ancient or primitive peoples, and the unique mixture of classical myth, fairy-tales, the phantastic, and the allegorical serve more to add effectiveness and variety to his artistic expression and pictorial stage settings (Schaumann, *Gestalt* 7–8).

The mythical thus helps determine the formal construction in that Rappelkopf's transformation is made visible through Astragalus' dual role. Linking the spirit world thematically to the plot results in greater unity than in those cases in which it was employed for parody or spectacle alone. However, when Raimund concentrated too heavily on the realm of the spirits and made that world the representative of abstract ideas (as in *Die gefesselte Phantasie*, *Moisasurs Zauberfluch*, and *Die unheilbringende Zauberkrone*), the plays also suffered. In fact, another of his strengths was in giving life to distinct local characters such as Rappelkopf. If he had subordinated Rappelkopf to an idea, dramatic action would have been lost.[12] *Der Alpenkönig und der Menschenfeind* could not have functioned effectively without either of its two title characters, and their coexistence results in dramatic tension rather than smooth harmony.

Since Astragalus functions principally as a mirror by which Rappelkopf can learn his own lesson and as a catalyst who enables this process to take place, rather than as a supernatural force who single-handedly effects the cure, the work gains in interest. The tension also serves as a reminder that no providence exists that will automatically resolve all disharmonies. The inability to cure misanthropy totally within the human world demonstrates the inadequacy of the current state of affairs, while the presence on stage of an individual, and perhaps provisional, amelioration points to the desirability of a changed world in which such problems do not occur. Providing an immediately omnipotent spirit-king would have presented a false utopia through a counterfeit solution. But omitting him altogether would have failed to solve Rappelkopf's problem, since no solution exists in the world at present. Raimund chose a dramatic medium that his audiences would understand, yet his changes point to the inadequacy of present conditions and the necessity of improvement.

Raimund's initial generic designation of this drama was "Ernst-komisches-romantisches Original Zauberspiel" [Serious-comic-romantic Original Magic Play] (*Säkularausgabe* 2: 470), and the awkward string of adjectives indicates the hodge-podge of elements that make up the work. Though he later dropped the word *ernst*, a term for which he sometimes interchanged the word *tragisch* (Wiltschko 50), the play consists basically of an interweaving of the comic with the deadly serious. This mixture represented a new feature in the *Volksstück* and can be considered a modern element in Raimund's dramaturgy. Although *Der Alpenkönig* was greeted favorably, many critics realized that they could not measure it by the usual standards, and certain parts remained sinister. Rappelkopf can hardly be called "realistic" in the sense of the term as used later in the nineteenth century, but the seriousness with which his problem is treated represents a change in emphasis from most previous *Volksstücke* and prevents *Der Alpenkönig und der Menschenfeind* from being a consistently funny (and perhaps forgettable) comedy. Although Theodor Graf Heusenstamm, who reviewed the play's premiere for the *Theater Zeitung* faults it for its mixture of the comic and the tragic, saying that both masks cannot be worn at once, a critic in Hamburg admires Raimund's ability to force the audience to laugh and weep at the same time.[13] In any case, Raimund was searching for means that could adequately express the complexity of Rappelkopf's condition, even if it meant confounding some segments of the audience by transgressing against their notions of what a drama should provide.

It becomes clear that pure comedy would have placed restraints on Raimund's portrayal. Making the misanthrope Rappelkopf into a laughing-stock because of his personal insufficiencies would have kept the play at the level of the burlesque and failed to address the problem in sufficient depth.

And the author could not have produced a satire or a comedy that delights in the joys of life because Rappelkopf's failure is not simply viewed as folly, but is referred to as a "Seelenkrankheit" [spiritual illness] (I.vii, 341), a problem much discussed at the time both in both medicine and literature (Zeman 300). Moreover, his problem is a social one, though this aspect receives less thematic analysis. In addition, Rappelkopf must be at least partially sympathetic in order for his cure to be meaningful to the spectators: a pure laughingstock is likely to call forth *Schadenfreude* on the part of the audience.

Laughter in *Der Alpenkönig und der Menschenfeind* has liberating, didactic, and critical functions, though none is predominant, and none can extinguish the potentially tragic undertones that persist to the end.[14] In a sense, any laughter liberates the spectators by freeing them from their worldly cares. A farce can thus provide a temporarily better place, though it merely represents an escape if no change is made in an inadequate reality. Some of the comic effect in *Der Alpenkönig* results from situation comedy, such as Rappelkopf's repeated falling out of his role as Silberkern: the real Rappelkopf recoils in horror as his daughter's fiancé is introduced (II.v, 385–86). The spirits engage in a form of didactic laughter, into which the audience joins, when they finally get to see the misanthrope that their king has repeatedly mentioned. In the place of the huge dragon they had expected, they find only a "dwarf" (II.i, 377–78). A more critical form of laughter is provoked through irony when Rappelkopf-Silberkern believes Habakuk, the servant whom he has mistrusted the most, rather than his loving family, because Habakuk is the first to criticize his absent master openly (II.vi, 388–89).

As Hein points out in "Gefesselte Komik," the radical re-orientation in Raimund's conception of his main characters and thus of the genre itself placed limits on the types and function of comedy in his plays: the seriousness of the plot, the more elevated style, and the tighter unity of the various parts such as inserted songs and poems make the security of liberating laughter more difficult, since the plays demand a greater identification with the world rather than an escape from it (84–86). Elements of a pseudo-utopian desire for an escape can be found in the entertaining comic features of this play, but the intrusion of the serious adds another perspective (parallelling Rappelkopf's new perspective as a result of the mirror-like play within a play) on the problems of the external world. The truly utopian must therefore be sought elsewhere.

Although the overt message calls for reintegration into a world that offers the possibility of harmony, the unexpected new formal elements negated certain public expectations, and thus the supposed unity of the world as well, since there is no exuberant laughter of satisfaction with existence at the end, despite the positive conclusion. Satire would have provided a comic means for dealing with the inadequacies of the world, but little would have been gained by making fun of the individual Rappelkopf, and satire would have tended to work against Raimund's belief in the possibility of attaining satisfaction in the here and now. Mixing the two forms was the only means possible to deal honestly with present insufficiencies while giving expression to a hope for wholeness, without succumbing completely either to despair or to the false utopia of a temporary escape. As a result, however, the form carries a message of negation.

Another important element, different from both the comic and the tragic, is the sentimental. Although this feature is perhaps the least acceptable to audiences of today, Sengle says that we should not criticize its presence, since for audiences of the nineteenth century it was a sign of the human (*Biedermeierzeit* 3: 40). It can thus serve to underscore the serious quality of the work, even though it might also function as a form of indulgence in providing a vicarious emotion. Malchen's sweet descriptions of the beauty of her native valley, her recounting of August's oath of fidelity to her, and her expressions of concern for her father's condition (I.iv, 332–33) thus characterize her in a positive way while offering the audience a pleasant diversion. The sentimental expresses a valid longing, even though its presence does not provide an actual fulfillment.

The basic rifts between the mythical and the everyday and between the comic and the tragic are further reflected in the mixtures of styles, levels, and inserted elements. The opening tableau displays a mountain panorama, introduced by an overture and a chorus of spirits (I.i, 324). After an exchange with the other spirits, Astragalus delivers his opening monologue in rhymed, High German verse expressing lofty sentiments and ideal virtues (I.iii, 331–32). The next scene in prose between Malchen and her chambermaid Lischen conveys the sentimentality of Malchen's love for August and the humor of Lischen's superstitious fear of encountering the King of the Alps (I.iv.332–35). August's entrance is marked by a song (I.v, 335–6), the first of at least ten in the play, from solos to sextets as well as several choruses. One of these, "O leb wohl, du stilles Haus" [Oh farewell, you peaceful house] was promptly taken up by the public and practically established itself as a folksong. Although Raimund integrated quite a number of diverse elements into a single whole, the end product is by no means seamless. No overarching view could impose a totality that would give the form and content a consistent unity. Since this play emerged from and remained grounded in a society that was not unified, it could not overcome all the contradictions. As a form of *Volk*-expression, *Der Alpenkönig und der Menschenfeind* is therefore an expression of diversity as well. Its mixture of forms indicates the desirability of unity while negating the notion of a unity that is achieved through the forced exclusion of any segment of the population.

The wide assortment of types of language in *Der Alpenkönig und der Menschenfeind* is one example of diversity that might fruitfully be investigated in this regard. The plays of the upper class *Burgtheater* tended toward an elevated, unified style, whereas the *Volkstheater* offered a wide spectrum of speech forms on its stages. One function of this variety is to provide an opposition that undercuts the unity of dramatic style as found at the court theater. In addition, the play's use of dialect, or more precisely, its contrast of dialect with standard literary language, also indicates marginalization. Although Viennese dialect is more a regional than a class vernacular, it was clearly associated with the *Volk*. Its use within the institution of the *Volkstheater* sets it apart from the literary language of the court theater and enabled it to function in a mild way as a form of identification or even assertion. There was little actual political conflict in Vienna in the 1820's despite the stratification of society. The emperor's habit of mixing among the people, like the attendance of the upper classes at performances of the *Volkstheater*, provided an illusion of egalitarianism (Prohaska, *Raimund and Vienna* 154–59). The apparent incorporation of the lower classes into the social whole helped stabilize the status quo, but the remaining differences between the classes and their institutions served as reminders that inequality remained in force. In general, Raimund retained the traditional dramatic distinction between the use of High German for spirits, lovers, the nobility, and the educated, and dialect for the lower classes: that is, in maintaining a social function for language by making a person's speech consistent with his or her rank in society (Wiltschko 10, 16). Yet he also introduced innovations and nuances for other purposes. In *Der Alpenkönig und der Menschenfeind* there is not a simple dichotomy between the two levels of language, but a range: the coachman speaks the strongest dialect, whereas the house servants speak on a level between pure dialect and the standard language. Habakuk's attempts to speak the elevated form serve to parody his striving. Rappelkopf's family speaks High German, as do the spirits.

The main exception is Herr von Rappelkopf himself, a wealthy landowner who would be expected to speak High German, yet he uses dialect throughout. Although Rappelkopf is in part a comic figure, he is not merely to be laughed at,[15] and dialect cannot be viewed simply as an indication of his ridiculousness, as it was in the case of Fortunatus Wurzel in *Der Bauer als Millionär*. It is used rather to set him apart, as appropriate to his role as an isolated misanthrope. It thus does not have an absolute significance, but is to be understood within the context of this play as an indicator of his alienation. Astragalus' behavior as Rappelkopf is even more extreme than that of his model, yet he never lapses into dialect, as either a "realistic" or a didactically comic portrayal would have demanded. He remains in this respect consistent with his character as King of the Alps, and his speech reminds us that we are not watching Rappelkopf himself, but a play staged for his benefit. Moreover, the differences in linguistic register serve as continual reminders of the disunity between Rappelkopf and his community and, by analogy, between the *Volk* and the ruling classes.

In addition to the distinction between the levels of dialect, there are also distinctions in levels of literary speech: verse is used in the songs and monologues and for the expression of lofty sentiments, whereas prose is employed for most of the conversations. But since the juxtaposition of these two stylistic levels would often be too abrupt or cause conversations between two unlike characters to be too jarring, Raimund introduced rhythmic prose as a third possibility to maintain the contrasts while smoothing the transitions (Wiltschko 36). Astragalus uses verse in his first appearance to Malchen and August (I.v, 338–39), but to ease the effect on the ear, he employs rhythmic prose in his first confrontation with Rappelkopf: "Du irrest, wenn du wähnst, daß du auf eigenem Boden herrschest. Mein ist das Tal, in dem die Alpe wurzelt" [You err, if you presume to walk on your own soil. Mine is the valley, in which the Alp is rooted] (I.xxi, 371–74). In the heated scene when Rappelkopf finally comes to his senses, the *Alpenkönig*, the family members, and the servants all speak in rhythmic prose, and again, Rappelkopf, speaking pure prose, is the only exception (Wiltschko 45). Dialect served as a continuous reminder that he was an outsider to his family and his society; here prose shows that he is outside the scene that is being staged for him. When he forgets himself and starts to defend his family, he begins to speak in rhythmic prose, but returns to his former speech pattern when he is reminded that he and Astragalus are playing roles (II.iv, 405–08). The unconscious switch represents a form of integration in the play within a play; his reintegration into the family at the conclusion of the frame is not accompanied by a similar switch in register, however. The text's use of language has a dual function, indicating the desirability of a utopian whole, even as it works against a unification that is unsatisfactory or unattainable.

As became evident in the discussion of the juxtaposition of mythical figures with everyday characters, *Der Alpenkönig und der Menschenfeind* is strengthened by the prominent central role of Rappelkopf. Although both the characters of the title are essential, Rappelkopf is made of flesh and blood, whereas the King of the Alps is a rather flat representation of an idea. And the seriousness with which Rappelkopf's problem is presented prevents him from being a mere laughable buffoon. For these two reasons he gains in sympathy despite his negative attributes, and his language, with which most of the public could relate, is thus viewed sympathetically as well. The members of Rappelkopf's family, who speak High German, pale in comparison, since they are rather sentimentalized and idealized. The servants Lischen and Habakuk, despite the faults of the latter, come across more strongly. Though not incorporated thematically as such, and though probably not intended as a rebellious act of class consciousness by Raimund, the juxtaposition of various types of speech serves as a reminder of the splits within society. Dialect, through its contrast with a "higher" standard language, signals the marginalization of the *Volk*, which has a parallel on stage in the outsider Rappelkopf. An integration that required acquiescence to the demands of the existing order would have been undesirable, and an integration on terms adequate to the *Volk* or through self-knowledge alone would have been impossible. The split that is expressed in this drama by means of differences of linguistic forms remains unhealed, despite Rappelkopf's cure on the level of content. The importance that different levels of language would play in later *Volksstücke* is already in evidence.

The rifts that pervade the play's form can also be found in its content. One of the most obvious sources of inconsistency concerns the nature of Rappelkopf's misanthropy. Grillparzer praised this theme and its treatment as psychologically true (94), and most critics since his time have agreed that the strength of this play resides in its ability to make the inner process of Rappelkopf's improvement visible through Astragalus's providing of a mirror for him. Yet the cause of his hatred for his fellow humans is never precisely explained. In an early expository scene, Malchen says that when her father lived in the city as a bookseller he was betrayed by false friends for large sums of money (I.v, 335–38). Their deception caused him to flee to the country, where he would not have to confront such behavior. But

Malchen does not condemn her father or think that his misanthropy represents the only side of his character. She recognizes his double nature in the following wish: "Wenn der *gute* Vater nur nicht gar so *böse* auf mich wäre!" [If only the *good* father weren't so *bad* toward me] (I.v, 337, italics in the original).

Both Malchen's attitude and the rather vague displacement of the cause onto false friends in another time and place (they are not mentioned specifically again in the play) are necessary for the play's moral: Rappelkopf's problem is a personal one, and the world into which he needs to reintegrate himself is a positive, ordered one. Thus he is surrounded on stage by a loving family, rather than an unjust society. Shakespeare's audiences see first-hand the deception and hypocrisy of those around Timon, who is unable to rejoin the whole, for the author would have first had to present a change in society to make that possible. Geißler convincingly argues, however, that the betrayal by false friends is more crucial than the brief mention would indicate. Rappelkopf had formerly perceived the human and business worlds to be unified: when he learns that they are not, his belief in a whole is shattered, and misanthropy is the result (158-9). But *Der Alpenkönig und der Menschenfeind* does not attempt to define a single cause: Rappelkopf's wife, when trying to reassure the rebellious servants who can no longer put up with their master's behavior, refers to his condition as a *Seelenkrankheit* (I.xv, 411). As mentioned above, such a concept was consistent with the importance that the era placed on *Seelenheil* [spiritual health] and thus makes a cure possible by forcing it to take place within the character. Rappelkopf claims that his condition is a result of deception and betrayal, but Astragalus says that Rappelkopf himself is the one who has left the circle of humanity (I.xxi, 372-73). His belief that his family and servants deceive him is clearly erroneous, but no answer is given as to whether his error in this regard is one of kind or degree. Through the perspective that he gains with the *Alpenkönig*'s mirror, he sees that he was wrong and says in the end that he is a "pensionierter Menschenfeind" [retired misanthrope] who has achieved the proper perception and who plans to live out his days with his family in the "*Tempel der Erkenntnis*" (II.xv, 411).

It would have been an oversimplification on Raimund's part to attribute a single, mechanical cause to Rappelkopf's problem: a condition such as misanthropy is no doubt overdetermined and is the result of a continuous and reciprocal relationship between inner and outer conditions. Thus the multiple hints without precise explanation are not necessarily inaccurate, and none should be overlooked, despite the emphasis on Rappelkopf's intense self-hatred that is transferred into a hatred toward all of humanity. The presence of social causes thus never goes away, even though the cure of overcoming *Zerrissenheit* [inner strife] must take place solely within Rappelkopf himself, according to Raimund's apparent message. The play's concluding song grants that deceivers exist, though it does not investigate possible economic or class causes for their behavior nor indicate what our response to them should be (II.xv, 411). Nor does it portray society on the whole as being characterized by such behavior. Rappelkopf has been cured because he has observed the play's moral, the ancient admonition to "know thyself," yet this advice begs the question. Although the implication exists that the more general human problem can be solved analogously, the rifts that remain in the text, despite the otherwise largely successful attempts at unity, leave the answer open. The play does not end with a picture of a completely unifiable world.

A second problem that is never completely solved involves the role of money. Though false friends are supposed to have cheated him, lack of money is not responsible for Rappelkopf's condition, since he is a wealthy landowner at the play's beginning. Yet money frequently serves as an expression of his damaged relations with others. Sophie defends her husband to her servants by saying that he often gives them presents, but the cook replies that such occasions serve as an opportunity for coarse remarks, and the money is delivered by being thrown at the servants' feet (I.viii, 342 and I.xii, 349). Money is here a literal reification of his relationship to them and becomes a demeaning weapon in his hands. He clings to money, because it is an abstract value that holds together a world that is otherwise characterized by non-identity (Geißler 161). It is also symptomatic of his own inability to be satisfied with himself: even though he has plenty of money, he feels that the amount is not sufficient and worries about the security of the investments he has made on the advice of Silberkern (I.xi, 345–47).

When Rappelkopf decides to isolate himself in the forest, the only thing he takes along is money, which would be of least use to him in that environment (Politzer 20). His remarks about money indicate his ambivalent attitude toward it, and the split in his own character: "Nur das tiefgehaßte Geld/ Die Mätresse dieser Welt/ Das bewahr ich mir allein,/ Das muß mit, das steck ich ein" [Only profoundly hated money/ The mistress of this world/ I'll keep for myself/ It has to come with me/ I'll put it in my pocket] (I.xiv, 355). In the second act Rappelkopf considers himself lost when a letter arrives from Venice announcing the failure of the commercial establishment in which he had invested (II.xiv, 407). Even after he has abandoned his misanthropy and is happily reunited with his family in the *Tempel der Erkenntnis*, he asks whether the King of the Alps can use his powers to restore his fortune, so that he might be able to forgive his brother-in-law, the only person that he still hates. One should note that Silberkern's advice was not given in order to cheat Rappelkopf and that the loss involved a normal business practice, rather than fraud. Money thus represents an obstacle on the path to Rappelkopf's complete recovery; self-recognition alone cannot remove this final cause for hatred.[16] But fortunately the real Silberkern arrives to announce that he had withdrawn Rappelkopf's investment just in time, and the happiness of the conclusion can become complete (II.xv, 409–10). An external factor thus intrudes on the harmony of Raimund's moral, since he was unable to avoid the use of this redeeming herald altogether.

The most obvious intrusion of the inadequacies of contemporary reality, also related to the theme of money, is the scene in the poor charcoalburner's hut (I.xv–xvii, 355–64). Itself a mixture of styles and elements, this scene has received a variety of interpretations and emphases and was a disturbing factor to some of the critics of Raimund's time. The mother tries to keep her hungry children from disturbing their inebriated father: rather than bringing home the money from the sale of charcoal, he has squandered it on alcohol. Rappelkopf, on his flight into the forest, enters as the scene becomes chaotic and offers a large sum of money for the house. Despite objections from the older daughter and the drunken father, who wants to hold out for more, the mother is compelled by necessity to accept the offer, even though it means leaving their home. Their departure is marked by their farewell song to the home that they love (I.xvi–xvii, 362–64).

Scholars disagree concerning the extent to which this scene can be characterized as realistic. Wiltschko, for example, says that it is the only scene of Raimund's to display a complete and realistic identification between characters and their setting; in this he believes it represents a foreshadowing of Naturalism. The children, he says, are not character types but social beings that are to be understood in terms of their milieu. Yet he is careful to add that this scene is not an accusation of society and that the situation of the charcoal-burner's family is viewed as both disturbing and comic (97).[17] Most critics correctly realize, however, that the soot on the walls of the hut is not enough to put it into the category of realism. The sentimentality of the songs and the humor of several puns prevent a consistently "realistic" picture from emerging. But even though social problems are not discussed, or even portrayed in terms of their economic basis, drunkenness and hunger intrude in a manner that is not purely laughable or sentimentally ennobling. And the mother who beats her child in desperation is part of the new, somber note that Raimund introduces; several critics of his time thought in fact that this scene should have been omitted (*Säkularausgabe* 5.1: 436, 464 and 467). Even though Raimund was by no means attempting to condemn society or even explain it, this scene mars the picture of a harmonious whole. The charcoal burner's family never returns, remaining permanently alienated from their former home. The money that Rappelkopf throws at them fails to provide an adequate exchange, and he thus commits his own act of social injustice.

Raimund was perhaps aware of these inconsistencies and intrusions on his picture of a *heile Welt* [intact world] and does not try to eliminate them, but rather bracket them. The play does not attempt to justify the existence of evil in the world in the sense of a theodicy, but it explicitly acknowledges that imperfections exist and implies that behavior consistent with the principle of proper self-knowledge can nonetheless result in a satisfactory life. In abandoning humanity for Nature, which is "so well-furnished," Rappelkopf still recognizes that parasitic caterpillars destroy foliage (I.xii, 351), and Astragalus reminds him that the logic of his fleeing humanity to escape deceivers would compel him to flee Nature as well because it contains misshapen trees, poisonous plants, and cloudy skies (I.xxi, 372). In other words, he should not condemn the whole for imperfections in its parts. Even the world of the *Alpenkönig*, which frames the play and serves as a higher example, is not perfect. The soft notes of the overture, expressing happy birdsongs, are interrupted by the strange, disturbing tones of hunting, accompanied by musket shots (I.i., 329). The mixture in this opening music is thus a signal for the play as a whole. In an aria cataloguing the absurdities of human behavior Rappelkopf says that the world remains the same despite its constant rotation, and that he is beginning to see that he is just another fool in this insane asylum (II.xii, 401–2). To Greiner, the world is insane and chaotic because the different realms of life have become separated, as have individual phenomena. He sees Rappelkopf's attempt to think the whole as positive, though such an attempt is doomed to be considered foolish in a situation in which "gesunder Menschenverstand" [common sense] requires an acceptance of the fragmentation (165). Raimund gives tacit acknowledgement to the rifts and imperfections, but intimates that they cannot be overcome. Acquiescence to such a world reveals the fatalism that for many is one of Raimund's chief characteristics, and in the end this call for acquiescence fails to be very convincing. The play's expression of negation remains strong, despite its overt call for submission to the inevitable.

In a discussion of the mirror-motif in this play, Heinz Politzer points out that Rappelkopf's self-hatred is so extreme that he attempts to destroy his own reflected image. However, since a mirror in reality also consists of glass, he gets a bloody hand as a result: "Wahnwelt und Wirklichkeit stoßen zusammen" [The world of madness collides with reality] (16). This scene may perhaps serve as a parallel for the artistic image provided by the play itself: not wishing to escape from this world altogether into a completely magical realm, Raimund has maintained a definite connection to it, but his picture of a place in which a self-produced harmonious reintegration is possible comes into conflict with reality. This collision is made manifest both in certain features of content, such as the causes of misanthropy, the role of money, and the existence of poor families who suffer the blight of hunger and alcoholism, and in the form, which tries to overcome contradictions through a unification of such a variety of inherited and original elements.

The ruptures and contradictions show how the play serves as a negative comment on its world, even though systematic social criticism almost certainly was not intended. There was little sense of class consciousness either in the *Volk* or the emerging bourgeoisie of the time (Erken, "Raimund" 309), and neither did they demand nor did Raimund seek to provide an expression of rebellion against the status quo. Any explicit criticism was intended to alleviate the flaws, rather than to overturn the whole (Urbach, *Wiener Komödie* 119). But a fuller understanding of *Der Alpenkönig und der Menschenfeind* must view the play in terms of its own text and its place in history, rather than in terms of its author's intentions, and as has been demonstrated, it represents an expression of negation on several levels. At its weakest, it rejects society by creating an alternative world of illusion through theatrical spectacle, to satisfy public demands for something besides the alienation and submission of their everyday lives, which they did not fully understand. Somewhat more strongly, it rejects an exclusive privileging of the upper levels of the social hierarchy by its identification with the *Volk* through its performance in their medium of the *Volkstheater*, its choice of characters with whom they can sympathize, and its affirmation of their values. Although Gerd Müller claims that the critical dimension of Raimund's plays lies in their portrayal of an ideal world whose workings are completely visible, in contrast to the real one, this aspect of their negativity is also rather mild, because the hierarchy itself is not questioned[18] and a solution is sought in terms of conservative virtues within a safely delineated private realm. Since *Der Alpenkönig und der Menschenfeind* offers more than pure entertainment or total escape, it grapples with the problems of contemporary reality in a manner that does not completely eliminate the occasional intrusion into the play's content of such matters as the social and economic roots of misanthropy, the reification of human relationships as a result of the increasingly important role of money as a system of exchange value, and the existence of social misery in the form of poverty. Neither the *Weltanschauung* of Raimund's epoch, the expectations of his public, nor his own talents and intentions could have produced a realistic portrayal of these issues, nor would such a treatment have necessarily been the most adequate one, but the contradictions of his age and the increasing tendency toward verisimilar representation in literature force their way into the work in a manner that disturbs the harmony that is otherwise portrayed.

It is in the form, however, that the expression of the negative comes through most strongly, and Sengle even claims that Raimund's style— which attempts to overcome the division between the serious and the comic and the fairy-tale and the everyday— makes him more radical than Nestroy (*Biedermeierzeit* 3: 20). His unwillingness to completely ignore the problems of his time, while at the same time remaining within the medium allowed him by the *Volkstheater*, demanded this solution, and he succeeds amazingly well in the combination.[19] Though the serious and the comic complement one another, they also exist in a precarious, dialectic tension that is never fully resolved. Urbach points out that Rappelkopf is not finally cured, but "pensioniert" [retired], and he speaks of Raimund's "agonizing, almost forced happy endings" (*Wiener Komödie* 103). Klotz's comment is similar: "Resistance consists of the frantic effort to clarify something on stage that pushes and shoves as a chaotic jumble in the everyday world outside. Such clarification must however fail for those who cannot see through it themselves" (*Dramaturgie* 71). The form thus negates the more simplistic aspects of the genre as practiced by Raimund's predecessors, as well as the smooth harmony of the play's own conclusion. Because the "chaotic jumble" of the outside world can be neither ignored nor penetrated, the ultimate lack of completion of the form serves in the end as the strongest negative comment on the status quo. Adorno's criticism of the weaknesses of overtly didactic plays applies to the stated message of this one. But the formal elements of *Der Alpenkönig und der Menschenfeind*, as the preceding analysis has demonstrated, succeed in conveying much more.

The other side of this dissatisfaction with the present situation is the desire for utopia. Because Raimund was ostensibly more interested in presenting a solution within society than in rejecting it, the attempt at a harmonious, formal unity and the explicit ideological message of self-improvement within the existing order make the positive elements more evident than the negative ones. Yet an affirmation of the present can close off the utopian and present a false goal for hope, rather than a genuine one. Though the play in many ways expresses such a limited affirmation, the utopian, or longing for the completely new, also proves to be a major impulse behind its creation. However, the precise depiction of utopia was even harder for Raimund to accomplish than the merging of disparate formal elements, and since utopia in general stands under a *Bilderverbot* (see p. 31 above) we are only presented with hints as to how it might appear.[20] In any case, the expression of hope for a genuine utopia cannot be totally suppressed.

Before examining the genuine forms that this hope takes, I will examine several false of inadequate utopias that the play presents and in turn rejects. For example, Habakuk repeatedly claims that he spent two years in Paris, hoping to earn respect in the eyes of others and gain superiority (II.xii, 400). Yet this assertion, which is most likely false, is based on *ressentiment*, and placing himself above others does not offer a solution to the problem of inequality. Lischen is at a disadvantage because she is a woman and repeatedly betrayed by men. Her wish, expressed in an *Ariette* in the subjunctive mood, is that she could be a man and lead an army in conquest of a *Weibchen*, to whom she would then remain true (I.xix, 369–70). Transformation into a creature who repeats the role of the dominant sex would similarly fail to resolve the problem of inequality between the sexes, though her dream represents an improvement in that she would pursue *Amor* rather than war, and instead of deceiving women like the men she knows, she would remain faithful. Thus a glimpse is given into the possibility of a better situation.[21] Rappelkopf's utopia is represented by the escape into Nature, but the belief that this offers a solution is a product of his erroneous outlook. As we have seen, Nature is not simply a harmonious idyll, but contains numerous imperfections. Thus Rappelkopf's wish is not even a nostalgic longing for an earlier, more innocent time, but a flight from humanity, within whose fold the only true utopia can be created.[22] But the utopias of these three characters are individual and partial: in ignoring the whole they prove themselves inadequate.

The "utopia" recommended in the play's moral encompasses a realm that is only a little larger: Rappelkopf's happiness is to be found as a result of self-knowledge within the modest, localized world of middle-class values. Just as August is prepared to leave the grandeur of Italy and its perfected works of art for a place with his love "im biederen Vaterlande" (I.v, 335–36), Rappelkopf finds his true contentment in the confines of his own family.[23] Since Rappelkopf's *Zerrissenheit* was viewed as a personal, psychological problem, its solution is sought within the microcosm. To Sengle, the tendency toward the small, the concrete, and the near-at-hand, as represented by *Heimat* and family, provide the strongest counterweight to the *Weltschmerz* of this era (*Biedermeierzeit* 1: 48). These two poles express the negative and the utopian, yet in a very limited and modest way.

But even this harmony is attained at the expense of harmony in the larger social world and only with the help of the spirit kingdom. It is the stage picture of this latter realm that serves as a vivid theatrical sign of a higher world: to the spectator this scenery no doubt carried a stronger message than the moral. Sengle says that one should not question the sincerity of Raimund's preaching of contentment, but he adds that Raimund is able to call for this precisely because he is so dissatisfied (*Biedermeierzeit* 3: 13). In Raimund's case, much of this dissatisfaction took the form of a portrayal of a majestic spirit world. In reply to Politzer, who thought that the conclusion was an ambiguous, forced resolution resulting from Raimund's personal "Angstvision," Prohaska says that it is in fact integrally related and that the play also represents a "Wunschtraum" [wish-fulfillment] ("Raimund's Contribution" 367). It is indeed both, as a result of its simultaneous negative and utopian impulses. Raimund is too modern to assume the presence of a perfect order behind the world of appearances, but because his audiences were still situated firmly enough in the Baroque theater tradition, these allegorical and mythical images can serve as intimations of something better, without having to function as precise models. They are like Bloch's *Spuren*, traces of the utopian that appear in the present. It is in this sense that the world of the *Alpenkönig* points toward utopia, rather than actually depicting it.

Similarly, the *Schlußgesang* [concluding song] is not in itself the final answer. It too is an intimation within a microcosm of what needs to be realized in the social whole. *Der Alpenkönig und der Menschenfeind* reminds us of the world that *is supposed to* exist; in Astragalus's opening monologue, the verb *soll* occurs in the first sentence to indicate the discrepancy between what is and what should be in the spirit world: "Wohl soll in der

Geister Walten/ Lieb und Großmut mächtig schalten" [In the spirit realm indeed/ Love and generosity are supposed to have the power] (I.xv, 411). Raimund avoided taking an overt political stance, but the tensions in the form that indicated the negative state of affairs may also serve as spurs toward what *should* be. In this sense, the negative, upsetting aspects of the form simultaneously act in a utopian manner. Otherwise, the pleasing stage pictures and the degree to which formal harmony is achieved could too easily serve as an evening's escape into an *Ersatz* theatrical utopia. The disturbing undertones are more likely to remain after the end of the performance and remind the public of present inadequacies, for which the enjoyable scenes provide a hope for an alternative. The drama is thus more open-ended than at first appears, and the gap between "soll" and "ist" is evidence of a dialectic that has not yet been resolved. Urbach claims that satisfaction, the explicit main theme of *Der Bauer als Millionär* and *Der Verschwender* can be realized only for a moment and must constantly be sought anew ("Zufriedenheit" 123–24). This allows for development and represents a form of hope: a fully realized utopia would no longer be a utopia.

The process of attempting to unify disparate forms and to reach a goal which here is only provisionally achieved does not end with the play's conclusion and therefore points beyond to something better. In the final scene, for example, the late-arriving Silberkern asks, "Aber wie hängt das alles zusammen?" [But how does it all fit together?], and is told by Rappelkopf that he will relate everything on the following day, "sonst möchte es den Leuten zuviel werden" [otherwise it would be too much for the people] (II.xv, 410). In addition to piercing the theatrical illusion for the audience, this remark spurs the spectator to reconsider how in fact everything does fit together and even to ask whether the play has provided a satisfactory explanation. This process is in the end more effective than the frozen, encapsulated statement of the moral "truth." Raimund's more complex form creates something new, and it takes its audiences seriously enough to place new demands on them without ignoring them altogether or succumbing completely to their wishes. It speaks in their language, in their particular dramatic form, without simply conforming to their expectations. And in fact, they were able to accept both the plays of Gleich and Meisl, who followed the path of least resistance in providing entertainment, and the more demanding works of Raimund (Klotz, *Dramaturgie* 49). This radicalizing of the form, rather than the incorporation of *Volk* as thematic material or the presentation of a didactic message (which, as the *Schluß-*

gesang indicates, is a truth "known" since ancient times [II.xv, 411]), is a more important indication of Raimund's relation to the people and of the utopian impulses within the play.

Scholars who try to place Raimund within a particular literary-historical tradition have had trouble reaching agreement on whether he is more properly to be considered a representative of the baroque, the romantic, the Biedermeier, or a beginning realism.[24] Part of the reason lies in the transitional nature of Raimund's age, which was finding it increasingly difficult to produce a unified world view, and it is little wonder that this play's search for harmony is unable to resolve the disunities that are manifest in the rifts in its style. Raimund was among the last who could still employ baroque elements within his dramaturgy, yet he could no longer isolate them from a serious and enlightened consideration of the everyday, into which bits of what would later be considered realism force themselves. *Der Alpenkönig und der Menschenfeind*, a historical manifestation of the ideology of accommodation typical of its time, simultaneously reveals the limits of that ideology. The play is more than its moral, which is both rather obvious and hard to accept, given the conditions that prevail in the external world. The play is also more than a decorative coating that allows the message to be delivered in an entertaining manner. Instead, both form and content express quite strongly a negative stance toward a system that breeds misanthropy and alienation, even though the causes of these conditions are not sufficiently analyzed or understood. The extent to which they permeate life is revealed in the structure of the drama, which cannot patch over the rifts by means of aesthetic unity or calls for individual moral improvement. At the same time, the seriousness of Raimund's attempt as a voice for the *Volk* and the literary demands that he makes show that the form and content of *Der Alpenkönig und der Menschenfeind* express a longing for a utopia, whose presence can be intimated, but not portrayed directly. Raimund's *Volksstücke*, so similar and yet so different from what had gone before and what came after, ultimately take their form from the dialectic between the negative that their author so desperately sought to suppress and the utopian, which he so strongly desired to achieve.

Chapter III

Signification through Insignificance: Johann Nestroy's *Der Unbedeutende*

> FRAU VON ERBSENSTEIN: Wahrheit wünsch ich, Wahrheit aus Ihrem Mund, ich hab' bereits eine Ahnung.
> SCHNOFERL: Dann haben Sie auch alles, denn die größten Gelehrten haben von der Wahrheit nie mehr als eine Ahnung g'habt.
> —Johann Nestroy, *Das Mädl aus der Vorstadt* (I.xi; SW 11: 28–29)[1]

LIKE FERDINAND RAIMUND, JOHANN NESTROY (1801–1862) began as an actor in the *Volkstheater* before writing his own plays, but although he was contemporaneous with the later Raimund and wrote in the same theatrical tradition and for similar audiences, he was different from his predecessor in many ways. Whereas Raimund's plays had been marked on the surface by allegory and magic, by a more conciliatory humor, sentimentality, and even resignation, Nestroy's were characterized by wit and satire that exposed the illusions of the world.[2] Critics of his day often expressed concern at his techniques, fearing that he was destroying what they considered the more positive achievement of Raimund (see Yates, "Idea" 464–65). Early scholars also tended to criticize him for destroying the tradition, though recent views have been more favorable, praising his changes for providing enlightenment. There is no need to set one of these playwrights over the other, however. Both created theatrically effective plays that provided something more than ephemeral entertainment.[3] Change of any sort represents both a destruction and a renewal of course, as well as a transition to something else. What is important here is to examine the changes that occurred both in the content and the form of Nestroy's dramatic texts as well as in their relationship to the public, and to determine the reasons behind these changes and their significance. What dramatic means does Nestroy use to express and deal with the inadequacies of the contemporary situation, and what hope do these plays hold for an improvement?

In Nestroy's case, the first of these questions seems easier to answer than the second, since there is general agreement among critics concerning his overriding skepticism and pessimism (Hein, *Wiener Volkstheater* 130–31). Any disagreement is mainly one of degree: that is, whether he is a cynic and nihilist (Hannemann 6, 144) or whether something more positive or humanistic can be found in his plays (Sengle *Biedermeierzeit* 2: 63; Berghaus 119). Tied in with the various interpretations of his general *Weltanschauung* are the disparate opinions concerning the political significance of his works: on the one hand Ernst Fischer considers him a "Jacobin of the Austrian suburban stage" (127), while on the other Preisner ("Der konservative Nestroy") and Sengle (3: 191, 263) find it incorrect to overlook the more conservative, bourgeois aspects of his plays. Another ground for contention concerns the essence of Nestroy's works. Mautner points out how literary scholarship has done Nestroy a disservice, either by emphasizing his wit alone without regarding its satirical function or by viewing him as a precursor of realism ("Nestroy. 'Der Talisman'" 41). As he mentions elsewhere, however, misinterpretations can also result when Nestroy is viewed solely as a satirist and not as an "author of comedy and lover of language" as well (*Nestroy* 92). Hein also criticizes a one-sided emphasis on the satirical, which has tended to occur since the famous essay by Karl Kraus stimulated new interest in Nestroy in the early twentieth century; in his own book, *Spiel und Satire in der Komödie Johann Nestroys*, Hein convincingly demonstrates that the playful is equally important (10). More recently, Decker has criticized Kraus for divorcing Nestroy's satire and verbal achievements from the social and political context and for assuming that form can be separated from content (47–48).

The divergence of views concerning the *Weltanschauung* expressed in Nestroy's plays, their political significance, the main elements of their form and content, and their place in the tradition can result from narrow critical perspectives or in reaction to previous, inadequate approaches, yet it can also result from the complexity of Nestroy's work, which cannot easily be reduced to a single element, viewpoint, theme, or genre. As with Raimund, quite a number of antitheses are in evidence, and to come to an adequate understanding of Nestroy's plays one must be aware of the large number of forces at work in their creation and the difficulty of the problems that his works attempt to resolve. Firmly fixed within the *Volkstheater* tradition with its links to the clown-like Hanswurst figure and the *commedia dell'arte*, he nonetheless made important original contributions and should be viewed both as a comedian who takes great pleasure in the creation of amusing dramas as well as a skeptic whose illusion-exposing satire is an equally important constitutive element. The contrasts within Nestroy's work might therefore best be explained as stemming from the urge to expose and condemn (the negative impulse) and the desire for the completely new (the utopian). The valid observations of previous scholars can be incorporated into a discussion that analyzes Nestroy's drama from this dual perspective.

One should also keep in mind that Nestroy's work was theatrical and that restricting one's investigations to the printed text fails to give a complete picture. The limitations of the text become especially apparent when one considers the genesis of a Nestroy play: after choosing a suitable source (such as a French comèdie-vaudeville — Nestroy rarely created his own plots), he would draft a scenario and make rough notes before finishing the initial manuscript. Copies would then be made for submission to the censor, who would often make revisions. Changes were also likely to be made by the composer of the music and by the author himself both during rehearsals and also later in response to public and critical reception. Thus a "text" in the popular theater was constantly undergoing development.[4] Yet printed texts are the principal surviving artifacts with which today's scholarship can concern itself: this study will of necessity concentrate on the literary text without, however, ignoring the theatrical nature of the entire work of art and the public response to it.[5]

The intellectual element within Nestroy's wit and linguistic inventions gives strength and value to the plays as printed texts, and his theatrical constructions enable the plays to take shape as effective stage productions. His place within the tradition explains his use of dramatic conventions, yet his place within a particular historical period gives his plays a new relationship to external reality as a result of changing conditions and changing public response. The *Zauberstück*, for example, proved no longer to be an effective means for Nestroy's creativity, and his first efforts, which still employ a magic frame, tend to parody this genre rather than taking it seriously as a vehicle for revealing inadequacies in reality or providing alternatives to it.

Because the public's role in the creation of plays for the *Volkstheater* is so important, it is necessary to examine changes that occurred in that institution during the 1830's and 1840's. According to May the public influenced both form and content because it was "employer, consumer, and object of the Viennese *Volkskomödie*" (87). In the period following the Congress of Vienna the suburban audience was comprised of spectators from the middle and lower-middle classes, and, despite differences among various groups within it, was relatively homogeneous. In the *Vormärz* period following the July Revolution of 1830, however, changes within society became evident with the increasing independence of the middle class, and differences between classes became accentuated. The beginnings of

industrialization that resulted in the rise of the middle class also brought a
change in the concept of the lowest group from "Pöbel" (rabble) to
"Proletariat" (Eder, 135). The *Volkstheater* author Friedrich Kaiser reported
that in this period the orchestra seats were filled by the families of
well-to-do industrialists as well as occasional representatives from the
aristocracy, whereas the second and third galleries were occupied by the less
well-off, who could nonetheless afford weekly visits to the theater because
of the cheap ticket prices.[6]

Although the middle class and the *Volk* both united in opposition to the
conservative Metternich system, a distinction began to be made in the 1840's
between the "better part" and the "inferior part" of the public (May 91),
and reviews of the time indicate that different plays pleased different
segments of the audience. The "lower" group was particularly appreciative
of the more aggressive genre, the *Posse*, whereas the more conservative
spectators and many newspaper critics preferred the conciliatory *Lebensbild*,
or "picture of life" (93). Whereas the old *Zauberspiel* had attempted to
"master structurally the vision of better middle-class norms in new social
attitudes," the *Posse* destroyed the philosophy and forms of the middle-class
phase of the popular theater and the *Lebensbild*, as written by Friedrich
Kaiser, tried to create positive artistic representations of the democratic
social structures of the *Vormärz* period (121).

The term *Volksstück*, as used in the 1840's, tended to be applied to
positive plays resembling the last of these genres (Yates, "Idea" 462–66).
In general, the *Volkstheater* sided with the new industrial middle class, but
because of the varied composition of the public, as well as the interests of
its authors, it could also be critical of the bourgeoisie. This dialectical
position, which places it between the two classes while allowing it at various
times to serve as a voice for each, is what makes it a *Volkstheater*,
according to May (63). Developments in the 1840's, however, such as
worsening economic conditions, which made it harder for the lower classes
to afford theater tickets, meant that audiences began to be composed more
and more of *Großbürger* and therefore no longer represented such a
cross-section of the Viennese public (97–98). The increased censorship
during the reaction that followed the Revolution of 1848 was also a factor
in diminishing the ability of the *Volkstheater* to function as a critical forum.

The changing public role should therefore be kept in mind in the
following discussion of Nestroy's plays. Karl Carl, the director of the
Theater an der Wien to whom Nestroy was contractually obligated after
1831, had made a fortune with his *Volkstheater* in Munich and came to

Vienna with the hope of repeating his success. Because the *Spektakelstück*, including the *Zauberspiel*, was expensive to produce, he preferred the *Posse* with its simpler sets.[7] This form was better suited to the talents of Nestroy, Carl's most popular author, and together they were successful at drawing large crowds. Whether or not Nestroy's real audience of the earlier period were the *Kleinbürger* who occupied the cheaper seats and appreciated his caustic attacks on the idyllic Biedermeier tradition (Berghaus 110) or the *Großbürger* who also attended his plays (Sengle, *Biedermeierzeit* 3: 198), Nestroy's artistic inventions were also constrained both by censorship and the need to provide successful plays to a mixed audience. Nestroy's texts have merit, however, because he did not merely give in to these constraints or accede to the expected demands of public or critical taste, even when he took them into account (see Hüttner, "Nestroy im Theaterbetrieb" 243; Yates, "Kriterien" 11).

Although many scholars find it more important to consider Nestroy's total output than to focus on a single play, too broad a focus runs the danger of gathering scattered quotations out of context. The best approach would be to refer to the entire corpus of plays when necessary while concentrating on one in order to observe in detail the crucial interrelationships between form and content, public and drama, and literary text and external reality. For this study, almost any of Nestroy's better-known and more frequently performed plays could be chosen. Many of his *Possen* from the late 1830's and early 1840's, such as *Der Talisman* (1840), are the most typical of his aggressive, creative satire, and an attitude of negation toward the status quo is clearly in evidence in them. Yet it would be worthwhile to examine a more "positive" text to see if the negative is present there as well, and, similarly, to find whether a positive portrayal can also express the utopian. I will therefore concentrate on *Der Unbedeutende* [The Insignificant One], subtitled by the author *Posse mit Gesang* [critical farce with music] but categorized by Otto Rommel as a more conciliatory *Volksstück* in his edition of the *Sämtliche Werke*. Rommel's decision is not without basis, since this play seems to take a more serious stance and attempts to present a moral with a positively portrayed, exemplary hero from the *Volk*. But a closer investigation will reveal that his evaluation is somewhat overstated and arbitrary, and that the negative and the utopian are not necessarily to be found in the expected places.

According to Rommel, after eleven years of nagging by the critics, Nestroy delivered a *Volksstück* of the type that they had requested: "a believable plot taken from real life, characters and situations from the life of the *Volk*, didactic tendency, and 'healthy comedy'" ("Johann Nestroy. Ein Beitrag" 244, 247). The critic from the *Wiener Theaterzeitung* of 5 May 1844 praised the premiere as follows:

> It is a *Volksstück* of the right sort, written *from* the perspective of the people and *for* the people, and of such a character as only a people's author in the original sense of the term could write it. Nestroy has blazed a new trail with this play.... He has solved the difficult problem of writing a play in which comedy and morality go hand in hand, not in separate serious and comic scenes, but in a heartfelt, harmonious union. (qtd. in SW 8: 339; italics in the original.)

It would thus seem that Nestroy succeeds in fulfilling the dual purpose of instructing and entertaining, which many have felt to be the primary function of the *Volksstück*. Later reviews in the same newspaper echo these sentiments, one even claiming that Nestroy has abandoned his dirty jacket for a clean "Bürgerrock" [burgher's coat] (SW 8: 344). Moritz Saphir also finds reason for praise (alongside his grumblings about weaknesses in the plot) and claims that for once all the critics and the public are in agreement (*Der Humorist*, 13 May 1846, qtd. in SW 8: 348–53). After the premiere Nestroy received 35 curtain calls, and the play was performed 63 times the first year.[8]

The apparent attempt to take public wishes into account is significant, as is the acclaim with which the play was greeted. Yet contemporary judgments should not be unquestioningly accepted as valid: the play needs to be examined more carefully to determine if it indeed represents the serious, positive work that was called for, and if so in what way. A positive Nestroy would represent a contrast to the negative skeptic and could perhaps give a more direct indication of any utopian dreams he may have had. Yet a closer examination will reveal that this play does not represent an abrupt break with the form of the *Posse* and that the most obvious "positive" elements are on the whole too weak and too ambiguous to serve as the representation of a better alternative. Ironically, the negative elements are the most positive, and, as is often the case with Nestroy's plays, the two are so closely intertwined through inverted juxtapositions that it is practically impossible to separate them. The call by critics for a positive portrayal of the *Volk* is itself ambiguous and could mean either the picture of lower classes who were moral and loyal to the status quo or the favorably depicted expression of a self-assured class, which, in delineating its own identity, presents a negative counter-image to an imagined homogeneous society that could appear unified only by repressing or assimilating elements outside the ruling powers. What picture of the *Volk* and of society is presented, and what is the play's relation to external reality? What is satirized, and perhaps more importantly, how does this process of satirization take place?

Over three-fourths of the characters that appear onstage in *Der Unbedeutende* are from the world of craftsmen and servants; the rest come from the nobility. The make-up of his cast of characters thus reflected the world in which Nestroy lived (Mautner, *Nestroy* 38) and corresponded to the audiences that visited his plays. Posters that stressed roles from the *Kleinbürgertum* were useful advertisements for drawing crowds (Eder 136). Yet Nestroy was not alone in portraying such social groups on stage: this practice was a well-established *Volkstheater* tradition. And the comic conventions of the tradition as well as aggressive satire's need to exaggerate prevent Nestroy's portrayals from being realistic in the later sense of the term (Rommel, "Nestroy, der Satiriker" 65; Eder 139). Though they consist of character types clearly grounded in the existing social world, they do not depict that world with psychological or sociological verisimilitude. Character names that indicate professions (such as the carpenter Span [wood-shaving] in this play) are often found in Nestroy's comedies and point to such a typology. Hein says that Nestroy's division of his characters into a good-bad, rich-poor dualism is purely a fictive contrast that allows a dramatic tension to develop, rather than a moral or social one, and that the characters are "Spielfiguren" [dramatic figures], instead of realistic reflections from daily life (*Spiel und Satire* 29, 35). But although the dramatic aspect is an important constituent, the portrayals are not limited to this. As a satirist, Nestroy wanted to attack reality rather than reflect it. The figures are therefore precisely connected to their reality. And by placing representatives of the *Volk* on stage, Nestroy was affirming their ability to function as spokespersons in public dialogue.

As the play opens, Baron Massengold's unscrupulous secretary Puffmann and cousin Ottilie help the baron's minor ward elope with her lover. Puffmann, who has forged the date on her birth certificate, fears that a marriage between the baron and his ward would diminish his own influence over his employer, and Ottilie hopes for a match between the baron and herself. In order to establish an alibi for himself on this fateful evening, Puffmann manages to convince a sleeping boy that he has seen Puffmann returning from a tryst at the home of Klara Span, whom the secretary does not even know. The boy's report spreads as gossip among the villagers, who ostracize the innocent Klara. Her brother and protector, the carpenter Peter Span, takes it upon himself to clarify this slander and to defend the honor of his sister and himself by exposing the behavior of Puffmann. As the play's title indicates, he is an insignificant person in comparison to the members of the Baron's coterie, but he is eventually successful, and a happy ending is achieved with the restoration of Klara's engagement to her fiancé. The entire truth about Puffmann is never publicly revealed, however: in order to save himself, the secretary makes up a story about an unhappy love affair with Ottilie. The Baron, attempting to restore the situation for Puffmann and his cousin, promises them a wedding which neither in fact desires, but which they cannot reject without re-incriminating themselves.

Satire is of course one of the most important features of Nestroy's works, whether it be the essence or one of two co-equal elements.[9] Satire in general attacks a threatening world, which it exposes by revealing the discrepancy between an inverted reality as it actually exists and the ideal situation that should exist. On the level of content, *Der Unbedeutende* reveals a world that is the inversion of the ideal in that a representative of the upper classes is able to ruin a person from the lower ones, or as the irony of the title suggests, that the true significance of such people is not recognized. The complicated series of maneuvers with which Puffmann attempts to extricate himself and their culmination in his fitting punishment make him look more and more ridiculous and result from an aggressive satire that refuses to give unqualified support to the existing order. Span's remark concerning the "angeborene Feindschaft zwischen arm und reich" [inborn enmity between poor and rich] in his heated exchange with Puffmann (III. xxiii, 90) and his rejection of the baron's attempt to allow Puffmann to cover up his doings are thematically related to this satirical target and provide further grounds for interpreting this play as an expression of revolutionary *Vormärz* sentiments. Examples of social-critical content can also be found in the less than respectful manner in which the servants talk about their employers (I. vii–viii, 13–14), the description of Hobelstadt as a town with eight hundred inhabitants, one palace, and three houses (I. ix, 15), or Peter Span's definition of "Standeswahl" as an apprentice's freedom to decide by which guild he wants to be exploited and mistreated (I. xiii, 23).

Nestroy's plot does not retain all the complicated intrigues of his source (Michel Raymond's novella "Le grain du sable" and Karl Haffner's dramatization, "Der Faßbinder;" cf. SW 8: 307–36), and he makes the secretary rather than a court minister the villain to get his work past the censors more easily (Charue-Ferrucci 65–67). His replacement of Klara's fiancé (who does not appear at all in the play) with the fiancé's father (Thomas Pflökl) allows Span to be the main actor, and thus a comic figure as well (Rommel, "Johann Nestroy, der Satiriker" 130–33). The definite satire directed against Puffmann and the clearly delineated antithesis between his position and that of Span indicate a negation of the status quo and prompt Berghaus to claim that "Adelskritik" [criticism of the nobility] is the main theme of the play (117). Yet the satire cannot be classified so easily and precisely.

Even though the Baron's lack of insight into the sycophantic character of his secretary and his willingness to stop the inquiry before justice has been done prevent him from being a positive figure, his position of power and authority remains basically unquestioned. The satire seems directed at the dishonest abuse of that power, rather than at the order itself. Puffmann, who stands between the classes, is the villain, and much of the accent has shifted from class to wealth (see Hein in Aust, Haida, Hein 147). And even though the play sides with Span in the conflict with Puffmann, not all of the representatives of the *Volk* come off so well. The gossiping and petty morality of the villagers is also subject to ridicule, and in this respect the play negates human weakness in general rather than simply the present social order. Sengle claims that Nestroy's satire is "occasional" and "punctuated" in that he does not try to maintain a dominant standpoint throughout a play (3: 215), yet skepticism concerning a number of phenomena, including figures from different classes, does not necessarily represent a shifting stance. What underlies all of the satire in the play is a criticism of the failure to recognize the truth; as in *Der Alpenkönig und der Menschenfeind*, the goal here is to achieve *Erkenntnis*. The lesson thus seems to be more epistemological in nature than moral or political.

Yet the title and other elements within the play link the criticism of this inability to see beyond superficial appearances with a more political satire of a society that employs false criteria to measure a person's significance. Puffmann uses an exaggeratedly humorous metaphor of clothing to explain that his self-interested behavior stems from a higher motive than pecuniary greed: "Mein Eigennutz hat etwas Respektables, seitdem er sich in den Salonfrack des Dominierens geknöpfelt" [My self-interest has something respectable about it since it put on the dress-coat of domination] (I.iv; 8), yet his choice of words indicates that self-interest still lies behind the disguise, which merely serves to lend the appearance of respectability. Clothing is referred to more directly when Peter enlists the aid of the boy Hansi to find the "gentleman" who supposedly visits his sister. Hansi at first fails to recognize Puffman because he looks for the clothes that the secretary wore rather than the man behind them (III. vi–vii; 66–67). Later, when

Peter in the presence of his sister reveals Puffmann as the source of the slander, the secretary attempts to hide behind stilted bureaucratic language about the "prevailing circumstances of a mistake" ["es scheint bei der ganzen Sache die Obwaltung eines Irrtums stattzufinden"]. By contrast, there is no dissembling for Peter: "Ich sprech', was ich denk" [I say what I think] (III. xxiii; 88).

Additional criticism of the nobles occurs when they are placed into a dilemma concerning their treatment of Ottilie, who is temporarily in disfavor. What is important to them is to present the proper *appearance* to the baron, in order to retain the advantages of their parasitic existence (III.vii; 67). The inability to distinguish reality from appearance is potentially quite serious in the neighborhood's ostracism of Klara as a result of her supposedly damaged reputation. If Peter had failed to stand by her and uncover the true state of affairs she could have suffered a fate similar to that of her namesake in Hebbel's *Maria Magdalene*. Even though members of the *Volk* are criticized for their slander of an innocent person, their fault lies in their behavior at a given instant. The aristocracy is more thoroughly condemned because its very existence is based on appearance.

Much of the treatment of the discrepancy between appearance and what lies behind it is given expression in Peter Span's entrance song and monologue (I. xiii; 21–25) and his *Couplet* in the sixteenth scene of the third act (74–80). These offer thematic parallels to the play's action and introduce Span in his role as commentator. In using a carpenter's rooftop perspective to contrast examples of the insufficiencies of human behavior with situations that would represent something completely new, Peter indicates extreme skepticism concerning the likelihood of their occurrence. The negation is here all-encompassing, since human weakness in general is criticized and not just the behavior of one class or the present form of the social order. Its breadth is indicative of the honesty of its analysis, however: a politically partisan criticism can only be partial because of the limitations it places on its own skepticism. In going beyond mere topicality, this criticism seems to fit Adorno's call for a thorough-going negation. The integrity of the critique thus provides a stronger condemnation of the status quo. Yet these examples are statements of a negative outlook within the play's content, and as such they are in themselves insufficient in providing enlightenment, in Adorno's sense.

In addition to the negative, satirical attacks on external reality and human insufficiency there are also positive elements in the play's content, the most obvious of course being the figure of Peter Span. As a craftsman who sees through appearances he provides a positive contrast to the corrupt Puffmann and thus a model for and affirmation of the "Unbedeutenden" in the *Volkstheater* audience. May's comments on the character Salome Pockerl in *Der Talisman* could just as well apply to Span:

> The inferior position in a society of antagonistic classes is replaced by the valid criterion of human worth: by the measure of one's productiveness for society. With this Nestroy, who was often considered a poet of negation, created around 1840 a real measure for the formation of positive characters. (161)

As illustrated above, Span's self-awareness in his profession leads to an enumeration of its advantages, which in turn express metaphorically his outlook on life. That such a perceptive character from the *Volk* is given so much time as a spokesman on stage challenges the notion that he is insignificant, and, according to Hein, such portrayals during the period of increased social tensions in the years before the revolution served to encourage the social and political self-consciousness of the audience ("Possen- und Volksstück-Dramaturgie" 131; see also Fisher 182–83). In his "Der utopische Nestroy" Hein says that "a bit of newly achieved social quality flashes in *Der Unbedeutende*" (21). Hein's essay tends to stress content in its search for utopian aspects, which it finds in a number of Nestroy's aphorisms, songs, and plots. Span's victory would exemplify the last of these and his song, contrasting inadequate behavior with the ideal, is another means for introducing positive content that points both beyond the plot of the play and present reality.

Klara too is a positive figure, and in fact it is her complete honesty, directly conveyed by the guileless expression of her countenance, that convinces her brother of her innocence (II. xii; 61–62). This openness, in contrast to Puffmann's dissembling, later convinces von Packendorf as well (III. xxx; 95). Yet Klara, of course, plays less central a role than does Peter, and the restriction of her character to the positive tends to idealize it and thus to weaken it. Positive is not to be confused here with utopian, however, though a world in which everyone had the perception of Peter and the ingenuous honesty of Klara would indeed approach the ideal. These figures exist in a dramatic world that suggests the imperfections of the real one, and no blueprint is given to change it.

In fact, Peter's struggle is an individual one and fails to display any awareness that his situation is socially determined. When Peter tells Thomas about the only two friends on whom he can depend, and Thomas asks if they aren't rich friends, Peter replies with a pun on the homonyms "poor people" and arms [Arme]: "Nein, Arme sind's— (seine Arme weisend) die zwei" [No, they're arms— (pointing to his own) these two] (I. xiv; 27). Although he criticizes the unreliabilty of the rich, it is his own two arms that can help him and not the members of his class, a fact that becomes evident during his later ostracism. His victory gives a glimpse of the positive, but fails to introduce utopia itself, because it does not extend beyond him. Since the victory is achievable, it resembles a "fulfillable affect" in Bloch's sense of the term, rather than an example of the radically new (see p. 27 above). It also seems similar to Raimund's attempt to seek a solution within the private rather than the public realm.

Although the importance of the positive in Span's portrayal should not be underemphasized, the negating aspects in his outlook, expression, and behavior are stronger. As Hinck observes of comedy in general:

> A comedy ... achieves its effects from the ridiculous lack of a norm— from the spectator's secretly correcting a character or condition in terms of the norm .... This norm can be one that obtains within a social system or it can be one that goes beyond it .... Norms of the latter type are set by utopia. ("Komödie zwischen Satire und Utopie" 8)

Nestroy is less capable of creating directly positive roles and situations and is more successful at conveying the positive through a negation of the negation, a process that occurs in a number of ways in the play. Foremost among these is Span's skepticism. This side of Span's character causes him to resemble figures such as Schnoferl in *Das Mädl aus der Vorstadt*, and the play remains very much a *Posse*. Despite the seriousness of the tone that is introduced by the positive elements, the comic predominates, and it is doubtful whether the play can be described as "im Ganzen ernsthaft" [basically serious] as Mautner does (*Nestroy* 286). This satirical quality makes Span appealing, and statements expressed in this manner are more convincing than direct utterances of the truth, as will become evident below in a discussion of the language in the play.

Span's skepticism even includes a shadow of doubt concerning Klara's innocence, and he decides to seek concrete proof. The method he chooses to find the truth involves, ironically, non-recognition: when he brings his sister and Puffmann together, it is obvious to him that they have never seen one another before (II. xx; 105). Negating what would have been a damning recognition proves her not guilty. The play's ending is a happy one for Klara, but she expresses her joy in negative terms: "Glücklich sein is viel, aber ich hör auf, unglücklich zu sein— das is noch mehr" [Being happy means a lot, but now I'm going to stop being unhappy— that means even more] (III. xxxiv; 105). Peter's neighbors also receive a good deal of time on stage, and the portrayal of the *Kirchweih* [church fair] has in certain respects a positive, festive air which is, however, negated in the end by their petty gossiping and suspicion. Yet even the criticism of the *Volk* can in a sense be regarded as positive — Nestroy knew them well enough and took them seriously enough to condemn as well as praise; an idealization would have been dishonest. Karl Holtei, a *Volkstheater* author whose sentimental *Lorbeerbaum und Bettelstab* was parodied by Nestroy, complains that supposedly progressive authors show the people as "niedrig gesinnt" [having abject views] and mock supposedly reactionary authors who ennoble the people (qtd. in Eder 140). This refusal to idealize on Nestroy's part was unacceptable even to such authors as Gutzkow and the Young Germans (Eder 140). They failed to understand how the negative could be stronger and in fact more positive than what passed for positive depictions.

As the begining of this chapter made clear, Nestroy's plays embody new artistic attempts, and it is in their form, both internal and with respect to the tradition, that the issues of negation and utopia are most sharply delineated and effectively conveyed. His abandonment of the *Zauberstück* may perhaps be regarded as an accommodation to changing public tastes, but his relation to the public was an ambivalent one, and his unwillingness to immediately embrace the *Lebensbild*, the genre favored by Friedrich Kaiser, shows that critical opinion alone was not enough to determine what form his plays would take. He makes fun of the *Lebensbild* in *Der Talisman* (II. xxiv; SW 10: 456), and in his approaches toward it in *Der Unbedeutende*, the critical quality of the *Posse* remains stronger. Of the various forms of popular comedy, the *Posse* was the most negative and was criticized by some for being too destructive without setting up any ideals, yet its satirical-aggressive character made it the most popular of the genres as well as the most suitable form of expression for Nestroy.[10] Although the educated of the day tended to look down on the lower style of the *Posse*, it was, according to Sengle, the best means of comic expression of the period, and he feels that it has failed to receive its deserved place in German literary history (2: 402–03, 438–39).

Whereas Raimund mixed the higher and the lower styles, Nestroy made a conscious decision to stick with the lower one (Sengle 3: 257), which he sharpened into an effective dramatic and literary instrument. Hannemann claims that since Nestroy doubted the possibility of revolution on the barricades he created one every night on the stage; thus his drama can be considered as negation or anti-theater (44–45). Although this view goes a bit far in its implication that the play serves as a sublimated replacement for actual social change, it is nonetheless true that the form of Nestroy's plays contains the greatest innovation and runs most clearly against the grain. It is here that Nestroy's "intellectual principle... of *antithesis*," always at work within the mechanism of his plays, is most evident (Mautner, *Nestroy* 95. Italics in the original). The choice of generic form thus takes a stand in opposition to the political and aesthetic establishment.

Negating innovations can be seen, for example, in Nestroy's relation to plot, which he rarely invented himself and which he subordinated to the relations between the characters and their speeches: downgrading the plot to a mere scheme strengthened the plays' social criticism (May 121). *Der Unbedeutende* has far fewer intrigues than its source, and the character relationships and the confrontation between aristocracy and commoner predominate over the artificial machinations.[11] This treatment of the plot allows the development of the well-known Nestroyan *raisonneur* who provides unity and offers comments that bring about an awareness of his own (and the audience's) insufficiencies. The first examples of this type, such as Titus Feuerfuchs in *Der Talisman* are still fixed within their own situation, but the later versions, such as Peter Span, stand clearly above the world and maintain no illusions (Rommel, *Alt-Wiener Volkskomödie* 970-71). Characters like Span thus play a role within the fictional world but also step outside it in order to comment on it. They are split characters whose dual function lends epic qualities to the drama of the sort later employed by Brecht (Slobodkin 51, 54–55; Preisendanz 11).

Thus a contact is established with the public that allows them to see through the theatrical illusion, and this begins a process that aids in piercing the deceptions of external reality as well. Peter Span provides criticism, not simply because he represents a positive contrast to a corrupt and decadent nobility, but because his superior position in terms of the theatrical fiction enables him playfully and dialectically to reveal false perceptions and to criticize a society whose illusions have become fossilized. The content of the statements from Span's monologue and songs quoted above is not the main vehicle for criticism of a world caught in the grip of illusion, but rather their context in the mouth of a character who uses them to destroy the closed unity of the dramatic fiction and to point to something beyond.

Songs had long been an important element in *Volkskomödie*, but whereas the *Theaterlied* tended to be simpler, more poetic, and more closely related to folksongs, *Couplets* had a satirical, reflective basis and were similar to the *Bänkelsang* [street ballad]. They appealed to the intellect, while the chorus, *quodlibet* and situational song had a mimic or burlesque character (Hein, *Spiel und Satire* 89–92). These last types could therefore function as safety valves, whereas the *Couplets* contributed to the satirical function of exposing the real world (117–18). Rather than unity, they conveyed dissonance, which was "supposed to lead to to the provocation of the suburban theater public" (May 343). In *Der Alpenkönig und der Menschenfeind* songs had a number of purposes: to advance the plot, to further character development, and to serve as examples of a desired harmony. Any commentary was usually in the form of advice that claims to promote congruity. Raimund had attempted to respond to the fragmentation of the world with a harmonious form, but Nestroy willingly plays with elements that open up form rather than closing it off. The two chief examples, which provide a carpenter's superior insights and which stress the unlikelihood of several positive occurrences, have only a tangential relation to the plot. They interrupt it, rather than helping it to a smooth conclusion. Nestroy's forms, which undermine the conventions of genre and plot and cast doubt on the dramatic fiction, create an antithetical relationship that effectively questions the make-up of the world at large, including the contemporary social order.

More important than Nestroy's questioning of genre, plot, and dramatic fiction is his relation to language. Although his language has the dual purpose of communication (exposition, advancing the plot) and comic play, the second of these functions takes on a critical character and becomes dominant, since the plot is less important than the reflective commentary.[12] The episodic character of Span's entrance monologue allows him to comment on society in general, and Nestroy's playing with language in the form of puns is more effective than direct criticism in opening the possibility of new perspectives. When Peter and Klara are instructed by Puffmann's servant to wait in the anteroom [*Vorzimmer*], Peter uses the common verbal link between the name of his profession [*Zimmermann*], which represents his social identity, and the designation of the room that represents a subservient position outside the realm of power:

Ich bin doch Zimmermann, aber in die Vorzimmer kann ich mich nicht finden. Ein Vorzimmermannn is halt eine ganz eigene Profession. Viele erheben s' zur Kunst, mancher bringt's bis zur Virtuosität darin, 's is schwer z' lernen, und doppelt schwer für den, den sein Unstern in sein' alten Tag'n erst zum Lehrbub'n im Vorzimmerhandwerk macht. (III.xxi; 86)

[I am, after all, a carpenter who constructs rooms, but I can't feel at home in the anteroom. An anteroom-man is, in my opinion, a completely different profession. Many elevate it to an art, some even achieve virtuosity in it, it's hard to learn and twice as hard for one whose misfortune makes him in his old age an apprentice in the anteroom-craft.]

The creative neologism "Vorzimmermann" represents an antithesis, which, in appealing to an intellectual insight, is stronger than a direct remark, such as the reference to the "inborn enmity between poor and rich." In reassembling language, the dialogue criticizes the construction of the existing hierarchy and provides a model for a possible rebuilding.

Like Raimund, Nestroy employs a number of levels of language, though not necessarily for the same reasons: speech that is flavored with Austrian dialect, conversational High German ("Schriftdeutsch"), and High German theater language, which tends to convey pathos to the South German listener (Mautner, *Nestroy* 66). Most of his main characters speak in dialect, which they control and, in Span's case, use for comic effect. In itself, dialect is not a sign that a character is ridiculous, as is the case with High German, which because of its artificiality for Nestroy's audiences, often marked a character as a target for mockery (67). Thus language operates on the level of content as an accurate reflection of Span's and Puffmann's ranking in society, but more importantly as a formal means for commenting on their character and on reality. Puffmann's resorting to stilted or bureaucratic language reveals his insincerity, especially when juxtaposed with the more natural-sounding dialect. According to Hein, "Dialect is the measure by which the genuineness of what is said is gauged" (*Spiel und Satire* 45). Since dialect is presented as the norm, the drama functions, as it did with Raimund, in asserting an outside voice that forces its way into the social dialogue. The verbal discrepancies within the play, which are repeatedly presented to the ears of the spectators, serve as a constant reminder of discrepancies and insufficiencies in reality. Discrepancy in numerous breaks of style, thousands of plays on words, and hundreds of expressed antitheses create, according to Mautner, the family resemblance among all the plays of Nestroy (*Nestroy* 69). Nestroy's plays thus do not go as far as Raimund's in attempting to maintain the fiction of an overall harmony.

In language characters can either reveal, as Span does with his verbal connections, or be revealed, as is the case when the gossipy neighbor Flachsin demonstrates her unthinking superficiality with the use of two contradictory clichés in practically the same breath: "Die Klarl! Aber hab' ich's nicht allweil g'sagt—?!" and "Nein, wer hätt' sich das denkt! D'

Mamsell Klarl!" [Klara! But isn't that what I said all along—?, and No! who would have thought it! Mlle Klara] (I.xiii.; 34). She is thus caught in the reified language that has, like the world, become paralyzed by convention. She accepts opposite sentiments as identical, just as supporters of the current order were blinded to its contradictions.

The exposing of clichés sometimes results from the situation, as when Puffman's offer to Thomas "statt dem Geld einen guten Rat geben, der mehr wert is" [instead of money to give some good advice, which is more valuable] (III.xvii; 81) is obviously an expression of his own self-interest rather than an ideal that he believes. At other times it takes the form of direct comment: when the innkeeper uses High German to quote a proverb about the satisfaction of his guests being his highest goal, Kübler interrupts to finish it for him and adds, "Die Redensart kennen wir" [We know the saying] (III.xxxi; 96). The words are thus revealed as not being the innkeeper's own, and Kübler's remark skeptically implies that they may not even reflect the innkeeper's sentiments or any truth at all. Span also unmasks "Floskeln" [flowery phrases] in the seventh stanza of his *Couplet* when he contrasts the empty promises of theatrical entrepreneurs with something that has not yet occurred in reality: an entrepreneur who says nothing yet uses all the means at his disposal to create the best spectacle possible for the public, and all at the usual price (II. xvi; 79).

Language reflects society, which determines the conventions that govern its use.[13] In exposing clichés, Nestroy's characters also expose the conventions of society. Decker is thus correct in seeing the "interrelationship between Nestroy's political and linguistic critiques," as opposed to Karl Kraus, who viewed the plays as metacritiques of language or satires about satire, divorced from their social context (48). In *Der Talisman* Titus Feuerfuchs ascends the social ladder by observing how the linguistic constraints of a class-conscious society maintain the current order. In Decker's words, this play "demonstrates how [Nestroy's] texts subvert social structures by turning their operative social codes against themselves" (51). Since society places such an emphasis on external, aesthetic forms, deception through language becomes possible, and Titus's success thus condemns a society that is based on appearance and is blind to its own contradictions (53, 55). His manipulation of mannered forms is a stronger criticism of the reification of society and its language than is the content of the words (Jansen 258; Brill 119, 128). Unlike Titus, Peter Span does not use language to deceive, though he is just as aware of its conventions and just as creative in manipulating them to achieve his goals. Since he stands outside the aristocratic order and has no desire to gain acceptance within it, it is necessary to investigate to what extent he is able to voice a positive alternative to it.

The attempts to state truths directly, which were greeted as positive by contemporary critics, fail to convince because the language in which they are stated remains fossilized within its own system, and the identity which these truths claim to achieve with external ideals is one of appearance only.[14] For example, the term "der Unbedeutende" is at first effective because it is an ironic use of a negative designation (through the prefix *un*) that denies the false use of the term as it was employed by convention, but this antithetical quality becomes paralyzed through repetition (twice in I.iv, 28–29; twice in III.xxiii, 88–92 and twice in III.xxxiv, 106). Moreover, it is sometimes coupled with an apparently unquestioned statement of a truth, such as the play's "moral" in Span's final remark to Puffmann: "Wenn Sie wieder einmal mit unbedeutende Leut' in Berührung kommen, dann vergessen Sie ja die Lektion nicht, daß auch am Unbedeutendsten die Ehre etwas Bedeutendes ist" [If you ever again come into contact with insignificant people, then don't forget the lesson, that even for the most insignificant person, honor is something significant] (III.xxxiv; 106). This is in effect a *Floskel*, which Span on other occasions has revealed as such. As Brill points out, attempting to state something as true without mediation reduces speech to empty talk instead of opening it up to new possibilities in artistic play (172). He points out that the demand of contemporary reviewers for the expression of such sentiments indicates a contradictory attitude with regard to the *Volk*: on the one hand, it greets what it regards as a democratic tendency within the play, but on the other, it uncritically assumes that the *Volk* is still so immature that it needs to be offered didactic truths from above and thus reveals a basically undemocratic way of thinking (171).

But even though direct statements of this type occur in *Der Unbedeutende* with greater frequency than in other *Possen* up to this time, they fail to outweigh the comic, skeptical outlook that Span conveys in most of his speeches, and in the end they become subverted by the questioning of language and clichés that obtains in the remainder of the play. This process of questioning is actually more democratic than simply dishing up the "truth." The motto that prefaces this chapter suggests skepticism concerning the ability to attain truth or to express it in words, which cannot possibly correspond to the ideal (see Harding 153).

Thus Klara's speechlessness says more than words when she is confronted with her supposed moral lapse. The neighbors take her silence as a sign of guilt, and her brother is at first amazed and even somewhat suspicious at her unwillingness to defend herself, but he then perceives the eloquence behind it: "Mir ist alles klar, Klara, ich versteh' dich; andere Leute sagen viel und 's heißt nix, bei dir aber heißt grad das sehr viel, daß du nix hast g'sagt" [Everything is clear to me Klara, I understand you; other people say a lot and it doesn't mean anything, but with you, saying nothing is what means a lot]. He then gives three-and-a-half paraphrases of the meaning of her silence, and concludes, "mit einem Wort, das alles hast du mit dem Nixsagen g'sagt" [in a word, you said all that in saying nothing] (II.ix; 59). The insufficiency of language is shown by Peter's inability to sum up his sister's meaning in a single phrase and by his eventual giving up the attempt altogether.

Nestroy could not construct a play of silence, however, but was forced to take the reified language of his society as material with which he worked to reveal negatively the insufficiencies of language itself and the world behind it (Brill 141). If truth is contained in the plays, it is only in the form of hints in which the negative elements expose the illusory as untrue (154–55). The nonidentity of the object with itself is an important component of Adorno's "negative dialectics" and in fact provides an entrance for the positive. It resembles Bloch's *Spuren*, or non-identical traces of utopia already visible within the present. Statements can only point toward the truth when they show that they are not identical with it: both Adorno and Benjamin believed in the unintentionality of truth (cf. Buck-Morss 76–81). Klara's silence is a strong example of the inabilty to encapsulate meaningful truth within a statement. Nestroy's ultimate refusal to identify truth with a moral prevents him from lapsing into the blatant and ineffective didacticism that Adorno criticized. Thus the greatest service rendered by this supposedly positive *Volksstück* is, paradoxically, its negation, and most effectively in the antithetical aspects of language, its most important component.

Comic convention, especially in the nineteenth-century popular comedy, requires a happy ending, which *Der Unbedeutende* supplies with Klara's vindication and restored engagement, together with Peter's successful ratiocination and maintaining of the integrity of his family before the intrigues of a person from the aristocratic camp. This coincides well with the "positive" outlook of this "new *Volksstück.*" Yet in several other plays Nestroy had revealed his discomfort at providing so satisfactory a conclusion: in *Lumpazivagabundus* and in *Das Mädl aus der Vorstadt* several different morals are suggested at the end, and the quantity thereby relativizes the truth of each and of the ability to state a moral at all. Though most of his plays have happy endings (as Klotz says, "In the end the wretched schlimmassel on stage cannot remain as unresolved as in real life" [*Bürgerliches Lachtheater* 45]), they are usually undermined in one fashion or another, and audiences could take the conclusion either way (cf. Höllerer 179). And in *Der Unbedeutende* the linguistic skepticism in much of the rest of the play makes it difficult to accept the final moral at face value.

There are several additional features that mitigate the neatness of the ending. Marriage, the reward of Klara, is also the punishment of Puffmann and Ottilie. Since it is shown not to be an ideal state in itself, it is called into question; Peter calls it "die Straf' Gottes" [the punishment of God] (III.xxxiv; 106). And even though enough truth is uncovered to acquit Klara, the whole truth of Puffmann's guilt is never revealed. In the end he is saved by an alibi that is pieced together from bits of information and suppositions supplied by four different people. The same process in which insufficient fragments of knowledge and lies were combined to slander Klara is at work here, and the only justice consists in the fact that guilty parties are punished by marriage rather than saved by it, as the baron believes. Truth cannot be achieved without mediation and can only be understood as the goal of a process. And marriage, the traditional solution in popular comedy, is not necessarily an ideal state: its significance depends on how it is attained. Truth's victory in this play is only partial, and the satisfaction of the ending is in many respects a negative one. Even though Peter's final line states a direct moral, his last speech but two continues his sarcastic questioning of encapsulated truths. When the baron states that he will only grant his cousin Ottilie Puffmann's hand in marriage, but refrain from a gift of money, Span comments, "Und Liebende brauchen wenig" [and lovers need but little] (III.xxxiv; 101). As mentioned above, the many episodic elements and the emphasis on witty, reflective speeches detract from the importance of the plot and therefore from the ending to that plot. The essence of this satirical comedy is process, rather than conclusion, and it cannot be summed up in a single verbal statement.[15] Even though Nestroy may have held many of the common beliefs of his period, the ending is certainly something more than a result of any character or his artistic limitations. We can only interpret from the dramatic texts, which contain an overriding, open-ended skepticism.

But it is important to note that the happy ending can have two functions, which, when taken together, can be much stronger than the positive or the negative alone would have been. Ernst Bloch discusses both the faults and the virtues of this type of conclusion in his chapter "Happy End, durchschaut und trotzdem verteidigt" [Happy Ending, Seen Through and Defended Nonetheless]. Bloch claims that people want to be deceived, not because they are stupid, but because they cry out for the joy that should be theirs and that they never experience in their lives. His chapter is in fact prefaced by a quotation from Nestroy's *Einen Jux will er sich machen* that describes the daydreams of a store clerk who only knows of sunsets through the accounts of customers and who longs for a way to fill this emptiness (*Das Prinzip Hoffnung* 512). Such a lack leads people to accept anything that glitters, even though it is usually something less than gold. Since false fulfillments of this type can be found in happy endings, there is much in the latter that can be condemned, especially their deceptive implication that a better future can be attained without any changes in present reality (512-13). But Bloch says that this is only one side of the matter, since betrayals of genuine fulfillment cannot refute people's real need for a satisfactory end. Exposing the false claim of present fulfillment does not necessarily destroy the pressing hope for a good end, which is too firmly rooted in humans and has provided the motor of history. In recognizing the spectators' urgent longing for a satisfactory conclusion, Span's victory and Klara's marriage represent a *Vorschein* [glimpse] of the utopia that will ultimately mean a genuine improvement. But the skepticism that calls this solution into question at the same time reveals that it cannot be achieved for all people within the structure of present society.

Even though *Der Unbedeutende* was greeted with critical acclaim and its author praised for fulfilling the demand of a positive *Volksstück*, Nestroy's general relation to the public was more ambiguous and not without important negative aspects. Nestroy was one of the most popular authors of the Viennese *Volkstheater*, yet Mautner reports that he did not love his public and quotes a reviewer from the year 1861 who says that one could not tell from the actor Nestroy's smile at a curtain call whether he was thanking spectators or ironically commenting on his relationship to them (*Nestroy* 42–43). Other contemporary observers also noticed this negative quality: the Prague critic B. Gutt wrote in 1844 that "the negation is thoroughly propounded," though he found that Nestroy was beginning to alleviate somewhat "das Ungeheuerliche" [the monstrous, outrageous] of his earlier plays (qtd. in Rommel, "Johann Nestroy, der Satiriker" 51–52). Members of the establishment were particularly offended: Friedrich Theodor Vischer objected to Nestroy's soiling of noble sentiments, and even Gutzkow accused him of robbing the *Volk* of two of its most precious jewels, "sittliche Grundanschauung aller Dinge und gläubiges Vertrauen gegen

Menschen" [basic moral outlook on all things and devout trust in fellow humans] (qtd. in Rommel, "Johann Nestroy, ein Beitrag", 200).

Der Unbedeutende was less provocative in its effect than many of the other plays, though critical opinions diverged and are not necessarily accurate assessments of the drama. The negative strain in Nestroy's attitude toward his audiences was actually positive in that it took them seriously as partners in the dialogue that sought to uncover illusions, rather than as recipients of a pleasing didacticism. Examples quoted above have shown that when the latter does occur in *Der Unbedeutende*, it is less than satisfactory. The reviewer for the *Wiener Theaterzeitung* on 13 May 1846 says that in sacrificing neither morality nor wit this play can provide a model for raising the *Volkstheater* "to a higher, more noble standpoint" and becomes a "unifying point for all classes of society" (qtd. in SW 8: 343). Yet to fulfill this demand the play would have to fulfill an ideal, whereas its basic position is to reject the notion of the possiblity of realizing ideals within the existing world. Nestroy knew that idealizations of the *Volk* from a superior vantage point are not genuine, and to posit an identity between an ideal and the dramatic form in which it is represented would have represented a false, aesthetic harmony that failed to respond adequately to the alienated reality outside the theater.

Most critics agree that the negative predominates in Nestroy's work as a whole. In content and in form this element even overrides the positive content of *Der Unbedeutende*, but it is now necessary to investigate whether the form of the play in any way indicates a hope for a world that is less trapped in illusion, convention, and reification. The main answer can be found in that element which Hein contrasts with satire and calls "Spiel" [play] or "das Spielerische" [the playful]. Rather than representing a discrete world that is the opposite of satire, it serves both comedy and satire. The rules of play as they are contained in comedy are not goal-directed; rather, play is engaged in for its own sake (16–17). In its lack of future orientation and its creation of a self-contained world, it would thus seem to provide a safety valve or escape that vicariously fulfilled public desires in the present, rather than directing them toward possible change outside the theater. And in many instances this was no doubt the effect of the plays. Yet comedy can be utopian in its world of free playfulness by presenting a formal model of a world that operates by different rules as it creates enjoyment, rather than in attempting to depict the content of an imagined better reality. Such an attempt would have had to transgress against the utopian *Bilderverbot*. Playfulness that takes such delight in its own powers of formation provides an intimation of a world that is free of restraint and worth living in its own right. The same "Spiel" that brings about a "Weltbewältigung" [overcoming of the world] demonstrates a standing-above-the-world that leads to reflection and thus to satire, which projects a negative picture of the world (17).

This playful creativity that takes on a critical function is of course most evident in the use of language. When the nobleman von Packendorf allies himself with Peter Span in order to circumvent Puffman's influence over the baron, he tells Peter that Klara had come to him (Packendorf) because she had mistaken him for the "Gutsherrn" [lord of the manor]. Punning on "Gut" [estate, good] and "Herr" [lord, gentleman], Peter shows that property and virtue are not necessarily conterminous: "Den Gutsherrn hat meine Schwester in Euer Gnaden verfehlt, aber den guten Herrn hat s' auf alle Fäll' getroffen" [My sister missed the mark in taking you for the lord of the estate, but in any case she succeeded in finding a good gentleman] (III.xxx; 95).

In Hein's words, "Illusion is juxtaposed with the overcoming of illusion, and the playful creation of a second world is placed against the satirical destruction of the the present world" (*Spiel und Satire* 17). And in another place he comments: "Beyond the play there is the view into a better future, which promises more freedom and self-determination than can become reality here and now. In their utopian dimension the historical component of Nestroy's *Possen* and their current effectiveness are sublated [*aufgehoben*] and maintained" ("Der utopische Nestroy" 22). Thus the two impulses use similar means to create both a positive, playful utopia and a negative attack, and the dialectical relationship between the two prevents the plays from becoming either entertaining escapes or cynical expressions of hopelessness. The combination also helps to explain their popularity in Nestroy's day as well as their continued appeal into the present. The two moments are so closely intertwined that they cannot be separated.

Nestroy's language, which uses its own components to question itself and satirize the conventions of reality, becomes a positive example of creative power as its users take the reified material at their disposal and form new insights, albeit destructive ones in most cases, by means of wit. Peter Span becomes a positive model not simply because he is incorruptible and forthright and triumphs over his enemies, but because of his ability to reflect and to act creatively. Sengle fails to find the comic alone positive, but thinks that the positive is represented by the degree of Nestroy's outrage, which could only result from his clinging to customary norms. Though this viewpoint too strongly stresses departure form the norm rather than skepticism about the norms themselves, Sengle is correct in finding a trace of humanism in Nestroy, even though this humanism is very narrow and skeptical. Dürrenmatt recognizes this as well when he suggests that his own *Der Besuch der alten Dame* [*The Visit*] be performed in the manner of Nestroy (181). Although *Der Besuch* is extremely critical of the world and the people that inhabit it, there is still an underlying respect for humanity that should be conveyed in its performance: "Die 'Alte Dame' ist ein böses Stück, doch gerade deshalb darf es nicht böse, sondern aufs humanste wiedergegeben werden, mit Trauer, nicht mit Zorn, doch auch mit Humor" [*The Visit* is a wicked play, yet for that reason it must not be rendered evilly but in the most humane way: with sadness, not with rage, but also with humor] (183).

Since the formal, positive conclusion of *Der Unbedeutende* is undermined in a number of ways, the "happy ending" can be only partially listed as an example of the positive here. In the words of Fülleborn's title, the play presents an "open event in closed form," an antithesis that works negatively through satire to point to the improbability of improvement in the world. Yet this same questioning of a neat conclusion assumes a positive direction through its very offering of direction rather than closure, in its emphasis on the process of the action, rather than its outcome. Nestroy made Klara's brother, rather than her fiancé, her savior. The hero is thus not as directly rewarded by the ending in marriage. The position of this central figure outside and above the action corresponds to his position above the givens of external reality and places more weight on the process. The ending here serves as a model for a genuine happy ending, which can only occur in the future. Evaluating the conclusion thus opens it up, and the model of creatively productive skeptical insight has stronger positive implications than the didactic or political statement about the honor of the common man. The latter message is fulfilled in the conclusion and thus fixed in the present, yet reality is seen to be insufficient and this encapsulation remains ultimately inadequate. It is only in a continued skeptical attitude in which the seeds of hope are to be found.

In the relation between this play and the public, as in most of its other aspects, there is a close interweaving of the positive and the negative that is extremely complex. As mentioned, Nestroy's apparent fulfillment of the demand for a "positive" *Volksstück* may not have been so positive after all, and if Carl's theater is an early capitalistic enterprise that attempts to carry out some of the same functions as the later culture industry in providing a desublimated form of entertainment in order to maintain itself, one should be especially cautious before granting a favorable assessment to public acclaim. What is positive is not that entertainment is being provided that corresponds to the public's expectations, but that the public is a co-worker in the creation of the play.[16] Though perhaps overestimating this aspect of its origin, Gottfried Keller praised the *Volkskomödie* as a form of expression arising from the people: "Das Volk, die Zeit, haben sich diese Gattung *selbst geschaffen* nach ihrem Bedürfnisse, sie ist kein Produkt literatur-historischer Experimente" [The people, the times, *created* this genre *themselves* according to their needs; it is not a product of experiments of literary history] (354; italics in the original).

But as an examination of the text has revealed, Nestroy's method is not always flattering toward his audiences, and he is unwilling to ignore totally the inadequcies in the behavior of the *Volk*. Complete change cannot occur only as a result of changes in behavior in individual members of the public: a qualitative change in society and consciousness will have to be brought about first. The complex dialectical relationship between the author and the public, and further, between the antithetical aspects of that relationship, is what comprises the positive aspect of the public's role. In entering into a playful dialogue with them, which he nonetheless takes extremely seriously, Nestroy implies that there is a purpose, and perhaps even future direction, to the discussion.

The *Volkstheater* of Vienna produced various types of plays that attempted to provide entertainment while dealing with the problems of the times: the magical betterment plays of Raimund and the satirical *Possen* of Nestroy represent two quite different formal attempts to reach a solution. For Raimund's works the formula *prodesse et delectare* still might be used as a descriptive designation of function. Though Nestroy's plays clearly demonstrate the latter purpose, their didactic intent is less obvious, and thus it is more useful to compare and contrast these two authors in terms of their stance with regard to negation and utopia. Both playwrights convey an awareness of the inadequacies of external reality, which they approach negatively, and both oscillate between this negative pole and a positive one, which contains at least a hint of a utopian hope.

In Nestroy's case, however, the negative has become more pervasive, and his dissatisfaction and skepticism prevent him from attempting to force his works so excruciatingly into a harmonious mold. Irony is more prevalent in the plays of Nestroy, who casts doubt on the ability to provide a final truth. The negative is to be found most clearly in Nestroy's satire, which in the context of the forum of the *Volkstheater*, represented opposition to the Metternich system. When the positive occurs in Nestroy's play it is closely linked with the negative and often appears as the opposite side of the same coin. Such is the case with the portrayal of the central figure of Peter Span, who, positive in his affirmation of the *Volk*, serves as a vehicle for opposition when he resists the intrigues that come from the side of the nobility. Comments within the plays can be found to bear out this social criticism, which might have been even stronger, had it not been for the thorough censorship of the time. But as his *Freiheit in Krähwinkel* reveals, lack of censorship did not bring about a significant change in the ability to express an explicit alternative in words, for Nestroy's criticism was more all-encompassing and could not simply be stated as a partisan political program.

Thus it is easy to read his plays as mockeries of human folly in general, rather than of conditions that have a historical root. One should not fault Nestroy, however, for lacking historical consciousness or failing to take an overtly partisan stance. An examination of *Der Unbedeutende* has revealed that the explicit statement of such positions is not as strong as the exercising of criticism through the form itself. By experimenting with the rules of the genre that he inherited, Nestroy established a pattern for questioning the currently accepted order. The *Couplets*, which interrupt the action, the ironic stance with relation to the happy ending, and the playful and creative use of language that calls into question the very linguistic structures with which people in his society attempt to communicate and to deal with reality are features of dramatic form that convey negation, though Nestroy's re-formation of them into new types of satiric comedy is an expression of the positive.

But as I have stated, the positive is not the same as the utopian. Because the negative is so strong and so all-encompassing, and the positive so weak as it exists on the level of content, most scholars express doubt that the utopian can be found here.[17] In the search for the utopian one must begin with the *Volk* itself, with the people that Nestroy took such delight in portraying and before whom he enjoyed performing on stage. The relationship is not altogether positive and is often fraught with ambiguity. This play does not content itself with apotheosizing the insignificant ones in their current reified state but in pointing to what they should and must become. The distance to that utopia is great, since a radical change in society and a qualitative leap in consciousness would be necessary before it could be attained. Though unable to affirm this world and these people as they are, this play uses them as the starting point for the creation of a fictional world that presents a playful intimation of a better alternative. In doing so it offers something other than an escape because of the manner in which it relates itself to the people and the world beyond the stage.[18]

This particular positive element is a very individual one, and is not without foundation in the developments of the period nor parallel in the individual action of Peter Span, yet Nestroy's creative expressions took place in the forum of the *Volkstheater* under a sort of co-production with the public, and this participation in a dialogue helps it transcend the purely individual. The dramatic literature that resulted was particularly effective and represents one of the greatest achievements of German comedy; in elevating the people's form of expression, it helped to elevate them as well. Nestroy, with his refined combination of satire and traditional elements, was the principal author to achieve this. The skepticism of his all-revealing wit kept his audiences from becoming complacent in their present situation or accepting falsehoods as true. Though he fails to sketch out a utopia or map the path by which it may be reached, the process with which he mercilessly unmasks illusions bears witness to the existence of hope. The truth cannot be stated directly: that is why the moral at the end of the play is less than satisfactory, and why no one gives evidence of having learned it. The interweaving of the positive and negative throughout the play provides the moments of a dialectic, opposing the unsatisfactory present and implying the eventual triumph of the utopian.

Chapter IV

Poetry or Realism:
Ludwig Anzengruber's *Die Kreuzelschreiber*

Ja, für die Verklärung des Lebens spricht alles und dagegen
nur eines — die Wahrheit.
—Ludwig Anzengruber (SW 15: 289)[1]

JOHANN NESTROY HAD FOUND THAT the old *Zauberstück* was no longer
viable, since it neither suited his particular talents nor provided an adequate
dramatic form for the audiences of his period. The kind of *Posse* that he
developed, as the last chapter pointed out, showed substantial differences
from the plays of Raimund. Critics of his time and later scholars have taken
varying stances with regard to his departures from the forms of his
predecessors: those who held that Raimund's art was exemplary lamented
Nestroy's destruction of the genre, whereas those that admired the power of
Nestroy's wit praised him for renewing what could have become a hollow
tradition. It should therefore not be surprising that playwrights who followed
Nestroy did not necessarily imitate his type of artistic achievement, or that
observers would again speak of a decline after his disappearance from the
scene. Changes did in fact occur during the latter part of the nineteenth
century within the population, in the institutions that performed popular
drama, and in the types of plays that they offered.

There are a number of reasons for these changes. The strongest
proponent for the notion of a decline was perhaps Otto Rommel, who held
that there was no author of Nestroy's talent and stature to replace him and
that the audience changed because of mass immigration to the inner city, the
division of the *Volk* into classes as a result of industrialization, and the
rising cost of theater tickets, which fewer and fewer people were able to
afford. In the latter part of the century the operetta became the dominant
form of entertainment on suburban stages (*Alt-Wiener Volkskomödie* 975).

More recent scholarship holds, however, that instead of a flowering and
a decline in the *Volkstheater* and its offerings, it would be more accurate to
speak of two periods. Crößmann, for example, believes that the idea of a
decline is based on a romantic exaltation of the earlier period and says that
the *Volkstheater* continues, but in a different way: Friedrich Kaiser's more
serious and edifying type of *Volksstück* proved less entertaining to the
public, who tended to abandon it for the operetta. This latter genre, in her

view, revives the musical and entertaining functions that the earlier theater had possessed (48, 54–63). Even though more research needs to be done in the area, the rise in ticket prices, especially after the severe economic crisis of 1873, and the increasing proletarianization of the lower classes did have an effect on the composition of the audience, and the theaters found themselves addressing a more middle-class public.[2] It is probably incorrect to say, however, that this change resulted in a sudden need to make money, since the suburban theaters had always been under this constraint (Hüttner, "Volkstheater" 130–31, 139). And even though a particular variation of the genre may have dominated at a given time, there had never been a single, clearly defined category under which all the dramas of the *Volkstheater* could be subsumed.

Additional political and economic factors no doubt played roles in the development of the popular drama: the triumph of bourgeois capitalism on a large scale and the Austrian goverment's *Konkordat* with the Roman Catholic church in 1855 proved to have major influences on many aspects of both public and private life, including marriage and education. Although the concordat was ended in 1870, the church's power remained substantial and limited the freedom of liberal authors to express criticism (G. Müller 50–51). There was, then, a definite change after Nestroy's death in the kind of plays being written, but this situation is not unique to the second half of the nineteenth century: all authors have had to address the problem of a changing populace and the corresponding problem of finding an adequate form.

Ludwig Anzengruber (1839–1889) sought a form that would address the *Volk* in a manner different from that of the operetta or the currently popular but trivial and often sentimental plays of authors such as Karl Elmar, O.F. Berg, and Karl Haffner. Although his plays show certain similarities to the *Lebensbilder* of Friedrich Kaiser, they differ from these as well. Anzengruber had his own ideas about what he wanted to accomplish, and he is the first of the authors discussed in this study to make consistent use of the term *Volksstück*. Having worked as an actor on rural stages for nine years, he turned to writing plays and achieved his first success with *Der Pfarrer von Kirchfeld* (The Pastor of Kirchfeld, 1870), which is set in a farm milieu. His popularity continued with *Der Meineidbauer* (*The Farmer Foresworn*, 1871), which he also called a *Volksstück*, and the peasant comedies *Die Kreuzel-schreiber* (The Cross-Makers, 1872), *Der G'wissenswurm* (The Pangs of Conscience, 1874) and *Doppelselbstmord* (Double Suicide, 1875). He chose an urban setting for *Das vierte Gebot* (Honor Thy Father and Mother,

1877), which also proved successful, though his works were infrequently performed after that. Both the rediscovery of his work by the Freie Bühne in Berlin in the year of his death and the performance of his plays by other groups associated with Naturalism have led many literary historians to consider him a precursor of that movement.[3] Anzengruber's portrayal of a farm milieu with characters that speak almost exclusively in dialect, as well as his professed materialism, atheism, and socially didactic intention to improve the lot of peasants provide at least superficial grounds for this classification.

Other scholars prefer, however, to stress how his plays embody elements from the older *Volkstheater* tradition. Claude David, for example, finds that his portrayals of farmers hardly depart from convention and that he actually shows more similarity to earlier authors than to his followers: "He essentially remains tied to the past and is a belated representative of the spirit of 1848" (*Von Wagner zu Brecht* 77). Though Friedrich Kaiser was the only "Volksschriftsteller" with whom Anzengruber acknowledged any familiarity and whose influence is perhaps strongest (Schmidt-Dengler, "Die Unbedeutenden" 140), Yates finds that Nestroy's skepticism provided an indirect influence, despite Anzengruber's more limited use of satire and wordplay ("Nestroysche Stilelemente" 292–96). Another important similarity is in Anzengruber's use of the *raisonneur*, an outsider who can provide insightful commentary from his extraneous position. In the use of instrumental musical accompaniment and songs, symbolic names, and theatrical effects, Anzengruber's plays resemble *Volksstücke* going back at least as far as Raimund and maintain links to the tradition. The extent to which Anzengruber employed traditional elements from the *Volkstheater* and the *Volk* and incorporated artistic means that were later to be associated with Naturalism will be analyzed in a more detailed investigation of his dramatic method.

According to many of his own comments, and in the opinion of many scholars that have written about him, Anzengruber's main purpose in writing plays was to enlighten the people (Rommel, "Anzengruber" 335). In order to enlighten, he realized that he had to approach the people in a form that they would accept, and his plays appear to exemplify quite well the dictum of "prodesse et delectare." Yet establishing a balance between enlightenment and entertainment was by no means easy for Anzengruber, and the means employed by his *Volksstücke* should be viewed as something more than dressing for the message: they provide insight into the characteristics of that message and of the conditions that they condemn. He despised the current crop of playwrights, whose light entertainment merely provided diversions for their middle-class audiences, and he did not want to become a "Possen Fabrikant und Roman-Ver-Dramatiker" [farce fabricator and novel dramatizer] (qtd. in Martin 112.)

Although influenced to a certain extent by Friedrich Kaiser, he could not force himself to deliver box-office successes as that author was contracted to do: his sense of mission was too strong. An additional complication derived from the split in the public: his relation to his audience was more problematic than had been the case for Raimund and Nestroy, who had considered only one public, their own. Anzengruber, however, had to decide for which segment he was writing (G. Müller 52). His ostensible message was also different from those of these two predecessors: Raimund's lesson is essentially an ethical one that enabled people to find satisfaction in life as it is. Nestroy's messages of this type seem merely a nod to the traditions of the genre, while his more epistemological skepticism concerning the world undermines the apparent message without stating a clear alternative. Anzengruber's didacticism in some ways resembles Raimund's individual ethical solutions and in others Nestroy's questioning of the world, yet he is more explicit than either in directing his criticism at actual conditions and implying the possibility of an amelioration within the current order. It is not just a change within the public that signals a difference between him and these two authors, but his attitude toward his task and his public. His concept of enlightenment becomes evident in a letter to Peter Rosegger, in which Anzengruber pictures himself as having climbed up out of the mass of the people and calling back to them the path he has discovered (qtd. 15.3: 331). This image of himself standing above the ones he wants to instruct has important implications for the direction of his plays: his voice is not so much *of* the people as directed *at* them, and the dramas attempt to offer a superior perspective.

Convinced of his purpose, Anzengruber was also specific in the aim of his didacticism.[4] In *Der Pfarrer von Kirchfeld*, for example, an enlightened village priest who strives for a freer humanity suffers at the hands of a conservative nobleman and of an unyielding clerical hierarchy. The play thus addresses themes of topical interest: the concordat in Austria and the related *Kulturkampf* in neighboring Germany, in which the church's role was at issue. Anzengruber took the position that the church caused harm through unnecessary interference in people's lives and promulgated a superstitious adherence to dogma in order to keep its subjects in a state of dependency. The criticism of the church and religion continued in *Der Meineidbauer*, a tragedy in which a farmer's fortune in life results from having sworn a false oath in order to gain possession of a piece of property: after attempting to kill his son to prevent his misdeeds from becoming known, he eventually dies of a heart attack under the pressure of his guilt, which he refuses to face. In this play the target of the criticism seems more individual than social and the solution appears to be an ethical one. Yet some observers find the criticism stronger here than in Anzengruber's first *Volksstück*: in *Der Pfarrer von Kirchfeld* a priest struggles on behalf of his conception of a more humanè church, whereas the misdeeds of the not entirely unsympathetic "Meineidbauer" are traced back to his religious education (Frenzel 107; Koessler 190). "Antireligious accents" are thus added to the anticlerical criticism (Böttcher 933).

The irrelevance of all religious doctrine is the principal issue behind *Die Kreuzelschreiber*, the *Bauernkomödie* (peasant comedy) that is the object of this discussion. At a gathering in a beer garden in Zwentdorf in Bavaria, the local farmers are approached by the *Großbauer*, a large landowner from a neighboring village, who wishes them to add their signatures to his petition opposing reforms in the church: conservative in all aspects of life, he also wants to hold fast to the old Catholic faith. He refers to an elderly theologian in the city whose authority he is citing; although the beliefs in question are not made explicit, he is is referring to Ignaz von Dollinger's opposition to the newly proclaimed doctrine of papal infallibility (1.4, 16–17).[5] Though few are particularly eager, almost all the men follow the example of Anton, a young farmer who owes his present position to the *Großbauer* and easily succumbs to the pressure. As illiterates, they sign with X's, or crossmarks ["Kreuzel"]: hence, the name of the play.

Exceptions include the young bachelors of the village and Steinklopferhanns, the old stonecutter who lives alone near his quarry. Incited by the outraged village priest, the wives agree, like those in Aristophanes's *Lysistrata*, to deny their husbands sex until they recant and make a pilgrimage to Rome. Although adherence to the old doctrines is not a belief that they strongly hold, the farmers are unwilling to change their minds publicly, and they refuse to relent. As the relations between husbands and wives become increasingly strained (and the sexual deprivation increasingly frustrating) the old farmer Brenninger, who has enjoyed almost fifty happy years of marriage up to that point, commits suicide, and the others approach Steinklopferhanns for advice. He says that they cannot go back on their word, but provides a plan for resolving the issue. The farmers suddenly appear eager to make the pilgrimage, and the women learn that it is because their husbands have convinced the village maidens to accompany them on their trip. This arouses the jealousy of the wives, who tell themselves that it would not be a sin to keep their husbands home under these circumstances, though the men are not now to be restrained. It is only when Josepha, the wife of Anton, urges them to go ahead, since she will find herself one of the young bachelors for temporary companionship, that the men change their minds. In the end both husbands and wives give up their allegiance to their respective dogmas in order to be reunited in what the play considers to be their natural relationships.

The situation that Anzengruber would like to see corrected is the current role of religion and the church: here, what should be a trivial matter damages the basic relationship between husband and wife. The author does not take sides in the infallibility dispute, and in fact both groups, the husbands and the wives, are viewed as foolish for holding so steadfastly to their respective beliefs. When the *Großbauer* introduces his petition in a rather pompous fashion, there are a number of different reactions: Anton agrees to read the document aloud, "wann dir damit a Gfallen gschieht" [if it's a favor to you] (1.4, 18), and it is clear that he feels somewhat pressured to return the favors that the *Großbauer* has done for him. Veit, the tavernkeeper, explains to his wife that if he does not add his mark, the signers will stop patronizing his establishment. Thus this supposed act of faith has varying meanings for different participants, and it is ironic that for many of them, what is supposed to represent an act of conviction is actually a giving in to pressure. For old Brenninger faith seems paramount: "Um'n Glauben geht's — um'n Glauben sagts? — Dös muß man schon anhörn! Da muß sich schon verschreibn!" [It has to do with the faith — you say it has to do with the faith? — That has to be heard! That has to be signed!] (1.4, 19). But at this point the petition has not yet been read, and it is likely that Brenninger's reaction would have been the same if the *Großbauer* had approached them with the opposite request, to support the doctrine of infallibility, since that would have been equally a matter of belief.

Brenninger, like many of the others, is simply basing his act on the superficial information that it has to do with religion and the example of authority, rather than an inquiry into or an understanding of the real issue. And that is precisely what Anzengruber is attempting to criticize: the peasants' surrendering of their own judgment to other authorities. The X-marks are an index of their ignorance, and because the marks are all alike they represent a surrender of individual identity. The similarity to the Christian symbol is a form of parody that is intensified by the word's diminutive ending (Kreuze*l*): the farmers' beliefs are small ones, and since it is not even clear which side in the dispute represents true Christianity, religion itself is belittled.

The farmers are unaware at first of the implications of their action; after the petition has been collected the *Großbauer* praises them for their strong wills and urges them not to relent when those whom they have opposed encourage them to change their minds. Klaus says to Mathies: "Ich hab gmeint, 's is abtan mit'n Schreiben, no sollt's erst drauf losgehn?" [I thought it was over with the signing; now it's just supposed to begin?] (1.6, 25). His companion is equally surprised, and says that they should refrain from telling their wives what they have done. They had assumed that the matter would end with the affixing of their signatures; instead, it was a performative act that provokes later consequences. Not wishing to become involved, the young bachelors let Steinklopferhanns do the talking, since he is the only one who is willing to speak out against the petition. Though he at first does not give his reason and dismisses the process with jokes, he is later more direct:

> Geht mich ja alles nix an! ... schau, Großbauer, wann d' macherst, daß d' Straß, soweit durchs Land geht, a freundlich Gsicht krieget, wann d' a Gschrift brächtst, wo drein stund: dö Großen solln nit mehr jed neu Steuerzuschlag von ihnerer Achsel abschupfen dürfen, daß er den arm Leuten ins Mehlladel, in Eierkorb und ins Schmalzhäfen fallt, sondern sie sollen ihn, wie er ihnen vermeint is, die's haben, auch alleinig tragn — ah ja, Großbauer, da setz ich dir schon meine drei Kreuzel drunter; das verstund ich dir schon — aber was du heut fürbracht hast, das mag recht gut gmeint sein, doch mich fecht's nix an.... (1.6, 26)

> [All that is none of my concern! ... Look here, *Großbauer*, if you saw that the road, as far as it goes through the country, got a friendly face, if you brought a petition that said: the mighty should not be allowed to shrug off every new tax increase any longer, so that it doesn't keep falling into the flour scoop, the eggbasket, and the drippings jar of the poor; but instead that those who have should bear it alone, as was intended — oh yes, *Großbauer*, then I would add my three X's; I would understand you very well then, — but what you have brought today, that may have been well-meant, but it doesn't have anything to do with me....]

In other words, the issue is completely irrelevant as far as he is concerned, and he gives instead examples of material concerns that he would support. His final remark names a very minor task which would have a more beneficial effect on daily life than the support of Dollinger: "Willst du uns aber dö Straßen säubriger machen, da sein wir dann schon dabei ..." [If you want to keep the roads in better shape, you can count on us ...] (1.6, 26).

Though opposition to religious control is the thematic target of the play's criticism, this speech also allows Steinklopferhanns to make explicit attacks on the behavior of the rich and powerful and indicate that exploitation does not occur only through religion. The stonecutter represents the voice of reason, a superior perspective that shows the audience how the *Großbauer*'s petition and the farmers' reaction to it should be viewed. His philosophy is essentially the materialistic atheism of Feuerbach, who thought that nature and human beings themselves represented the proper object of study, not religion and metaphysics. His explanation makes clear his argument for not signing: he is by no means siding with the official church position, as are the wives. Like the author, he finds the whole controversy irrelevant, and not just clerics but any religious beliefs to which adherence is coerced through authority are potentially damaging. It is significant that the actual text of the *Großbauer*'s petition is not included within the play itself: Anton reads it offstage, while Steinklopferhanns and the young bachelors joke and sing about the beauties of the world and of his work (1.4–6, 20–24). Although this omission no doubt resulted from censorship's prevention of the airing of specifics and the author's wish to make the issue more general, the effect is to remove completely the irrelevant text of the petition and to replace it with a more positive vision, represented by the views of Steinklopferhanns.

But it is not only the husbands who bear the brunt of the criticism: the wives are made to look equally foolish. They too are stirred by a figure of authority, the village priest (2.1, 28). Josepha tries various wiles to get Anton to recant (2.3, 32–39), but her use of a white lie (that she is expecting a child, who should not have to be born with a father in a state of sin) casts doubt on the moral superiority of her position. When the wives learn that the village maidens are going to accompany their husbands, it requires little convincing to get the wives to change their minds about the necessity of a pilgrimage. Once again the voice of Steinklopferhanns serves as commentary that offers a perspective different from that of the two conflicting doctrines. It cannot be a sin to hold the husbands back from the pilgrimage, "weil nie sündig sein kann, wann in Zucht und Ehr und Arbeit beinandbleibt, was zueinand ghört!" [Because it can never be sinful, when what belongs together stays together in propriety and honor and work!] (3.3, 82). His song, which follows immediately, indicates that they need only follow their own hearts, rather than the doctrines of either the Old Catholics or the Vatican Council.

In Raimund's dramas, the moral had been ostensibly targeted at an individual flaw, which needed to be corrected in order for the character to reintegrate himself into a basically virtuous society. But like Nestroy, Anzengruber views society itself as intrinsically flawed, though "he attributes this to the fact that man's innate goodness has been distorted and misused" (Howe 143), rather than basing it on a more general skepticism about human nature. In any event the topicality of Anzengruber's criticism aims at more specific social conditions than did the criticism of these two predecessors and implies a close linkage between milieu and the behavior of the villagers. Yet the negation of *Die Kreuzelschreiber* is not limited to just one tendentious aspect: Karlheinz Rossbacher claims that if Anzengruber's oeuvre had been limited to *Der Pfarrer von Kirchfeld, Der G'wissenswurm,* and *Der Meineidbauer*, which criticized the church's power in the caricatured power of a few individuals, his importance would have ebbed with the *Kulturkampf* between church and state in the 1870's. Yet *Die Kreuzelschreiber* goes beyond the issue of papal infallibility, dealing "with questions of village community and the exercise of power, with social divisions as historical fact and appeals to unity as an instrument of the powerful in the village" (232). Not just dogma and the church need to be changed, but the villagers' susceptibility to authoritarian power, as indicated by the husbands' obsequiousness toward the *Großbauer* and the wives' obedience to the priest. Steinklopferhanns explicitly reveals that the method of unification advocated by the *Großbauer* and the church is inadequate.

The ostensible way out of all this is to follow the example of Steinklopferhanns, the outsider who is in harmony with himself and who feels no need to go along with either the *Großbauer* or the priests. An illegitimate child and an orphan, he has been brought up at the cost of the community, whose members resent the extra financial burden. This resentment toward him makes it difficult for him to find employment, and an injury precludes a career in the army. He goes off on his own as a stonecutter, and while leading an eremitic existence he receives a special "Offenbarung" [revelation], in which he experiencess a deep inner peace and a oneness with nature. He suddenly realizes, "Es kann dir nix gschehn!" [Nothing can happen to you!] (3.1, 70–74]. This sudden awareness gave him a feeling of gaiety, and he believes that one only need remain "lustig" [merry] to get along in life. That an outsider, who occupies a socially inferior position, is here superior to others in his insight and attainment of satisfaction should provide hope for the others. Thus the positive is to be found in the outsider, who is cast into that role because he refuses to go along with the negative state of affairs or to submit to an orthodox metaphysic (McInnes 139).

A major difference between Steinklopferhanns's position and those of the priests and the *Großbauer* is that his is based on his own awareness, rather than imposed from without. And he does not intend to institutionalize his teaching nor force others to submit to it. Since it is highly personal, the recounting of his "doctrine" is contained in a lengthy narrative about his own life. Personalizing the message tends to add credibility to what would otherwise be hollow words. Anton perceives a difference between this message and religious doctrines when he says that Steinklopferhanns is "kein Christ und kein Heid und kein Türk" [not a Christian and not a heathen and not a Turk] (3.1, 74).

But the stonecutter's experience must be generalizable as well if others are to apply it to their own lives. If the farmers could become as aware as he about the folly of allowing themselves to become so enslaved, and if they could rely on their own inner voices while maintaining a social conscious-ness and a cheerful attitude, something resembling a utopia could be achieved. Just as the outsider is here the hero, the farmers, traditionally the outsiders of literature, are made the principal characters. And even though Anzengruber does not completely free himself from the old stereotypes, and in this play portrays farmers' behavior as foolish, he makes the rural proletariat fit subjects for literature (Rossbacher 241; cf. Martin 114). He is not making fun of them because of their origin: in fact, the exemplary figure comes from the same background (see Jones, "Variations" 158). By incorporating them as principal content of the drama and encouraging their emancipation in real life, Anzengruber is creating an image of a more utopian society that does not exclude some as outsiders.

As with Raimund's misanthrope Rappelkopf, a dislike for humanity leads Steinklopferhanns into the wilderness, yet in the earlier play the fault lies with Rappelkopf, who achieves contentment when he realizes he has falsely judged his fellow humans. Here, Steinklopferhanns is justified in criticizing the uncharitable attitude of the villagers who resented having to pay for his upbringing or the folly of those who are duped into supporting questionable positions. Although he undergoes a personal betterment in overcoming the resentment and bitter egotism that he had apparently felt in his younger years, he does not reintegrate himself into society as it is. Neither does he abandon his critical judgment in favor of resignation, but promotes without compromise the vision of society as it should be. As Howe points out, general education, rather than individual moral improvement, is the message in the plays of Anzengruber (143–45). Though Koessler goes too far when he claims that a new morality triumphs over the old barbarism at the end of *Die Kreuzelschreiber* (268), the possibility of a utopian vision is clearly introduced.

Yet there is always a danger that the utopian will appear as affirmation of the existing: although Steinklopferhanns rejects society, he achieves contentment within this world. In contrast, Josepha presents a picture of a utopia that is not genuine, if one subscribes to a materialistic *Weltanschauung*. She claims that the church was able to remove her sins and her cares through confession and absolution (2.2, 30–31), and thus her salvation is found in a higher world. But as pointed out above, this supposed state of grace does not prevent her from proposing an uncharitable solution to make her husband recant — the state ushered in by the wives upon the urging of the priest is actually a dystopia so severe that it brings on the death of one of the men. Steinklopferhanns introduces a vision that contains the seed for improvement, but one must ask if his teaching is any less illusory as a utopia. This problem ties in with the third of Marx's "Theses on Feuerbach," in which Marx criticized the latter philosopher's materialistic doctrine on the changing of human conditions because Feuerbach forgets that the educator must be educated. In taking this type of didactic attitude, the advocate of such a doctrine divides society in two, one part of which is then superior to the rest (MEW 3: 5–6).

Anzengruber is not totally unaware of this problem, which he attempts to solve in part by letting a "revelation" be the source of Steinklopferhanns's insights, yet this merely displaces the problem one step, and he here followed a practice for which Marx also criticized Feuerbach: "But the fact that the secular basis raises itself above itself and establishes for itself an independent realm in the clouds can be explained through the cleavage and self-contradictoriness of this secular basis" (MEW 3: 6; *Portable Karl Marx* 156). Steinklopferhanns's "Du ghörst zu dem alln, und dös alls ghört zu dir! Es kann dir nix gschehn!" [You belong to the All, and all belongs to you!; 3.1, 73] is a pantheism that here represents a transcendental ground, as do the two forms of Christian theology in dispute within the play. The stonecutter realizes that his lesson could become another dogma and takes pains to avoid that. He finds it necessary to explain to Anton the reason for his constant good humor, but cautions him not to spread this message around the village, "sonst meinen s', ich wöllt ein neu Glauben aufbringen, und da könnt mich leicht der Landjager zwegn Gwerbstörung aufs Gricht

holn!" [Otherwise they might think I wanted to introduce a new faith, and
then the bailiff could haul me into court for unfair trade practices] (3.1, 70).
His calling his teaching a "trade" seems to secularize this teaching, but does
not really cover over its superior source. Nor does his unwillingness to
preach alter the quality of his message: the play itself attempts to propagate
such a message, and the characters themselves are supposed to learn it in
order to free themselves from clerical superstition.

Because of its urging of acceptance this message is in many ways
reminiscent of Raimund's, and in fact seems in some respects just as
fatalistic: "Ob d'jetzt gleich sechs Schuh tief da unterm Rasen liegest oder
ob d' das vor dir noch viel tausendmal siehst— es kann dir nix gschehn!"
[Whether you're lying six feet deep under the ground or whether you see it
before you a thousand times more — nothing can happen to you!] (3.1, 73).
A major difference of course is Steinklopferhanns's preaching acceptance of
the natural world while criticizing social institutions that interfere with what
he considers natural practices: his message therefore does call for change.
Yet this change seems to be one that can be individually induced in the
immediate world through a pantheistic awareness; this teaching "does not
comprehend the significance of 'revolutionary,' of 'practical-critical'
activity" (Marx, MEW 3: 5; *Portable Karl Marx* 155). In many respects it
seems a metaphysical rather than a programmatic solution. It is also a liberal
idea, in line with the thinking of the emerging middle class, and thus
affirmative of the order that would soon triumph, though it remains negative
in its criticism of the current status quo in Catholic Bavaria and Austria (cf.
Lengauer, "Anzengruber's Kunst" 400). Steinklopferhanns resembles
Nestroy's Peter Span: both are "insignificant" individuals who maintain their
own independence and succeed in attaining a satisfactory station in life for
themselves. One can of course validly question to what extent their
individual successes could be generalized within society as it existed at the
time. If not, the utopian is then subverted by an affirmative trend within the
drama, one which implies possibilities that do not actually exist.

The content thus displays a clearcut negation as well as a utopian thrust
that contains more than a hint of the affirmative. But it is necessary of
course to consider the form employed in order to see how these elements are
in fact conveyed: Anzengruber wanted to enlighten, but like Steinklopferhanns, he realized that simply stating his message would not necessarily be
effective. His awareness of this problem anticipates Adorno's objections to
didacticism stated as content. To reach the people, he thus turned to the
genre of the *Volksstück*, which he hoped to change and renew. Though

David says that Anzengruber's dramas remain close to the people while at the same time presenting a thesis (77), McInnes, more correctly, I think, stresses their disjointed quality, which results from the difficulty of combining a given theatrical convention "with a view of dramatic possibilities which was determined by skeptical, positivistic assumptions." As McInnes points out, the relation to the tradition was necessarily ambiguous, since the conventions on which it was based no longer appealed to audiences to the extent they once had (135–36). Anzengruber's plays contain familiar elements, but their variations mark them as dramas of a new type.

To a large degree, the familiar elements express affirmation of the offerings of *Volkstheater* and thereby convey a more general sense of affirmation as well. Anzengruber employed both instrumental music, exemplified by the overture in which strains of church music are gradually drowned out by merrier folk-melodies, and songs, such as the one at the opening in which the youths proclaim that they are a little bit pious in church, and a little bit godless with the girls (1.1, 3–4). The songs typically comment on the action, but their entertaining quality also serves to make the theater experience a positive one. Audience satisfaction is also maintained by the genre of comedy, which provides, at least on the surface, a happy resolution. Many of Anzengruber's other plays are tragedies or contain greater mixtures of the comic and the tragic. In them the discrepancies and disunities are greater, because the author depended on his own aesthetic imagination to fulfill his purpose. The comedies, according to McInnes, show "more consistent control," since the author could rely more heavily on the inherited forms of the popular dramatic tradition (145–46). In other plays, more than in *Die Kreuzelschreiber*, Anzengruber was not averse to employing sentiment and melodrama, even when these did not add to his criticism or even worked against it (cf. McInnes 146–47, G. Müller 44).

Another *Volksstück* element, already mentioned above, was his decision to treat the *Volk* as characters, and his most successful plays were ones that employed farmers as subjects. As with any type of character, the portrayal of farmers can vary from the stereotypical to the naturalistic to the romantic: the means Anzengruber chose to depict them have a decisive effect on the "message" of his plays. The farmer had traditionally been a comic figure, even in the *Volkstheater,* and had usually provoked laughter by appearing as a foolish bumpkin in contrast to a more sophisticated city-dweller. In *Die Kreuzelschreiber,* set entirely within the village milieu, there is no contrast of this type. As pointed out earlier, the farmers' folly is not linked to their status, and it is not they who are satirized, but religious interference. Since the language is entirely in dialect, it carries no internal message of comparative superiority or inferiority. In order to direct the audience toward the goal of his criticism Anzengruber had to distance his portrayals from the old stereotypes, and he tried for a closer correlation between his figures and actual farmers of his day.

The stage directions that describe Steinklopferhanns's appearance, for example, fill a paragraph. Mention of certain details, such as his worn-out clothes, are not included to make him look ridiculous, but to attempt verisimilitude, in the manner of the nineteenth-century realists and the later Naturalists. He was to be viewed as a rural figure, but one who was to be taken seriously, rather than humorously. And the hammers that he carries also correspond to the function of verisimilitude instead of merely tagging his profession, as did the identifying proper names as used by Nestroy (1.1, 4–5). This seemingly exact observation is one of the features that made Anzengruber popular on Naturalist stages. The context within which the farmer is presented serves to negate previous stereotypes, which resulted from the historical fact of class and social division. Anzengruber does not ignore these divisions, but seeks to overturn them by elevating a lower class to the sole subjects of drama (similar to the earlier development of middle-class tragedy) and by criticizing the forces that have kept them in a state of dependency. Although these characters are participants in a comedy, the mixture of means employed by Anzengruber demonstrates the seriousness with which he takes them and their problems and has a decisive effect on what he conveys. It affirms them as human beings, while commenting negatively on their current situation and pointing toward a better future.

Affirmation of farmers as worthy subjects for literature with dramatic means that take pains to show them as they are runs the danger of affirming existing conditions and of failing to stress sufficiently the necessity for change. And when verisimilitude is pursued in a superficial manner for its own sake it is of course subject to the criticism that Lukács directed against Naturalism in his essay "Erzählen oder Beschreiben" [Narrate or Describe]: that it simply records external impressions of reifications without analyzing the connections behind them or realizing that humans can be both subjects and objects of history. However, an examination of the play and of Anzengruber's purpose and method, expressed in his letters and essays, shows that his portrayals do not display such close observation after all. Although he had worked for a number of years as an actor on rural stages, he claims his real purpose for choosing this type of literature and subject was to portray universal, human problems, and a country locale would provide a more poetic setting than a cityscape for illustrating them.

In addition, he believed that a rural environment interfered less with a person's innate character and thus enabled it to be viewed more clearly (SW 10, 369–70). In fact the sentimental Black Forest village tales of Bertold Auerbach were as much an inspiration as his own experiences (Rommel, "Anzengruber" 392, 401). Anzengruber commented on his method in numerous conversations and letters: "Ich meinerseits ... schuf meine Bauern so real, daß sie ... überzeugend wirkten — und soviel idealisiert, als dies notwendig war, um im ganzen der poetischen Idee die Waage zu halten" [For my part, I created farmers real enough to give a convincing effect, and idealized as much as necessary to balance the poetic idea in the whole] (qtd. in Rommel, "Anzengruber" 392). He claimed that seeing a farmer from afar and hearing him speak a few words were enough to enable him to know the man thoroughly (390). His method thus appeared to be as much an example of romanticism as of naturalism or realism.

Since there can be no complete convergence of signifier and signified, no immediate representation of reality, what is construed as realism at a given time is largely a matter of convention. Anzengruber went farther than his predecessors in the *Volksstück* genre in employing specific details to link his portrayals to contemporary people and locales, yet he shied away from such linkages if they resulted in too much unpleasantness or detracted from his didactic intentions, for he saw no point in merely recording observations for their own sake. An examination of the figures in the drama reveals that the author's own assessments in this regard are basically accurate: the aesthetic does indeed play a decisive role in their characterization. Anzengruber can thus be more properly grouped with the poetic realists than the Naturalists: according to Lengauer, he sets the "poetic" as a formal principle in opposition to the "real," which, he claims, contains no poetry when immediately reproduced ("Anzengruber's Kunst" 389). Lengauer finds that attempting to combine the two results in poetry's imposing of a unity onto reality, which it nonetheless attempts to portray without transfiguration. To Lengauer, the phrase "poetic realism" is an oxymoron (400).

The quotation at the head of this chapter thus cannot be applied to *Die Kreuzelschreiber* for a number of reasons. Numerous features, such as Steinklopferhanns's song "Schön blau is der Himmel, Schön grün is der Klee" [The sky is a beautiful blue, the clover a beautiful green] (1.5, 18), give a transfigured picture of reality in poeticized form and tend to view the proper sort of village life as an attainable idyll. Yet departures from verisimilitude could also have a different effect. The author imposes a unity on observed appearances, but it is one more influenced by art, rather than the relationships that govern, or supposedly govern reality. The intrusion of reality prevents the dramatic work of art from attaining the desired unity. The attempt to create the positive is in the end subverted by the difficulty in combining the "poetic" with the "real," since the former tends to conflict with the latter's more negative assessment of the status quo.

A similar subversion of the didactic process is found in the language spoken by the characters, which is not real either, but is actually an artificial mixture created by Anzengruber from several Alpine dialects. Just as he created generalized characters to illustrate human problems, he crafted a generalized language that would fit his plays whether they were set in Austria, Bavaria, or Switzerland (Rommel, "Anzengruber" 393–94). Though he felt flattered to be considered a dialect writer, he knew that this designation was only partly accurate: he refrained from tying his dialect to one narrow region, so that he could be understood by a greater number of people (SW 15.1: 294). As Gerd Müller points out, this did not necessarily achieve the desired result (54). Mountain people could tell that the author was only pretending to speak their language, and the middle-class urban public thought he was writing for someone else. Neither group felt specifically addressed, and the didactic intent, with its negative and utopian thrusts, is dampened. Instead of unifying by increasing the play's comprehensibility to a larger number of people, "it ... suggests a gap between language and experience that real dialect seemed to bridge" (Howe 148). Raimund and Nestroy had used real dialect (albeit it in a unique, artistic way), and their audiences had felt that the plays spoke for them and affirmed their identity. The content of Anzengruber's message was more specific in its opposition, but the dilution of its language was less effective in expressing this, since its artificiality worked against specificity.

Other aspects of the form are more successful, however. The comedy, as well as the farcical nature of the plot, which provides at least a superficial resolution, is undermined in a number of ways in order to keep the harmony within the drama and enjoyment within the theater from co-opting change outside the theater. Anzengruber's two previous plays, which he labelled *Volksstücke*, more closely resemble tragedies with their unhappy endings that result in death. On a less superficial level, tragic elements also include the introduction of fate and of heroic, mythic qualities into plot and character (Böttcher 934). The use of tragedy was a new departure for the *Volksstück* and gave a different sort of force to Anzengruber's plays. Combining the tragic with inherited elements from popular drama was not easy to achieve, however, and both dramatic traditions tended to work against Anzengruber's professed aim of realistically revealing social processes.

According to one critic, it was easier to avoid such contradictions in comedy (Böttcher 934). Even though the designation of *Die Kreuzelschreiber* as comedy is essentially accurate and the exaggerated situation of its plot appropriate for the *Volkstheater*, this play cannot be simply categorized either. The suicide of old Brenninger strikes an anomalously discordant note and emphasizes the seriousness of the matter in which the church has involved the villagers: it is not a trivial matter that can be completely dismissed with the final laughter. In fact, this play's first audience was not sure whether or not it was watching a comedy or a tragedy: Anzengruber's "directness, the robust language, the monumental characters, the moral earnestness of his ideas, were perhaps discomfiting to a city where drama had used humor to achieve indirectness" (Howe 150).

Not only the tragic, but also the epic is included here to a larger extent than before: this too detracts from the overall dramatic unity and was a feature that was favored in the later plays of the Naturalists (cf. Cowen 84). Epic features are evident in the lengthy stage directions of the written text, but also in narrative passages spoken by several characters. The *Groß-bauer*'s long speech serves to characterize him better, both straightforwardly according to the face value of his words and ironically because of the exaggeration with which they are delivered. The speech introduces more details about the milieu in which the play is set and provides a better idea of the background from which these characters emerge. Brenninger's story gives a more precise indication of the effects of the conjugal rift and lets the spectator become better acquainted with him in order to intensify the news of his death later. Steinklopferhanns's story of his revelation and its interpretation similarly retard the dramatic unity in giving a philosophical explanation that could not be introduced otherwise. The text of the play thus strives for something more than the enjoyment to be gained from the potentially farcical sitation of the plot and its happy resolution.

The nature of the harmony at the end and how it is achieved must be examined more precisely. The essential conflict is between the church and the villagers, yet it here takes the form of a conflict between husbands and wives, who stand as surrogates for two different dogmas. The play does not reconcile these two dogmas, nor does it reconcile religious institutions with the peasants, but only the husbands with the wives. The church is excluded from the final harmony. The stonecutter, who brings about the resolution, is not an "equalizing mediator" who strives for a synthesizing harmony. Neither does Anzengruber view such a synthesis as the basis of true poetry. According to Rossbacher, his is a "poetry of dissonance, in which recognition, precise representation, and implied criticism of contemporary reality take the place of harmony and transfiguration" (233). Steinklopferhanns is and remains an outsider within the play's content: he has no need of compromise, and the resolution takes place outside the initial conflict. His remarks, even when humorous, are not at all soothing, but border on the caustic. The stonecutter, called a "Monbua" (a 'man-boy' or old bachelor) has the detachment of bachelorhood and the wisdom of age, and thus the ability to remain free of the restraints that confine the others. He is both man and boy, but also neither.

The harmony that he has found through his earlier revelation and partially conveyed through his lesson will not be achieved to the same extent by the farmers. Though the couples are reunited, the problem of church dogma does not go away: it is doubtful that the villagers will simply be able to ignore it in the future, and thus the ending remains open and the harmony incomplete. This is underscored in the play's last lines, in which Anton's proclamation that the men were able to stick to their intentions by keeping their word provokes paroxysms of laughter from Steinklopferhanns, who says, "Dös heißen s' in der Stadt *Gewissensfreiheit*" [That's what people in the city call *freedom of conscience*] (3.4, 73; italics in the original). He still occupies a superior position, and the others have not yet reached a state of maturity sufficient to achieve true freedom of conscience. The mixture of comic and tragic elements, the use of epic inserts, and the incompleteness of the final harmony are aspects of the form that cast the current state of affairs in a negative light.

In Anzengruber's case, the utopian is closely linked to his conception of the didactic, though of course he may not have accomplished what he intended. *Die Märchen des Steinklopferhanns*, a series of prose tales in which this same stonecutter serves as narrator and main character, present a number of persons who figure out implied advice and adjust their lives accordingly. In Rossbacher's opinion, readers are supposed to regard themselves as continuers of this process: thus literature is the anticipation of possible action (238). In the case of *Die Kreuzelschreiber*, the spectators should no doubt follow the example set at the end by freeing themselves from the stranglehold of religious dogma and interference. The reunification and laughter of the conclusion should point to a future utopia, though the negative formal elements discussed above should disabuse the audience of the notion that this state has already been achieved. In choosing a form that he calls *Volksstück*, Anzengruber tries to address and integrate the excluded, whose continued exploitation prevents the creation of a better world. Yet he avoids many of the conventional features that could be found in the genre up to that point, since some of them might provide a utopian vision in an all-too distant realm. Howe says that the old *Zauberstück* had made the metaphysical mechanical as "an excuse for spectacular feats of stagecraft," but that Anzengruber turns the form of the other world back into theme and shows the misery of people who think God is there to fulfill their wishes (145). He removes not only the *deus ex machina*, but also the *deus*. Steinklopferhanns relies on his own devices to achieve harmony with the world and himself, and he implies that others can do likewise. Any effectiveness his message may possess derives not from the saccharine pantheism of his song "Schön blau ist der Himmel" or the explanation of his revelation, which is not transferrable, but from the attractiveness of his ex-centric position, his integrity, the sharpness of his remarks, and his actions. Yet he can only reveal, not fulfill for others: the gap between his position and that of existing society is the distance that still needs to be traversed. The play illustrates Bloch's philosophy in that the various fulfillable affects attempted within the play prove to be inadequate: the true and qualitatively different utopia remains a goal of hope.

At the heart of all this consideration of the form and content taken by the particular brand of Anzengruber's *Volksstücke* is the public for whom he was writing. Difficulties and inconsistencies in addressing an audience have already been alluded to, as have differences between intended public and actual reception. The range of spectators was supposed to be expanded through the farm milieu and the artificial dialect. Farmers were not only the goal of the didacticism, but were chosen because their simpler milieu could more clearly convey the message. But as we have seen, neither actual farmers nor educated city-dwellers felt specifically addressed. These factors seem to limit the group at whom the message was directed. Rommel reports that even Anzengruber in his later years believed less in the "purely human" which he had observed in the simple figures of farmers and more in the material forces that determined life. He thus felt that his view of farmers had in fact been a romantic one ("Anzengruber" 551).

An additional problem resulted from Anzengruber's strong anti-clerical tendency: he himself expected that neither "old nor new, nor even middle-of-the-road Catholics" would take delight in his portrayal (qtd. in Böttcher 934). Yet this discussion of obstacles to a favorable reception should not obscure the success that the play did in fact enjoy at the Theater an der Wien in 1872 and shortly thereafter in both southern and northern Germany (Böttcher 934). Anzengruber managed to reach an audience whose members included representatives of the Viennese *Volk*, yet he also went beyond this group; his earlier play *Der Pfarrer von Kirchfeld* was even performed as far away as Detroit within two years of its Viennese premiere (Rommel, "Anzengruber 357).

In writing for and about a class that was excluded from power, Anzengruber was continuing the tradition of expressing negation with regard to the status quo, and in attempting to achieve an emancipation and integration he was aiming for the utopian. The results show both failure and success: failure, insofar as the plays attempt to negate the insufficient through explicit didactic content and to foreclose on the truly utopian by implying an adequate solution through a modification of present conditions. Both Adorno and Bloch would have doubtless criticized these plays for such shortcomings. The aspect of Anzengruber's didacticism that stemmed from his concept of himself leading the people from above ran the danger of creating a larger gap than it was able to bridge. In his last years he was disillusioned because he felt that he had not written for the *Volk* after all, but for a small group of educated people, and he doubted the effectiveness of literature as a means for teaching.[6] Yet for a time Anzengruber did enjoy popular success, and his plays continue to attract deserved attention because of the new ways in which he addressed dramatic and social problems. The formal constructions of *Die Kreuzelschreiber* ultimately go farther than the limitations of its content in condemning the status quo and expressing hope for a utopia that is still to come.

Anzengruber remains an important figure in the history of the *Volksstück* for reasons other than his didacticism, which was ultimately less than successful. He was confronted with a new situation, in which "the organic connection of the popular stage to the people" no longer existed (Rommel, *Alt-Wiener Volkskomödie* 973). The early Viennese comedy had been closely tied to its time and place, but Anzengruber's plays loosen this particular rootedness.[7] The texts of Raimund and Nestroy, though collectively produced and not necessarily intended to maintain lasting value, have been repeatedly performed into the present because audiences have continued to find literary merit in them. Although Anzengruber relied more heavily on the inherited tradition than any other author of *Volksstücke* has been able to do since, he began a process in which the plays are considered a more autonomous form of literature from the outset. To Howe this means that popular drama begins to "prefer individuality to familiarity" and to seek the status of great art "in the universal rather than in the local and particular" (150). But although the majority of plays in the *Volkstheater* had delivered the generically familiar, the greater writers had always offered something new, and such plays take on an individual character, whether or not their content and form result from a single author or from collective forces within the theater. And Anzengruber's plays would have been less successful if they had not retained a certain amount of particularity. Yet that particularity is not to be found in "exact" portrayals of farmers, any more than the strength of their universality is to be found in the stated message.

Anzengruber had to search for an appropriate dramatic solution, just as Raimund and Nestroy had, even though the theatrical and social conditions were so different. It was now less easy to address a homogeneously encapsulated "Volk," and his plays were sent out to a wider public, though this by no means implies that the new audience had become more integrated. The divisions were still there, and if anything, the groups more fragmented. Attempting to address them all may have made his plays more "universal," though any universality contained within the phenomenon is more representative of a utopian impulse than an accomplished fact, whether in reception or social reality.

The form and content of Anzengruber's plays free themselves from the local confines of the early Viennese *Volkstheater* as genre and institution, yet the form, and its relation to content, is no less a response to the historical circumstances of time and place, regardless of the degree of verisimilitude attempted or achieved. Gerd Müller claims that the later history of the *Volksstück* shows that Anzengruber's uncertainty with respect to the function of the genre is what forms its structure (155–56), and after Nestroy any choice to employ the genre *Volksstück* became more self-conscious and arbitrary. Through modifications of inherited forms, Anzengruber's plays attempt emancipation from the alienating and exploiting forces that prevailed in late nineteenth-century Austria and Germany. His message was a progressive one, but he realized that merely stating it was not sufficient. Steinklopferhanns's teaching is to be found not only in his words, but in the relationship between his character and the other figures of the drama, and between this *Volksstück* and the tradition that it addresses, re-forms, and works against. Anzengruber's dramatic voice serves as an expression negating the status quo and calling for a utopian improvement, even though it never completely achieves the latter because of the contradictions that it was unable to resolve.

Chapter V

The Transition: Ludwig Thoma's *Magdalena*

Ach, die bildsauberen Deandln mit der sittig verschämten, manchmal auch so sündhaften, aber immer gar so rührenden Liab, die auf den Defreggerbildern lächeln und in den Ganghoferstücken schnäbeln — warum hast du sie, o Ludwig Thoma, in deinem neuesten Volksstück aus der Welt der Bauern eliminiert?[1]

THE CHANGES BROUGHT TO THE VOLKSSTÜCK by Ludwig Thoma (1867-1921) continue in many ways the ones introduced by Anzengruber, and there are similarities as well in the backgrounds of the two authors. The families of both were rooted in the Alpine region, and both had occasion to observe rural life at close range. But whereas Anzengruber worked as an actor (as had Raimund and Nestroy) before writing his plays, Thoma received a university education and started his career as a lawyer in the town of Dachau near Munich. He soon realized, however, that he was more interested in the rural people themselves than in their legal problems and that he preferred writing short stories and poems to juristic briefs. After moving his practice to Munich, Thoma wrote a comedy, *Witwen*, which he completed in 1899. He also published in the newly founded satirical journal *Simplicissimus*, and when offered the editor's position in 1900, he gave up the legal profession altogether to devote himself full-time to journalism and writing. He is perhaps most famous today for his amusing *Lausbubengeschichten*, a collection of children's stories, though his plays are still frequently performed on stage and television, and his satirical pieces and regional novels are still widely read.

Despite the range of genres displayed by his output, most of Thoma's works reveal several common characteristics: social criticism, verisimilar portrayal of Bavarian peasants, and artistic accomplishment. Thoma usually employed satire for his criticisms of society, and in fact one poem ("An die Sittlichkeitsprediger in Köln am Rhein") [To the Morality Preachers in Cologne on the Rhine, 1904] was so forceful in its attack that he was sentenced to spend six weeks in prison. All but two of his major plays are comedies, and most are satirical. *Die Medaille* (The Medal, 1901) takes aim at the condescending attitudes of bureaucrats, and *Die Lokalbahn* (The Local Railway, 1902) makes fun of village officials who behave hypocritically as they let themselves be trampled by the powerful. *Moral* (*Morality*, 1908) attacks supposedly solid citizens who establish watchdog committees to guard public morality through censorship, but who find their own weapons turned against them when it is revealed that they have simultaneously been patronizing a local prostitute. In such plays Thoma politicizes the farce, though he directs his criticism at precise shortcomings rather than at the social order as a whole (Kaufmann and Schlenstedt 263-4).

Even though Thoma did not explicitly link his comedies with any of the various types of *Volksstücke* up to that point and was not attempting to renew the genre, as Anzengruber had done, many of these plays share elements associated with the tradition of popular comedy, and today's public tends to think of them in that connection (cf. Dewitz 100). Thoma had on occasion even used the term *Volksstück* pejoratively, criticizing for example the inferior Viennese *Volksstücke* that were being performed at Munich's Residenztheater (LB 75)[2] and parodying it himself in "Der Sieger von Orleans" [The Victor of Orleans], a four-page scene that he called a "patriotic *Volksstück* in two acts" (GW 5, 450-54).[3]

But in 1908 Thoma was so impressed by a performance of Anzengruber's *Die Kreuzelschreiber* at Michel Dengg's *Bauerntheater* on the Tegernsee that he was determined to write a play in the same vein. The term *Volk* thus refers to a group similar to that addressed by Anzengruber. This rural population was different from the suburban theater-goers of nineteenth-century Vienna, yet it was also a group situated below the upper and middle classes. Thoma tried to encourage Dengg's attempts to perform Anzengruber both at home and in North Germany (LB 212) and began seeing and reading as many of the works of his Austrian predecessor as he could (*Ausgewählte Briefe* 97). His first product for Dengg was the peasant farce *Erster Klasse* (First Class, 1910), but after a number of false starts he was able to complete *Magdalena* in 1912, the only one of his plays that actually bears the designation *Volksstück*. Thoma had written non-comic works before, such as his *Heimat*-novels *Andreas Vöst* (1905) and *Der Wittiber* (The Widower, 1911), but *Magdalena* was his only tragic play.

In the opening scene of this *Volksstück*[4] the farmer Thomas Mayr, also known as Paulimann, and his dying wife Mariann learn that their only daughter Magdalena, called Leni, is being expelled from the city after her arrest on charges of prostitution. Mariann wonders if they as parents might not have been partially responsible for this outcome by letting her go to the city in the first place when she proved too weak for farmwork. As Leni arrives at home accompanied by a gendarme, the whole village turns out in force to gloat at the spectacle. And the new priest, who has come to comfort

Mariann in her illness, hurriedly leaves to avoid being seen in the presence of the fallen girl. Thomas, intensely feeling the shame that he must henceforth endure, treats his daughter harshly, but Mariann displays sympathy and tries to draw her daughter closer. Leni reveals that she was lured into a proposal of marriage by a young man who then took all her savings and disappeared. Without a penny to her name, she turned to selling herself in order to earn some money.

By the second act Mariann is already dead, and father and daughter lead a rather tense life at home. Leni continues to display her characteristic stubbornness, though she also appears at times to want to succeed at housework and farmwork. The mayor offers to buy their farm, but the insulted Thomas throws him out, suspecting with good reason that the mayor is actually stirring up village opinion against him in order to increase the pressure for him to sell. The farmhand Lenz, with whom Leni starts flirting in the hope of gaining a husband, gives notice, and Thomas feels the ostracism intensifying.

In the third act Barbara Mang tells Leni that the new priest has preached a sermon that was obviously directed against the fallen girl. Slowly realizing that she will never be able to rehabilitate herself in the community, Leni offers to sell Barbara an old coat of her mother's for enough money to enable her to leave the village. Worse news comes with the revelation that Leni had taken Martin Lechner, the son of a village farmer, into her room at night and then asked him for money before he left. The outraged mayor and villagers storm the house in order to force Leni from the town. Her father, shattered by the effect that this latest revelation will have on his position in the community, and bound by his promise to the dying Mariann never to turn Leni from the house, draws a knife and stabs his daughter to death.

Although Anzengruber was not the first author associated with the *Volksstück* to write non-comic plays, the success and endurance of his dramas mark him as an important proponent of this direction. *Magdalena* follows this course, though it is a much more intense and closely knit tragedy than any of the earlier author's plays. As described in the previous chapter, Anzengruber wrote most of his works before Naturalism had taken hold; Thoma wrote *Magdalena* after this literary movement had passed its peak. Both were skeptical of writers who followed this movement simply because it was fashionable, since it often served as a pre-formed stencil for lesser authors who believed they had found the recipe of their greater counterparts. Because the Naturalistic portrayal of stark social contrasts was quite popular, directors gave in to public wishes, and Thoma sarcastically referred to this element as "dieses undefinierbare, aber rentable Etwas" [this undefinable, but profitable something] ("Theater- und Literaturbrief" 6-7). Nonetheless, Thoma, like Anzengruber, employed features that link him to Naturalism and that have an important effect on the construction of *Magdalena*, though the combination of forms and materials displays complexity and has a variety of implications.

Since Naturalism imitated in certain ways the observational and experimental techniques of the natural sciences, there was a tendency for the artist to stand above his disadvantaged characters and draw implications from their behavior as to how their lot might be improved. Gerhart Hauptmann was aware of the dangers of this method, which he makes manifest in the character Loth in *Vor Sonnenaufgang*. As a sociologist Loth studies poor people and alcoholics and provides ideological answers for their plight, yet he has little personal understanding for individuals from this background or awareness of their views. Although Thoma wanted to analyze the inadequacies of rural conditions, he also wanted to avoid providing a pathology of a sociological group from a superior perspective. Thus he employed some of the elements of Naturalism but combined them with a genre that was of the people and not just about them. A genre that remained outside their discourse altogether would not have been able to give voice to the inclusive unity that would be characteristic of utopia. This combination of elements gives a new form to the *Volksstück*, just as it also gives expression to the utopian and the negative.

To many spectators Naturalism meant the portrayal of social misery, a function that is also evident in the thematics and social criticism of *Magdalena*. Like Anzengruber, Thoma gives a precise depiction of current conditions in rural areas and does not refrain from making the picture bleak, despite his affinity for rural Bavarians. And like Anzengruber, he aims criticism at the church, though this institution is a secondary target in *Magdalena*. It is the dangerously narrow-minded attitude of the village that provides the main focus of criticism: the stifling system of moral norms so rules the community that neither Thomas nor Leni is able to escape a tragic outcome. Although Leni's supposed transgression occurred in the city, the urban milieu itself is not viewed here as the cause of her downfall. A commonplace of much sentimentalized *Heimatliteratur* contrasted a corrupt, city environment with the idyllic and unspoiled life of the country, but *Magdalena* is set entirely in the village, and it is the rural community that is most thoroughly damned.[5] Leni is not allowed to return quietly and pick up the pieces of her life: she is greeted by a crowd of farmers, who, notified in advance of her arrival, leave the fields early in order to view and participate in her humiliation (1.4, 20).[6]

What they condemn is her taking money for sex: when Thomas wants to know the difference between Leni's situation and that of the daughter of the mayor, who has an illegitimate child, the mayor responds that his own daughter made a stupid mistake not unusual among young people, and that she is otherwise upright and a hard worker whose plight is of no concern to anyone else. When Thomas asks why Leni's situation cannot be equally ignored, the mayor informs him that Leni's transgression results from immorality rather than stupidity, and that he as mayor has a responsibility to protect the village's reputation. His argument that neighboring towns are already making fun of Berghofen demonstrates that the appearance of morality is paramount. The moral code to which all these villages subscribe tends to perpetuate itself and to exclude the perceived threat (2.5, 37-9).

The villagers make a distinction between a natural giving in to mutual attraction and the charging of money for the same act. However, no one notices a similar distinction later when it is revealed that Leni asked Martin Lechner for money as he was leaving, rather than making monetary exchange a condition at the outset (cf. Kaiser). Instead, this second example more strongly convinces the villagers of Leni's incorrigibility and, seeking to drive her away, they never consider that they may have reversed the actual cause and effect. Rather than continuing with prostitution as a livelihood, Leni merely seeks a means for escaping a situation that community norms make extremely confining. When accused by Thomas of lying about the matter with Lechner, one of the villagers responds, "Dös werst du wiss'n, daß mir richtige Leut san ... Da gibt's nix mit Lüag'n und a so ..." [You must know that we're upstanding people ... We don't have anything to do with lies and such ...] (3.8, 60; ellipses in original). He is technically correct, because Leni did in fact ask the young man for money, but the villagers' attitude is dishonest, since they show no concern for her or her family, sacrificing her instead to a rigid norm.

Morality is here an abstract principle that legitimates injustices instead of eliminating them (Kluge 594). Bavarian communities did in fact on occasion use mob action in an attempt to correct what they considered deviant behavior. Thomas refers to the mayor's threats of mobilization of opinion as "Haberfeldtreiben" (2.5, 40), a practice defined by Schmeller as the public marking of a person for a real or imaginary transgression that is beyond the concern of ordinary laws. He points out that it is often motivated as much by jealousy or personal revenge as by moral outrage, and that it is often tacitly condoned by the clergy as a means of enforcing morality (Gierl 140). In *Magdalena*, the unyielding attitude of the community toward Leni creates a very negative picture of narrow-mindedness, superficiality, and hypocrisy as it often existed in Bavarian villages of Thoma's time. Though the play offers no spokesman, such as Anzengruber's Steinklopferhanns, to express a preferable alternative, Thoma obviously thought that these were attitudes from which the people needed liberation. *Magdalena* bears a certain thematic resemblance to *Die Kreuzelschreiber*, since the two plays take aim at a similar targets.

Although community opinion is fairly cohesive here, the play makes clear that in this instance it is not merely a spontaneous expression of moral outrage, but has been encouraged by the mayor, who can benefit economically if Thomas is forced to sell his farm at a low price. Community relations are not just personal bonds among neighbors, but the nexus of economic interests. Thomas is aware of this at the very beginning: when his wife expresses surprise that the whole village is aware of Leni's return, he says, "Waar i a großer Bauer, na hätt ma's vielleicht hoamlicher mach'n könna, aba so derf ma de Leut a Freud lass'n" [If I were a wealthy farmer, we maybe could have done it more secretly, but as it is, we have to give the people their fun] (1.4, 19). He is merely a "Gütler" (a smallholder) and not as powerful as the mayor, who owns a lot of property. Later, when the mayor comes to suggest that he sell his farm, Thomas says, "Di kenn i guat. Du host ma's nia verziech'n, daß amal der kloa Bauer Recht kriagt hat geg'n den groß'n ..." [I know you well. You've never forgiven me, because once the small farmer was judged right, and not the large one ...] (2.5, 39). Here he refers to an earlier lawsuit that the mayor had brought against him and lost, and indicates that they both are aware of the importance of class interests. Thomas sees through the hypocrisy of the mayor's claims that he merely wants to protect the village from uproar and a bad reputation.

In the end, the mayor claims he cannot be responsible for what the mob of young men does if Thomas refuses to expel Leni, and refuses to answer Thomas's question about whether he intends to uphold the law. Instead, he replies that his duty is to insure that calm prevails in the community (3.8, 63). In other words, order is more important to him than justice, and more important than either is his own advantage. But of course, he is not maintaining order either, but fomenting the opposite when he tacitly encourages the action of the mob. Thomas also feels compelled to restore what passes for community order, with which he basically agrees, even though it means breaking the law and killing his own daughter (cf. Dewitz 218, G. Müller 63). Just before stabbing her he says, "Und host *mir* dös to!" [And you did this to *me*!], indicating that the effect of her actions on him, as they provoke community outrage, is paramount (3.12, 67; my emphasis).

One of the principal institutions interested in maintaining the current order was the church, which is here seen as an ally in the community's ostracism of Leni. Its negative qualities are embodied in the figure of the new assistant priest Köckenberger, an example of a group whom Thoma frequently opposed for considering their offices political and their congregations constituents (Stark 75). This young clergyman is described as having a "singing, unctuous" tone, and his lack of sincerity is further indicated when he says, "Man hat mir aufgetragen, einen Besuch bei Euch zu machen" [I have been assigned the task of paying you a visit] (1.2, 14). In other words, he has come to console the dying woman because he has been told to, not because he wants to or thinks he should, and he speaks in liturgical phrases in order to keep from having to console Mariann in a more personal fashion.

It is only with great difficulty that she gets him to listen to her problem about her daughter, and again he is only able to offer slogans: "Müßiggang ist die Quelle schlechter Begierden" [Idleness is the source of evil cravings] (1.3, 17). He sees Leni's behavior as completely predictable and believes that nothing more can be done or said about it. His attitude is in stark contrast to that of the understanding and unselfish Mariann, who says, "Weil i mir denk, unser Herrgott ko net so schnell ferti sei mit an Mensch'n, und es müaßt eahm selber's Herz weh toa, wann er siecht, daß so a G'schöpf nimmer in d' Höh derf" [Because I think the Lord God can't write off a person so quickly, and it must pain him in his heart when he sees that such a creature isn't allowed to go to heaven] (1.3, 17). A distinction is thus introduced here between clerical behavior and a form of religious faith that is more tolerant.

Religious institutions are criticized further when Thomas doubts that Leni would even be allowed in church to get married (2.4, 33) and when Köckenberger attacks Leni personally with a sermon that preaches, according to Barbara's paraphrase, "Daß diesen Übles geschiecht, die wo Ärgernis geben" [That harm comes to those who cause trouble] (3.1, 48). This message exculpates the community in advance from any harm they may cause Leni or her father by singling out her behavior as the root of the evil. The church and the community work hand in hand to insure that the existing state of power relations remains intact; this collusion resembles that found in *Die Kreuzelschreiber*. Thoma's condemnation of the church is also political, since the linkage of community opinion and interests to church interests was also practiced on a larger scale in the connection between the Catholic Church and the Center Party. Though *Magdalena* does not make this relationship explicit, as Thoma's topical satires often did, the message would have been clear to audiences of the time, and the predominant effect of this tragedy is to give a very negative view of the church's role in maintaining the status quo.

Even though the narrow-minded attitudes of the community and the church are thoroughly condemned, they are not directly responsible for Leni's behavior in the city, and Thoma presents her situation as being quite complex. Anna Stark notes that the three most important things in the lives of farmers of the Dachau region are the community, religion, and their work (47); an inadequate relation to the last of these also plays a role in the direction taken by Leni's life. As a small farmer, Thomas has had to establish his position in the community through a lifetime of hard labor. In trying to determine why their daughter has turned out bad, he mentions that they were unable to keep her from going to the city because farmwork was always too difficult for her, and Mariann attributes this difficulty to her physical weakness (1.1, 11). Later Leni herself doubts that she will be able to survive on the farm because her mother always claimed that she was not strong enough. Mariann wishes she had never made this remark, indicating perhaps that a perception of weakness may have played as great a role as any inherent lack of strength (1.7, 24).

In any event, Leni does not participate in work the way they do, and this makes her situation harder for them to comprehend. Her transgression against honest work, by employing a different means to earn money, is what damages the family in the eyes of the community. Thomas says: "Sieb'na- dreiß'g Jahr hamm mir hart g'arbet und san rechtschaffen g'wesen, und hat uns jeder de Ehr lass'n müass'n ... und jetzt, weil mir alt san, g'hör'n mir zu de schlecht'n Leut!" [We worked hard for thirty-seven years and were always upright, and everybody had to pay us honor ... and now, because we're old, we're counted among the bad people] (1.1, 12-13). According to Gerd Müller, Thomas can only consider humans upright when they are work-oriented, and he attributes his favored position in the community to his appreciation of this fact (60-61). Leni is unable to incorporate herself into the world of work, the religious congregation, or the community as a whole. The play represents not just a criticism of isolated conditions but a clear negation of the portrayed milieu by displaying how village attitudes in these three areas serve to create a dystopia.

The villagers of course think that the problem results from Leni's individual transgression, and she does in fact reveal certain weaknesses. More obvious to the spectator than any physical weakness on her part is her lack of intelligence, which prevents her from gaining any insight into her situation or taking any steps to do anything about it. She fails to comprehend the gravity of her situation and unrealistically thinks that by flirting with Lenz she can obtain a proposal of marriage, which will make everything all right. Only at the end, when she seeks money for escape, does she seem to realize how impossible her situation is within the village. In justifying her asking Martin Lechner for money, she says, "Weil i furt hab woll'n ... weil's ma do nix hilft ... weil i schlecht bleib'n muaß ... [Because I wanted to get away ... because nothing helps me anyway ... because I have to remain bad ...] (3.12, 67; ellipses in original). In other words, no matter what action she takes, she would always be considered a bad girl in everyone's opinion. Her own weaknesses and the inability of the church, the community, and her parents to prepare her for life either in the village or the city contributed to the situation that led to Leni's downfall. Upon her return, a narrow-minded system of village norms and hypocrisy, aided by self-serving clerics and the economic self-interest of the mayor, prevent her from extricating herself.

Although the web of causality is complex, most of the blame can clearly be attributed to the milieu, and the negative predominates. In this tragedy there seems very little of either the utopian or the affirmative. Yet these elements are to be found where they were in Anzengruber: in the precise setting of this serious drama. By making his figures correspond as closely as possible to the actual Bavarian peasants that he knew, Thoma strongly indicated that they were fit subjects for tragedy, rather than comic buffoons or pitiful creatures worthy of denunciation. In plainly showing their limitations, however, he introduces a modern element into his tragic *Volksstück*. According to Dewitz he helps inaugurate the tradition of later authors who portray excluded figures from the very margins of society (223). But even though important aspects of the characters' lives are condemned, they themselves are not. This distinction is an important one that carries over into the twentieth-century *Volksstücke* of Fleißer, Horváth, Sperr, Turrini and Kroetz.

Looking back to the past, many consider the rural *Magdalena* as the culmination of a line of middle-class tragedies that began with Lessing's

Emilia Galotti, but such comparisons should not simply be based on superficial similarities of plot. Although Emilia Galotti is also murdered by her father when he sees no other alternative to her bringing shame on the household, and even though the father in Hebbel's *Maria Magdalene* drives his daughter to death because of his fear of the disgrace that would be placed on him from her bearing an illegitimate child (the similarity in the titles of Thoma's and Hebbel's plays is no doubt intentional), the real resemblance lies elsewhere. The main similarity is in the treatment of tragedy in its social manifestation as it arises from a character's background and milieu, rather than in the plays' correspondence to a classical tragic archetype (G. Müller 57-8). In addition, the plays of all three authors display an assertive portrayal of a previously subordinate class as suitable material for drama.

The opening stage directions of *Magdalena* give a precise desciption of a farmhouse with simple furniture, tile oven, and crucifix that would be recognized by rural spectators and serve as an affirmation of their way of life. Similar attention to the dialect, not merely Bavarian but more precisely localized to the Dachau region, shows that these people are taken seriously. A number of scholars have attested to the accuracy with which this speech has been rendered (Ronde 65, G. Müller 66-9) and in this respect Thoma goes farther than Anzengruber, who created an artifical dialect by mixing elements from different regions. Work, the community, and religion, the predominant elements in the farmers' lives, also display possibilities for the positive. Work itself is not condemned, merely an attitude that fails to find alternatives for those who are unable to perform in the accepted ways. A spirit of community would also be beneficial if it aided its members, rather than confining them.

Mariann, the only character who shows any understanding for Leni, is an example of how concern for the person is preferable to an adherence to norms. Her previously mentioned remark on how a sympathetic God must view Leni runs counter to dogma, but indicates the possibility of a religious faith that is less destructive than the current practices of the church. If this means the return to an earlier, truer faith, it could represent an attempt to find a solution in nostalgia. Dewitz in fact claims that *Magdalena* marks the rejection of the modern world and that Thoma creates for himself a unviverse turned toward the past (230-31). But the awareness of an attitude that could lead to a true community, whether or not such an attitude ever existed in practice, can provide an impetus toward a future utopia in Bloch's sense. A certain sympathy must be generated for these characters and their way of life in order for the seeds of the utopian to exist at all, but the negative aspects of their milieu, which are so strongly stressed, prevent the predominance of the false affects of nostalgia or affirmation of the existing *Heimat.*

Since there is no supernatural vision of a better realm, as in Raimund's *Alpenkönig,* nor a *raisonneur* like Anzengruber's Steinklopferhanns to point the way out of the stifling environment, the task is left to the spectator to see not only the shortcomings of the existing society, but also the manner in which it might be overcome. No apparent authorial opinions are inserted as morals into the mouths of characters. The didacticism is less overt, though it still exists in the negative example of the content, rather than explicitly in words. The play offers only glimpses into overcoming the limitations of the status quo. These can be found in the mixture of good and bad within most of the characters and in the gap between what is and what could have been. In their first discussion about Leni, Mariann expresses hope that Leni can remember the prayers that she memorized when she learned how to talk, and she recalls an incident from her daughter's first Corpus Christi procession:

Wia s' 's erst'mal mit da Prozession ganga is, da is sie hinter'n Pfarra daher trappelt, so fromm als wie de andern. Und wia'r i ihr dös weiße Kleidl anzog'n hab, da fragt sie mi: Is wahr, Muatta, daß i mit'n Himmivata geh derf? Ja, sag i, Lenerl, heunt gehst amal mit'n Himmivata. (1.1, 13-4)

[When she walked with the procession for the first time, she tramped along behind the priest, just as piously as the others. And when I put the little white dress on her, she asked me: Is it true, Mother, that I will be allowed to walk with the Heavenly Father? Yes, I said, Lenerl, today you're going to walk with the Heavenly Father.]

Thomas fatalistically doubts that these early beliefs will have any effect at this point, though Mariann thinks that they can be rekindled. The picture of an innocent child in her white dress serves as a contrast to Leni's present "fallen" state and gives a utopian image of wholeness within a true religion and true community, even though these had never actually prevailed in the village. At the end of the first act Mariann recalls similar scenes of childhood to Leni, though Leni sees little point in remembering them and fails to have her faith revived (1.7, 25-6). Religion provides an image of utopia in *Magdalena,* rather than offering a path to that goal.

Though Leni on most occasions stubbornly resists her parents' efforts toward reintegration, she is not to be viewed as completely bad, and her plight is more a result of weakness and stupidity than of evil. Her few attempts are doomed to failure, not so much because of her own inability to change as the refusal of the others to believe that she can change. Just as the causes of the tragedy are revealed to be quite complex, most of the characters show a mixture of good and bad. (The only exceptions are Mariann, who is purely good, and the new priest, who has no redeeming qualities).

When Lenz, for example, gives notice, Thomas believes that his farmhand wants to get away from the disreputable household as quickly as possible. Lenz disputes this, saying he can earn more money through piecework at a sawmill (2.2, 30-31). Though his motivations are never completely clear to the audience, Lenz seems sincere in his expressing pride at having Thomas's recommendation in his service book, and he is obviously not part of the group of young men that have fun at another's misfortune (2.7, 41-42; 3.4, 52-54). He is decent enough to want to stay on good terms with Thomas, but not strong enough to stay in his employment. Similarly, the neighbor Plank wants to help Thomas by warning him of the new rumor concernig Leni. He does so only with difficulty, and though he is motivated by a desire to do the right thing by his neighbor, he cannot disagree that the community is justified in getting upset by Leni's most recent action (3.8, 57-60).

These two figures thus show some decency, though they are unable to oppose community opinion in either thought or deed. They merely serve as reminders of the possibility that humane behavior might flourish in a different environment. The closest that any character can come in acting to try to bring about a change is in the negative activity of flight from the current dystopia: Leni desires to get away, but it is doubtful that her life would improve as a result of a change of setting. And it is certainly true that intolerance and injustice would prevail in Berghofen, even after Leni left.

In *Magdalena* Thoma employs a form different from those used in his shorter situation comedies, his farces, and his satires. This is a full-length play, which allows time for the development of character and complex situations, but most significantly, it is a tragedy. This differentiates it from his satire *Moral*, which also dealt with the potential harm that could be caused by a hypocritical emphasis on surface morality, as well as from most previous *Volksstücke* of other authors. Thoma's choice of the term *Volksstück* to designate the play was confusing to the distinguished Berlin critic Alfred Kerr, who nonetheless praised the work for its similarities to classical tragedy:

> Kein Volksstück. Vielmehr das Gegenteil eines solchen: in knapper Wucht. Im lautlosen Hinstellen eines Sachbestandes. Im festen Zurücktreten des Bildners. Gefugt, geschweißt, gebändigt. (Im Volksstück liegt Beschönigendes, Trostvolles, Einrenkendes, Begütigendes, Schwindelhaftes: hier nichts dergleichen). (76)

> [Not a *Volksstück*. Rather the opposite of such: with concise force. In the quiet placement of a set of circumstances. In the firm withdrawal of the portrayer. Joined together, welded, controlled. (In the *Volksstück* one finds mitigating, consoling, rectifying, soothing, dizzying qualities: here, nothing of the sort.]

Kerr's conception of the *Volksstück* is based of course on the entertaining farce, which may have predominated in actual performances, but which fails to describe the plays of Raimund, Nestroy, and Anzengruber. Though *Magdalena* is also quite different from any of these works, with the exception of certain plays of Anzengruber, Thoma's choice of genre designation fulfills a definite purpose and makes sense. In order to write the type of *Volksstück* that he felt was adequate to his time, he combined elements from a number of different literary movements: the middle-class tragedy, Naturalism, and the *Volkstheater*, especially as it was manifested on rural stages. For content he chose a particular class of people, the small farmers of Bavaria, yet rather than situating them in a farce or even a sentimental play, he employed tragedy. This choice had a number of effects: since it was somewhat unexpected, it caused urban audiences to consider more closely the relation between the form and the content in the drama they were viewing (as in Kerr's case). As a form of serious drama, it underscored the notion that the problems of the people of the rural underclasses or of individuals with serious limitations were also worthy of attention.

But in *Magdalena*, the negative function of the tragedy is much stronger than the affirmative. The villagers confront Thomas Mayr with a dilemma in which he can neither send his daughter away nor hope to improve her lot by keeping her at home: restricting the sole solution to filicide casts the current state of affairs in an extremely negative light. The ending is carefully motivated and the play more tightly constructed than in other plays that have been considered here. There is not much of an opening within the conclusion that gives grounds for hope or alternatives: the form of *Magdalena* thus provides a more through-going negation. The tragic form seems appropriate to the portrayal of social misery, although Thoma himself denied that *Magdalena* was a "Strindberg'sche Trostlosigkeit" [Strindbergian dreariness] (LB 243). Referring to his own novel *Der Wittiber*, Thoma also remarked that he wrote better than Zola, who attempted to write veristically rather than with style and who lacked "the best thing of all, humor" (LB, 385). Although comedy is one of the dominant elements of Thoma's oeuvre, it is totally missing in *Magdalena*, a play that offers less consolation than its author seems to think. Comic effect had provided one of the most entertaining features in many previous *Volksstücke*, but that form of enjoyment is denied the public here, as is the inclusion of music and songs.

An additional element that tended to give in to audience expectations, but which was more often found in trivial *Volksstücke*, was sentimentality. Thoma had discarded his first attempt at a *Volksstück* in the Anzengruber manner because of the "cloud of sentimentality" that surrounded it (*Ausgewählte Briefe* 105-5), and he is careful to avoid this quality for the most part in *Magdalena*. An avoidance results partly from an attempt to render accurately the speech of farmers, who rarely expressed their emotions in words. In the first scene of *Magdalena* Thomas uses short, unemotional sentences when speaking with his dying wife. Although he is certainly quite moved, his strongest verbal expression of feeling toward his wife is, "Bist mei guate Kameradin gewesen" [You've been my good comrade] (1.1., 11). In the first manuscript version of the play he simultaneously dabbed at his moist eyes, but this stage direction was omitted in the final text, for Thoma always took pains to avoid exaggerations in the actual performance (cf. Jones, "Tradition" 218-9). Sentiment does crop up more strongly, however, in the scenes where Mariann reminisces with her husband and Leni (1.1., 10; 1.7, 25), yet the play as a whole is rather restrained in this regard.

Comic effect, songs, and sentiment, all components of many previous *Volksstücke*, are almost completely avoided in *Magdalena*, for they would have detracted from the characters and their situation, and this omission hinders a reception that lets an enjoyable theater experience serve as a surrogate for change in society. The only element that could promote such a vicarious function results from *Magdalena*'s resemblance to classical tragedy. Since the play is so tightly constructed and refrains from any commentary that might provide distance, there is a danger that it could evoke a cathartic effect or a feeling of inevitability on the part of the spectator. Such a reception would be more likely, if audiences regard this drama as a mythic enactment of fate in farmer's clothing, but to do so would mean ignoring the analytic plot that so carefully develops a complex causality.

Another element that has been discussed in terms of its naturalistic content, and one that marks the *Volksstück* in general, is the use of dialect. The accurate reproduction of the vernacular of the region around Dachau serves to convey verisimilitude and specificity, since Thoma believed that he could not characterize these people with any language other than the one they actually spoke, nor would he be able to capture their manner of thinking (LB 446). Dialect does not seem to have the oppositional function that has been observed in other plays (including Thoma's own *Die Medaille*): here it is neither superior because of some sort of naturalness and integrity, nor inferior because of shortcomings in comparison with the standard language. Since the environment of its speakers is condemned, it is not to be viewed as offering possibilities that High German lacks: otherwise there would have been no tragic situation. But since its characters are taken seriously, it cannot mark them as stupid buffoons, as dialect often did in comedies portraying stereotyped farmers. Although the dialect of *Magdalena* inevitably carries different connotations to different spectators, it seems intended merely to represent language in general as it is actually spoken, reflecting of course the particularities of people of a definite background and region. Recent linguistic analyses of the elements of Thoma's dialogues point out that they have a strong basis in Bavarian reality, even though they have been artistically crafted (Betten 183-86). High German is used rarely: in the mouth of Köckenberger, it is stilted and insincere and thus serves to criticize the priest's character, but when Thomas reads aloud the attestation he writes in Lenz's service book, it appears more neutral, since Thomas apparently means what he writes (3.4, 54).

It is therefore necessary to examine the way the language is used, rather than simply to identify it as dialect. For Anna Stark, the qualities found in the language of Thoma's characters are important because of their close correspondence to the actual speech of a particular linguistic group. Although she makes valid observations about certain features of language, the implications of these features for the characters themselves are more significant for our purposes. She indicates, for example, that farmers do not think in long sentences with some parts logically subordinated to or contained in others: they tend to use many short clauses arranged paratactically (86). This is evident in narration, as in Mariann's recounting of an event from Leni's childhood (1.7, 25), but it also occurs when Thomas attempts to explain that he and Mariann need not consider themselves guilty for the way Leni turned out: "Hamm mir net lang gnua g'red't, und sie hat net anderst mög'n, und d'Bauernarbeit is ihr allaweil z'hart g'wesen"

[Didn't we talk long enough, and she didn't want to do anything else, and farmwork was always too hard for her] (1.1., 11). Several of the factors involved in this complex process are singled out and connected to one another by the conjunction "and," rather than being related in any sort of logical fashion.

Similarly, when Thomas outlines his dilemma to the mayor at the play's end, the thoughts are merely strung together. Though the ellipses marking the pauses in his speech result partially from anger, they are also a sign of his difficulty in comprehending and explaining his plight:

> Z'erscht bringt mir der da ... *auf den Bürgermeister zeigend* ... dös Weibsbild ins Haus ... schreit mei Schand im Dorf rum ... bringt s' da rei zu da krank'n Muatta ... i derf mi net wehr'n ... na! I muaß s' hamm ... und heut kummt er, i derf s' in mein Haus nimmer g'halt'n ... i muaß leid'n, daß s' draußd im Dreck derstickt ... Derf mi der zum Narr'n halt'n? Schaugt's mi z'erscht o! I vertrag nimma viel ... (3.9, 62)

> [First he ... *pointing to the mayor* ... brings me the hussy into the house ... spreads my shame all over the village ... brings her in to her sick mother ... I can't defend myself ... Well! I have to take her ... and today he comes, I can't keep her in my house any more ... Is he trying to take me for a fool? Look at me! I can't take much anymore ...]

As Betten points out, Thoma achieves a natural-sounding taciturnity not only through ellipsis, but also through attention to oral patterns of repetition, paraphrase, and self-correction (185).

When he and other characters discuss the concrete, everyday concerns of farmwork, they are more articulate, but the matter with Leni is one that he cannot grasp, and language fails him. Abstract concepts in general are foreign to the thought of these farmers, and when words expressing such notions are employed, they tend to be mispronounced (e.g. "Kuraschi" for "Courage," 2.5, 37). Thus when they have a choice, they talk about the things they know, but it is perhaps equally accurate to say that they know the things they talk about. Leni's situation, as it affects both her and the other members of her family, is an unfamiliar, alienating one which they are unprepared to confront and incapable of controlling through language. Leni is the character most limited in her intelligence and in the choices open to her, and her limitations are reflected in her use of language. When the gendarme delivers her to her parents and her father greets her roughly, she is only able to reply with "n ... no!" [well now] (1.6, 20), a phrase that she uses twice more in the next two pages and on repeated occasions throughout the rest of the play. Her failure to find a more suitable response is similar to the use of the word "genau" [exactly] in the later plays of Franz Xaver Kroetz, even when the word does not fit.

Fenzel claims that unlike recent researchers who subscribe to a theory of language barriers, Thoma did not view his characters as disadvantaged and thus gives them a broader palette with which to express themselves (132). Although this observation may hold true for the comedies, the questioning of language's ability to give a character insight into his or her situation and to communicate it to others is a new element introduced into *Magdalena*. In Anzengruber's *Kreuzelschreiber*, Steinklopferhanns was able to articulate a philosophy of life, and the two warring factions were able to reach an agreement in the end through discussions. Even Brenninger, who could not understand why his wife of fifty years would suddenly shun him, was able to express himself to the others. Though he too speaks in short, paratactic utterances, he does not stammer before the inexpressible, and his lack of comprehension of his plight is not matched by a similar failure of language itself to describe or communicate. Such a failure would later become a dominant feature of the *Volksstücke* of Horváth and Kroetz.

Gerd Müller claims that unlike the problems in a play such as Gerhart Hauptmann's *Die Weber*, which can be more or less solved through an intervention of legal authorities, those in *Magdalena* can only be solved when they are successfully articulated. The concept of tragedy is thereby liquidated, if it can be shown that the tragic conclusion can be avoided through a discussion of the participants (66). The characters in this play never achieve such an analysis, however, because their language is not adequate, and nothing indicates that they could ever carry on such a discussion. In several instances they themselves doubt that talk ("red'n") can produce results. Leni tells her father at one point that he should have tried harder to convince Lenz to stay, but he replies, "Da is nix mehr zum red'n!" [There's nothing more to talk about] (2.3, 31). In an argument with the mayor, Thomas protests the treatment he and his daughter are receiving from the community, and the mayor replies, "Dös Dischkrier'n hat koan Wert" [There's no sense in discussing it] (2.5, 37). The play does not discuss this problem either, but simply displays it. When Leni says she sought to escape because she would only remain bad in the villagers' eyes, she indicates that the narrow moral code does not change; neither, however, do the words with which it is expressed. Language does not provide a way to an alternative, and Thomas's final response, when words and all else fail, is to kill her. The inadequacy of the characters' speech does not rule out the possibility that spectators might be able to achieve an adequate discussion, but within the play, the failure of language to provide insight and communication is one of its most strongly negative features.

In its formal aspects *Magdalena* offers little opening for hope, except in its analytic structure. At the play's beginning, Leni has already committed the act which seals her fate (its later repetition is merely an intensification that insures the inevitable), and her family and neighbors in the village are all aware of it. This differentiates Thoma's tragedy from Hebbel's *Maria Magdalene*, in which the father only learns near the end about the "shame" his daughter has brought on him. What follows in Thoma's play is an attempt on the part of Leni's parents (though not on the part of the villagers and the priest) to understand why this has come about and to see if the situation might be ameliorated, or at least salvaged. But since no one, with the exception of Mariann (whose early death removes her from the picture) reaches any significant degree of comprehension or sympathy, the attempted analysis by characters within the play fails. To Kaufmann and Schlenstedt this means that Thoma's earlier optimism concerning the possibility of exercising effective criticism of society had disappeared in this tragedy, which portrays a conflict as irreconcilable (264). Yet the careful process of revelation and development enables the spectator to observe how this situation has come about and to reflect on how a tragic outcome might be avoided.

While it is certainly true that these characters as they are presented would never achieve a reconciliation, the possibility that audiences might reach a degree of insight or even move toward change is not entirely ruled out. The author, after all, was not enslaved to the normative influence of a type of rural society of which he was quite fond, and the implication remains that others might liberate themselves as well. Gerd Müller observes that since the *Volksstück* in general tended to be less openly didactic than *Lehrstücke* [instructional plays] or even classical German drama, its entertaining aspects frequently obscured its lesson. Although *Magdalena* contains no comic effects to get in the way of a message, it too refrains from providing a practical application as to how the village milieu might be changed (64-5). Müller contends that this play thus fails to provoke the spectator to change the world outside the theater, but I would assert that the strength of its negation and its analytic structure provide an impetus in this direction. Because it does not give a specific answer, however, spectators are forced to draw conclusions themselves.

Some may see the solution in an individual commitment to open-mindedness, whereas others might perceive a necessity for change in the basic economic structure and its relation to the cultural superstructure.[7] Whether or not Thoma had a political solution in mind, the play makes this aspect evident, and no solution could be complete until it is addressed. The analytic structure that portrays how a complex set of causes results in a disastrous situation implies that the end might have been averted. If characters could gain insight, they might see how they could change some of the factors that govern their lives. In this the form allows a slight opening for a utopian hope.

In the history of its reception, *Magdalena* further broadens the concept *Volksstück* in providing theater for audiences beyond the region that it portrays. Although early Viennese plays had been written with specific audiences in mind, Nestroy took his plays on the road to northern Germany, and his works are still widely performed on numerous stages. Anzengruber was faced with institutional changes within the suburban theaters and specifically aimed at a wider audience with his artificial dialect. His plays were successfully received by adherents of Naturalism in the cities as well as by rural spectators, and Thoma's *Magdalena* met a similar response. Thoma realized that farmers rarely read dialect and would therefore be unfamiliar with his peasant novels, but that they had an active theatrical tradition and would be more likely to appreciate a dramatic work. He therefore wrote *Magdalena* in the language they spoke and intended that it be performed at Michl Dengg's *Bauerntheater*. It received its premiere, however, at Viktor Barnowsky's *Kleines Theater* in Berlin, and critics from all over Germany were on the whole quite positive in their evaluations of it; the review by Kerr, for example, has already been quoted. Most of the reviewers were pleased that *Magdalena* was different from the sentimental variety of trivial *Volksstücke*, and many found that its author surpassed Anzengruber. Even though the strong Bavarian dialect is difficult for other Germans to understand, the language did not seem to hinder its reception.

Thoma refused to soften the dialect in order to make concessions to non-Bavarians, though his keeping the orthography as close to High German as possible facilitates the reading of the play.[8] Rural actors would of course retain the proper pronunciation, and local farm audiences were thus confronted with a play whose characters spoke the language that they did. The strongly negative elements of the play did not seem to hinder a reception on their part, however. Dengg's successor Bertl Schultes, for example, called *Magdalena* "the most significant *Volksstück* that was ever written" (94). In the 1950's traveling performances by these rural actors met with acclaim in other regions (cf. Jones, "Tradition" 237-8), and a 1975 revival at Munich's *Residenztheater* was greeted with strong applause (Kaiser). Giving lower class rural people a dramatic voice on stages throughout the country and providing them with a secure place in literature resulted from a utopian impulse that also envisions the possibility of their living adequate lives in an integrated society.

Magdalena represents a step in the transition to the *Volksstücke* of the present century because of its more autonomous stance with regard to the tradition, its more thorough-going negation, its portrayal of the limitations of its characters, its tentative treatment of the insufficiencies of language in providing insight and communication, and its hesitancy in offering a concrete solution. Leni cannot be reintegrated into the world that is portrayed here. The play condemns the artificiality of a unity that is forced through conformity, yet it does not condemn the characters, for whom it maintains a degree of hope. The difference in balance between the overtly negative and the overtly positive provides the chief contrast between the *Volksstücke* of the nineteenth and the twentieth centuries, though both groups of plays find means to express the inadequacies in the existing condition of the *Volk* as well as a utopian hope for the future.

Chapter VI

Neither Heaven nor Hell: Marieluise Fleißer's *Fegefeuer in Ingolstadt*

> Er war und wurde Außenseiter in einem Dorf. Der Knabe lernt keine Liebe kennen, entbehrt sie aber, sein ganzes Leben lang hängt ihm dies Liebesbedürfnis nach, treibt ihn zu seltsamen Entschlüssen.
>
> —Marieluise Fleißer, "Findelkind und Rebell: Über Jean Genet"[1]

WITH THE NATIONAL SUCCESS OF PLAYS by Anzengruber and Thoma the concept of the *Volksstück* took on broader applications. It began to be used for more socially critical and literarily demanding plays that refrained from simply repeating variations on farcical entertainment with local color, and it became less closely linked to a specific theater or audience. The genre was no longer associated only with its origins in the Viennese *Volkstheater* or other *Volkstheater* in South German areas, although these regions and their traditions continued to serve as important sources.[2] Several playwrights without specific links to a popular theater tradition tried their hand at this type of play; as a result *Volksstücke* of the Weimar years are less closely connected to any predecessors. But the conscious association with the *Volksstück*-tradition, either through the use of the term as a genre designation or of elements frequently found in plays of this type, points to a certain continuity, despite the variety of approaches by different authors. An analysis must determine whether the resemblances are merely superficial, however, or whether they are more substantial.

The simplest criterion for comparison is content, and most of these plays portray the classes below the educated bourgeoisie with a certain regional specificity, yet their methods and reasons for doing so are often quite different. Certain plays of Ödön von Horváth and Bertolt Brecht can also be considered *Volksstücke* because their authors consciously linked their work to this tradition in an attempt to renew it. In the case of Marieluise Fleißer there is an additional, retroactive reason for such an association: more recent authors of *Volksstücke*, including Faßbinder, Kroetz, and Sperr, regarded her as a model for their work, and this renewed attention actually resulted in more performances of her plays in the 1970's than she had received when she began writing fifty years earlier. Hein's summary of Fleißer's accomplishment is an accurate one: she "counters the amusing provincial idyll in the old *Volksstück* with the anti-illusionistic '*Heimat*-play'".[3] The destruction of the illusions contained in the old clichés of the popular *Heimat*-drama is perhaps the most striking feature of Fleißer's texts; it is what distinguishes them most from nineteenth-century *Volksstücke* and makes her such an appropriate starting point for a discussion of the modern variant of this genre.

Born in the lower Bavarian city of Ingolstadt in 1901, Marieluise Fleißer attended a boarding school for girls and later studied drama in Munich. She began writing plays herself during the 1920's in Berlin. Here she became acquainted with Brecht, whose encouragement and help with staging no doubt furthered her career, though his influence was not always entirely positive. She received critical acclaim for her plays and short stories, but was prohibited from further publishing when the Nazis came to power in 1933. She married a shopkeeper in her native town and wrote little else in the following years. Except for a few performances in the early 1950's, her plays were largely forgotten until their "rediscovery" shortly before her death in 1974.

The use of the name Ingolstadt in the titles of her first two plays and in her signature as "Marieluise Fleißer aus Ingolstadt" on the title page of her first collection of short stories connect her closely with her native region, but her texts deliver something other than the comforting and familiar that usually characterized local-color writing, and they display an author quite different from the "callous, reactionary spirits" that typically produced this kind of literature (Benjamin, "Echt Ingolstädter Originalnovellen" 189). Walter Benjamin calls the language in her stories "der aufsässige Dialekt, der die Heimatkunst von innen heraus sprengt" [rebellious dialect that explodes *Heimat*-art from within] (190), and Herbert Ihering says she remained true to her "Heimat" by creating "inexorable counter-works" to the "localized stupidity, philistine arrogance, and criminal haughtiness" that characterized the "Blut und Boden" [blood and soil] ideology of the Nazis (*Mat.* 229).[4] Even when "Heimat"-literature was not so blatantly and dangerously perverse, the sentiment and superficiality of the more "harmless" variety tended to present a false picture of an already attained utopia, a secure native region whose qualities and timeless values were to be defended against all threats of change. The form of such plays aided this lulling into complacency by offering a vicarious escape into a harmonious realm that was supposed to correspond with outside reality.[5] Fleißer, however, provided something quite different: she reveals the falseness behind a timeless, mythical notion of *Heimat* by showing the inadequacies of a specific historical situation (Gerd Müller 91).

In order to delineate more sharply the changes that Fleißer and Horváth brought to the genre, many studies contrast the plays of these two authors with Carl Zuckmayer's *Der fröhliche Weinberg* [*The Merry Vineyard*, 1925], a very popular comedy about boatmen and vintners along the Rhine that affirms a healthy sensuality and ends with four engagements, including that of the daughter of a wealthy wine-grower to a robust, vital man from a lower class. The play includes comic effects, singing, dancing, dialect, and recognizable portrayals of the the customs of Zuckmayer's Rhine-Hesse homeland; a critic at the Berlin premiere pointed out its filiation to previous authors of *Volksstücke* such as Niebergall, Anzengruber, and Thoma. But the play essentially affirmed the entertaining, expected aspects of the tradition, rather than offering new perspectives. It in fact displays many of the very features that Brecht later wanted to overcome in his attempts at a renewal of the *Volksstück*: scandalous morality, which reduces sexual problems to healthy instincts, nature that cannot be dominated, and irrelevant subconflicts. It provides entertainment through songs and effective theatricality in which the characters show no evidence of problems with language, but rather a complete unity between speaking and acting (Rotermund 22–23). Even though Marieluise Fleißer voiced no theoretical program such as Brecht's, her plays also shun most of the features that he criticized (cf. Rühle, "Leben" 22).

In criticizing Zuckmayer, Erwin Rotermund cites Karl Mannheim's *Ideologie und Utopie*, which describes the 1920's as characterized by an "absorption of utopia," or "the gradual decrease of utopian intensity." For Mannheim this is evident in the disappearance of the humanitarian in art, which resulted in a resigned acceptance of the existing (20). Rotermund finds that the reception of *Der fröhliche Weinberg* signalled this loss of utopia: "it is precisely the 'hey, we're alive' attitude based on the new prosperity that Ernst Toller criticized so intensively." Zuckmayer's play is unhistorical and does not point to anything besides existing social reality (24). Any attempts at satire are blocked by making the Dionysian timeless and absolute and by portraying a nature that can be immediately experienced (26).[6] *Der fröhliche Weinberg* thus shares many superficial features of the commonly held definition of the *Volksstück*, yet it ultimately fails to live up to the attributes embodied by the plays discussed in this study. Its affirmative qualities keep it from expressing utopia or negation, either in form or in content. In this regard it fails to deal adquately with the need for change in creating a truly unified society.[7]

For Marieluise Fleißer, on the other hand, *Heimat* did not have the connotations of a vital, healthy, intact world: the picture presented in her first play *Fegefeuer in Ingolstadt* [Purgatory in Ingolstadt, 1926] was extremely unflattering, and reports of the Berlin performance of *Pioniere in Ingolstadt* three years later were greeted with outrage in her home town, where the mayor accused her of fouling her own nest.[8] In Fleißer's plays the *Volk* consists of lower middle-class citizens of provincial towns, rather than the craftsmen and tradesmen of the big city or the farmers of the country-side. Instead of finding a solution by following timeless instinctual drives in an unsullied regional environment, her characters face an alienation that they do not comprehend, brought on by conditions and forces that they feel powerless to change. Her play might therefore be considered an anti-*Heimat* play because of the manner in which it subverts audience preconceptions. The *Volksstück*, long viewed askance by those in power, takes on a different relation to the audience as well in the form provided by Fleißer and certain other twentieth-century authors of the genre. Very little comfort is provided in the theater experience, for the frustration in the lives of lower middle-class people in small German towns is confronted directly in both form and content. The place we encounter here is much bleaker than Zuckmayer's Rheinland, though it does not quite represent a trip into hell, for the hope of deliverance is never completely extinguished. It is purgatory, in this case a historical dystopia whose characters long in vain for a transformation into a utopia; it is *Fegefeuer in Ingolstadt*.

Although the play's current title was not chosen by Fleißer, her own choice *Die Fußwaschung* [The Footwashing] having been replaced by the director Moritz Seeler before he had her full permission to do so, it is nonetheless appropriate. Seeler claimed that its two parts combine the real, earthly landscape with the metaphysical landscape of the soul (*Mat.* 27). The former aspect is indeed important to an understanding of the play, since the concrete historical environment of the characters is crucial and since the town's name suggests the type of *Heimat*-play against which Fleißer's text is to be read. Fleißer's later claim that "Ingolstadt stands for many cities" does not contradict this, for the important aspect of the specificity is retained in her explanation that the name refers to a "gesellschaftliche Lebensform" [social form of life] (*Mat.* 352–53). Purgatory need not be interpreted metaphysically, however, but rather metaphorically as both a characteriza-tion of the torment contained in the present earthly environment and an expression of an expectation that redemption will occur in the future.[9] Like the present title, which points to an inversion of the traditional concept of *Heimatstück*, *Die Fußwaschung* uses a Biblical term to point to a redemption that becomes subverted in the course of the play. Both titles give expression to a utopian hope, though *Fegefeuer in Ingolstadt* additionally indicates that utopia is not to be found in the contemporary world as it is and hints at a concept of genre against which the play must also be considered.

The purgatory encountered in this Ingolstadt is characterized by a seemingly endless cycle of domination, violence, and inability to engage in any sort of meaningful communication. The play lacks a unified plot, a traditional dramatic structure, or a satisfying resolution. In the first of the play's six scenes, or *Bilder*,[10] the audience learns that the main character, Olga Berotter, has considered aborting her child by her erstwhile lover Peps until she learns that the town's back-street abortionist has given up her practice. Although her father, brother, and sister Clementine are not yet aware of her plight, it is clear that she would be unable to find any understanding within her family: the father receives no respect from his children, and Clementine resents the fact that it was Olga who got the better education.

When Olga realizes that she has no future with Peps, she seeks refuge in Roelle, a weakling and outcast whose *ressentiment* leads him to try to raise himself above all the others through visions of angels, which he induces by fasting. Roelle is constantly degraded by the others: at one point two altar boys drag him into a crowd of waiting fellow high school students, eager to see him in an ecstatic visionary state, and when he is unable to fulfill their wishes, they stone him. After his wounding, Olga seems to be most sympathetic to him, yet even though Olga and Roelle are both victims who seek a way out of their predicament, they victimize each other in turn. Olga does not attempt to hinder Clementine's humiliation of Roelle, who has a phobia about water, by leading a group in dunking him in a tub. Even Roelle's later rescue of Olga from a suicide attempt in the Danube does not serve to establish a better future for either of them; at the play's end, each is alone as at the beginning.

Continuous and continual victimization characterizes the play from start to finish and constitutes the punishment inflicted on the inhabitants of this earthly purgatory. In the 1970's Fleißer summarized *Fegefeuer* as a play about "the law of the pack and about outsiders" (GW 1, 438; cf. also *Mat.* 368). In this respect Olga's position resembles that of Thoma's Leni, the victim of a community "Haberfeldtreiben." Victimization is accompanied by overt and covert violence in both form and content; what occurs in the first scene is typical for the rest of the play. At the beginning the widower Berotter is engaged in conversation with Olga and Clementine. The former is home from boarding school, and the latter, who is in charge of running the Berotter household, promptly expresses her envy. It becomes clear that in this particular triangular configuration Olga is subordinate to the other two; here for example, they accuse her of not cooperating in their preparations for the visit of Hermine Seitz. Although this relationship of domination and subordination is typical of every scene in the play, the same people are not always victims.

Domination usually results from superior numbers or knowing how to take advantage of a given situation in order to create an outsider as victim. Because she is outnumbered, Olga attempts to strengthen her position by enlisting the aid of her deceased mother: she says that the latter would not have approved of Hermine's coming to the house. But a state of equilibrium tends to be extremely unstable in this play: Clementine attempts to appropriate her mother's aid herself by countering that Olga did not even cry at the funeral. Later, she again bolsters her position with a moral argument by making a first reference to Olga's intended abortion (and an indirect reference to the play's title): she hopes for a final victory, which she displaces into a metaphysical realm, by saying that she will attain heaven, whereas Olga will burn in hell (68).

Roelle makes an appearance at the end of the scene; even before he walks on stage we learn that he too is on the giving as well as the receiving end of victimization, for he once stuck a needle in a dog's eye, thus cruelly mistreating a weaker creature. Olga tries to maintain her position of superiority over Roelle, while he attempts to invert it. When he eventually succeeds by making a reference to the abortionist, Olga consents to walking arm in arm with him in public in order to prevent him from spreading the story. Roelle tries to escape his own plight by the victimization of another through blackmail. Olga now feels confined on all sides, and when asked by Roelle to deny that she wanted to get rid of the child she replies. "Hätte es meine Mutter an mir getan!" [If only my mother had done it to me!] (72).

Even though Olga and Roelle are the principal victims, no one is free of mistreatment at the hands of others. Domination finds its expression and fulfillment in violence, either in the obvious onstage brutality exemplified by the stoning of Roelle or through subtler forms of force, such as Roelle's attempted blackmail. But any advantage a character may have is only temporary, and the sole escape open to these characters is to attempt to dominate someone else. Olga's sarcastic remark to Berotter (when referring to his treatment of his late wife) that she knows that violence represents a form of salvation to him could similarly be applied to others (66). The only means of escape that these characters are capable of imagining is to perpetrate on others the same mistreatment that they suffer; the cycle simply continues unbroken.

Violence is so pervasive that characters speak of almost everything in violent terms. For example, when dreaming of freedom, Olga expresses herself in the following way: "Wenn die Freiheit kommt in einer schönen Gestalt und es schlägt über einem zusammen —" [When freedom comes in a beautiful form and everything engulfs you —] (73). Roelle takes advantage of this expression to approach Olga physically, "Meinen Sie — so?" [Do you mean — like this?], but the forceful threat of possessive desire is stronger than any amorous tenderness, and she can only shudder. The language and gestures of violence do not let up throughout the play, nor is any relief nor redemption achieved through its means. Even the stoning of Roelle does not represent any sort of catharsis, since it is followed by the scene in which a smaller group strips him and forces him into the tub at Berotter's house, where he has sought refuge (111). In almost all cases domination is experienced corporeally by the characters, rather than simply observed (Dimter 233). According to Rühle, society itself is a body ("Leib") in which the individual is trapped and from which he or she has no escape ("Leben" 14).

Although individual psychological explanations might account for some of this behavior, these characters act largely according to social norms that they have internalized. According to Kurt Pinthus in his review of the premiere, the outer world is revealed not in external details describing Ingolstadt, but in the inner world of these pitiful creatures (*Mat.* 368). It is in this that the content most strongly serves as a negative condemnation of society. The most obvious example is religion, whose language, beginning in the play's title, runs as a subtext throughout and provides expression to the utopian impulse while at the same time subverting it. It both counters and supports the cycle of victimization. On the one hand, the religious is the traditional language of hope and salvation: those in purgatory long for eventual release, and characters like Clementine believe that through suffering and a moral life they will achieve salvation in the next world. This traditional belief fails to find fulfillment within this play, however, for religion is unable to provide a satisfactory solution for any of the characters. On a superficial level, the presence of religious terminology and imagery in everyday speech is an accurate reflection of the language and culture of the inhabitants of a provincial town in Catholic Bavaria, but in this play it has thematic and formal dimensions as well. Here, the characters can expect salvation neither from the institution of the church nor from metaphysical faith, and hopes placed in the latter seem to be only investments in an imaginary utopia that does not redeem present earthly existence.

Religious beliefs as exercised through the institution of the church retain their power in enforcing conformity, yet clerical figures do not appear onstage as targets of criticism, nor do specific dogmas and practices of the church. Anzengruber's *Die Kreuzelschreiber*, for example, had contained explicit satire on the doctrine of papal infallibility, and Thoma's *Magdalena* had criticized the behavior of a young priest who, though he could mouth doctrine, was unable to offer solace to a person in need. In Fleißer's play, however, the institution of religion is more thoroughly condemned precisely because it is so absent in content, even though its forms are so pervasive. Its assimilation into the speech and behavior of the characters indicates the strong influence of the church and the degree to which it participates in the continuing victimization.

The system of control exercised by the confessional is taken over by the characters; in their behavior they reflect the normative restraints imposed by the church (cf. Dimter 234–35). They condemn others as sinners, accusing them, for example, of not having been to mass, so as to maintain their own positions. The un-Christian manner in which religious practices are employed indicates that what the characters have learned best from the church is a system of authority and repression. Hoffmeister rightly contends that characters appropriate such conventions by internalizing prescriptive thinking and relying on authority figures, rather than thinking critically about the socio-political reality around them or the issues that they must face (*Theater* 41). The institution is thus indirectly but thoroughly criticized by means of the characters' imitation of it and resorting to it as a higher power to which they themselves are subordinate, but which legitimizes and provides a model for their domination of others.

The church is not the only force that holds the characters in its grip: school, science, and the economic system are made manifest in the behavior of the characters, even though the institutions themselves remain absent causes in the play. The audience does not see any dominating teachers, for example, although Hermine enlists their authority when she threatens to get Roelle expelled by tattling about his treatment of the dog. Similarly, we are aware of the control of the mysterious Dr. Hähnle only through his two assistants, who try to exploit Roelle's aberrant behavior for Hähnle's experiments. Fleißer says, "Der Doktor ist ein Mann, der wissenschaftlich arbeitet über die Formen des 'Irre-Seins' in ihren verschiedenen Stadien und der sich seine Objekte zum Zweck der Befragung durch Handlanger zutreiben läßt" [The doctor is a man who works scientifically on the forms of 'being insane' in their various stages and who lets his henchmen drive his objects to him for purposes of investigation] (qtd. in Kässens and Töteberg, *Fleißer* 48). Rather than improving humanity's lot, science manipulates and abuses by turning individuals into objects, and it does so at an anonymous distance. In addition to persecuting Roelle themselves, the doctor and his assistants provide further justification for the other characters to do likewise.

The economic sphere is also significant, even though it is hardly mentioned explicitly. The play demonstrates from start to finish a group of people so incapable of comprehending their alienation that they embrace and perpetuate it, rather than attempting to overturn it. Clementine, whose resentful attacks on Olga have already been described, is so desperate that she at one point seeks to escape through a marriage with Roelle. She tries to convince him that he should marry her, because his mother had approved of the match, giving as a reason, "weil Sie gar so ein fleißiges Mädel sind und das ist wie ein Kapital. Und das stimmt. Auf mir ruht das ganze Haus" [because you're such an industrious girl, and that's like capital. And that's true. The whole house rests on me] (93). In equating her own value with that of a capital investment, she is engaging in an extreme form of self-reification which is indicative of her own self-alienation.

In order to escape the drudgery of being a maid in her own family's household, she can only repeat this type of occupation somewhere else. The location changes, but the determining relationship remains the same. It is obvious that this form of escape is a delusion and that she would be just as subject to victimization there. The prospects of employment are not mentioned for most of these teenagers nor presented as a hope for a future improvement in their lives. Whatever occupation they eventually follow will simply be a fungible alternative to what they now experience in school. All of the institutions and systems, even when they are hated, are accepted as givens; there is no attempt to change them or escape from them all together. Instead, characters merely adapt their methods to their own ends while being abused by them. The fact that no one achieves any insight is a comment on the degree to which the conditions of existence affect consciousness.

The process of alienating individuals and making outcasts of them has a number of additional causes and pretexts. Roelle is an outsider because he is physically unattractive (he has a goiter) and because his behavior borders on the psychologically aberrant; Olga and Clementine are outsiders because they are women.[11] When Olga becomes pregnant, she is the victim of a biological occurrence for which this stifling environment provides no acceptable solution. Although Clementine chooses to submit to the assigned roles, she faces a life equally devoid of prospects. In this respect, Fleißer's play illustrates the male chauvinism typical of the provincial world at that time. But Cocalis says that Fleißer does not simply offer a reflection of the traditional view of men and women, in which the woman's "natural function" is either to deliver the man from his cares through forgiveness and consolation or to risk expulsion from society as a Lilith, witch, or *femme fatale* ("Weib ist Weib" 205–06). Olga's inability to provide consolation for Roelle does not mark her here as one of those evil, mythical types but results from her refusal to submit to the male practice of manipulating female sympathy for purposes of sexual exploitation. A redemption that requires a sacrifice from her alone would not be a real redemption; once again both characters behave according to internalized norms. Simply being a woman provides ample grounds for victimization in this play, though the position of woman does not necessarily free a character to see through the conditions that perpetuate mistreatment or to behave in a better fashion herself. Neither does being a man result in the avoidance of suffering (Cocalis, "Weib ist Weib" 205). To Sauer, the main theme is the necessity, but also the intolerability of love between the sexes, played out before the "false" background of existing conditions (22). All characters behave according to the law of the pack that Fleißer summarized as the basic content of the play.

Although the author does not offer specific explanations for the inadequacies of life in this Ingolstadt and even refrains from portraying representatives of the institutions of power on stage, the behavior of the characters, especially to the extent that they have internalized the prevailing norms, indicates the criticism inherent in the play's content and the very negative attitude that it takes toward existing social reality. More effective in expressing this negation, however, is the play's form. The difficulty in escaping from the cycle of domination and exploitation in this earthly purgatory is conveyed through the repetition of the basic pattern, which, despite the shifting character configurations, remains the same. The lack of causal or even chronological connection between scenes serves to further emphasize the stifling atmosphere within each one: the viewer is not granted any reprieve from the cycle either, for no final status is ever reached.[12]

Fegefeuer in Ingolstadt breaks off, rather than ends, and the form thus seems to deny the possibility of a positive alternative. The failure to offer a satisfactory resolution or experience within the theater is one of the chief reasons behind the disappointment of those seeking an affirmation of the traditional notion of *Heimat*.

The most striking and significant aspect of the form is the play's speech, whose critical force is to be found somewhere beyond the thematic content of the words.[13] The language is also much more than a mimetic representation of the speech of a certain milieu. To Donna Hoffmeister, Fleißer's plays have "a more economical, more vivid impact than their predecessors in Naturalism" because of the "acute attention their [author has] paid to the structure and rhythm of dialogue" (*Theater* 2). Hoffmeister's entire study focusses on the language in the plays of Fleißer (and Kroetz), which she calls "speech act plays, whose subject matter is the very possibility of human communication" (12). Franz Xaver Kroetz, for whom the dramas of Fleißer provided an early model, said the brutality that permeates her work is made visible through "den Ausstellungscharakter der Fleißerschen Sprache" [the display character of Fleißer's language] ("Liegt die Dummheit" 525).

This language, which seems at first such a simple, sparse, rendering of actual middle-class speech flavored by regional dialect, is in fact quite complex and serves the purpose of both commentary and characterization (cf. Rühle, "Leben" 43, 45). Lutz (*Stellung* 123), Roumois-Hasler (40), and Betten (207) all point out that the language is an aesthetically calculated mixture of elements from dialect and the standard language; Fleißer's particular combination results in both the suggestion of realism and a puzzling, alienating effect. Less is told by what is said than by how speech is used: the struggle to gain the verbal upper hand and the internalization of the norms of authority provide good examples. The restrictions and exploitations of society are revealed through its victims, who become known through a speech that they fail to master or penetrate. The group badgers Roelle, for example, because a priest has refused him absolution. They are not interested in the real meaning of absolution, however, but in how this situation makes him an outcast of an institutionalized authority and of their own group as well. Their remarks on the subject demonstrate this limited perspective:

HERMINE: Das ist einer, der hat zum Beichten müssen, und dann haben sie ihn im Beichtstuhl nicht fertiggemacht.

ROELLE: Das ist bei mir keine Schande.
HERMINE: Ist sie schon.
ROELLE: Ich gehe einfach zum anderen Pater.
HERMINE: Das müssen Sie mitbeichten, wenn Ihnen der Frühere die Absolution verweigert hat.
ROELLE: Ich beichte nie wieder.
PEPS: Was machen Sie dann, wenn Sie mit der ganzen Klasse vorgehn müssen zur Kommunion?
ROELLE: Das geht nur mich was an. (74–75)

[HERMINE: He's one who had to go to confession, and then they didn't finish with him in the confessional.
ROELLE: That's no reason for me to be ashamed.
HERMINE: It is too.
ROELLE: I'll just go to another priest.
HERMINE: You'll have to confess that too, if the first one refused you absolution.
ROELLE: I'll never confess anymore.
PEPS: What will you do, when you have to go to communion with the whole class?
ROELLE: That doesn't concern anyone but me.]

Language is a weapon, rather than a means for achieving insight.

Dialect is an important feature of this play, but its use varies from that in the *Volksstücke* examined thus far. Pure dialect would be difficult for non-Bavarian audiences to understand; therefore, *Fegefeuer in Ingolstadt* principally uses a High German that corresponds to the structure of dialect and makes use of certain of its features.[14] The use of a regional vernacular lends an air of verisimilitude, though Fleißer claimed that she mainly employed dialect because it allowed greater powers of expression and creativity than the standard language (*Mat.* 345, 352). This is doubtless true for the characters in the heated exchanges, yet dialect here serves a function different from that in many plays, in which it distinguished between the speakers of two linguistic groups, one of which was made laughable by the contrast. In sentimental *Heimatstücke* it was supposed to indicate with its feigned naturalism the unspoiled world of the province, but Fleißer reveals that such a notion of an intact world is an illusion. Dialect is here no more able than any other language to give the characters a measure of insight and control over their lives.

Roelle, for example, utters the following awkward lines concerning his situation: "Wenn man wo drin ist und ich sage, da ist man schon immer drin gewesen, so daß man sich wohl hinauswünschen kann, und kann sich aber nicht vorstellen, wie das ist an einem anderen seelischen Ort —" [When you're inside someplace, and I say you've always been caught inside someplace, so that you can maybe wish yourself out but can't imagine how it is in some other psychological situation —] (108). The characters are alienated from language to the same degree that they are alienated from society, and their plight leaves them open to further abuse (cf. Christoph Kuhn, *Mat.* 311; Kässens and Töteberg, *Fleißer* 53). The inability to achieve understanding through language was already a prominent feature of Thoma's *Magdalena*. The failure of Fleißer's characters to achieve or express anything other than what they already know is indicated by the degree to which they appropriate the language of religion: the textuality of the institutions of religion becomes incorporated into their own speech and influences their endeavors to exert power. The language in this play reveals its own inadequacy and explodes the type of genre that propagates an idyllic view of the province by offering an escape through its own form. In addition it reveals the alienation of the characters while serving as their means of abusing others.

Language as content in the lives of the characters provides a negative comment on the society in which they live, but it offers a more effective negation when it works together with the open-ended form that fails to lead anywhere. Like the scenes themselves, the verbal exchanges tend to be self-contained and to provide continual bits of an on-going purgatory.[15] No resolution is ever attained; apparent victories merely serve as starting points for other characters to try to get the upper hand with new dialogues. Such maneuvering continues until the play's end, offering little let-up in the confining language of abuse. As Roumois-Hasler observes, the dialogues are not the representation of a specific expression of content, they are the expression. The characters' inability to communicate is not the subject of conversations, but it is communicated to the audience through their linguistic behavior (143f.). Hoffmeister also observes the effect on the spectator: although the language of *Fegefeuer* is basically mimetic, it is more forceful than a merely reflective type of dialogue, because it "compels the audience to equate the strict confinement of the dramatic frame with the sociological confinement of the characters' lives and to articulate the very perspectives that are inaccessible to the characters themselves" (*Theater* 151).

Buck, on the other hand, finds that Fleißer is able to add more explicit commentary at certain points by entering into her characters and speaking along with them in a sort of "indirect irony," which has the effect of making a a non-literary language literary ("Kleinbürger" 50–52). This is used for criticism in the knife scene, for example, when Roelle requests of Olga, "Stoßen Sie zu, daß es mir die Augäpfel endgültig nach oben dreht" [Thrust it in, so that my eyeballs finally turn upward]. Olga calls this act "Vernichtung" [destruction] and he replies, "Erlösung" [salvation] (118). The use of antonyms in the mouths of two characters provides contrasting interpretations for the same act. The juxtaposition offers commentary that goes beyond what either character could otherwise supply. This quality is noticed by Kroetz in the "Ausstellungscharakter" of the language: "Although the plays, in my opinion, can be considered realistic, they seem to be continuously supplied with subtitles, which observe and explain the dialogue at a distance" ("Liegt die Dummheit" 526). Whether the commentary is supplied by the audience alone or indirectly conveyed by the words themselves, the language is a careful construction that provides much more than a naive mimesis. The difference between Fleißer's dialogues and the traditional affirmative type of dramatic speech in dialect that is taken for realism provides the opportunity for negative criticism.

Those, like Kroetz, who view society as inadequate consider Fleißer realistic because she conveys this inadequacy.[16] On the other hand, those who subscribe to the more romantic, mythological view of the lives of the inhabitants of the provinces fault her for not being true to the "Volk" and for not providing genuine *Volksstücke* (*Mat.* 80; cf. Gerd Müller 90–91). Different observers thus have different criteria for determining what is "realistic," based on their own ideological starting points, which, in most cases, involve the fallacy that assumes an identity between signifier and external referent. A recognition of the relativity of concepts such as realism, or the attempts in the preceding paragraphs to demonstrate that the portrayals in the play are not to be naively taken as mimetic reflections of an extra-textual reality should not lead to the conclusion, however, that there is no reality outside the text or that the text has no way of relating to it; it simply makes the determination of that relationship more complex.

Although precise information about this society's institutions is left vague, the play has a precise geographical and historical location. There is a reason for setting the play in the "Ingolstadt" of the title, but what is the nature of its connection to the town in which its author grew up?[17] One need not assume the existence of an objectively definable Ingolstadt that is then reproduced in words in order for one to claim a referential relationship between the text and external reality. "Ingolstadt" consists to a large extent of what people agree in their discourse that it is. It is a concept created through social language and formed of shared expressions of *Heimat*, and the notion of *Volk*, as well as the roles of such elements as religion, the economy, and the sexes. *Fegefeuer in Ingolstadt* colludes with the verbal expressions of its community insofar as it is an addition to a genre that carries an expected meaning of the notions of "Volk" and "Heimat" (as opposed to a meaning that is objectively true), but Fleißer's utterances in the generic dialogue work against these expectations to produce a new meaning. Her "Ingolstadt" is not the same as the Ingolstadt outside her play, since the actual existence of that place cannot be conveyed without mediation. Yet her dramatic creation has a very definite relation to it, which it expresses in the difference between itself and the "Ingolstadt" of those who subscribe to the myth of the provincial idyll.

Her language can rightly be called realistic both for its surface ability to reflect a regional, class idiom and for the more complex way in which it relates to accepted notions about its supposed referent, which it calls into question by its form and by the link between form and content. This dual aspect is what Herbert Ihering noted in his review of the premiere: "Marieluise Fleißer writes factual, seemingly dry reports. But a strange power of suggestion emanates from her reportage. Word has again become image. Representation has become likeness. Marieluise Fleißer has the decisive talent of the poetic narrator: to present a message immediately as expression" (*Mat.* 40). In conveying her message of negation through the play's form, rather than through mimetic, didactic content, Fleißer provides a more powerful vehicle, using means later advocated by Adorno.

So far the discussion has centered on this drama's negation of the social and textual environment from which it emerges; the utopian has been very little in evidence. The World War and inflation had contributed to the destruction of the ideals of the previous generation; according to Fleißer in 1972, "Alles Vorgeformte stimmt nicht mehr. Sie [die jungen Menschen] können aber nichts Neues dagegen setzen. Sie suchen sich zu erlösen und können sich nicht erlösen" [All preformed ideas are no longer valid. However, they (the younger generation) cannot replace them with anything new. They seek to save themselves but are unable to do so] (*Mat.* 364). Most manifestations of the utopian that occur in the play are pseudo-utopias, fulfillable affects that offer no hope of improvement or that even turn themselves into dystopias. In so doing, they further strengthen the negative direction.

The most obvious of these, including the internalization of social norms as a means for exerting control over others and the attempt to fit one's life into existing structures, have already been mentioned. Others include the

characters' outright attempts at possession of something that does not belong
to them in order to make up for their feelings of alienation from what should
properly be theirs. For example, Roelle tries to pass himself off as the father
of Olga's child in order to fill a void in his life and to prove his abilities to
his classmates (115; cf. Ulrich Schreiber in *Mat.* 284). Toward the end of
the play, Olga longs for someone who will take her to America, where no
one knows her (122). But all of these efforts represent false utopias because
they merely appropriate or exchange elements of the existing situation,
rather than introduce something completely new.

Hope that seeks a solution beyond the immediately existing is expressed
throughout the text by the religious, biblical language and the ecstatic
visions that Roelle claims to be able to bring on. Up to now I have stressed
the inversion of these elements, since the effect of their negation is
dominant. The purgatory of the title, like Fleißer's original "Footwashing,"
turns out to be an earthly punishment rather than a harbinger of eventual
heavenly rewards. Some see this as the only content of these words (Buck,
"Kleinbürger" 44). The author's refusal to demonstrate a traditionally
accepted religious truth behind such words and to acknowledge the
metaphysical in revealing the discrepancy between the language of religion
and the situation in which her characters live seems to exclude utopian hope
altogether.

Hoffmeister, however, points out that dialogue has a "double reference"
as communication between the characters and also as communication
between dramatist and audience. This makes it possible to stimulate critical
thinking (*Theater* 41). Though she is here referring to an increased
awareness concerning social conditions that is elicited in the spectator but
not in the characters, the double reference can also point in a different way
to the use of the language of religion. Although ablution, the traditional act
of humility, is turned into its opposite in the humiliation of Roelle (Rühle,
"Leben" 12), just as purgatory, the place that should offer the opportunity
of redemption, is transformed into a locus of seemingly endless degradation,
the original meanings are not completely expunged, but rather retained even
as they are cancelled. Hope does not disappear from the text, even though
the possibility of its fulfillment seems rejected at every turn, as for example,
when Roelle's rescue of Olga from her attempted suicide in the Danube
(112) fails to realize the possibility that the two outcasts will understand one
another. Roelle's condition at the conclusion seems to his mother to be one
of outright insanity, and she seeks a priest to save him from his evil spirits.
Alone on stage, Roelle confesses his sins, but when no one hears or delivers

him he eats the piece of paper on which his confession was written. The word that here becomes flesh fails to bring any salvation from elsewhere, although it continues to express the very real hope of the characters and probably the spectators as well. The characters' failure to locate an object for that hope and the author's refraining from intervening to indicate where such an object might be found does not however diminish the play's position in the dialectic between negation and hope.

Another faint hint of an opening for the utopian is observed by Susan Cocalis in Fleißer's mimetic retention of the picture of a patriarchal world marked by the continually occurring "helplessness, passivity, and bondage" of the female characters ("Weib ohne Wirklichkeit" 65; "'Weib ist Weib'" 201). Although these qualities do not offer a solution, they serve to question that world and to call for an alternative. This critic also says that an additional impetus toward the search for a different order is provided by Fleißer's refusal to let her male characters come off any better than her female figures ("'Weib ist Weib'" 205). Both groups are caught in a web of abuse and domination, and neither the men, nor the women in their imitation of the men, are able to get ahead by practicing aggressive behavior. But since Fleißer does not explicitly point out how a world free of exploitation and domination is to be attained, most scholars and critics find the utopian only faintly present, if at all.[18]

Kroetz contrasts Fleißer with Brecht, for example, pointing out that the ability of Brecht's characters to articulate enables them to start in the direction of a positive utopia. "If the workers at Siemens had the linguistic level of Brecht's workers, we would have a revolutionary situation," he comments. In this particular essay Kroetz considers such portrayals a fiction and finds Fleißer more honest because she refrains from giving her characters an extensive command of language or a superior perspective on their situation ("Liegt die Dummheit" 525). The consensus seems to indicate that there is very little of the utopian to be found in *Fegefeuer in Ingolstadt*, and indeed it is not to be sought as content which would provide a model for the spectator. Its glimmer may be observed, however, and an important starting point is Kroetz's observation that the "Ausstellungscharakter" (display character) of Fleißer's dialogues serves to denounce the society in which the characters live but not the characters themselves (525). Their behavior is appalling, but their cries for deliverance are genuine. The utopian is not revealed, but it lies in the gap between the language of religion that fails to provide the content of salvation and the constant torment of this earthly, provincial purgatory.

If the utopian is something more than an illusion, and if the spectators indeed attain an insight that the characters fail to achieve, how is this process brought about and what effects should it have? Since the play received only one performance in the 1920's, its effect was necessarily small, though it attracted a good deal of attention from reviewers, even from beyond Berlin. Both Kerr and Ihering praised it, whereas Fechter and Jacobs panned the play, presumably because they misunderstood the criticism. The latter reviewers also allude to the applause that greeted the actors and the hisses that were aimed at the author (*Mat.* 36–50). The positive side of the reception results from Fleißer's skill in portraying the characters' language and the atmosphere of inescapable degradation in which they live; the negative reaction can be explained by her unwillingness to provide a precise authorial commentary and by the discomfort resulting from the intensity of the portrayal. This last feature is one of the changes in the genre that ran against audience expectations; in this respect Fleißer goes even farther than Thoma. Her refusal to provide a comforting, merely entertaining picture of her *Heimat* hindered a widespread, enthusiastic response, yet her honest treatment of the problems of this milieu make Fegefeuer a type of *Volks-stück*.[19] Sociologically and thematically, her plays show a link to previous *Volkstücke*, but their form presents something altogether different.

The advantages of Fleißer's changes enable the play to confront an inadequate reality more effectively and call into question the notion that a utopia can somehow be found in a return to the idyllic, unspoiled life of the people or in a mythical other world. The disadvantages, of course, are that such plays are unpalatable to much of the middle-class public and unlikely to be performed at regional *Volkstheater* before the types of people whom they take so seriously and attempt to integrate. This dilemma represents an inversion in the genre in the twentieth century. Those nineteenth-century authors who searched for more literarily demanding forms tended to remain firmly rooted in a popular theater tradition and attracted audiences even as they confounded their expectations. Yet *Fegefeuer in Ingolstadt* has the same function as plays of this type, even though it carries this out in a different form that is necessary and appropriate under the historical conditions under which it was written. As a dramatic text that takes a stand for people from the provincial middle classes who remain outsiders because of their inability to achieve integrated lives, it denounces the conditions that pervade their existence, while holding out the hope for a society in which they can be redeemed.

Chapter VII

With the Tongues of Men (and Angels?): Ödön von Horváth's *Kasimir und Karoline*

Daß das Interesse am Theater im breiten Volke nachgelassen
hat, liegt wohl daran, daß wir kein richtiges Volkstheater mehr
haben — aber auf dem Wege zu ihm sind wir.
— Ödön von Horváth, "Interview" (GW 1, 15)[1]

ÖDÖN VON HORVÁTH (1901–1938) WROTE at least eighteen different plays,
three novels, and various prose pieces and sketches, but his five *Volksstücke*, most of which were written between 1930–1932, have received the
greatest amount of critical attention and been most frequently performed.
His theoretical remarks consciously relate these plays to a *Volksstück*
tradition, which, according to the scholarly consensus, he both destroyed
and renewed. Critical opinion diverges, however, on another crucial aspect
of these plays: whether or not they are to be considered realistic documents
of their times or metaphysical texts. This issue forms a central part of the
critical debate and is closely related to the approach taken here. Urs Jenny
set up this polarity between the realistic and the metaphysical in the title of
his 1971 article, which states that although the plays do indeed present a
rationalist analysis of current conditions, they are ultimately graspable not
in Marxist but in religious categories such as guilt and innocence, sin,
repentance, and the expectation of redemption (291). Since then many other
scholars have stressed one side or the other in this seeming dichotomy.[2]
    The disagreement is partly due to a change in Horváth's emphasis from
the earlier plays, which contain elements of a Marxist perspective, to the
later works, which tend to stress the individual and the timeless. In his
well-known radio interview of 1932, Horváth said that the content of his
first *Volksstück*, *Die Bergbahn* [The Mountain Railway, 1929], is the
"struggle between capital and labor power" (GW 1, 10), but his last play,
Pompeji, is set in the past and seems to find a solution to humanity's
problems in the newly arisen religion of Christianity.
    Another source of the difficulty stems from the fact that Horváth's
attention to the particularities of his own society, coupled with his unwillingness to deliver overtly simplistic causal explanations, also led to an emphasis
on the individual as well as the social. Horváth himself said that he wrote
his play *Glaube Liebe Hoffnung* [Faith Love Hope, 1932] "in order to be
able to demonstrate again the gigantic struggle between individual and

society, this eternal slaughter, which can never result in a peaceful solution — at most, that occasionally an individual enjoys for a few moments the illusion of a cease-fire" (GW 1, 327–28). It is not that Horváth is unable to decide between the two, but rather that he recognizes the essential role of each. However, his emphasis on the individual has led some scholars to believe that his answer must be a personal or even metaphysical one. Even though such a solution is neither explicitly provided nor ruled out, it will become clear from this discussion that individuals will not be able to find fulfillment until society is changed, but also that society cannot be considered adequate as long as it ignores individual fulfillment.

My study contends that the elements that have been called the realistic and the metaphysical are both present, but rather than defining them in such potentially misleading and mutually exclusive terms, it will continue its investigation by viewing Horváth's *Volksstücke* from the perspective of utopia and negation. It will not try to decide between the two, since, as has been demonstrated in other authors, both are present in a dialectical relationship, even though the utopian may seem less obvious in these twentieth-century versions of the *Volksstück*. Nolting (20) and Dimter (231), for example, go so far as to say that Horváth's plays lack utopian content altogether. Horváth's refusal to provide an explicit alternative to present conditions has been recognized by most scholars and has caused problems for those who seek to categorize him, but the utopian could not be portrayed directly in the earlier *Volksstücke* either, and it is in fact a process that is only to be grasped in its interplay with the negative and in the relation between form and content. Moreover, providing a consistent social response that affirms a single ideology would in fact deny the utopian by foreclosing on it.

Although Horváth's theoretical statements are to be taken with a certain amount of caution, since they are at times self-contradictory or even inaccurate, he is indeed a "chronicler of his times," as he proclaims himself to be (GW 8, 662; see also GW 1, 12). His *Volksstücke* can be understood only in terms of the social conditions of central Europe during the period between the wars, conditions that are implicitly criticized through his insightful analyses: instead of portraying eternal human problems, he dealt with historically relative ones.[3] But the various forms of the *Volksstück* that had been offered over the years, including the more naturalistic plays of Anzengruber and Thoma, were no longer adequate to Horváth's conception, and his more stylized dramas took a negative stance with regard to the theatrical tradition as well as to contemporary reality.[4] Though the plays are clearly grounded in the social and economic situation, their conciously artificial form renders the term "realistic" an incomplete and less than accurate description. It is thus the form that needs to be stressed.[5]

The presence of two seemingly conflicting opposites may also be observed in Horváth's claim that that his plays consist of a "synthesis of seriousness and irony" (GW 1,12; GW 8, 663; *Mat.* 103).[6] The motto to *Kasimir und Karoline* (1932) is certainly to be understood as such: "Und die Liebe höret nimmer auf" [love never ends]. This unattributed quotation from I Corinthians 13: 8 is seen by the end of the play to be an ironic comment and has most frequently taken to be only this (Fritz 201), since the "love" of the title characters goes on, but with different partners, and, as in Fleißer's play, it seems to be the cycle of victimization that never ends. The social conditions that prevail in a time of mass unemployment hinder the existence of love as understood by St. Paul, whose message hardly seems able to be taken as a description of the possible. The motto damns rather than affirms the world in which these characters live. Yet Horváth's characters are not mocked, but taken seriously, as are their dreams, no matter how *verkitscht*. The motto therefore serves at the same time as a faint sign of what that world should be.

Since a negative stance toward existing conditions makes up such an important component of Horváth's texts (whether or not its presence is to be considered an example of "realism" or social criticism), it is necessary to investigate Horváth's explicit incorporation of the situation of the late Weimar years as content before analyzing his formal methods. Horváth's own often-quoted remarks state that the subjects of his plays are the *Kleinbürger* [petty bourgeoisie], who he claims made up ninety per cent of the population of Germany in the years following World War I (GW 8: 662). Horváth's analysis, it must be noted, departs from a purely economic class analysis because it subsumes the proletariat into the middle-class and presupposes constantly shifting class boundaries. It also stresses moral and intellectual components that are not necessarily dependent on economic status, since the various members of this sunken middle class hold fast to a middle-class mentality, whether they are on the ascent or the descent (Fritz 120–21). An important psychological attitude of this group appears to be the despising of those perceived to be just beneath them (133). Adapting the genre to changes in the population, both with regard to material and audience, is a necessary and important feature of Horváth's *Volksstücke*.

These observations concerning attitude and behavior, while retaining an awareness of economic factors, give a more complex picture. Previous scholarship has covered the area of social criticism and Horváth's relation to reality quite thoroughly.[7] Horváth himself drew explicit connections to the situation of his time and in some of his plays even incorporated factual materials: the rise of the fascist "Schwarze Reichswehr" in *Sladek*, a criminal case history in *Glaube Liebe Hoffnung*, an actual construction accident in *Die Bergbahn*, and a brawl between Nazis and socialists in *Italienische Nacht*. Though *Kasimir und Karoline* (1931) makes no such use of factual documents, it has a very precise geographical and historical setting: according to the stage directions, "This *Volksstück* is set at the Munich Oktoberfest, and in fact, in our time" (10).[8] The original subtitle was "Sieben Szenen von der Liebe, Lust und Leid und unserer schlechten Zeit" [Seven Scenes of Love, Desire, and Sorrow and our Bad Times] (*Mat.* 81). The adjective "schlecht" that is added to describe "our times," reveals the author's basic reaction to the contemporary environment: negation (Schneider 59).

The title characters are Kasimir, a chauffeur who was laid off the preceding day, and his fiancée Karoline, an office worker who refuses to admit that her clerical job can be classified as proletarian (94, Sc. 36). The "plot" involves their increasing alienation and eventual break-up. They and their relationship are to be understood in terms of the economic conditions of the depression years, yet even though Horváth wanted to give an accurate rendition of the general situation, it is not "Masse Mensch" [the man of the masses] that he portrays, but "Durchschnittsexistenzen" [average existences] (Kienzle 8). They are representative types in the form of individuals, and both aspects are necessary in order to comprehend them. Other characters in the play include Kasimir's friend "der Merkl Franz," a petty criminal; Franz's girlfriend Erna, who has also served time in jail; Schürzinger, a tailor whom Karoline meets at the Oktoberfest; Rauch, an important businessman, and his friend Speer, a judge; the prostitutes Elli and Maria; and the members of a carnival freak show.

"Our times" are "bad" because of the prevailing economic conditions, of which the play provides continual reminders. Kasimir's loss of unemployment prevents him from enjoying the Oktoberfest and provokes his resentment of the twenty captains of industry who can afford a ride in the zeppelin while millions hunger down below (70, Sc. 3). Karoline's wages of 55 marks a month are not very high, but she feels fortunate to have them "under present conditions" (119, Sc. 83). Merkl Franz adds a social justification to his stealing from parked cars: they are capitalist limousines that belong to tax dodgers (120, Sc. 86). Maria and Elli present a clear equation between human being and monetary exchange value: they promptly abandon Kasimir when he cannot even buy them a beer (108, Sc. 67). The freaks represent the most blatant example of humans enslaved to money. When they rush outside their tent to view the zeppelin, their dwarf-manager orders them to return: "Was braucht ihr einen Zeppelin zu sehen — wenn man euch draußen sieht, sind wir pleite! Das ist ja Bolschewismus!" [Why do you need to see the zeppelin — if people see you outside, we'll go broke! That's Bolshevism!] (97, Sc. 45) As his grotesquely humorous remark reveals, they represent a form of capital for him, to be exploited in the making of money.

The economic situation is also pointed out in the stage directions, which provide more information to the reader than to the spectator: "Rechts eine Hühnerbraterei, die aber wenig frequentiert wird, weil alles viel zu teuer ist" [To the right a roast-chicken stand, which is infrequently visited, however, because everything is much too expensive] (85, Sc. 21). Most seem trapped in a situation that they do not fully comprehend, although Schürzinger seems to provide an explicit correlation between external conditions and behavior when he says, "Die Menschen sind weder gut noch böse. Allerdings werden sie durch unser heutiges wirtschaftliches System gezwungen, egoistischer zu sein, als sie eigentlich wären" [People are neither good nor evil. To be sure, they are forced by our current economic system to be more egoistic than they really are] (72, Sc. 4). Karoline later says that people should be able to separate the general crisis from the private, but Schürzinger replies that the two are "unheilvoll miteinander verknüpft" [disastrously linked together] (87, Sc. 24). Such remarks, however, need to be examined more closely in terms of the relationship between language, consciousness, and the external economic reality in order to determine whether their "message" is to be considered that of the play.

The characters react to their miserable situation in several ways. As indicated, Kasimir's dissatisfaction results in feelings of *ressentiment* toward the wealthy, but also in self-pity (70-71, Sc. 3; 78-79, Sc. 11; 80-81, Sc. 15; 93-94, Sc. 36; 105, Sc. 62). When Karoline realizes that her own attempts at advancement have failed, she resorts to name-calling (131, Sc. 107). Such drives become more forceful when they seek to provide self-esteem by victimizing those who are weaker or in an inferior position. The pleasure taken by "normal" people in viewing the freak show provides one of the simplest and most primitive opportunities to demonstrate superiority (Karasek, "Kasimir" 68), but women are the most frequent victims. Merkl Franz regularly insults women in general (78-79, Sc. 11) and Erna in particular (84–85, Sc. 18), and he accuses Kasimir of masoch-ism for not standing up to Karoline and her newly acquired friend Schür-zinger (81–82, Sc. 15). Later Kasimir joins in the denunciation of women, and even Erna agrees with them, perhaps in attempt to curry favor (104, Sc. 60; cf. Bance 256). But this sign of weakness makes her an even more likely target of victimization: Karoline tells Schürzinger that Franz beats Erna, even though she obeys him (77, Sc. 9). Just as in *Fegefeuer in Ingolstadt*, victimization of a character is most evident when that character victimizes others in the same fashion. Economic conditions result in the males' degradation, which they then pass on to the weaker party, women. Their behavior is basically reactive, no matter how much they try to appear dynamic and in control of the situation.

The degrading treatment of women extends of course to their pursuit as sex objects. Speer and Rauch have come to the Oktoberfest in search of sexual adventure: they look under the skirts of passengers descending the toboggan before trying to pick up two of the women (85–86, Sc. 21–22). Karoline is reduced to a part of her anatomy when Rauch admires her "Popo" and says, "Ein Mädchen ohne Popo ist kein Mädchen" [A girl without a fanny isn't a girl] (87–88, Sc. 25). His wealth makes other forms of coercion unnecessary, and Karoline is willing to go off with him in his limousine in the hope of advancing her own status. But when his heart condition makes him too ill to remain interested in her, he cruelly abandons her, even though she has probably saved his life by preventing his car from running off the road (131, Sc. 107). Aggressive expressions of frustration that find their objects in victimizing the weak are the most common attempts at escape in *Kasimir und Karoline*. They result in the creation of an atmosphere that demonstrates a thoroughgoing dissatisfaction with present conditions and thus a clear negation of them. As attempts to create an alternative they can hardly be called utopian because of their simple-mindedness and dehumanizing cruelty; like the similar manifestations in Fleißer's play, they are further evidence of the current dystopia.

The characters also search elsewhere for possible solutions to their plight, though in the end most of these objects are fulfillable affects and therefore inadequate goals of utopian hope. The most accessible are those provided by a capitalist society in general and the culture industry in particular. The setting itself, the Oktoberfest, stands as a constant visual and auditory reminder of the characters' search for happiness amidst various sensory offerings in an atmosphere of ostensibly shared togetherness. Alcohol plays a prominent role, of course, but represents little more than an escape. The carnival rides, the hippodrome, and the freak show also entice the characters, but are likewise mere diversions. All are to be had for money, but the businessman Rauch is the only one that can afford to let Karoline ride the horses as many times as she wants (111–13, Sc. 73–76). For him, the money represents an investment, whose return he expects in later pleasure.

The zeppelin that sails over the festival meadow has not been specifically created as entertainment for the masses, but Kasimir correctly analyses how it serves the same function of providing the illusion of possessing something better: "Der Zeppelin, verstehst du mich, das ist ein Luftschiff und wenn einer von uns dieses Luftschiff sieht, dann hat er so ein Gefühl, als tät er auch mitfliegen — derweil haben wir bloß die schiefen Absätze und das Maul können wir uns an das Tischeck hinhaun!" [The zeppelin, you understand, is an airship and when one of us sees that airship, then he feels as if he were flying along too — meanwhile we're down at heel and and can sink our teeth into the wood of the table] (70, Sc. 3). The zeppelin is a symbol of desire, which is visually cut down to size (as are the hopes of the characters in general) at the end of the play, when Schürzinger appears with a balloon fastened to his lapel by a string (136, Sc. 115). All available means of fulfilling the characters' desires prove insufficient.

A more obvious product of the culture industry is the music that comprises an important part of the play's form and also its content, as cultural material from the late Weimar years. Music is heard in at least 21 of the scenes, and in some of them it is the only element. The selection includes folk songs (104, Sc. 61), *Heimat*-songs (69, Sc. 1; 103, Sc. 59), marches (100, Sc. 51; 102, Sc. 57; 123, Sc. 91), drinking songs (105, Sc. 63; 107, Sc. 66), songs from operettas and opera (127, Sc. 102; 131, Sc. 108; 101, Sc. 54), and currently popular tunes (76, Sc. 7). Although not all of these musical selections are newly created hits that satisfy a consumer demand for constant innovation, all are to some extent popular and have the same function as the hit song.

According to Adorno, the social role of hits is to provide frameworks of identification: "Not only do hits appeal to a lonely crowd, to fragmented people. They count on people who are not yet fully mature; those who do not have control over their expression and experience.... They deliver a substitute for feelings in general" (*Musiksoziologie* 36). When the listener identifies with the fictive, musical subject, he or she feels less isolated through incorporation into the community of fans: "Whoever whistles such a song to himself bows to a ritual of socialization" (37). This is made manifest in the scenes in which a crowd joins in a drinking song, though there is always at least one character who does not sing along (105, Sc. 63; 107, Sc. 66). The familiar music provides a comforting background for the characters; the repetition of the always-the-same leads to uncritical assent (Adorno, "Resumé" 62–63). The ultimate effect is thus the same as that of the hit song: "It seduces according to the basic custom of the culture industry, the affirmation of life as it is" (*Musiksoziologie* 47). Its sentimental, repetitive, sterile qualities are also shared by other forms of kitsch that appear throughout Horváths *Volksstücke* and that represent a similar lack of development of consciousness (Jarka 564). The effect of the popular song might also be compared with Emile Coué's repetitive, autosuggestive formula, which Schürzinger introduces to Karoline as a means of improving her life: "Es geht immer besser, immer besser" [Things are getting better and better, better and better] (137, Sc. 115). Horváth did not include musical material to lull audiences into affirmation but to reveal this type of music as a surrogate that provides an illusion of happiness (cf. Karasek 68); how he reveals it as such will be discussed below.

In addition to looking for happiness in the readily available products for entertainment and diversion, the characters sometimes take what appears to be a more active role in improving their plight. Karoline confusedly thinks she can somehow better herself through the right connections: in answer to Kasimir's question as to why she has chosen to associate with "Herrschaften" [gentlemen] like Rauch and Speer, she replies, "Eine höhere gesellschaftliche Stufe und so" [A higher social level and such] (94, Sc. 36). Schürzinger hopes to ameliorate his position as well and is even willing to abandon Karoline to his employer Rauch in return for a promotion (117, Sc. 80). But such methods only copy the system that has abused them in the first place and offer no hope for freedom from it.

Karoline appears to realize this when she says near the play's end: "Ich habe es mir halt eingebildet, daß ich mir einen rosigeren Blick in die Zukunft erringen könnte — und einige Momente habe ich mit allerhand Gedanken gespielt. Aber ich müßt so tief unter mich hinunter, damit ich höher hinauf kann" [I simply imagined that I could get a rosier view into the future — and for a few moments I played with all kinds of thoughts. But I would have to stoop so low beneath myself, in order to rise higher] (135, Sc. 113). Her self-contradictory metaphor indicates that attempts to elevate herself only result in the opposite. The break with Kasimir is now final, and she is left with Schürzinger more or less by default. Her reception of his kiss shows more resignation than participation: "Karoline does not resist"

(137, Sc. 115). Rather than bettering herself, she simply finds another version of her initial predicament.

Kasimir is less hopeful of finding some form of advancement for himself; he has a driver's license but no job and thinks that things might be better if he knew what political party to vote for. But Merkl Franz attempts to disabuse him of the illusion that political parties can provide a solution by saying that he has been a member of all of them (109, Sc. 68). His own solution is an individual one, to provide for himself through petty crime. He is arrested one too many times, however, leaving Erna to take up with Kasimir (133–34, Sc. 111–12). Erna sometimes imagines a revolution with the poor streaming through a triumphal arch and the rich in paddy wagons, "weil sie alle miteinander gleich soviel lügen über die armen Leut — Sehns, bei so einer Revolution, da tät ich gerne mit der Fahne in der Hand sterben" [because they all tell so many lies to one another about the poor — See, in a revolution like that I'd gladly die with a flag in my hand] (121–22, Sc. 88). Yet this is a dream rather than an achievable political program and is composed of bits of *ressentiment*, the famous Delacroix painting, and a nostalgic turning back into history (Bruns 124). It is more a vague expression of a utopian longing than a portrayal of how a better state might be reached, and the quality of this dream differs little from an attempted escape into the sentimentality of popular music.

The failure of politics to offer a path toward utopia is a result of Horváth's assessment of the Weimar situation. The Nazis promised false solutions, and the Communists failed to address the everyday needs of the people (Bruns 121). In his plays Horváth focused on such needs, which are not to be dismissed, even when revealed as embracing inadequate forms of sentimentality, self-pity, and kitsch. According to Bruns they can, "when released, generate a utopian power" (124). The words "generate" and "power" are perhaps too strong to describe what is presented in this play, though one should not overlook the urgency with which these characters seek an alternative to the reality that they know and the strength of the utopian hope that drives them. Although their aspirations seem absurd and doomed to failure, the mere willingness to struggle redeems these characters in Bance's eyes ("Kasimir" 92). The various solutions that they attempt are false, but their hope, which Karoline describes more vaguely as "so eine Sehnsucht in sich" [more or less a desire one has], permeates the play, even when characters break their wings in their attempts to escape (136, Sc. 114).

All of this pent-up aggression, social-climbing, changing of partners, and searching for diversion centers around what is constantly lacking, despite the motto's assertion of its continuous presence: love. If the characters' situation were to improve it would be marked by love, which is an essential constitutent of utopia and is the absent goal of all their frustrated searching; a world in which love is possible would also be a world of "a humanity that has not yet been achieved" (Doppler 12), of solidarity among human beings (Joas 58–60), and of freedom from the present interdependence of love and money which results in victimization (Hildebrandt 168). It would, in other words, be a genuine community.

This utopia is not portrayed, nor is the possibility of its achievement either through political and economic action or individual, metaphysical means sketched out. But its importance is revealed through the emphasis on those characters in whose fate the dichotomy between the world as it is and the world as it should be is made manifest — the women. As the most frequent objects of victimization, they serve to expose the negative conditions of external reality, yet in their disillusionment with the brutality around them they remain passive, either resigned or broken.[9] Bance finds that they can adopt one of two strategies: to embrace the kitsch about "romance," or to prey on the male. Karoline moves from one alternative to the other, but neither is able to provide any autonomy for her ("Sex, Politics" 255–56). Bance contends, however, that there is a qualitative difference in the "Uneigentlichkeit" [lack of authenticity] of the males and females: in women it is secondary, since they are exploited before they exploit, and in this there is "a glimmer of hope for the future" (254). Although the women of the *Volksstücke* are not able to provide a better way, their plight most clearly reveals the imperfect nature of the existing world and expresses the yearning for the utopian dream.

It is a mistake, however, to view the social reality that is treated thematically within the play as equivalent to the play itself, which is an aesthetic text that mediates reality through its choice of form.[10] Horváth's choice of the *Volksstück* genre was a provocative one that addressed specific expectations of his public, expectations that he foiled with changes that treated this traditional genre both seriously and ironically (GW 8, 663; GW 1, 12). Arntzen rightly warns that misunderstanding can result from overly stressing the genre designation and from taking Horváth's theoretical remarks too seriously, since he finds that the *Volksstück* is a sociological category based on content and reception (248–49). One cannot deny that content and reception are important components of the concept and are specifically addressed by these plays, yet one should neither restrict discussion to them nor exclude them altogether. As mentioned earlier,

Horváth said that the part of the population that enacted the plots of the old *Volksstück* had changed considerably in the previous two decades, and he felt compelled to bring this new lower middle class on to the stage (GW 1: 11) and to treat their problems and "simple concerns" in a manner that is as appropriate to them as possible ["eine möglichst volkstümliche Art"] (GW 8: 662).[11]

But naturalistic, documentary, and even radically experimental plays could all deal with "the simple concerns of the people," and the question arises as to what he means by "eine volkstümliche Art," or whether his *Volksstücke* actually accomplish this. Many scholars thus correctly recognize that a proper analysis of these plays centers on their form.[12] Not all *Volksstücke* of the Weimar period treated the genre in the same way. The differences between Zuckmayer's popular *Der fröhliche Weinberg* and Fleißer's *Fegefeuer in Ingolstadt* were discussed in the last chapter. *Kasimir und Karoline* also differs from Zuckmayer's play, though it shares more similarities with it than Fleißer's drama does. For example, Horváth also includes music, erotic motifs, and comic effects, but he does so in a way that reveals their insufficiencies. How content gives a negative portrayal of existing reality has already been demonstrated; more effective is the negative treatment that Horváth's changes bring to the old generic form.

François says that Horváth's originality lies in his putting social and economic reality into a genre whose audiences usually wanted to forget that actuality (*Histoire* 176). Yet the unmasking occurs not because of the presence of external reality as content in the *Volksstück*, but through Horváth's formal mediation of it. In negating, rather than affirming things as they are, he avoids the absorption of the utopian that characterizes *Der fröhliche Weinberg* (see p. 131 above). Horváth's genre designation is to be understood ironically, insofar as his play destroys the old form along with audience expectations, but it is also to be taken seriously as the description of a new form that is adequate to the conditions with which it deals.

After observing audience reactions to several performances, Horváth realized that his attempted synthesis of realism and irony was not always understood: his plays were frequently taken as fulfillments of the unpretentious, purely entertaining form of the genre or as parodies of it. He thus felt compelled to write his "Gebrauchsanweisung" [Instructions for Use] to explain that he intended neither and to give directions for staging. In order to avoid the first extreme, he stresses that the plays should be performed in a stylized manner, since naturalism and realism destroy them (GW 8: 663–64). But irony and destruction of the old *Volksstück* do not aim at a parody of the genre either, for the *Volksstück*, when properly employed, can provide an adequate medium for the treatment of the very real and serious problems of the *Volk* (GW 8: 660). A careful reading of the text bears out these assessments of the author; like the motto, the choice of genre is a synthesis. As a *Volksstück*, *Kasimir und Karoline* stands on its own and reacts to external reality and literary tradition. Its form negates the existing, while expressing utopian hope in its taking the *Volk* seriously and in actively creating a new form to deal with their lives.

The play is divided into 117 scenes and has an intermission in the middle. The longest scenes cover less than three pages, and many contain only a few words, or no dialogue at all. Scene One, which precedes the opening of the curtain, is purely musical, consisting of the familiar Munich song "So lang der alte Peter." The second is visual and presents the hubbub of the Oktoberfest meadow with the zeppelin flying overhead. The plot centers around the dissolution of the relationship between Kasimir and Karoline, but the two appear together on stage in only six of the scenes, and the events leading to the break-up are by no means dramatic. None of the steps taken in the play is irrevocable as is normally the case in tragedy, since the characters can always go back, and only at the end is the break final (Hummel 54).

The play thus has an epic structure, or, in Horváth's words, "mehr eine schildernde als eine dramatische" [more of a descriptive than a dramatic one] (GW 1: 12). This feature leads him to compare himself more to *Volkssänger* than to earlier *Volksstück* authors (GW 8: 663).[13] There is no longer a main "plot," but a general levelling of plot and subplot (Hummel 71). The scenes have become so small that they no longer possess their typical function of articulation but tend to merge back into a continuum (81). This merging effect is greater on the spectator than on the reader, though there are at least eight examples of overlapping scenes, in which one scene continues after the interruption of an intervening scene (e.g. Scenes 13–15; 24–26; 94–99). The epic disintegration of plot into minute scenes corresponds to the fragmentation in society, and this form seeks to draw attention to the drama that is occurring within a character, rather than in the play as a whole (cf. GW 8:659–60).

The string of scenes may be regarded as circular as well as linear since the characters, particularly Kasimir and Karoline, depart and return, and even though they are not reconciled at the end, their basic situation is little different from what it had been at the outset. Economic conditions have remained the same, and these figures have been unable to develop their communicative capabilities on an individual level (Bartsch 48). Moments of insight alternate with the more persistent lack of awareness, and the characters cannot establish a common ground on which to better their lot. The ending seems to provide a satisfactory resolution, but in fact represents an inversion of the traditional favorable conclusion. Bance finds that Horváth uses a "parodistically contrived happy ending," similar to that employed by Nestroy ("Kasimir" 83). Although the one found here is less upbeat than Nestroy's, it is similar in function in its avoidance of a final pronouncement. The play opens rather than closes with togetherness in a festival setting; the final pairing off of Kasimir with Erna and Karoline with Schürzinger is almost by default and accepted more with resignation than with affirmation (Hein 56). Kasimir tells Erna that "Träume sind Schäume" [dreams are made of foam], and she replies, "Solange wir uns nicht aufhängen, werden wir nicht verhungern" [As long as we don't hang ourselves, we won't starve]. After a pause he addresses her with "Du Erna —," but in reply to her "Was?", he merely answers "Nichts" (137, Sc. 116). The dialogue literally ends with "nothing."

The final musical selection, a love song that had previously been introduced in Scene 71, is seen to be romantic kitsch (Joas 60), yet in its yearning continues as a faint expression of hope. The finality of establishing two new couples is an illusion, since the circularity that has occurred up to this point indicates that these too will dissolve, only to be replaced by something qualitatively similar. The open ending is thus ambiguous: in pointing to the process beyond the conclusion (Hein 58) it leaves an opening for the new, while it skeptically implies the continuation of the same.

As the scholarly consensus indicates, the most original feature of Horváth's *Volksstücke* is the language that he puts into the mouths of his characters. Rather than containing information about contemporary reality, it conveys that reality and its effect on the characters by its very form.[14] The term that Horváth used for the language of his characters was *Bildungs-jargon*, a type of artificial speech that he felt had replaced dialect. Through its use the characters hope to consolidate or advance their positions by feigning educated talk, though this jargon gives only a poor camouflage at best.)[15] Horváth employs *Bildungsjargon* to give a realistic portrayal, but since it is a symptom of alienation and the lack of identity between word and deed, it is revealed to be inadequate as a means of communication and is also criticized: "Der Bildungsjargon (und seine Ursachen) fordern aber natürlich zur Kritik heraus — und so entsteht der Dialog des neuen *Volksstückes*, und damit der Mensch, und damit erst die dramatische

Handlung — eine Synthese aus Ernst und Ironie" [*Bildungsjargon* (and its causes) naturally provoke criticism — and in this way the dialogue of the new *Volksstück* arises, and with it the human character, and only then the plot — a synthesis of seriousness and irony] (GW 8: 662–63).

This type of speech is included not simply for reasons of mere verisimilitude, as was dialect in many traditional *Volksstücke*; it simultaneously provides a means for revealing the insufficiencies of the characters and their environment. Attention is called to the language through stylizations in the structure and staging of the play. Dialect of course provided several different functions for Raimund and Nestroy, and Horváth follows in the tradition of the more demanding *Volksstücke* in his conscious treatment of language. As a sign of the gap between speakers of the standard language and the lower class, dialect was able to offer a reminder of the disunities in reality, but when joined with an entertaining plot and a satisfactory resolution in inferior plays, it could soothe audiences with a repetition of the familiar and serve in the end as an affirmation of the status quo.

The *Bildungsjargon* of Horváth's figures is disturbing, however, and does not readily promote identification. Although Horváth advises that not a single word of dialect is to be spoken (GW 8: 663), the language of his *Volksstücke* is strongly marked by the features of Bavarian-Austrian speech patterns. Yet the traces of dialect included here are not supposed to represent some sort of prelapsarian idyll: even when the characters' language contains dialect, they are equally unable to comprehend themselves or their situation (cf. Nolting 43, 49). For Klotz, the presence of dialect is necessary as a scaffolding that Horváth needs to erect in order to disassemble as part of the process of continuation and destruction of the old *Volksstück* (188). The remnants of dialect make the artificiality and inadequacy of the new *Bildungsjargon* more evident.

Bildungsjargon consists of clichés, slogans, quotations, educated vocabulary, and borrowed phrases that are often connected through association rather than logic. It is kitsch on a linguistic level, whose expression is not adequate to its content (Jarka 575). Erna's remark, when she views the constellation Orion, is sentimental and lacks reason: "Wissens, wenns mir schlecht geht, dann denk ich mir immer, was ist ein Mensch neben einem Stern. Und das gibt mir dann wieder einen Halt" [You know, when I feel bad, then I always think, what is a human being compared to a star. And that always gives me something to hold on to again] (79; Sc. 12). In his advice to Kasimir, Merkel Franz tries to compensate in language for his precarious social position, but the high-sounding words are merely clichés, and his aggressive nature comes through in the final clause to provide a stark contrast:

Ich hätt ja einen plausibleren Vorschlag: laß doch diesen Kavalier überhaupt laufen — er kann doch nichts dafür, daß jetzt die deine mit ihm da droben durch die Weltgeschichte rodelt. Du hast dich doch nur mit ihr auseinanderzusetzen. Wie sie auf der Bildfläche erscheint, zerreiß ihr das Maul (78, Sc. 11).

Might I offer a more plausible suggestion: let this cavalier go — he can't help it that your girlfriend is running off with him through the world. She's the one you have to have it out with. If she appears on the scene, let her have it on the chin.

Bildungsjargon is fragmented and shares many of the features of the "Jargon der Eigentlichkeit" [Jargon of Authenticity] criticized by Adorno, even though Adorno was criticizing the inauthentic language of intellectuals who should know better: "Der Jargon ... benutzt als Organisationsprinzip die Desorganisation, den Zerfall der Sprache in Worte an sich" [Jargon uses disorganization as its organizing principle, the deterioration of language into words in themselves] (10). Whoever speaks in jargon does not need to say what he thinks, or even to think it, "jargon does that for him and devalues the thoughts" (11). Karoline expresses this same idea rather naively and blatantly when she says in reply to Schürzinger's denial that he is calculating in love, "Ich denke ja gar nichts, ich sage es ja nur" [I'm not thinking anything, I'm only saying it] (101, Sc. 52). Substitutions for an actual understanding of the world occur in speech that replaces thought: Kasimir sums up the complex matter of Franz's arrest and the conditions that led to it with the trite "So ist das Leben" [Such is life] (133, Sc. 112). Erna can only follow such a remark with another proverbial expression: "Kaum fängt man an, schon ist es vorbei" [One hardly begins, and it's already over]. These clichés have little reference to the specific reality in which Kasimir and Erna find themselves. Their conversation offers the appearance of communication, but it is really more an agreement about what one can say about things than about the things themselves.

Like the characters in Thoma's *Magdalena* Horváth's figures cannot comprehend their situation because they have no adequate language with which to grasp it. Instead of attempting to name a reality that has not yet been fixed in language, they refer back to one that has already been named (Kurzenberger, 16). Kasimir attempts to explain Karoline's taking up with Schürzinger by using a term that already exists: "eine Oktoberfestbekanntschaft" [an Oktoberfest acquaintanceship] (83, Sc. 17). Fixing it with this substantive makes further attempts at comprehension unnecessary. General-izations provide additional means with which to order empirical experiences. Karoline says, for example, "Aber die Oberammergauer sind auch keine Heiligen" [But the Oberammergauers aren't saints either], and "Alle Zuschneider bilden sich gleich soviel ein" [All tailors get a lot of conceited ideas right away] (73, Sc. 4). Ideologies can also offer ready-made replacements for insight into the external situation. Schürzinger's remark that people are neither good nor bad but simply forced into an egoistic position by the contemporary economic system may contain a certain amount of "truth" (72, Sc. 4), yet the remark does not stem from a raised political consciousness on his part. It is a fragment, tossed off in conversation, and he himself behaves egoistically in abandoning Karoline in the hopes of a promotion.

　　It would be a mistake to view individual characters as mouthpieces for the author, or the plays as exponents of an ideology. Despite his generally anti-fascist tendencies, Horváth mistrusted the "dogmatic rigidity in the political jargon of the social democrats and communists as well as of the fascists" (Bruns 125). In *Italienische Nacht*, for example, the critical anti-Nazi Martin is himself criticized by linguistic means (Reinhardt 345–46). And in *Kasimir und Karoline* the real criticism of capitalism is not contained in Schürzinger's platitude, but in a "criticism of the critical platitude" (Nolting 166). In other words, capitalism has produced alienated people who neither know themselves nor possess the capability of expressing themselves in meaningful communication with others but instead rely on borrowed verbal fragments to feign a pseudo-individuality (cf. Adorno, "Jargon" 19; Doppler 17).

　　Karoline's attempts to sort out her own situation are filled with contradictions because they can occur only within an inadequate language. She says she is abandoning Kasimir for Rauch because in hard times, a woman "muß einen einflußreichen Mann immer bei seinem Gefühlsleben packen" [has to grab an influential man by his feelings]. She claims to have done this with Kasimir, but when he says he believes her desire for advancement is something new, she contradicts herself by saying that she was previously confused, "weil ich dir hörig war" [because I was bound to you] (94, Sc. 36): she is apparently unaware of the discrepancy between her two remarks about who was emotionally bound to whom. Kasimir thinks he is describing a situation but actually gives his language a performative function when he accuses Karoline of abandoning him and adds, "Ich konstatiere eine Wahrheit" [I'm confirming a truth] (75, Sc. 5). Yet it is his statement of "confirmation" as much as her previous action that serves to drive them apart. Language becomes action, but a random, powerless action that is unable to achieve results; thus the plot runs in circles and simply breaks off in the end. Arntzen's conclusion that the relation between Marianne and Alfred in *Geschichten aus dem Wiener Wald* is only a "manner of speaking" can also be applied to *Kasimir und Karoline* (263).

These characters, their situation, and their actions coincide to a great extent with their language, whose lack of identity with consciousness presents a negative rather than an affirmative picture of contemporary reality in a manner that is hard for audiences to overlook or escape. Yet achieving an awareness of the exact relationship to that reality and the conclusions that can be drawn from it are more difficult. Adorno stressed that language was the means of negation in Beckett's plays; Horváth's language also negates, yet it is restricted to the phenomenon of *Bildungsjargon* rather than language in general. In Horváth's play the possibility of a mediating function for language is not ruled out, even though it is not specifically portrayed as an alternative.[16] The language of *Kasimir und Karoline* thus leaves a small opening for hope.

The question remains, however, as to how that hope may be made manifest, since the characters' language is both a symptom of their false consciousness and a means for continuing that consciousness. And how does the audience become aware of an alternative, since no outside commentary is introduced into the plays? Horváth said that his only goal was a "Demaskierung des Bewußtseins" [an unmasking of consciousness] (GW 8: 660): it is necessary to look closely at the text to see how and to what extent this is achieved.[17] This unmasking is largely carried out through the use of *Volksstück*-elements in a way that runs counter to the prevailing expectation:[18] this is a method of implicit *Verfremdung* [distancing] that hinders identification and provides an opportunity for the spectator to think about the contradictions between what is and what should be.

Another technique for distancing concerns the play within a play, represented by the freak show where Karoline and the others make up an audience for the fat lady, the man with the bulldog head, and the gorilla girl (95–102; Sc. 39–55). During the performance the dwarf marches across the stage with a sign reading "Intermission" that refers both to the freak show and to the performance of *Kasimir und Karoline*: the real audience's actions are incorporated into the peformance by making the 56th scene the intermission itself (Hummel 72). This breaks the illusion and encourages the spectators to think about what they have been seeing.

Because very little external perspective is offered from the stage, much of the task of unmasking consciousness must be carried out within language itself. The spectator is prodded into awareness by the irritating features of the dialogue such as the clichés, the insults, the characters' frequent self-contradictions, and the fragmented conversation that jumps at random from topic to topic (see especially 82–84, Sc. 17). The audience is supposed to be struck twice: in their own lives as contemporaries who speak this kind of language and as irritated witnesses to the dissonant dialogues on stage (Klotz 188). Since this language reflects actual usage to a great extent, Horváth was forced to include another formal element as an additional reminder of the inadequacy of *Bildungsjargon* as an expression of thought and feeling, namely the numerous spots marked "Stille" [silence] in which the struggle between consciousness and the subconscious should be made visible (GW 8: 664).

After Karoline answers Kasimir's question about Schürzinger's identity by saying, "Das ist ein gebildeter Mensch. Ein Zuschneider" [He's an educated man, a tailor], the directions for silence are given (83, Sc. 17). This gives the spectator time to consider how these words fit as a categorization of Schürzinger and as an expression of Karoline's comprehension of him. The similarity and contrast between her present description of him as "gebildet" [educated] and her previous generalization that tailors are "eingebildet" [conceited] is striking and emphasizes the importance of language in affecting her consciousness and actions. It is not clear to the spectator (or even to Karoline herself) whether she is making a personal judgment based on her brief acquaintance with Schürzinger or a new generalization about his profession. What is crucial in this context is that dropping the prefix "ein" provides a positive adjective, which she needs to supply here in order to defend her behavior. She makes her remark seriously, but the irony in the use of two similar-sounding words calls her language and, by extension, her thought process into question. The phrase can hardly serve as a step to a deepened understanding between the two title characters, and after wrestling with his own reactions in the pause, the self-pitying Kasimir interprets the remark as a personal attack; the limited language causes the dialogue to take a further turn for the worse.

The means employed to unmask the characters' consciousness are subtle and easily missed by the spectator, but when they are noticed they point out not only that conditions are bad, but how they are bad. To Doppler this "hidden antagonism between the image [*Abbild*] and counter-image [*Gegenbild*]" constitutes the dramatic process of Horváth's *Volksstücke* (12).

The image is of course the depiction of society that is conveyed through the use of *Bildungsjargon*, and the formal features that negate it evoke (without depicting) a counter-image of an "Erlösungsmöglichkeit" [possibility of salvation] (12). Negation and the urge toward utopia are both present in the same moment.

As discussed earlier, music constitutes one of the most important elements in *Kasimir und Karoline*, and, like language, its components are to a large extent propagated by the media and its form molded by the culture industry. Its function also parallels that of language by providing a depiction of contemporary society while simultaneously revealing certain of its currently popular forms as invalid means of expression. Music's function can be fully comprehended only by examining its formal use within the play, not just by viewing it as content. But whereas the play's language irritates the spectator, popular, familiar melodies invite identification and a shared experiencing of the sentimental kitsch that makes up a large part of the characters' lives.

Music is present on several levels: as in many films it provides background accompaniment, which sets a particular mood, and serves a naturalistic function, which establishes the setting and reflects what is actually sung at a particular festival. The author of a trivial *Volksstück* would perhaps have been content to let these two uses suffice, but since Horváth is more interested in analyzing the relationship between music and contemporary consciousness, he thematizes the former and treats it ironically through its formal incorporation.

When the melody of "So lang der alte Peter" is played before the initial opening of the curtain, its message is one of "Munich-ness" and "Gemüt-lichkeit," since at that point no additional context has been presented to indicate otherwise (69, Sc. 1). But when the beer drinkers sing the same song immediately following the intermission (103, Sc. 59), the text, "Solang stirbt die Gemütlichkeit/ Zu München nimmer aus" [Then conviviality in Munich will never die], is called into question, because the Oktoberfest has been anything but pleasant and cheerful for Kasimir, and the "Gemütlich-keit" at which Karoline has grasped is forced and artificial. The timeless categories of the song seem rather abstract when confronted with concrete, historical reality: the stage directions state that Kasimir sits there "melancho-lisch," as the only one who does not sing along, and the ensuing conversa-tion reveals his lack of prospects. The juxtaposition should show that the sentimentality of the song provides a mere escape.

Similarly, the orchestra plays Lehar's waltz "Bist du's, lachendes Glück?" [Is that you, smiling fortune?], whose title comments ironically on the pantomime that occurs simultaneously: wounded people with bandages emerge from the first aid station (127–28, Sc. 102). The breaking off of the music in the middle of the measure emphasizes the dialogue that follows and also implies a negative answer to the song's title. The next scenes indicate that there has been a general brawl whose causes are known by few of the participants, and also show Karoline's rejection by Rauch. The continuation of the waltz in Scene 108 should further demonstrate the illusory nature of the happiness that the music signals.

But like the techniques that were included to point out the non-identity between *Bildungsjargon* and what it was supposed to communicate, the criticism of these musical selections may not have the desired effect on the spectator. In a 1986 performance in Freiburg the brass band got more applause than any of the actors: the audience obviously enjoyed the infectious character of the music, which was more in keeping with their idea of an evening's entertainment than the dreary lives of the characters. This is partly Horváth's fault for using a medium that so readily invites identification and thus affirmation of the status quo. Adorno doubted the parodistic function of music in Brecht's *Threepenny Opera*: even though it caricatures opera and operetta, it stolidly imitates them without providing any enlightenment of these forms (qtd. in Kurzenberger, 111). There is a parallel in Horváth's plays: when artists reach back to incorporate decayed forms in their works, there is a great danger that they will succumb to them.

Despite the dangers of misinterpretation or the tendency to overemphasize one aspect, music is contained in Horváth's plays both as an expression of utopian longing that uses a traditional means of signalling hope and as a condemnation of the attitude that the object of that hope can be found within sentimental music itself. For Ernst Bloch, music could definitely express the former function. Hans Mayer sees a similarity between Walter Benjamin and Ernst Bloch in their attraction to concrete expressions for their genuine visions: in Benjamin's case it was Paul Klee's painting "Angelus Novus," and in Bloch's the trumpet signal from *Fidelio*. With these notes in Beethoven's opera, the prisons of the past are swept away, says Mayer, and what has always been hoped for begins. "Die Utopie wird plötzlich konkret.... Ohne Beethovens 'Fidelio' wäre das Konzept des 'Prinzip Hoffnung' undenkbar gewesen" [Utopia suddenly becomes concrete.... Without Beethoven's *Fidelio* the concept of *Das Prinzip Hoffnung* would have been unthinkable] (71–72).

The music of *Kasimir und Karoline*, while giving expression to such a hope on a smaller scale, should simultaneously reveal the error of seeking fulfillment of that hope in this type of music alone. It should not serve as a surrogate for language or an affirmation of the status quo, but should also be revealed as a "means of obscuration" and a "fraudulent promise of hope" (Doppler 18), of something that is "objectively false and promotes the atrophy of the consciousness of those who are exposed to it, no matter how difficult it is to measure the atrophy in individual effects" (Adorno, *Einleitung* 48). The final song, in which Kasimir and Erna long for the approach of spring, is obviously a sentimental *Ersatz*, but it is at the same time the expression of a genuine hope in a world that presently contains only false objects for that hope (138, Sc. 117). The play's first half also concludes with a number that should make both functions clear: a musical quotation, the "Barcarolle" from the *Tales of Hoffmann* is given a plaintive rendition by Juanita the gorilla girl to a hackneyed piano accompaniment (101–102, Sc. 55).

All authors of the *Volksstücke* considered thus far have found it difficult to resolve the tension between the negative and the utopian. Ferdinand Raimund's *Der Alpenkönig und der Menschenfeind* was unable to provide a purely liberating comedy: the contradictions and inadequacies of the world were too great to be excluded from the drama. Similarly, *Kasimir und Karoline* presents a mixture of the comic and the tragic without falling completely into either category. Horváth claimed that all his plays were tragedies, that they only become comic because they are "unheimlich" [uncanny] (GW 8: 664). In another draft of the "Gebrauchsanweisung," however, he wrote that tragedies are comic as a result of their "humanity" (*Mat.* 101). At the 1932 premiere there was a difference of opinion among critics: Alfred Kerr found that the play had a comic power surpassing that of the earlier *Volksstück*-authors Thoma and Ruederer (*Mat.* 40), whereas Monty Jacobs said that it was not a comedy because it was too merciless and lacked humor (*Mat.* 88–90). These divergent interpretations result from the synthesis of elements contained within the play, which seem to have different effects on different viewers.

Horváth writes that misinterpretations result from asking *against* whom his plays are written, rather than *for* whom (GW 8: 666). Since the play is for the *Kleinbürger*, who also stand at its center, and since Horváth refrains from offering a monocausal analysis, the play does not contain a program of consistently directed satire as a source of comedy. Yet satire is very much present in isolated instances. Although the characters may be unaware of its critical force, its barb should be evident to the spectators. For example, the dwarf makes fun of German technological achievement in the form of the zeppelin with his remark, "Wenn man bedenkt, wie weit es wir Menschen schon gebracht haben" [When one considers, how far we humans have progressed] (69, Sc. 3), and the doctor satirizes nationalism indirectly with his comment on the brawl: "Ein schöner Saustall sowas! Deutsche gegen Deutsche!" [That's a real pig-sty! Germans against Germans!] (129, S c. 104).

Satire serves Horváth's purposes more directly when it helps reveal the emptiness and inconsistencies of Bildungjargon. When Kasimir responds negatively to Merkl Franz's question "Parlez-vous française [sic]?", Franz says that it is too bad, "Weil sich das deutsch nicht so sagen läßt. Ein Zitat." [Because you can't say it the same way in German. A quote] (78, Sc. 10). The absurdity of language that exists for its own sake to impress through quotations rather than to communicate is made evident here.[19] In general, however, the audience is too constricted by present reality and its inadequate language to laugh at the conditions on stage from a position of superiority, but neither is it able to laugh with the characters: their situation is too depressing to generate a robust laughter similar to that produced by the Dionysian *Der fröhliche Weinberg*. When Karoline makes a pun with a mixed metaphor in her remark about having to stoop pretty low in order to climb up in the world (135, Sc. 113), she is unaware of what she is saying. The laughter that results can only be partial and slighty embarrassed.

Kasimir und Karoline is neither a comedy nor a tragedy but contains elements of both. They exist in a precarious, dialectical relationship in which the former holds out utopian hope while the latter serves as a constant reminder of the implacable conditions of the present.[20] To have offered a comic resolution would have been impossible and artificial in light of the contradictions within reality, for it would have frozen the utopian object into a form of kitsch. But to resort to pure tragedy would have run the danger of creating a cathartic melodrama (François 228). The grotesque humor should distance the spectator from the events and offer a sort of commentary. This "mélange des genres" (231) may hinder an unambiguous reception, but, as in Raimund's case, it was the only adequate solution for dealing with a not yet completed process that both negates the present and points to a better future. And no progress can be made toward utopia if no demands are made on the spectator.

Several varying reactions to *Kasimir und Karoline* have already been mentioned. The synthesis of seriousness and irony that manifests itself in the speech of the characters, in the music, in the play's relation to the traditional *Volksstück* genre, and in the mixture of comic and tragic is often subtle and subject to varied interpretation by directors, critics, and spectators alike. Hummel points out three additional problems that a twentieth-century *Volksstück* has to overcome: the formal one of entertaining a broad mass of the people while at the same time comprehensibly portraying complicated sociological and psychological conditions, the problem of finding the right content for a play that is *for* the *Volk* but not necessarily about them, and the institutional problem of putting such a play on a middle-class stage because a true *Volkstheater* no longer exists (114–15). Although Horváth confronted all three, he was not always successful at solving them as far as audiences were concerned. His ironic treatment of elements from the *Volksstück*-tradition and popular music was often misunderstood and tended to prove irritating. The lives of the *Kleinbürger* were discontented enough, and they did not necessarily appreciate having uneasiness provoked further from the stage (Hummel 131). Horváth indicated his awareness of this problem when he responded to criticism in the press that he was too coarse, disgusting, sinister, and cynical by saying that he simply tried to portray the world "wie sie halt leider ist" [as it unfortunately happens to be]. Although this statement of intent is overly disingenuous, he claims that spectators who react with distaste recognize themselves on stage and are unable to laugh at their own driving instincts (GW 1: 13).[21]

It is not so much the choice of content, but the revealing formal means that cause difficulties in the reception of these *Volksstücke*. Horváth himself recognized that genuine *Volkstheater* of the type found in nineteenth-century Vienna had largely disappeared and that the lower middle classes rarely attended plays. Much of the educated public expects aesthetic enjoyment and does not appreciate criticism or the destruction of its illusions, although extremely one-sided interpretations of Horváth plays are no longer as frequent.[22] The problem of audience and reception has not been totally overcome, though Hinck considers Horváth's achievement a positive one, because, like the *Volksstücke* of Raimund and Nestroy, his plays grasp the world from the perspective of the lower strata of society while remaining open to the outlook of the other classes. "Horváth's best plays exemplify how a *Volkstheater* of distinction, without ignoring class differences, can nonetheless attempt to overcome them — that in other words the *Volksstück* aims at a public in which the 'people' are represented in the broadest and most unrestricted sense" (*Das moderne Drama* 132). This assessment is perhaps overly optimistic and refers more to the intention than to the accomplishment, yet an important element of the utopia in these *Volksstücke* is the attempt to provide demanding literary entertainment for a broad mass of the people and thus of taking a stand on their behalf. The discontent felt by many members of the audience is an indication, however, that Horváth did not set out to conquer major stages in the same manner as Zuckmayer, but in a way that refused to ignore the insufficiencies of the present. He thus took his audience seriously and aimed for a form of entertainment that was more than a mere diversion or poor substitute for an insufficient reality.

In a letter praising the play's successful reception in Vienna (in contrast to the Berlin premiere, where audiences had taken the play to be a parody of the Oktoberfest), Horváth wrote that Kasimir and Karoline "streben nach Wahrheit, trotz der Illusion, daß es eine solche nicht gibt, oder nicht geben darf" [strive for truth in spite of the illusion that no such thing exists or is permitted to exist] (GW 8: 666). Truth might mean an interpretation that is correct in the author's opinion, or the statement might also be a criticism of those who found Horváth cynical and coarse as a result of their unwillingness to be confronted with the truth of actual conditions, with things "as they unfortunately happen to be." But it must be noted that Horváth speaks of a *striving* for truth and believes that it should at least be allowed to exist, even if it does not appear to exist now. As has been pointed out, the text of the play presents no truths in the content of its utterances: even apparently accurate statements are called into question, and Horváth might have added "for our knowledge is imperfect and our prophecy is imperfect" (1 Corinthians 13: 9; *New Oxford Bible*). Schürzinger's statements seem to assess accurately the effects of the economic situation on individuals, but his possession of the "truth" hardly results in a higher consciousness on his part. Kasimir's awareness is more penetrating, yet he too is a victim of conditions, his own self-pity, and self-fulfilling illusions.

The *Bildungsjargon* is particularly incapable of conveying wisdom directly: it is through the form that this *Volksstück* and its language begin a process toward truth (cf. Hummel 17). Unmasking consciousness is a pedagogical task, but Horváth's plays are not didactic in the manner of Lehrstücke: the author does not try to change consciousness or teach audiences what they should think, but rather only to reveal the falseness of present illusions (V. Wiese, "Horváth" 10). This explains the lack of ideological tendency, a lack which is annoying to those who expect an answer for a way out of the current impasse but which represents a strength to those who consider programmatic answers inadequate (cf. Kurzenberger 122, Handke). It also explains the refusal to offer a simplistic, monocausal explanation of the characters' situation. Karoline's various attempts to give a reason for her own behavior call this type of causality into question:

> Eigentlich hab ich ja ein Eis essen wollen — aber dann ist der Zeppelin vorbeigeflogen und ich bin mit der Achterbahn gefahren. Und dann hast du gesagt, daß ich dich automatisch verlasse, weil du arbeitslos bist. Automatisch, hast du gesagt (135, Sc. 113).

> [What I really wanted to do was eat ice cream — but then the zeppelin flew over and I took a ride on the roller coaster. And then you said that I would leave you automatically because you're out of work. Automatically, that's what you said.]

Her explanation proceeds temporally and by association; the break with Kasimir is actually not mechanically "automatic," but proceeds out of the situation in which both are inextricably caught and can neither understand nor control. Although economic conditions play a major role, they do not represent the single cause. Horváth does not attempt to present the complications and contradictions of reality explicitly within his plays and sort them out in a message to the audience. Society is depicted through its language, which contains these contradictions.[23] Kasimir and Karoline are both individuals and social beings, despite the fact that they are not able to realize either part of their nature adequately. In the ideal world toward which they strive, both would be possible.

Horváth remarks in the "Randbemerkungen" (glosses) to *Glaube Liebe Hoffnung* that all of his plays could bear this title of "Faith Hope Love" (GW 1: 328). The reference to the thirteenth chapter of 1 Corinthians links it to the motto of *Kasimir und Karoline*, as do the themes of love and hope. Despite the bleakness of the characters' outlooks and the author's unwillingness to ignore present evils, the play is permeated with the hope that the characters hold out for the future.[24] This hope, like love, is expressed in the title, in which the names of the characters are linked by the conjunction *and*. In the final scene, however, they are separated and have resigned themselves to new partners; a realistic compromise seems to be the only possible course of action. But the hope for love never ends, even though that love is not fulfilled in the play itself.

As Joas states, the hope for a unique, lasting individual love is part of the hope for non-alienated relations between human beings, and thus love and solidarity are part of the same problem (60). In attempting to stress the possibility of an adequate life in the present, Ferdinand Raimund seemed anti-utopian, though the inherent contradictions in this stance allowed an opening for the utopian drive in his plays. In showing a present that seems incapable of providing an adequate life for human beings, Horváth appears anti-utopian in a completely different way. Neither Raimund nor Horváth could paint a picture of a future utopia or chart a specific path in its direction, yet Horváth leaves room for a possible approach in the dialectic between the jargon, which is portrayed, and its opposite, which is not (Nolting 24); it is not in the content of the characters' speech that utopia can be discovered, but in the movement toward genuine speech (161).

Neither should the letter to the Corinthians be taken as an expression of the truth behind the play nor as a key to the interpretation of the text. It is rather a separate text from a different perspective that deals with similar problems. Thus Horváth only hints at scripture in ironic fashion instead of quoting it as an authority. His more explicit inclusion in his final play of "der Herr" who bears a close resemblance to the Apostle Paul is often taken as a sign of his increasingly metaphysical standpoint, yet the roots are already present in his earlier plays.[25] Kasimir and Karoline would not be able to achieve the lives that they seek through purely individual acts of will that are divorced from the social situation as a whole. The "Herr" of *Pompeji* advises characters not to talk so much in order that they might collect themselves. He does not command silence, but a correct speech that conceives of the personal as the community, as is shown by his writing letters to "entire cities" (Arntzen 268).

Kasimir und Karoline is firmly rooted in the specifics of contemporary reality, which it thoroughly negates, yet the characters, whom the author understood and must have loved (Kroetz 92), continue to hope for a more genuine existence within reality. Expressing hope is not easy, and in Horváth's play it is by no means encountered in the form of a rosy optimism; it is hidden between the lines. Günter Grass, who said that the characters in his novel *Die Rättin* continue to carry on even though there is no hope, finds that clinging to false hopes represents a greater danger than hopelessness and that it is the writer's task to expose false hopes as counterfeit.[26] Horváth similarly reveals the hopes of his characters as false when they seek fulfillment in domination of others or in the consumption of ready-made products of the culture industry, though he does not altogether rule out the possibility of escaping from this cycle. The characters' language is like a noisy gong or clanging cymbal, they can only see themselves and the world through a glass darkly, but their hopes, continually dashed within the play, remind the spectator of the eventual possibility of seeing face to face.

Chapter VIII

The *Volksstück* as Epic Theater:
Brecht's *Herr Puntila und sein Knecht Matti*

> Die armen Leut brauchen Courage.... Schon daß sie Kinder in
> die Welt setzen, zeigt, daß sie Courage haben, denn sie haben
> keine Aussicht.
>
> —Bertolt Brecht, *Mutter Courage und ihre Kinder*[1]

OF ALL THE AUTHORS CONSIDERED by this study, Bertolt Brecht (1898–
1956) seems the most like an outsider to the genre, since the majority of the
plays for which he has become well-known are not usually considered *Volksstücke*. Even though some of his early one-act plays, e.g., *Die Kleinbürger-
hochzeit* [The Middle-Class Wedding, 1919], were clearly influenced by the
Munich *Volksschauspieler* Karl Valentin and Konrad Dreher (Schumacher
93–94) and although many of his major dramas display techniques borrowed
from popular dramatic forms that are designed to appeal to the people (cf.
Hinck, "Mutter Courage"), Brecht wrote only one full-length play that he
called a *Volksstück*. Nevertheless, the *Volksstück* seems a particularly
appropriate form of drama for Brecht because of his views on the necessity
for change in a class society and on the didactic purpose of drama. And in
fact, his attempt to employ this form was quite serious. Always innovating,
Brecht did not take over any of the existing forms of the genre, but made
modifications to suit his own purposes. His essay "Anmerkungen zum
Volksstück" ["Comments on the *Volksstück*," 1940] explains what he
considered wrong with previous plays of this type and points out how
adaptations could produce a more valid drama. *Herr Puntila und sein Knecht
Matti* (*Mr. Puntila and his Hired Man, Matti*), which was written at the
same time, provides a concrete model for his ideas.[2]

His observations in "Anmerkungen zum Volksstück" apply more to the
frequently performed farces that he had experienced in the 1920s than to
plays like those of Nestroy, Anzengruber, and Thoma, or to more recent
authors such as Fleißer and Horváth.[3] He considered farcical *Volksstücke*
"crude and unpretentious," a description certain regimes wish to think
applies to their lower classes, and they contain "derbe Späße, gemischt mit
Rührseligkeiten, da ist hanebüchene Moral und billige Sexualität. Die Bösen
werden bestraft, und die Guten werden geheiratet, die Fleißigen machen eine
Erbschaft, und die Faulen haben das Nachsehen.... Es genügt eine tüchtige

Portion der gefürchteten Routiniertheit des Dilettantismus" [coarse jokes, mixed with sentimentality, there is preposterous morality and cheap sexuality. The wicked are punished, and the good are married off, the industrious get an inheritance, and the lazy have their trouble for nothing.... All that is necessary is a generous portion of the dreaded routine of the dilettante] (GW 17: 1162). Brecht therefore was not trying to revive an obsolete form, yet his insistence on the generic designation recognizes an existing need that the trivial *Volksstück* was addressing without being able to fulfill (Speidel 319). This was a need for a theater that was "naive but not primitive, poetic but not romantic, close to reality but not topically political" (GW 17: 1163).

Though Brecht was more explicit than any previous author of *Volksstücke* in expressing theoretically the need for renewal, he follows Raimund, Nestroy, Anzengruber, Horváth, and others in taking a given tradition as a starting point while making substantial changes. But despite his major contribution to the genre, early Brecht scholarship tended to devote less attention to *Herr Puntila und sein Knecht Matti* than to other plays. By now, however, this drama is generally conceded to be one of his major works, and a number of important studies have been devoted to it, especially the articles by Hermand, Speidel, and Poser and the book by Mews, which provides a useful introduction and compilation of significant interpretations. Although these investigations bring out the most important aspects of the play, it is necessary to look at Brecht from the point of view of the changing dynamics of the *Volksstück* and not just at the latter from the perspective of Brecht. The unique formal aspects of *Herr Puntila und sein Knecht Matti*, especially as they relate to the proclaimed genre, provide the principal reason for considering it more closely in this study.

One noticeable surface difference between this drama and others investigated here involves its non-German setting. During part of his exile in Finland in 1940–41, Brecht and his family stayed at the home of the Finnish author Hella Wuolijoki, who had written a short story with comedy and filmscript adaptations entitled *Sahanpuruprinsessa* [The Sawdust Princess], based on an incident in the life of her uncle. Like Brecht, she was interested in the *Volksstück*, and incorporating modifications that he suggested, the two of them revised this script and submitted it to a Finnish playwriting contest under the title *Herr Puntila und sein Knecht Kalle*.[4] Wuolijoki's text was essential in launching *Herr Puntila und sein Knecht Matti*, but Brecht transformed it in basic and important ways. He recorded in his work diaries in September 1940 that it was necessary to change what was essentially a comedy of conversation into something else:

> What I have to do is to work out the basic farce, to tear down the psychologizing conversations and gain space for tales from Finnish folk life or for opinions, to construct scenically the antithesis 'master' and 'servant' and to give back to the theme its poetry and comedy. The theme shows how H[ella] W[uolijoki], with all her cleverness, experience, vitality, and poetic talent, is hindered by conventional dramatic techniques. (*Arbeitsjournal* I, 64)

Brecht made the contrast between master and servant more ideological by portraying Puntila in his role as capitalist and more central by relegating an episode involving Puntila's "brides" to a minor subplot. Most importantly, he made Matti an aware member of the working class, who is in the end unable to marry his employer's daughter. In Wuolijoki's original version, Kalle is actually a sophisticated intellectual disguised as a proletarian and is therefore capable of carrying out such a union in a happy ending (Deschner 119–22). But most of Brecht's remarks in the *Arbeitsjournal* are concerned with form, and it is in this area as well that his changes shift the focus of the play quite significantly.

Although many of the play's early critics dismissed it as harmless entertainment and denied that it had any political message,[5] and although some have considered it a very loosely constructed collection of scenes,[6] it is actually quite clearly focused on the dialectic between master and servant expressed in the title, a relationship that Hinck calls a "soziales Grundverhältnis" (basic social relationship, *Dramaturgie* 33). The two principal characters or sets of characters, the relation of form to content, the relation between didactic theater and popular theater, and the expressions of negation and utopia are all connected to this dialectic, with which Hegel dealt in his *Phänomenologie des Geistes* [*Phenomenology of the Spirit*] (141–50). Here Hegel argued that even though the servant is dependent on and bound to the master, the master is also dependent on the servant, since the servant acts directly on an object, which the master can only experience as enjoyment or consumption through the mediation of the servant's activity (146).

The relationship between the two is unequal, but not in the sense that is commonly held. Since activity leads to self-awareness, the servant has the advantage: "Die *Wahrheit* des selbständigen Bewußtseins ist demnach das *knechtische Bewußtsein*" [The *truth* of independent consciousness is accordingly the *consciousness of the servant*] (147; italics in the original). The master can only enjoy and passively experience what is, whereas the servant changes things through his activity. Only the servant, in Knopf's words, "sorgt dafür, daß die Geschichte 'gemacht' wird" [provides that history is "made"] (218).[7] Hermand observes that no better example of a dialectic process can be found than in the relationship between master and servant, who seem to define one another in reciprocal necessity. Brecht's question, he says, is whether such a relationship must be perpetually maintained, or whether it should be resolved in favor of something better ("Herr Puntila" 132–33). In *Herr Puntila und sein Knecht Matti* the master is the one who enjoys while the servant acts. The chauffeur Matti is superior to Herr Puntila not just in terms of intelligence, as was often the case in the stock roles of the *commedia dell'arte*, but because he has more insight into the antagonistic structure of capitalism (Poser 192). Matti's final rejection of this particular relationship points to a future overcoming of the antithesis.

Critics have frequently pointed out that the master-servant relationship is a feudal one and therefore an anachronism in Brecht's play that does not exactly apply to a capitalist society. Brecht is, after all, a Marxist rather than a Hegelian. As Hans Mayer observes, Hegel's use of this terminology represented a middle-class protest against feudal conditions, which still existed in some places in 1807, but its retention by subsequent authors seems regressive, since the major class conflict had switched to one between capital and the proletariat (qtd. in Mews 12). Giving *Herr Puntila und sein Knecht Matti* a rural setting allied it more closely with the existing *Volksstück*, but Brecht had additional reasons for this choice of relationships and locales. Placing the drama more directly among factory workers would have made the simultaneous juxtapostion of the two contrasting title characters at work, play, and in family life more difficult and thus detracted from the advantages gained through ironic inversions. Seeing the two side by side in so many different situations increases the possibility of employing effects for distancing. In both the medieval and the twentieth-century relationships there is a relative imbalance in the positions of the one in power and the one who is exploited, an imbalance that is made more graphic in Brecht's choice of portrayals. The extent to which the relationships of capitalism parallel or have permeated the world of the large landowners is both implicitly and explicitly expressed within the play. The setting need not make the model irrelevant to today's situation; rather, the distancing could promote insight. Just as Finland represents Germany, the rural underclass represents the proletariat as a whole. This latter group, rather than craftsmen, farmers, or *Kleinbürger*, is the *Volk* that Brecht is addressing here.

This play in its final version consists of twelve scenes framed by a prologue and epilogue in verse. Single stanzas of "Das Puntilalied," with music by Paul Dessau, are sung after appropriate scenes. Puntila's inebriation in a tavern at the beginning introduces a further antithesis that is basic to the play: when sober, Puntila is a calculating capitalist, but when drunk, he socializes with his employees and expresses noble, philanthropic sentiments. In order to solidify his position in society, he has his daughter Eva engaged to an attaché, who has his eye on the dowry. Eva, however, finds the virile Matti much more attractive, and when drunk, even her father agrees that his chauffeur would be a better match than the spineless attaché.

Matti's staging of a suggestive scene with himself and Eva in the sauna fails to scandalize the proposed bridegroom, however, and Puntila's insults are similarly slow to take effect. In the meantime Puntila manages to get himself engaged to four early-rising women in a pre-dawn search for legal alcohol. Later, his inebriation prompts liberal sentiments at a market for farmhands but prevents him from signing the contracts that would be in the workers' interest. When Puntila's insults at the engagement party become so clear that the attaché finally takes his leave, Matti is supposed to become the new bridegroom. But through a series of demonstrations the chauffeur reveals that Eva is too unpractical to be wed to a member of his class, and she herself renounces the engagement when he gives her an affectionate slap on her backside. Puntila gets drunk once more and orders his servant Matti to construct a Mount Hatelma in the study from books and pieces of furniture. Puntila waxes enthusiastic about the view of his native land from the top of this artificial mountain, but Matti's remarks deflate their falseness. On the following morning Matti leaves without even waiting for a certificate of recommendation from his employer, giving as a reason "Weil sich das Wasser mit dem Öl nicht mischt" [Because oil and water don't mix] (1709).

The basic dialectic between master and servant so permeates all aspects of the play that it is hard to separate negative and positive elements, since they are inextricably linked. To Semrau, the drama is the product of two contradictory efforts: the criticism of aspects of an ugly reality, which needs to be made less harsh, and an affirmation of happy farm life (36–37). But this estimation falls short of the mark, for Brecht's criticism is even more radical: *Herr Puntila und sein Knecht Matti* demands not just an amelioration of existing reality, but a thorough negation of the basic social order. And although the play must start with an affirmation of certain aspects of the lives of the people that it is addressing, these conditions cannot be viewed in an entirely positive fashion as they now exist, but rather to the extent that they point to the qualities of a future utopia.

As in the other plays discussed thus far, utopia is not portrayed directly, but only glimpsed. According to Ralph Ley, a scene such as the one in which the snobbish wife of a minister carries on a perfectly natural conversation with the cook about their mutual interest in mushrooms affords "the spectator a minute glimpse of the world that is not yet, that world to come which must still be portrayed within the limits of the present reality" (454–55). This is an example of Bloch's "Spuren," or traces, that give an intimation of utopia without actually portraying or inaugurating it. In this play the truly utopian elements are mixed with false fulfillments, as well as with the negative, and the resulting portrayals are almost always fraught with contradiction.

Brecht is the only author treated in this study (except for Kroetz, at certain stages of his career) to have advocated a definite political goal. Many observers therefore expect him to provide a precise representation of the Marxist paradise in his dramas, although some have claimed to find a confirmation of their own views when he fails to do so. Preconceptions concerning the Marxist political economy and Marxist aesthetics could be found in countries of both the capitalist West and the Eastern bloc. In both camps there was (and is) a tendency to equate Marxism with Soviet Communism and to confuse political message with explicit content, which is considered incompatible with experimental artistic form. A typical expression of the view that sets up a false dichotomy between form and content, aesthetics and politics can be found in "Der Dramatiker Bertolt Brecht" by Benno von Wiese, who finds it fortunate that in the supposedly inevitable conflict between Brecht the playwright and Brecht the theoretician, the former usually wins. Brecht's greatest figures, he claims, are effective through themselves alone because they are politically realistic and not simply examples for a lesson. He illustrates his point with Puntila, whom he finds "convincing in the theater as a result of his juicy vitality and alcoholic playfulness," despite Brecht's attempts to pillory him as a capitalist property owner. This in contrast to the servant Matti, "who is of course supposed to embody for Brecht the intellectually superior lower class, but who in fact is almost always pushed out of the limelight by the lively, exuberant Puntila" (*Zwischen Utopie* 261).

But such interpretation faults Brecht for starting with the contradictions of the present and for incorporating in both form and content the dialectic in the relationship between master and servant. If Matti had been a purely positive figure and Puntila totally negative, utopia would be presented as more easily attainable than is actually the case, and the path toward it would be short-circuited: the dialectic would be prematurely resolved, and audiences would more readily accept or condemn the play on the basis of their current beliefs. Thus the portrayal of a vitally attractive Puntila does not simply represent a triumph of the "dramatist Brecht" over the message of the "theoretician Brecht": both triumph, though the contradictions will not be completely overcome until some future point. Benno von Wiese's remarks about Brecht's *Das Leben des Galilei* show greater perception and might be applied to *Herr Puntila und sein Knecht Matti* as well: "This drama not only proceeds dialectically, it makes dialectics itself its object. From this can be explained the numerous contradictions that can be found everywhere in Brecht" (271). Brecht, with his specific political vision that consciously perceived the *Volk* within a Marxist *Weltanschauung*, was no more capable than other authors of *Volksstücke* to make utopia itself the object of his portrayal. But the occasional glimpses resulting from the utopian impulses need to be examined more closely, to the extent that they point to genuine solutions or indicate the inadequacy of false ones.

Many figures from the *Volk*, including Matti, other servants on Puntila's estate, and Puntila's four "fiancées" (a telephone operator, an drugstore employee, a cowmaid, and Smuggler Emma) are viewed positively, but even though Brecht's sympathies clearly lie with the *Volk* he refrains from apotheosizing them. As mentioned earlier, *Herr Puntila und sein Knecht Matti* differs from many typical German *Volksstücke*, which tend to concentrate on the people of a particular region of Germany or Austria, and which, in the sentimental, trivial examples of the genre, tend to exalt them as ideals. Especially in 1940, the favorable portrayal of rural Germans by Brecht would have run the danger of misinterpretation through a possible confusion with the veneration of a "völkisch" ethnicity as found in Nazi propaganda. Although the characters speak with a hint of South German colloquial dialect, they are clearly cast as Finns. Brecht avoids the temptation of portraying this Finnish farm world in an unhistorical, folkloristic way but always stresses the concrete situation of class conflict (Hermand, "Zwischen Tuismus" 21). Thus any perceived similarity to or difference from members of the audience results from class position, rather than the accident of place.

Giving the play a different setting from that which was customary in most *Volksstücke* points this out more explicitly.[8] Together with the title and the configuration of characters, the setting should facilitate a Brechtian interpretation of the *Volk*: an exploited class occupying a particular historical situation rather than a timeless, ethnic group embodying certain genuine, natural qualities which an over-sophisticated majority should seek to reattain. But the actual portrayals do not always facilitate such an interpretation. For example, several representatives of the *Volk* still come off so much more favorably when compared with the ruling classes that it would be tempting to see in them the repository of an innocent, natural integrity. The wit and practicality of the "early-risers" make them more endearing and sympathetic than the upper-class guests at Eva's engagement feast. To Brecht they are the "noblest figures of the play:" they are richer in kindness and are actually prepared to show generosity to the landowner Puntila, who, when sober, reneges on his promises to them (*Theaterarbeit* 23; qtd. in Mews 42). Their role is not major enough, however, to allow them to be developed as ideals.

It is Matti, of course, the chief representative of the *Volk* on stage, who serves as the spokesman for this group. Unlike Puntila, whose commentary about his own self-interest varies with the amount of alcohol consumed, Matti always remains cognizant of his own identity and that of his class and how they stand in relation to their masters. Though Puntila addresses his chauffeur with the familiar *du* and insists on friendship and brotherhood, Matti always uses the formal *Sie* and speaks instead of acquaintance, not from servility, but in order to keep from deluding himself that barriers have been overcome when his master fraternizes with him: he knows that the relationship will ultimately remain unequal (1614–15).

At the employment market, Puntila treats the workers like commodities that he needs for his estate. But as the morning progresses, and he has consumed more and more alcohol at the café, he begins saying that he is more interested in getting to know his future employees and providing them with a home than in cold-bloodedly offering them a job with wages. As this delays the signing of the contracts, and the applicants fear that they will be without a job when the market closes, Matti in business-like fashion urges Puntila to dispense with making friends and to complete the transactions. Again, he is under no illusions. It is not that he is looking out for Puntila's interests but those of the workers to the extent that they exist under present conditions: a job that puts bread on the table is more important than the semblance of harmony between classes (1633–41).

In similar fashion he urges the early-risers to form a "Federation of Fiancées" to defend their interests before Puntila, since the chauffeur is one who "recognizes the voice of the masses" (1667). Matti thus appears to have the proper class consciousness and would therefore seem to be in a position to lead his comrades to a better future. Yet in fact, he is unable to accomplish anything. His "agitation" on behalf of the fiancées fails to get them a seat at the dinner table, and in the end he himself leaves Puntila because he is aware that no adequate, entire life can be lived on that estate, whether his master is drunk or sober. Insight results in negation of the existing, rather than creation of the new.

Susan Buck-Morss points to three different responses taken by Brecht, Adorno and Lukács to theory and its relation to a praxis that changes the world. For Georg Lukács in *History and Class Consciousness* the solution was to be sought in a vanguard party that would lead the as yet unaware proletariat to revolution. In contrast, Brecht in many of his plays addressed the proletariat directly in their current state, imputing to them a consciousness that would have positive results. Adorno rejected both solutions, since he thought Lukács's position would limit the freedom of the critical theorist by subordinating his thought to the practical goals of a party that claimed already to be in possession of the truth, and he could not agree that the workers had arrived at a sufficient level of development to produce real social change (Buck-Morss 30).

Brecht, on the other hand, considered Adorno and most of the other members of the Frankfurt School "Tuis," who spent their lives theorizing but were incapable of action (Fetscher 16). In *Puntila* Matti, the early-risers, and the "red" Surkkala possess greater awareness than the masters, but since they are unable to institute change, they more closely resemble, at least at the level of content, critical theorists who reveal the falseness of the ruling ideology than they do model revolutionaries. Thus Hans Mayer observed that Brecht in his last years actually came closer to the position of the Frankfurt School, especially as represented in Adorno's *Negative Dialectics* (Tatlow 23). The servants in *Herr Puntila und sein Knecht Matti* represent a starting point and provide glimpses of a future in which contradictions have been overcome, but they fail to map out an explicit road to that goal.

The servants thus provide positive examples through their negative reaction to the status quo. The behavior of the masters works in a different way to make current injustices explicit. Puntila's treatment of the job-seekers has already been mentioned, as has his general tendency when sober to preserve and increase his capital. At the beginning of the banquet scene the choice of honored guests and the content of their discussion reveals the alliance of property, the church, and the judiciary. In addition, the lawyers' speeches satirically reveal this group's own hypocrisy when they claim that the current greed of farmers is ruining their careers, because the latter hesitate to bring suits to court when they realize that trials cost money. The portrayals are not simply black and white, however. Though Puntila and Matti are indeed representatives of their respective classes, the split in Puntila gives him a certain depth which lends him sympathy and makes him more interesting than the less sharply profiled Matti.

Speidel perceptively observes that this split is not between a "good" side and a "bad" side, however, since even when drunk Puntila remains a capitalist. His enjoyment when he is inebriated still presupposes the existence of masses of servants to provide him with sources of pleasure. Thus he does not exchange false values for true ones, but exploitation for material gain versus exploitation for pleasure (325–26). He is likeable when drunk, but alcohol can only be a false path to utopia: currently available forms of pleasure cannot be divorced from their social context. Almost without exception, Puntila continues to behave according to the interests of his class, even when drunk. His carousing with servants does not endanger his position, though it blinds him to the realities of life, since he does not even have to win their friendship in order to engage in this activity (327). His two sides reveal the basic contradiction that prevents the unity of humane behavior and the capitalist order, but the juxtaposition also provokes the imagination of what things would be like when this contradiction is overcome.

Another perversion of the route to a genuinely desirable goal is Puntila's attempt to construct a *Heimat*. In dismissing the left-leaning farmhand Surkkala, Puntila accuses him of being a rootless person for whom *Heimat* means nothing (1703). He still considers Matti his friend, however, and wishes to share with him the view from the summit of Mt. Hatelma so that the servant can see what a fine country they live in. The Finnish landscape is indeed spectacularly beautiful, but beneath one's gaze from the mountain-top lie not only the forests and lakes, but also human beings and their present forms of organizing class and production. That these are in fact less complete than in Puntila's dream is made clear when Surkkala, in a foreshadowing of Matti's final departure, leaves without shaking the hand offered by the landowner. Hurt by this rejection, Puntila attempts to overcome it with his climb to the summit, which is exaggeratedly grotesque and unreal. For instead of ascending the actual Mt. Hatelma, Puntila, with Matti's help, constructs an artificial one in his library by destroying grandfather clocks, chairs, and cabinets and piling the rubble onto the billiard table (1704–07). From the top of the heap Puntila waxes ecstatic about the beauties of the province of Tavastland, and his paeans carry a number of messages simultaneously. In a just world characterized by integrity individuals would be able to glory in the homeland's sights, sounds, and smells that Puntila is able to enjoy so sensuously in his imagination. His return to Nature is regressive, however, in that it ignores the products of human hands.

His praise of the unique beauty of Tavastland marks his vision as incomplete in its exclusion of other countries and regions. Since most of this play's spectators would be German, they would be in a better position to consider Puntila's comments more critically. Yet Puntila's concept of his *Heimat* closely parallels a fascist, blood-and-soil outlook that demands mass political allegiance to a mythically conceived, unchanging landscape that is equated with the current authoritarian power. Puntila demonstrates the affinity with such an outlook when he criticizes Surkkala for not sharing his master's appreciation of *Heimat* and observes how such opposition mars his vision of the landscape: "Das Schloß übergeh ich, da habens das Weibergefängnis draus gemacht für die Politischen, sollen sie sich nicht hineinmischen in die Politik" [I'll overlook the castle; they've made a women's prison out of it for the political prisoners; they shouldn't get themselves mixed up in politics] (1707). The aware Matti refrains from joining in the singing of the national anthem, and in response to Puntila's final question about his reaction to the skies, lakes, people and forests of Tavastland replies with the ambiguous "Das Herz geht mir auf, wenn ich Ihre Wälder seh, Herr Puntila!" [My heart leaps up when I see your forests, Herr Puntila!] (1707). One's concept of the land cannot be divorced from the current system of ownership.

The members of the master class thus portray both undesirable characteristics and positive ones that reveal themselves as false utopias. The contradictions in Puntila that make him more interesting and attractive than the more one-sided and serious Matti do not represent a victory for his class or an unchanging human nature, but point to a future in which all human beings could enjoy life in a just society instead of in the exploitation of others. At that utopian stage there would no longer be master and servant, but only "der Mensch" [human being], a theme that is introduced in the first scene, entitled "Puntila findet einen Menschen" [Puntila finds a human being]. When Matti, who has been waiting for two days in Puntila's Studebaker while his master drinks in the tavern, finally complains that Puntila cannot mistreat a human being so, Puntila resonds: "Was heißt: einen Menschen? Bist du ein Mensch? Vorhin hast du gesagt, du bist ein Chauffeur. Gelt, jetzt hab ich dich auf einem Widerspruch ertappt!" [What do you mean, human being? Are you a human being? A moment ago you said you were a chauffeur. Now I've caught you in a contradiction, haven't I!] (1614).

To a member of the ruling class the two terms do perhaps represent a contradiction, because under present conditions only the elite can enjoy the leisure and resources to develop themselves as fully as they might. But Puntila is desirous of overcoming the contradiction: after looking his servant over "like a strange animal," he admits that Matti's voice does have a human quality about it and he invites him to have a drink. As we have seen, however, alcohol represents an inadequate means of bringing about an improvement. The theme of "Mensch" and its opposite, expressed in terms of animal imagery, runs throughout the play.

In the Prologue, written in 1949 after a Communist state had been established in East Germany, the speaker, played by the cowmaid, addresses the audience as members of a society that has transcended the negative features of the one portrayed in the play. Even though such a transformation had not really occurred, the effect of the speech is to provide a certain distance and thus a different perspective on what is being performed. The cowmaid says that we will see a certain "prehistoric animal" which she identifies taxonomically as *Estatium possessor*, or landowner, characterized by its tendency to gorge itself and its lack of useful function (1611). This inverts Puntila's concept of animal and human by making the property owner the one who has not yet achieved full human status, and it therefore parallels the picture of the master in the Hegelian dialectic.

Puntila gets an intimation of the uselessness of his class when he realizes the attaché's unsuitability as a bridegroom and admits his mistake in attempting to engage his daughter to a "grasshopper" instead of to a human being (1682). This prompts several of the guests, including a cabinet minister, to stalk off in disbelief, for they cannot agree with the drunken Puntila that Matti is a "good human being," both an "able chauffeur and friend." But they are not the only ones who believe that a union between Eva and Matti can succeed: Matti himself is skeptical of Puntila's promise to give him a sawmill as a source of income, for he knows that his master follows his own financial interests when sober. Moreover, Matti is aware that such a marriage cannot exist in a vacuum: it is dependent on the ownership of property in order to support the type of life to which the bride is accustomed. Even if Puntila's offer were genuine, the result would be a personal triumph for Matti alone and would not be generalizable to other members of his class.

The other alternative, for Eva to share a life based on a meager income, is shown to be unworkable in the test to which Matti submits her. His test, which is meant to demonstrate Eva's unsuitability for proletarian life, unfortunately emphasizes instead the extent to which the male chauvinist tendencies of patriarchal societies are retained in the behavior of men of any class. Eva is expected to fetch him a sandwich, darn his socks, wash his clothes, and keep her mouth shut so as not to disturb him after a hard day at work. But what convinces her finally of the lack of compatibility is his "affectionate" pat on the posterior, which offends her sense of decorum 1686-92). Matti's expectations no doubt accurately reflect those of other males within his class, so it would be wrong to consider that state of proletarian consciousness a model for emulation, whether Brecht intended such or not. Matti, like, his master, has not yet fully attained the status of "Mensch."

Wolfgang Butzlaff analyzes the occurrence in different forms and contexts of the word "Mensch" throughout the play to reveal its "image of humanity and its ideological essence" (qtd. in Mews 60). He notes the difference between the substantive used alone and when modified by an adjective, which often turns the noun into its opposite. These contrasts force the spectator to consider the meaning of the term more closely by throwing it into relief (57–58).[9] In the first scene Puntila says that although it is low [*niedrig*] to talk of money, he and Matti are entitled to do so because they are "freie Menschen" [free human beings] (1618-19). He quickly reveals himself to be unfree, however, when the conversation reveals his dilemma concerning a dowry for his daughter. To come up with enough funds he will have to sell either his beloved forest or himself, that is, offer himself to the wealthy widowed aunt of the attaché. When Matti suggests the former alternative, Puntila recoils in shock and accuses his chauffeur of callously viewing a forest as a quantity of lumber rather than as a "grüne Menschen-freude" [green joy for human beings] (1619).

But the choice with which he is faced makes it clear that neither is he a "Mensch" nor the forest a "Menschenfreude," since both have become reified commodities that need to be sold in order to secure a favorable match for his daughter. When drunk in a later scene he renounces the attaché as a suitor and says that he is not going to sell his forest after all, claiming that his daughter has her dowry "between her thighs" [1642]. But this too is a reification of human sexuality that reduces it to its exchange value. Marriage, like everything else, is a set of property relationships. Puntila is not free, but defined in terms of a capitalist system from which he cannot escape, even when drunk.

Although humans as they exist in the reality of the play fail to live up to the concept *Mensch* that they extol, this concept nonetheless offers the most precise goal for the future. In their behavior, we are sometimes offered glimpses into a realm in which current divisions have been transcended. For example, class distinctions seem to have been overcome at the engagement dinner when the drunken Puntila mixes the seating order between master and servant and the parson's wife enjoys a long, sincere conversation with the cook about mushrooms (1683–93). In a utopia unmarred by class divisions, association would take place on the basis of actual predilection rather than social order, and although this conversation represents a situation that cannot be maintained within the play's present, it provides an intimation of how things could be. Puntila's vitality and his love of the land are positive qualities that are likely to be found in the future *Mensch*, albeit in a historically different situation unmarred by exploitation.

The lack of such overt displays of vitality in the more sober Matti should not be construed as implying that Matti's current character represents the ideal or that members of his class would be unable to partake fully of pleasure. He refuses to yield to Eva's request to row out to the island one sultry summer night not from prudishness, but because he honestly does not want to raise false expectations. The scene begins after all, with Matti's similar invitation to the housemaid Fina, together with an expression of his willingness to ignore Eva's call (1656). The time is simply not yet ripe for all of these individuals to be able to treat one another as human beings. In their actions and words, both Puntila and Matti reveal why neither is fully a *Mensch*, but they also indicate how and why that peculiar creature represents a desirable goal.

In admonishing directors not to rob the title character of any of his natural charm, Brecht said that his *Puntila* was anything but a tendentious play (GW 17: 1168). He did not want to convey the superficial message that landowners are bad and their servants are good, especially since he wanted to show that the problem lay within the system itself, rather than in the character of particular individuals. Also, he did not merely want to preach on behalf of the single issue of agrarian reform. His remark can refer not just to the explicit lack of a clear-cut political solution in the content, but it also implies the importance of the chosen form for the entire work. In fact, the dialectic is no less significant for the form than it is for the content.

Brecht purposefully selected the designation *Volksstück* for this drama, and the relation of this text to the tradition of the genre as well as the relationship that the parts of the structure have to one another can only be understood dialectically.[10] Such a form proves to be adequate for Brecht's content, as might be pointed out in comparing this drama with some more narrowly tendentious plays of the period: although the attacks on the anti-abortion laws found in Friedrich Wolf's *Cyankali* and Paul Crede's *Paragraph 218* resulted in the free distribution of contraceptives, Brecht thought that the Aristotelian form of these plays prevented them from questioning the structure of society as a whole (Dickson 245). A thorough-going questioning is what Brecht attempts in most of his works, and such an undertaking cannot be achieved through oversimplification or through spoon-feeding of content. He therefore looked to a dramatic genre that was enjoyed by the *Volk* and which addressed them in their language, yet he refused to employ the form as it was currently found in the majority of productions.

His attitude towards the *Volksstück*, which he felt was in need of significant modification, further shows that he did not at this point simply consider the proletariat in their present stage of consciousness as the ultimate repository of a solution. Hermand explains, for example, that "dem Volk aufs Maul schauen" [to listen closely to the speech of the people] is something different for Brecht than "dem Volk nach dem Munde reden" [to repeat what the people want to hear]. He wanted to address them in a language they understood without reinforcing them in their false conscious-ness, and he rejected what he considered pseudo-forms of the people, such as operettas, musicals, or boulevard comedies that were dished out to them in order to increase their ignorance ("Zwischen Tuismus" 22).

At first glance *Herr Puntila und sein Knecht Matti* seems to have the necessary requisites for the cruder type of popular comedy, such as sex, drinking, and cursing, which seem to arise from eternal basic instincts (Hermand, "Herr Puntila" 120–21). Yet a careful examination of how these elements are included reveals that they are historical and calls into question their use in literary tradition and their place in extra-textual social reality. This play also fulfills the functions of *prodesse et delectare*, which are customarily considered the hallmarks of the literary *Volksstück*, but not in any simple way. The lesson is not smuggled in past the background of a roaring good time, but is inextricably linked with its manner of presentation. Puntila's portrayal does not simply consist of his inclusion as content as a member of a certain class, but also of the formal relationships between this depiction and other elements in the drama.

Brecht adapted elements of both trivial and demanding *Volksstücke* for his *Herr Puntila und sein Knecht Matti*. Songs are an important feature that can be included principally for diversion or entertainment, though Brecht, like Raiumund, Nestroy, Anzengruber, and Horváth used them to comment on the action as well. The eight strophes of the "Puntilalied" follow the appropriate scenes and add to them. In the first, for example, we hear that the waiter at the hotel where Puntila had been drinking for three days refuses to bid him a polite adieu: he cannot admit that the world is amusing, since all that he notices of the incident is soreness in his feet from having to stand so long (1710).

At the end of the engagement scene the audience hears the voice of Surkkala singing a gruesome ballad about a countess who falls in love with a forester (1694). The latter is afraid because he knows that the relationship is doomed, and he apparently kills her with an ax before fleeing. The final stanza compares this situation to the love between a female fox and a rooster, whose feathers are left hanging in the bush at the end of the night. The antithesis, but also the similarity between the two couples in the song, expresses in another way the words of Matti's final verses, "Wer wen?" [Who whom?] (1708). In other words, who is the subject and upon whom does he or she act? The song also presents the alternative of a more terrifying conclusion to the scene between Matti and Eva, which ended in a harmless slap, and thereby further underscores the depth of present differences. By using songs to provoke a new awareness, Brecht places greater demands on the *Volksstück* than do more trivial authors, although we have seen how earlier authors of the literary *Volksstück* also used musical numbers to provide additional perspective. For example, Nestroy's use of songs to comment and to attack represent a break with previous tradition, in which musical numbers had been directly related to the content (Slobodkin, "Nestroy und die Tradition" 112).

Comedy provides a source of amusement, but like the songs, it can help the spectator gain insight as well. Often based on inversion, it calls the current order into question. Puntila's remark about being afflicted with occasional attacks of "total, senseless sobriety" evokes laughter, but also comments on a world that can only be endured when one is drunk (1615--16). In addition, comedy for its own sake is relevant to the principal theme of the play. As Puntila says, "Ein Mensch ohne Humor ist überhaupt kein Mensch" [A person without a sense of humor is not human at all] (1679).

In the form of critical wit, comic effects negate the importance with which the existing order takes itself, and its constant accompaniment of the action reminds of the *joie de vivre* that a better world should possess.

The same applies to the off-color passages, which are usually funny as well. There is no reason to conceive of a utopia as a perfectly functioning, prudish place. When Puntila wants to insure that Matti will make an acceptable partner for Eva he asks him, "Kannst du anständig f...?" [Can you f... decently?], and Matti answers, "Ich hör, daß ja" [I'm told so]. Puntila then responds, "Das is nix. Kannst du es unanständig? Das ist die Hauptsache" [That's nothing. Can you do it indecently? That's the main thing] (1684, ellipsis in the original).

These passages are not merely a symptom of Brecht's anarchic fun that has gotten away from his political side and rules it invalid. For example, the remark quoted above about Eva having a dowry betwen her thighs questions the current concept of the institution of marriage as a business arrangement. And in one important passage the suggestive lines occur in a play within the play staged by Matti, rather than representing his actual feelings. In order to make the attaché renounce his engagement, Matti and Eva intend to scandalize him by making him believe that the two are on intimate terms. In their rehearsals for this scene and in the actual staging, comedy arises not just from the suggestive references, but from the fact that the situation portrayed is not the real one. Before entering the sauna, Matti fetches a deck of cards, because he wonders how the two would otherwise kill the time as they wait for the sober Puntila and the attaché to overhear their supposed love-making. Before Eva rushes out at the finale, Matti carefully tousles her hair as she unbuttons the top button of her blouse. The sexual content is thus neither a wish-fulfillment of prurient audience desires nor a titillation disguised as gratification, but serves as a comment on itself and the play's larger themes.

When the greedy attaché fails to take the least bit of offense at what happened, Matti makes a remark that points out the crucial role of money relations: "Seine Schulden sind noch größer, als wir geglaubt haben" [His debts are even greater than we thought] (1647–56). Jürgen Hein, who regards the *Volksstück* as poised between the poles of didacticism and enjoyment, finds that the playfulness in Brecht's theater aids the satire by unmasking the illusions and contradictions of Puntila's society. Nestroy's wit had served a similar purpose, though Hein feels that the public can more easily accept Nestroy's comedy as pure entertainment, since he was more pessimistic about the possibility of change and thought one could at most laugh at the imperfections of the world. Hein thus believes that Brecht's comedy goes farther toward activating the spectator (*Spiel und Satire* 128–31; cf. Slobodkin, "Nestroy und die Tradition" 115–16).

Herr Puntila und sein Knecht Matti distances itself more from trivial farces than from the literary *Volksstücke* discussed thus far. Brecht wanted of course to address the popularity (in the sense of being of and for the people) of the former type of play without pandering to a fulfillment of current expectations. According to Jost Hermand, Brecht's play represented a deliberate counter-model to Zuckmayer's *Der fröhliche Weinberg* [The Merry Vineyard, 1925], which also featured the daughter of a wealthy landowner who prefers to marry a robust man of the people rather than an effete, upper-class youth who has been arranged for her. In a comedy full of both coarse humor and lyric hymns to nature, Zuckmayer's heroine experiences reconciliation with her father and a happy marriage to the man she desires. Unlike Brecht's play, which emphazises the social conflict, Zuckmayer's maintains the myth of "Volksgemeinschaft" [community of the ethnic group].[11] McGowan says that even though *Der fröhliche Weinberg* "satirizes excessive militarism and nationalism" and was banned by the Nazis, it remains within the tradition of the trivial *Volksstück* ("Comedy" 75). It thus represents a good example of the ineffectiveness of critical content when borne by an inadequate form. Like other authors considered in this study, however, Brecht wanted to introduce a critical perspective within a literarily demanding form, and this meant that he had to invert many traditionally accepted usages. In his formal intent Brecht is most similar to Horváth, although the means that he employs attempt to go further in analyzing the causes behind the current situation of the lower and lower-middle classes (cf. McGowan, "Comedy" 77; Hinck, "Mutter Courage" 176).

Brecht's transformation of traditional *Volksstück* elements is largely based on his principle of *Verfremdung*, the technique of distancing the spectators from the events onstage so that instead of accepting these events as illusions of reality, they are provoked into questioning and analyzing them on their own. If this technique is successful, spectators should be less likely to accept either the existing order as it is or the play as a pleasant substitution for it. The direct commentary found in the prologue and the stanzas of the "Puntilalied" serve this function, as do the linguistic inversions and contrasts that have been mentioned above, such as the varying uses of the term "Mensch," the irony with which the lyric parts are presented, and the double function of the humorous and bawdy passages.[12]

In addition, the play contains many elements from Brecht's own "epic theater." Most obvious perhaps is the epic structure, which is so pervasive that Knopf calls *Herr Puntila und sein Knecht Matti* the "most epic of Brecht's plays:" not only does the organization of elements display this quality, but actual narratives are also delivered on stage (225). One entire scene is entitled "Tales of Finland" and presents four seemingly unrelated stories narrated by Puntila's "brides." These stories comment on the master-servant relationship in the manner of Surkkala's song and provide additional perspectives that the main plot is unable to convey by itself. Matti himself inserts narrative passages into his conversations with Puntila and Eva, which at first glance, according to Knopf, seem to underscore the master's assertions while actually adding a plebeian alternative that expresses resistance (225). When explaining that he lost his previous job through no fault of his own because he, like the other servants, had seen ghosts, he says that fewer ghosts would have been spotted had the estate provided better meals for its servants. His assertion to his previous employer, Herr Pappmann, that he had indeed seen a ghost crawling out of the stable maid's window and into Herr Pappmann's on the very nights when Frau Pappmann was in the hospital to deliver a baby, indicates not superstitious ignorance but cunning awareness of the hypocritical behavior of the ruling classes (1617–18).

The way in which a narrative is evaluated changes in the course of the telling, when Puntila encourages Matti to recount Puntila's dressing down of a fat man at the labor market for mistreating a horse. Puntila loves hearing repetitions of his own witty insults and colorful descriptions of the angry man's scarlet countenance, until the sauna and the coffee begin taking their effect. At this point Matti also adds information, ignored by Puntila while drunk, which shows that the landowner has harmed his own interests, since the fat man owns the only stallion within eight hundred kilometers that would be able to breed with their mares. Matti continues to relish the recounting, as Puntila grows angrier. At the beginning, they had reinforced each other's narration, but at the close there are two different perspectives (1643–46). The form in which this epic element is presented underscores the impossibility of unity between their positions. In addition to the inserted narratives, the use of various plays within the play also contributes to the epic structure. Most of these are directed by Matti and have already been mentioned: his scene with Eva in the sauna and his directing her activities as the future wife of a working man are the chief examples.[13]

Dialectic constructions are found not only in the way the disparate parts relate to one another and to the whole but also in the use of opposing character configurations and split characters. In the master-servant opposition the chauffeur is a *raisonneur* like Nestroy's Peter Span who provides insight that the master class lacks. Yet his comments and his control over the plays within the play represent only a limited ability to direct outcomes, since he cannot improve his position in the end, but only reject Puntila's.[14]

An additional opposition results of course from the split of Puntila himself into two personalities. This split provides a negative model of the current state of affairs and also a utopian stimulus, even though his gregarious, drunken behavior fails to offer a model for emulation. In appealing to the active consciousness of the people, Brecht's plays do not present finished, total models, but rather "stimulation for intervention." Brecht's comments on dialectics underscore the notion that it is wrong to offer complete portraits represented by only a single motive (GW 20: 157, 169; see Tatlow 26). The character of Puntila is part of a double dialectic, in opposition both to his servant and to another side of himself. These configurations reinforce the other distancing effects in the play's epic structure in their provocation of critical thinking. The method of *Verfremdung* has been much discussed: what is important here is to see that it can be fruitfully employed in a critical play aimed at the *Volk*. Its formal combinations enable amusing theatrical techniques to serve as something more than diversion, and its stimulation of thought, as opposed to the presentation of a completed thought, shows that it takes its audience seriously and encourages their participation.

As in most of the other *Volksstücke* discussed thus far, the ending provides a great deal of insight into the play's relationship to present reality and a future utopia. Unlike Wuolijoki's *Sawdust Princess* or Zuckmayer's *Der fröhliche Weinberg*, both of which end with double weddings, *Herr Puntila und sein Knecht Matti* concludes with the chauffeur's rejection of both marriage to his master's daughter and reconciliation with the master himself. Such a non-traditional ending, along with the irreconcilable split within the character of Puntila, has prompted some critics to view the play as more tragedy than comedy. Yet failing to see its comic essence is to overlook its basic direction. McGowan finds that Brecht's view of comedy is central to his work because it contrasts the way things are with the way they should be. Unlike farces, which produce comedy for its own sake through the avoidance of critical thinking, Brecht's critical comedy "presupposes a Utopia," with which it compares the present ("Comedy" 63–67). If Puntila's inability to become good is absolutely impossible, then the play is indeed tragic, as Sokel says (127–28, 133). But as this critic also points out, tragedy in this instance does not result from an unchanging human nature but from circumstances, which can be altered (133–34). Thus Sokel's use of the term "tragic" is not the most accurate one.

Comedy is consistent with Brecht's notion of history, which he envisions as one day transcending the bourgeois state to produce a society in which individual tragedies are no longer possible. Dickson observes that Hegel and Marx are "intrinsically comic" because a dialectic system is "based on the notion of inherent contradiction," and the "revelation of a basic contradiction tends to have a comic effect" (250–52). The prologue introduces the play with a comment on the function of its comedy:

> Geehrtes Publikum, der Kampf ist hart
> Doch lichtet sich bereits die Gegenwart.
> Nur ist nicht überm Berg, wer noch nicht lacht
> Drum haben wir ein komisches Spiel gemacht. (1611)

> [Honored public, the struggle is hard
> Yet the present is already getting brighter.
> Still, whoever can't laugh yet isn't out of the woods
> That's why we've made a comic play.]

It is utopian and human, and provides an insight into both, even though it cannot fully deliver either as yet. All the while, it is critical. Rather than working against the numerous comic elements within the play, the open ending is actually consistent with the genre of comedy as Brecht perceived it. And instead of letting the traditional form of this genre impose a closed, happy ending that would also impose an unwanted content, he chose an open one. The actual comic conclusion is still to be constructed beyond the play's finish. In its use of an open ending Brecht's play resembles most of the *Volksstücke* that I have discussed thus far, while differing from the trivial representatives of the genre whose main purpose was entertainment. The function of such an ending is to negate the status quo by denying the possibility of an acceptable situation under present conditions and to continue dialectically the process toward the utopian by demonstrating that the next step must come from the spectators. Providing a happy ending on stage would tend to subvert that process.[15]

Laina is surprised at Matti's early-morning departure in the twelfth scene: indeed, there has been no additional conflict to provoke such a step, and this scene is not a necessary result of the plot as it has developed to this point, but is one possibility among many (Hinck, *Dramaturgie* 82). Because the play has a loose, epic structure, no single result can be viewed as inevitable. The plays within the play, the songs, and the narrative inserts suggested other outcomes, and the intimation of several possibilities further stimulates critical thinking, and perhaps action, on the part of the audience. Surkkala's song, for example, presents the very real possibility of a brutal finale, although this is not the one that the play itself happens to choose.

Matti represents a model for the audience insofar as he has achieved insight, but he does not offer a lesson in praxis. That "oil and water do not mix" may be true, but if this saying is taken as an eternal verity, it has tragic connotations for the plight of the servants of this world. The character Matti will probably get another job with a master who may not be any better nor any worse than Puntila, yet the play points beyond this to a better situation more applicable to other members of the lower classes. As Matti says,

> Den guten Herrn, den finden sie geschwind
> Wenn sie erst ihre eigenen Herren sind. (1709)
>
> [They'll find the good master quickly
> As soon as they are their own masters].

Unlike Raimund, who proclaimed that reconciliation within the limitations of the present world was possible and desirable, or Nestroy, who was aware of the shortcomings around him but skeptical of the possibility of changing them, Brecht had a more specific program in mind. But like the dramas of the two nineteenth-century authors, *Herr Puntila und sein Knecht Matti* was unable to chart a specific path to the goal or to present its truth as encapsulated content. Raimund attempted a harmonious conclusion but was unable to cover all the rifts; Nestroy's supposedly satisfactory finish was offered tongue in cheek; and Anzengruber's lessons provided concrete answers to specific problems.

The twentieth-century plays discussed thus far did not even try to offer comedy in the traditional form: Thoma's drama is a tragedy and Fleißer's can almost be considered one. Horváth's intermixing of the comic and the grotesque provides a humor that leaves a feeling of pervasive malaise rather than liberating laughter. Brecht employed comedy in *Herr Puntila und sein*

Knecht Matti, but he had to alter it in such basic ways that it too refrains from providing a harmonious conclusion or a precise description of a truth that must be followed. The truth is rather part of a process, of which this play makes up a dialectic component. When Matti bids farewell to the sleeping Puntila, he does not bear any grudges. The point of the play, after all, is not to demonstrate how evil this individual is but that the system must be changed.

> Gehab dich wohl, Herr Puntila,
> Der schlimmste bist du nicht, den ich getroffen
> Denn du bist fast ein Mensch, wenn du besoffen. (1708)

> [Farewell, Master Puntila,
> You're not the worst I've met
> For you're almost human when you're drunk.]

Almost human is as close as this play can get to a conclusion. Neither Puntila nor Matti can attain this stage, but it is the goal which they, and the audience, are seeking.

Since the *Volksstück* is very much a part of the society in which it is produced, and since Brecht wanted his plays to be effective in bringing about change, it is necessary to explore in more detail the relationship between *Herr Puntila und sein Knecht Matti* and society. This entails an examination of the play's means of representation and of its concept of realism. A dispute about the appropriateness of various types of artistic means was at the heart of a series of aesthetic debates on realism and modernism in which Georg Lukács, Ernst Bloch, Brecht, and others participated during the 1930s.[16] These discussions dealt not just with realism of the type that had been practiced in the nineteenth century, but also with variants such as naturalism and the newly emerging socialist realism, as well as with other more experimental formal methods such as expressionism. Mews believes in fact that Brecht's choice of the "Volksstück" genre for the play under discussion should be seen in terms of these theoretical literary debates (5).

In these discussions Ernst Bloch had criticized Lukács for taking a closed and integrated reality for granted: if actual reality is in fact a discontinuity, Bloch says, then a modernist movement such as expressionism that shows real fissures is more than the subjective, willful act of destruction that Lukács claims ("Discussing Expressionism" 22). In response Lukács appealed to Marx's statement that "the relations of every society form a whole" and says that discontinuities portrayed by modern artists are reproductions of immediate surface manifestations and fail to convey the "correct dialectical unity of appearance and essence" that is necessary in true realist art ("Realism in the Balance" 31). Both James Joyce and Thomas Mann portray contemporary disintegration, but in Lukács's opinion the method of the former is inadequate because of its subjective, associative montage of superficial details in the consciousness of the characters, whereas the latter "knows how thoughts and feelings grow out of the life of society and how experiences and emotions are parts of the total complex of reality. As a realist he assigns these parts to their rightful place within the total life context" (35–36). For Lukács even Naturalism was inadequate, since it shared with other modernist forms the perception of factual immediacy rather than the "mediated, not immediately perceptible network of relationships that go to make up society" (38).

Brecht agreed with Lukács that the bourgeoisie of the time was in a state of decline, but unlike Lukács he was not surprised that its major art form, the novel, should be in a similar predicament (GW 19:296–97; "Essays of Georg Lukács" 68–69). Brecht also agreed with Lukács's criticism of Naturalism's mimetic technique as mere superficial reflection, and he opposed the milieu theory of Naturalism because it continued the fatalism of the tragedy through a belief in the determinism of a reified environment (Nägele 119). Yet he disagreed with the narrow limits of the realism that Lukács prescribed: because it was based on only a few nineteenth-century novels and ignored the lyric and the drama, it was in effect formalist in nature (GW 19: 298–99; "Formalistic Character" 70). Here Brecht defends the soliloquy of Molly Bloom and states that Tolstoy's method is not the only permissible one: one has to decide on a case by case basis which methods art should employ, including newly developed contemporary skills (GW 19: 303–06; 73–75).

Brecht's 1938 essay "Volkstümlichkeit und Realismus" [Popularity and Realism] demonstrates his interest in developing an effective realism that is allowed to incorporate any elements that may prove adequate in its search for a popular audience. He thought it essential to join among the people as an ally against barbarism, and since one had to speak their language to succeed in this, he did not feel that one could easily dismiss demands for a realist style (GW 19: 323). Fascism was currently making inroads with the people with a concept of "Volkstümlichkeit" [ethnic character, popularity] that Brecht condemned as false because it presents the people in a superstitious way with unchanging characteristics. Brecht, however, says that "popular" means "intelligible to the broad masses, adopting and enriching their forms of expression/ assuming their standpoint, confirming and correcting it ... relating to traditions and developing them/ communicating to that portion of the people which strives for leadership the achievements of the section that at present rules the nation" (GW 19: 325, "Popularity and Realism" 81). This notion of the people and their role is crucial to his concept of realism. Since people are in the process of struggling to change reality, artists cannot simply "cling to 'tried' rules of narrative, venerable literary models, eternal aesthetic laws" (81). Like history itself, it is a process and cannot be expected to adhere to a fixed model.

For Brecht, realistic means

> discovering the causal complexes of society/ unmasking the prevailing view of things as the view of those who are in power/ writing from the standpoint of the class which offers the broadest solutions for the pressing difficulties in which human society is caught up/ emphasizing the element of development/ making possible the concrete, and making possible abstraction from it. (82)

Since realism is part of a process, one set of formal methods could not be prescribed as an unchanging model, and the artist cannot simply produce works that exactly correspond to that with which the audience was familiar. In his words, "Es gibt nicht nur das *Volkstümlichsein*, sondern auch das *Volkstümlichwerden*" [There is not only such a thing as *being popular*, there is also the process of *becoming popular*] (GW 19: 331; 85; italics in the original).

The uniform style demanded by the advocates of socialist realism was similarly rejected by Brecht, who thought that art should offer criticism instead of ideal images and a stress on feeling (Tatlow 25). And he no doubt wanted to avoid the dishonest oversimplification that such an approach would entail and to avoid equating reality with the content of the literary work or assuming that it could be conveyed through a simple, repeatable style. Brecht's notion of realism was more complex, both in theory and in practice. According to Klaus-Detleff Müller, it was not just a passive reflection, "but a constructive, model-building aesthetic production that makes insights into reality possible" (243). Such insights are less likely if the literary text provides a finished product that corresponds to an already defined world view or attempts to reproduce mere appearances, rather than a "production" that takes the contradictions of society into account and attempts to reveal them. Demonstrating the historical nature of class divisions was more important to Brecht than portraying the details of daily reality, even though his artistic means prompted some of his opponents to label him a "formalist."

Since Brecht was primarily an artist, rather than a theorist, it is necessary to investigate how *Herr Puntila und sein Knecht Matti* relates to these issues. Although it can hardly serve as an example of verisimilar realism, it does display realism in the Brechtian sense. Like many previous *Volksstücke* this play refers to the reality from which it emerges without trying to reproduce it photographically. But its referral is even more distant and abstracted, in order to avoid a confusion between signifier and signified or a hypostasis of the signified. As mentioned above, there were current ideological reasons for providing a Finnish setting, which is indicated with numerous concrete details, though never completely fleshed out. An example is the indirect portrayal of the Finnish landscape through Puntila's words during his imaginary mountain climb. Like many other elements in the drama, this description is placed within quotation marks because it is not an actual ascent. It therefore contrasts Puntila's description of the way things are with the way they should be. Because of the distancing, "Finland" also serves as a second-hand representation of Germany to the German-speaking audiences and places a further emphasis on the social relationships rather than the specifics of place: it demonstrates that "Nature" may in fact be "second-nature," or an historical concept rather than an unchanging given.

Another problem with which realism has to deal lies in the attempt to portray the workings of general conditions through specific examples, or in other words, from the simultaneous representation of type and individual in a single stage character. This issue, moreover, introduces a further source of contradiction into the play. As both Martini (*Lustspiele* 242) and Hinck (*Dramaturgie* 33) point out, Brecht did not attempt to get around this dilemma but incorporated the contradiction directly into the character of Puntila, who, rather than being a hypocrite trying to cover up his true nature with a false front, lives both his roles to the fullest. The lack of "realistic, psychological consistency" does not however detract from the realism of the work (cf. Martini *Lustspiele* 242), which tries to convey the existing social contradictions that it hopes will one day be overcome.

Brecht also rejected arguments that great art should present a social "totality" in which the apparent contradictions within the development of society are overcome, since he thought that treating characters as "'round-ed,' 'harmonic,' and integrated personalities" was merely a solution on paper (GW 19: 316). As he said in his "Anmerkungen zum Volksstück," "Der Gegensatz zwischen Kunst und Natur kann dann fruchtbar gemacht werden, wenn er im Kunstwerk zwar zur Einheit gebracht, aber nicht ausgetilgt wird" [The opposition between art and nature can only be made fruitful when it is unified in the work of art but not eliminated] (GW 17: 1165). His instruction that the early-risers be portrayed poetically rather than naturalistically (GW 17: 1168–69) indicates that he wants to affirm the humanity of these women rather than stress the misery of lower-class life, but the simultaneous inclusion of the "Pflaumenlied" ["Song of the Plums"], which runs like a counterpoint throughout the scene, points to the impossibility of the union desired by Puntila under current class conditions (1626–33).

Brecht's choice of popular comedy meant that he had to provide an amusing play with which mass audiences could identify and which they could enjoy but which would not run the danger of simply affirming the conditions of their present lives through a form with which they were completely and comfortably familiar. As the discussion has shown, both the form and content of *Herr Puntila und sein Knecht Matti* reach them in a way that relates to the reality of their situation, although the play introduces aesthetic changes into a popular genre in order to deter the people from retaining the current perception of reality as the one that must necessarily persist.[17]

From the beginning, the spectators have played an important role in the creation of plays for the *Volkstheater*. This genre could not have existed in a vacuum nor as an autonomous product apart from the intended audience. For Brecht the audience was important for practical reasons of theatrical production, but it also played an important role in his theories of history and society. As mentioned above, he thought that it was particularly necessary to speak the language of the people in order to ally oneself with them against barabarism (GW 19: 323). Part of his method involved working against a trend that had been underway in the theater for quite some time. Hinck writes that the reality of spectator and actor, which was still unified in Greek drama, has become increasingly separated in recent times, as evidenced by the tendency to make the stage into a "Guckkastenbühne" [peep-show stage] that exists for its own sake (*Dramaturgie* 122–23).

Such a concept of the theater coincides with increasing alienation in capitalist society, and it is significant that the *Volkstheater* usually did not participate in this trend to the same extent. This institution tended to view its audience and characters as part of the same group and the performance as an act of communication among them. In doing so, it stood in opposition to much of the theatrical practice of the establishment. As we have seen, however, this degree of unity disappeared in the *Volkstheater* during the twentieth century, and Fleißer and Horváth were unable to attract a public like Nestroy's for demographic as well as aesthetic reasons. Farcical *Volksstücke*, which did have more mass appeal, owed much of their success to an image of the *Volk* and to a dramatic form that comforted through familiarity but which provided no valid means of progressive expression. Since Brecht's epic theater had a concept of its own relation to its public that resembled that of the early *Volksstück*, it was fitting that he should choose a modified version of the genre for his *Herr Puntila und sein Knecht Matti*. Brecht viewed this "Volk" as partners in dialogue: his plays not only spoke for them but with them, and encouraged their further speaking on their own.

The history of the reception and effectiveness of *Herr Puntila und sein Knecht Matti* provides an ambiguous comment on its theoretical intent, however. The public greeted the 1948 premiere at Zürich's Schauspielhaus with applause, although critical response to this and subsequent performances in other places tended to find fault with its lack of dramatic action or with its perceived communist tendency. It nonetheless became one of Brecht's best-loved plays and the big hit of 1949, playing on large and small stages in at least fifteen different West German cities. In Mews's opinion, this drama helped make Brecht one of the most frequently performed playwrights in Germany during the next two decades (74, 79). It must be remembered of course that popularity in this context is not necessarily a sign of reaching the "Volk" or of being understood intended. Much depends on the manner of the individual production (cf. Mews 80). Performances in the West frequently treated it as a coarse comedy in which Brecht's love of creating racy, original character types got away from his ideological intentions (Hermand, "Herr Puntila" 119). Brecht himself criticized the film version as a "feine Salonkomödie" [elegant drawing-room comedy] (qtd. in Mews 78).

Although the state and municipal theaters in the Federal Republic are public institutions open to all, their audiences tend to be drawn from the educated middle and upper classes. These are certainly groups who should be provoked into learning a lesson in economic reality, but their acceptance of the play does not necessarily mean that they do. The Marxist literary historian Ernst Schumacher observes that "a late bourgeois public that does not confront an immediate threat to its rule can also delight in its own decline, if it is presented in the form of art" (qtd. in Mews 80). More recent productions in 1975 and 1983 have been marked by resignation, and a 1985

Berlin performance was judged a "half-hearted attempt."[18] This is perhaps indicative of the current lack of imaginative alternatives in a late-capitalist society in which corporatism has become entrenched. The "Volk" as it existed in Nestroy's day no longer existed after World War II, and of course Brecht did not pretend that it did. The lack of a thriving *Volkstheater* institution and the minority status of the lower classes in the composition of most audiences underscores the continuing split between "master" and "servant" in today's society more than it represents a weakness in Brecht's form of presentation, however.

The play also enjoyed a great amount of success in the German Democratic Republic, where Brecht chose it for the opening performance of the Berliner Ensemble on 12 November 1949. In that country the communist message was stressed, and the reasons for performing it in a state that had supposedly overcome the contradictions depicted in the play are given both in the play's prologue (see above p. 184) and in program notes to the East Berlin premiere. In these, Brecht quotes Marx's lines that the last phase of a world-historical form is comedy, "[d]amit die Menschheit heiter von ihrer Vergangenheit scheide" [so that humanity may cheerfully depart from its past] (MEW 1: 382). In this context such a perspective would also seem to stress the enjoyment of the performance over any relevance to contemporary reality.

Similarly, equating its "message" with the ideology of the existing state would suppress criticism. To underscore this, this performance employed masks so that the evil side of Puntila would not get lost (Mews 76). But this staging technique uses an extra-textual means (albeit one allowed by Brecht) in an attempt to subvert the direction of the play's text, and a critical reading would lead to the question of whether or not a revolution from above had in fact replaced capitalist masters with masters of another sort. If true humanity has not yet asserted itself, the charge of "mangelnde Aktualität" [insufficient relevance] from GDR critics would not be accurate either. Whatever Brecht's intentions may have been, the play has experienced varied reception and effectiveness in both East and West, and many of the performances seem to ignore crucial aspects of the text. It is therefore difficult to determine from the history of actual performances alone whether or not it is possible for Brecht's form to provide an effective means of presenting a socially critical play.

The changes that Brecht brought to the genre of the *Volksstück* also provided one response to the controversy within left aesthetics between "'high' and 'low' genres — the one subjectively progressive and objectively elitist, the other objectively popular and subjectively regressive" (Taylor 66). In attempting to retain the appeal of a popular genre while adding a progressive dimension, Brecht seems to be attempting two things at the same time: to make it "realistic," so that it will be understood by the people, and to experiment with changes so that the play will not simply provide uncritical entertainment that confirms existing reality. As the discussion thus far has indicated, this *Volksstück* does indeed do both, but it is necessary to determine whether or not this compromise was successful, especially in light of Adorno's criticisms of Brecht in "Engagement" ["Commitment"]. As I pointed out in my Introduction (p. 25), Adorno said that all art originates in empirical reality, but art which has the true relation to reality is autonomous in its formal negation of it. Using Kafka and Beckett as examples he says, "Als Demontagen des Scheins sprengen sie die Kunst von innen her, welche das proklamierte Engagement von außen, und darum nur zum Schein, unterjocht" [By dismantling appearance, they explode from within the art which committed proclamation subjugates from without, and hence only in appearance. The inescapability of their work compels the change of attitude which committed works merely demand] ("Engagement" 129; "Commitment" 191).

Because *Herr Puntila und sein Knecht Matti* does not possess the same "inescapability" of the texts of Kafka and Beckett, the play does not have the same force of compulsion, and it is therefore easier both for theaters to stage it as entertainment and for audiences to overlook any overt political message. But a close examination revealed that the text itself does not support such responses. The "message" is not delivered through the content alone, and the form does not simply provide conformity to the horizon of expectations of an unsophisticated audience. The dialectics of form and content and of this play to its predecessors in the genre insure that the play conveys something deeper and more forward-looking than a sermon to the converted. Adorno is correct in condemning Brecht for such a stance in his didactic plays *Die Mutter* [The Mother] and *Die Maßnahme* [*The Measures Taken*]. Is he justified, however, in criticizing the playwright for dramatic abstractions that attempt to reveal the essence of society but instead convert it to theatrical appearance? Concerning Brecht, Adorno says: "Aber der ästhetische Reduktionsprozess, den er den politischen Wahrheit zuliebe anstellt, fährt dieser in die Parole" [the process of aesthetic reduction that he pursues for the sake of political truth gets in his way] ("Engagement" 117, "Commitment" 183).

In fact, we observed above that the feudal relationship depicted in the play is an oversimplification and even an anachronism and can only be understood metaphorically as it applies to present reality. As Adorno charges, Brecht fails here to portray all the mediations and complexities of the inner nature of capitalism. As in *Die heilige Johanna der Schlachthöfe* [*St. Joan of the Stockyards*], he refrains from dealing directly with "the appropriation of surplus-value in the sphere of production" and presents instead "episodes from the sphere of circulation" which miss the essence of capitalism, since they are only "epiphenomena incapable of provoking any great crisis" ("Engagement" 118–19; "Commitment" 183). Although the workings of capitalism may not be revealed, the effects of maintaining a system of capitalist relationships are: neither Puntila nor his servant Matti can get around the obstacles presented by the private ownership of capital.

The play's political analysis is only partial, but it is not false, as Adorno says of the "Lehrstücke" [didactic plays], which are in addition undialectic (120; 185).[19] And in *Herr Puntila und sein Knecht Matti* Brecht avoids the flaw that Adorno criticizes in *Arturo Ui*, which against its will renders fascism harmless by making its chief representative an object of ridicule (119; 184). In fact, Puntila is considered by many observers to be so sympathetic a figure that he overrides the play's criticism. But if one notes the inner dialectic of this character, as well as of the play, one can see that sympathy does not mean agreement with his views or his current status. Making him either a laughable buffoon or a personal villain, however, would have been a blatant way of telling the spectators what they should believe and opened this play to similar criticism.

Hermand points out the dialectical nature of Brecht's concept of knowledge with which he countered the "knowledge is power" position of the intellectual "Tuis:" for him the ideal was a learning-teacher and a teaching-learner. Knowledge thus did not proceed only from the party to the people but went the other way as well ("Zwischen Tuismus" 15). To reach the utopian one has to start with present conditions, though to do so by no means implies that one should accept them as they are. Brecht's grasping of reality and his addressing the people did not mean that he considered the latter a group that had reached the necessary level of achievement or consciousness, but neither did it mean that he considered himself in a superior position that warranted dictating a truth to them.

The relationship to reality underlies the main difference between Brecht's dramas and Adorno's theories. In his arguments Adorno emphasizes formal negation, but an important part of the dialectic of *Herr Puntila und sein*

Knecht Matti is its utopian impulse that exists beside the negative: Puntila is a negative figure but contains an intimation of the utopian in his momentary "almost human" quality. The play as a whole negates in its refusal to embrace the affirmative aspects of the genre, but it is utopian in its starting with the *Volk* in their current state in order to point to a radically different future.

Others have noted the utopian aspect in Brecht without analyzing it in detail through the course of one play. Speidel, for example, notes that there are many brief instances of a "genuine trans-social experience" that contain an element of promise (332). Dickson attempts in his study to "demonstrate Brecht's belief in the perfectibility of human society, of which the classless Utopia is an attainable, though by no means inevitable goal" (v), and Hinck finds that Brecht's *Verfremdung*, which is basically comical, is based on Bloch's *Prinzip Hoffnung*: Brecht, he claims, replaces the Aristotelian fear and pity with spite and hope (*Dramaturgie* 11). By combining the utopian with the negative and not presenting finished conclusions that portray the goal as inevitable, Brecht avoids the danger of accepting or ameliorating the status quo. His answer, as well as his entertainment, is part of a dialectic.[20]

Adorno, too, did not think aesthetic works should simply deliver a doctrine, but the degree of negativity that he advocated could result in a disengagement from reality that might allow it to continue as it is. Capitalist society has always been able to appropriate subversive works in its need to supply novelty and diversion. This applies both to didactic works and to negative texts that proclaim no doctrine in their content. Brecht's attempted solution represents a balance among numerous considerations and can only be successful if the dialectic is properly understood. It is neither an ideological sermon nor an evening's escape. Its lesson is not contained in the words or plan of a political doctrine that already claims to know the entire truth, but is part of a process that is found in the interaction between form and content, inherited forms and aesthetic experiment, master and servant, present and future, playwright and audience, and the negative and the utopian. It is a process that is directed to the goal of attaining full human status.

Chapter IX

From the Margins toward the Mainstream: *Stallerhof* and *Nicht Fisch nicht Fleisch* by Franz Xaver Kroetz

> Das Überraschende hat mich auch überrascht: in einem Jahrzehnt, in dem das Theater hauptsächlich von dem Autoren-Gespann Jammer und Hohn beliefert zu werden scheint, ist einer fast ununterbrochen liebreich und konkret. Er hat so wenig Aussicht und Änderung anzubieten wie sonst einer.
> —Martin Walser, "Bericht einer Aufführung" 224–25[1]

In the late 1960s and early 1970s a number of young playwrights such as Martin Sperr, Rainer Werner Faßbinder, Wolfgang Bauer, Peter Turrini, Harald Sommer, Wolfgang Deichsel and Franz Xaver Kroetz began writing social-critical plays with contemporary regional settings that employed dialect or language strongly colored by the speech patterns of dialect. By their own use of the genre designation *Volksstück* or their professed obligation to the dramaturgy of the newly revived Ödön von Horváth and Marieluise Fleißer, they indicated a connection between their work and the renewal of the *Volksstück* during the Weimar Republic.[2]

In 1971, the year of the premieres of his controversial one-act plays *Hartnäckig* [Stubborn] and *Heimarbeit* [Home Work], Kroetz wrote essays on these two predecessors. He praised Fleißer for her understanding of "the ones who matter" and for powerful scenic techniques that radically reduced dialogue to the essentials and provided a comprehensive model ("Liegt die Dummheit"). He admired Horváth for conveying reality through the characters' loss of the ability to speak ("Horváth"). Although Kroetz's contradictory theoretical statements in various interviews and essays indicate that his critical abilities are less advanced than his dramatic talents,[3] the qualities praised in Fleißer and Horváth are indeed ones that he himself employed in the plays that first attracted the attention of the critics. According to Fleißer, Kroetz was the "dearest of [her dramatic] sons," the one who dug the deepest into her work and found the essential (86).

Even though Kroetz more obviously belongs in the critical tradition of Fleißer and Horváth than in the line of the more widespread, entertaining variety of *Volksstück*, the latter tradition also played a role in his development. For two years he was a member of the cast of the Ludwig-Thoma-

Bühne in Rottach-Egern, where he even wrote a *Bauernschwank* [rural farce] entitled *Hilfe, ich werde geheiratet!* [Help, I'm Being Married!], complete with situation comedy and stereotyped roles.[4] In an interview he went so far as to say, "Everything that I have learned about theater, I learned from the Bavarian *Volkstheater*" (qtd. in Blevins 239). This is no doubt an exaggeration, yet the experience gave him the opportunity to observe at close range a certain type of people and their dramaturgy, a public about whom and for whom he wished to write (240–41). In an interview with Wilfried Scheller he stated that a *Heimatdichter* should write "plays appropriate and close to the *Volk*…. In any case he would have to have a critical outlook with regard to contemporary problems" (qtd. in Blevins 29). But providing critical insight made his plays unacceptable to the more farcical repertoire of the *Bauerntheater*, and his initial success was among a quite different sort of public.

As Hein correctly observes, German comedy after World War II had a difficult time establishing itself as a critical medium, since it had been misused as "survival comedy" during the Third Reich: a renewal of the comic *Volksstück* was thus all but impossible (5). An additional problem was the increasing tendency to separate art from society. In order to oppose this trend as found in the entertainment business, many young authors in the 1960s and 1970s thought of their plays as "Anti-Theater" (6), a type of drama to which Kroetz's early plays are closely related. Although the old *Volkstheater* had also represented an "other" theater, Kroetz's dramas set themselves apart from those of establishment theaters in a different way.

The purpose of this study, however, is not to emphasize superficial genealogical connections: even when influences exist, new *Volksstücke* cannot be written according to an inherited formula. As Kroetz himself points out, the world of the *Kleinbürger* portrayed by Horváth no longer exists and the manner of speaking employed by Horváth's figures was not available to his own characters ("Horváth" 93). New content, but also new forms, had to be employed. To force a playwright into the mold of the critical *Volksstück* as it had been understood to that point, as Evaluise Panzer accuses critics of doing to the newly discovered Kroetz (10–11), or to evaluate him in terms of the recently formulated concept "Horváth" (Schmid 246), is to run the danger of overlooking important aspects unique to his dramatic texts.

Like the other authors who have been discussed thus far, Kroetz both uses the tradition as one of his points of departure and works against it to create a new drama that is adequate to the new social and literary situation.

Once again, the concept *Volksstück* takes on an expanded meaning. In Kroetz's case the beginnings were quite controversial and the plays so pervaded by the negative that hope seems all but ruled out. This type of drama, which went further than the works of either Horváth or Fleißer in refusing to provide any kind of escape, has failed to find a large audience among the type of *Volk* that it portrayed. The critical acclaim, however, though not consistent (cf. E. Panzer), has been mostly favorable, and the reception at both little theaters and major stages has made Kroetz, in the words of *Theater heute*, "the most successful German author since Brecht" ("Ich habe immer nur" 72). Kroetz's career has shown continual development and change. Choosing a single play for analysis would be unrepresentative, and attempting a general summary would not provide sufficient detail. Thus this study will focus on *Stallerhof* (*Farmyard*, 1972), from his early period, and the more recent *Nicht Fisch nicht Fleisch* (Neither Fish nor Fowl, 1981).[5]

Stallerhof

The reason that the première of *Hartnäckig* and *Heimarbeit* was greeted with stinkbombs and demonstrations can be attributed to reactions to advance reports of the plays' content, since the protesters had not yet had a chance to see exactly how subjects such as masturbation and attempted abortion were incorporated into the drama.[6] Typical of most of the plays that Kroetz wrote between 1968 and 1972 was *Stallerhof*, whose premiere in Hamburg solidified his breakthrough as an author for the German stage (FXK 322).[7] Like the controversial one-act plays, it deals on-stage with traditionally taboo subjects such as masturbation, defecation, sexual intercourse, and preparations for an abortion. Violence, if not portrayed directly, lurks just beneath the surface.

The play's main characters are drawn from what critics originally referred to as the "Randgruppen," or marginal groups of society: a luckless farmhand nearing the age of retirement and the thirteen-year-old, semi-retarded daughter of the farmer Staller and his wife. Kroetz himself used the term "Randgruppen" and claimed that he wrote about such people because they were the ones he knew best ("Lust" 599–600). Volker Panzer points out that the term "marginal groups" is not to be understood here to mean groups with a set of values opposed to society's, since these characters maintain society's values and try desperately to fit in (52). They are, however, at the bottom of the social ladder, and their extreme incapacity for self-expression or meaningful achievement makes it difficult for many spectators to consider them a representative cross-section.

Kroetz had praised the "Ausstellungscharakter" [display character] of Fleißer's work and attempted to incorporate that principle himself in *Stallerhof*: any social criticism that the play contains is to be gathered from the presentation of inadequate conditions rather than from explicit commentary. *Stallerhof* confronts us with the picture of Beppi, who stumbles through the basics of reading and continues to play with dolls when most of her contemporaries are entering trade school. Her parents regard her condition with shame (13), and her mother responds with slaps to Beppi's mistakes in reading aloud (10). Sepp, the aging farmhand, looks forward to the retirement that he believes will free him from the pressures and restrictions put on him by his employers in various short-term jobs. He is able to attribute his unfortunate circumstances only to bad luck (12). At a rural carnival to which he has taken her on an outing, Sepp deflowers Beppi (16), and the sexual relationship is continued until her pregnancy is discovered. Sepp is driven away by the furious Staller, who also poisons Sepp's dog, and the parents begin preparing to abort their daughter's child, though the mother is unable to carry this out. In the final scene, Beppi's labor pains begin (32).

The utter hopelessness of these characters and the thematics with which their situation is portrayed gives a picture quite different from the pleasant and, in the end, orderly world of the trivial *Volksstück*. And even though an earlier serious author such as Raimund could not suppress the negative in his plays, he was nonetheless able to tack on a moral that urged the characters to be satisfied with their lot. In Kroetz's play even the semblance of such a stance is next to impossible.

The content, then, presents a quite negative picture: people who are intellectually, verbally, economically, emotionally, and sexually crippled, and who are able to do very little about it. In presenting such a view Kroetz breaks the illusion that the Federal Republic of Germany is an enlightened society that provides for all its members (Buddecke and Fuhrmann 151). Like the other young *Volksstück* authors, Kroetz felt that it was insincere for a writer to portray proletarian figures as perceptive, articulate, and class-conscious as long as the social system holds the lower classes in a state of ignorance and passivity (Cocalis, "Politics" 295). The effect is shocking, and the choice of such subject matter seems to offer little opening for the utopian or the affirmative. Yet the latter is made possible in two ways, and its presence can in fact endanger the proper reception of the plays, if the author's intent is to provide social criticism and to instigate a learning process on the part of the spectator.

Although Kroetz can hardly be considered a representative of the culture industry, the theater business is by no means free of the latter's needs to constantly offer the appearance of something new while actually promoting the continuation of things as they are. Part of Kroetz's success can be attributed to his brand of drama, which provided something quite different in the early 1970s, when the theaters were filled with absurdist and documentary plays (V. Panzer 49–50). His shocking realism could thus offer an aesthetic experience that in itself satisfied audience demands for novelty and, in precluding the necessity for commitment to change outside the theater, might affirm the status quo. Kroetz criticized the on-stage violence in Edward Bond's *Lear* for this very reason: it satisfies the public's *Schaulust* [craving to see spectacles] and reinforces a fatalistic view of history, implying that things cannot be changed ("Lust" 603–04). He himself does not include taboo subjects in order to provide such gratification: they are necessary evidence of the multiple injuries and the pent-up aggression that the characters undergo (Carl, *Kroetz* 52). Yet he probably cannot compeletely prevent an audience reaction that ignores the need for change; such a reaction would partly depend on viewing the characters as marginal figures that had little in common with spectators, as creatures that satisfied their voyeuristic urges in a sort of Bavarian freak show.

A second opening, which could lead to either the affirmative or the utopian, is offered by Kroetz's tendency to sympathize with his characters rather than to denounce them. He had praised Horváth for the love and understanding that he showed for his figures ("Horváth") and Fleißer for dealing with (in Horváth's words) the "people that matter" ("Liegt die Dummheit" 526). Kroetz also thinks such people matter and claims that one of the impulses behind his writing came from a Christian-humanitarian concern for showing what society does to the poorest of the poor ("Schwie-rigkeiten" 605). Indeed, the relationship between Sepp and Beppi cannot be dismissed as his abuse of her: in his own awkward way he shows concern, apologizing for possibly having hurt her (19; 23) and buying her presents, which he offers in an impersonal way: "Da ist ein Schoklad kauft worden für deiner" [Here's some chocolate that was bought for you] (27).

His inarticulateness and inexperience make him incapable of engaging in an adequate and fulfilling relationship, yet these pitiful attempts with Beppi represent the beginning of something that is more positive than either of them has known before. For the first time Sepp does not have the feeling of being the underdog, though this does not mean that he can become spontaneously communicative after a long, disadvantaged life. It is also significant that he does not simply copy exploitative behavior, which characterized the attempts of many of Fleißer's and Horváth's figures to get ahead. Beppi too grows as a mother in the play's sequel *Geisterbahn* and develops a degree of self-consciousness (Carl, *Kroetz* 65).

This slight progress on both characters' parts seems to indicate that the isolation of outsiders could be avoided if people who suffer congenital affliction or early mistreatment do not receive an intensification of these through repeated injuries (67). Even though failure is inevitable,[8] the hint of something better is included. This could possibly be construed as affirmative of the status quo, if audiences perceive that betterment can take place on an individual level: Volker Panzer, for example, accuses critics at the premiere of praising only the tenderness and charm with which the characters were portrayed and of overlooking the social criticism (52-53). But compassion and commitment, which have provided one of the most frequently used contexts for an analysis of Kroetz's plays, are probably both necessary elements in a social-critical *Volksstück.*[9]

If in addition to sympathizing with the characters, audiences recognize the degree to which society is responsible for keeping the Sepps and Beppis of the world in a condition of dependency, the direction is set towards a utopia where this is no longer the case. It is not Beppi's retardedness that makes her an outsider, but the environment in which she has to put up with this affliction (Carl, *Kroetz* 60). By taking a stand for the class that has not achieved full emancipation and by indicating that its members are capable of development, Kroetz refrains from a purely fatalistic negativism whose paralysis leads to affirmation by default.

The desire to change conditions could come not just from the intellectual awareness of social and economic obstacles to emancipation, but also from a sympathy that results from the awareness that these characters actually represent a cross-section, rather than marginal cases. Though they are extreme manifestations, they embody incapacities possessed to a certain extent by all members of society. According to Ernst Wendt, the shock comes not from seeing an old man seduce a retarded minor, but from the realization that this is neither a fiction of the theater nor the result of conditions unique to marginal groups ("Bürgerseelen" 99). The shocking, then, could "challenge the audience's wish to escape into an intact, ordered, and allegedly natural world" and force it to confront a situation that it would prefer to ignore (Cocalis, "Politics" 298). If this effect is achieved, the force of the negative might then in fact serve as an initial impetus toward genuine change. It would then promote the utopian, instead of providing either a de-sublimation through voyeurism or a sympathetic affirmation.

Much of the criticism of the early Kroetz stems from the inability of his X first plays to make the social connection explicit, since the plays merely offer scenic depictions without providing external commentary.[10] How in fact are such connections conveyed? And what is the difference between a Kroetz play and a newspaper account of the same event? Kroetz claims that he got his material from the newspaper ("Dramatiker Umfrage"), and the director Ulrich Heising quotes the entire brief account that followed the tabloid headline "60jähriger Knecht schwängert minderjährige Geisteskranke," [60 year-old farmhand gets retarded minor pregnant], upon which *Stallerhof* was based (FXK 201–02). To the director, as well as the author, it was important to get behind the headlines and present the context of the event without denouncing the characters or portraying them as exotic objects for voyeurs.

The newspaper contents itself with the latter purpose: by restricting its portrayal to the sensationalistic, it marginalizes the participants and distances them from the readers, thus gratifying the latter's desire to participate vicariously in the "demented" behavior of the other while simultaneously receiving the opportunity to denounce him. Certain aspects of the tabloid's factual style appear to present the appearance of objectivity, though its inclusion of terms such as "sex-crazed," "blackmail tactics," and "crime" facilitate the readers' interpretation of the event as the act of an individual transgressor. The newspaper thus diverts the condemnation away from social conditions since it is interested in preserving the status quo. To determine why there were demonstrators outside the theater and not outside the offices of the *Bild-Zeitung*, it is necessary to look more closely at Kroetz's type of realism and the form of the play, since its content, which can to a certain extent be found elsewhere, is not sufficient to stand as a negation of society or the expression of a utopian impulse.

Again, Kroetz's own early explanations of the realism that he practiced are somewhat naive and fail to provide a throrough analysis: he seems to think that he mirrors the people whom he knows best and who make up a large portion of the population.[11] Like the authors of late nineteenth-century Naturalism, the creators of the new critical *Volksstück* concentrated on a cross-section, emphasizing the milieu and using colloquial language that was tinged with dialect. Lukács's criticism of Naturalism could also apply here: merely describing, Naturalism remained on the surface and ignored the dialectics of essence and appearance (see p. 195 above). The "new realism" of the recent critical *Volksstück* describes the effects without explaining the causes, though in implying the social causes of alienation it points beyond itself. Unlike the realism advocated by Brecht, however, it usually fails to provide a positive moment of development (cf. Wapnewski, qtd. in Schregel 12–13).

In the essay "Form ist der Teller, von dem man ißt" [Form is the plate from which one eats], which was included in the program to the premiere of *Stallerhof*, Kroetz claimed that the difference between the two forms of writing was that Naturalism discovered the "Volk": i.e., it recognized the lower classes as an adequate subject for drama, whereas Realism discovered society by analyzing the social whole behind the individual surface effects (91). This essay points to the crucial feature that must now be explored further in this connection, though Kroetz's discussion here is not without contradictions: namely, the relation between form and content.

Kroetz criticizes authors who stress the priority of form, which, according to the essay's title, merely holds the food. Though he writes that it has usually been formal innovations that have shocked the public and cites Beckett's *Endgame* for its effectiveness in actually putting people into garbage cans, he warns that it is wrong to make form an end in itself; this only destroys the balance between the "how" and the "what." When form has an adequate relation to content and keeps it in sight, then art can become "a possible, better reality, i.e.; social criticism becomes at its best the vision of a better society" (89–90). Yet in the concluding sentences, Kroetz seems to grant priority to content, saying that at present, what one eats (the information carried in the work of art) is more important (91–92).

Adorno points to the danger of realist aesthetics, which can actually work in opposition to what Kroetz ostensibly wishes to achieve: "The reactionary nature of any any realist aesthetic today is inseparable from this commodity character. Tending to reinforce, affirmatively, the phenomenal surface of society, realism dismisses any attempt to penetrate that surface as a romantic endeavor" ("Transparencies" 202–03). Evalouise Panzer in fact says that many critics, in their fascination for the "photographic realism" of the early plays, were relieved that Kroetz only wanted to show things as they were and not comment on them (16).

Stallerhof is, of course, not simply the transposing of "real content" to a location where the audience may view it: it works with very precise formal means that exist in a dialectical relationship to the content. Kroetz's own plays contradict the questionable form-content and affirmation-information dichotomies that he sets up in his theoretical writings (Kurzenberger, "Negativ-Dramatik" 18–19). Emphasizing that the content is most striking to many critics and spectators ignores the content's mediation through form. As with Horváth and Fleißer, the question of form becomes apparent in the consideration of the play as a *Volksstück*, the genre with which it is associated.[12] The contrast between traditional expectations concerning this genre and what *Stallerhof* provides has a negating effect similar to that found in certain of Kroetz's predecessors. The form negates by destroying the illusion of the intact, orderly world of the *Volksstück*, even as it dialectically turns the genre designation into a utopian impetus to overcome the present state of affairs.

In the plays of Nestroy, language itself was more important than the incorporation of realistic details from the social milieu as material. He created his characters through the dialogue that they spoke. Language similarly determines and reveals the characters of Kroetz, though instead of displaying control through creative wit, they show themselves to be socially damaged. Portraying limitations through the treatment of language also marks the strongest similarity between Kroetz's plays and those of Thoma, Fleißer, and Horváth. It is thus not surprising that language is the feature that has attracted the most attention from scholars and critics: my investigation will demonstrate how these observations apply to Kroetz's language as an expression of negation or utopia.

The point of Hoffmeister's study, which is based on linguistic criteria, is to show that "the socio-political and linguistic, analytical structures converge: the presentation of a petit-bourgeois world and the criticism of a petit-bourgeois world are revealed through one and the same linguistic act" (*Theater*, "Foreword" n.p.). Benjamin Henrichs, in a review following the premiere of the two one-act plays, described Kroetz's dialogues "as the sparsest, most tight-lipped that have ever been written in German drama (qtd. in FXK 75).[13] They are marked by short sentences and sentence fragments in Bavarian dialect; responses that often fail to refer directly to the previous remark; explanations or affirmations that are less than convincing in fulfilling their intended functions; the quotation of ready-made sentiments, such as proverbs that the characters have heard elsewhere and cite as authorities; and frequent pauses that set in when language is no longer able to deal adequately with a subject or problem.

Most of these characteristics are illustrated in the beginning of the dialogue in Act I, Scene 4:

SEPP	Kein Glück hab ich ebn ghabt im Lebn, das is es. Wenn einer kein Glück hat, kann er nix machn.

Pause

STALLER	Jeder is seines Glückes Schmied, heißt es.
SEPP	Net jeder.
STALLER	Ausredn.
STALLERIN	Wenn er es sagt, wirds scho sein. (12)

[SEPP	I ain't had no luck in life, that's what it is. If you ain't had no luck, you can't do nothin.

Pause

STALLER	Every man is master of his fate. That's what they say.
SEPP	Not everybody.
STALLER	Excuses.
STALLERIN	If he says it, it must be so.]

This is a language that no longer functions, either in conveying meaning or establishing relationships. When speech fails, violence is the only recourse for the elimination of a problem, whether it is the actual poisioning of the dog or merely the thought of doing away with Beppi.[14] The characters' *Sprachlosigkeit* does not result from their powerlessness to form sentences but from the inability of their language to express their emotions or to allow them to come to terms with what they have not comprehended (Carl, *Kroetz* 38–39). As Kroetz observed of Horváth's plays, the catastrophe occurs "between what the characters say and what they mean, between that which they have to mean, because it is what they have been trained for, and that which they are not in a position to mean, although they want to mean it" ("Horváth" 91). Their situation is thus presented in extremely negative terms, not with an expressive language that comments on and describes their plight, but through the form of a crippled, non-communicative language that reveals by what it fails to do.

To those unfamiliar with the speech of the rural underclasses, the language found in Kroetz's plays seems extremely mimetic. One of the functions of the dialect is indeeed naturalistic, an attempt to reproduce the speech of a distinct group of people. It is both a regional speech, and also a sociolect, the language of a particular social level.[15] Yet naturalistic portrayals can work against critical intent through an affirmation of the existing. Bavarian audiences might find a positive confirmation in the representation of their speech, despite the other unappealing features in the language and content of the play that work against such a reception. There is also a greater danger that non-Bavarians would view the characters as

exotics because of their dialect and thus as more likely targets of denunciation. This is a possible reason for the stage direction indicating that in other
parts of Germany the language should be considered artificial (9). The use
of dialect is thus ambivalent because of its ability to provoke different
effects.

Kroetz's own comments (and directions in different plays) are contradictory,[16] and it must be concluded that dialect in the play's text has at least
two functions. The social-critical *Volksstück* must situate its subjects in their
actual social and historical setting, and dialect provides this referential
function. As in all the *Volksstücke* considered to this point, it cannot help
but serve as a reminder that society contains outsiders. The speech of these
characters should not convey too general a message on human existence,
like the figures in Beckett's plays, but should display handicaps that result
from historical conditions.

To prevent the criticism from remaining too limited (i.e., to remote rural
areas of Bavaria as opposed to more representative elements of the
population of the Federal Republic), it is important that dialect in general be
conveyed, rather than one specific dialect (cf. Burger and von Matt 272).
Yet to keep this language from repeating the affirmative message of the
merely entertaining *Volksstück*, namely the equation of dialect with the
idyllic expression of naive and genuine honesty, Kroetz fashions it into
extremely sparse and uncommunicative dialogues that hinder immediate and
unreflected sympathy on the part of the spectator.

Careful examination by linguists has in fact revealed that Kroetz's
language is not simply an unconsidered transcription of the language of the
people, but a careful construction that carries great force through its
techniques of economy. Although he does employ empirically observable
features of Bavarian dialect, he sharpens the use of some while omitting
others (Burger and von Matt 288). An example would be the multiple uses
of the conjunction *weil* (because), which feign causality where none exists
and which indicate that speakers are following their own train of thought
rather than referring to the remarks of their partners (Hoffmeister, *Theater*
101, 110–11). Unlike Naturalist authors such as Gerhart Hauptmann,
however, Kroetz does not include the many false starts, slips of the tongue,
and rewordings that actually occur in everyday speech (274). He gives the
impression of verisimilitude in language, since the various elements do
indeed come from reality, yet the language that he creates is quite artificial
(288). His characters nonetheless illustrate a theory of actual language
barriers, since they can speak only in a fashion that is restricted by their

specific class situation (270). Hess-Lüttich finds a similar selection process at work in the use of phonetic and grammatical characteristics, indicating that comprehensibility among speakers of the standard language is more important to Kroetz than pure mimesis (305–08). These studies indicate that attention to form was more important to Kroetz the playwright than to Kroetz the theoretician and that these characters consist of something more than unchanged reflections of reality.

A discussion of language in *Stallerhof* must also examine a feature that appears to be the opposite of language — the pauses, whose strict observation, according to the stage directions, should make this play from a farm milieu transparent and translatable (9). The second scene, for example, contains fifteen such pauses, the third contains no dialogue at all, and the fourth has seven pauses. In the stage manuscript, Kroetz indicated the length, from five to thirty seconds, that these should last (Schmid 251). If the directions are followed, the performance of the thirty-two pages of text fills the evening.

Kroetz's pauses are similar to the spots that Horváth designated "Stille" (silence), yet they occur even more frequently and have a somewhat different function. In a Horváth play, these were supposed to indicate the struggle between consciousness and the subconscious within a character, but in Kroetz the characters are not conscious enough nor sufficiently capable of reflection for such a struggle to take place (Motekat 121, Schmid 252). Horváth's figures often cover up their verbal inadequacies with phrases from *Bildungsjargon*, but the people in *Stallerhof* do not have such an extensive ersatz-language at their disposal, and when language fails, silence results (Schaarschmidt 212). Pauses indicate that the attempt to understand a problem has been forced to come to a halt; the continuation of the conversation goes around the problem, for which a solution is often found in violence (214; Burger and von Matt 278). Burger and von Matt (290) dispute Kroetz's claim in the stage directions to *Geisterbahn* that the pauses can lead to a "humane possibility of understanding" beyond the verbal (35). They correctly doubt that these characters can find themselves in silence when language fails; what often follows a pause is not an increased degree of understanding but a false means of help from a second-hand cliché (290).

This is what occurs in the passage quoted above (p. 334): Sepp pauses when he becomes unable to penetrate the problem of his "misfortune" any further. Staller replies with a proverb, an authority that is supposed to explain the situation. A dialogue that is incapable of communication cannot be made paramount, and the affirmative tendencies of dialect are muted as it here becomes the representative of an inadequate speech. The characters do not seem to be able to achieve any sort of change through their own reflection. The only possibility remains with the spectator, who, during the pauses, may reach a degree of insight into the characters' situation, which is otherwise presented without comment. The degree to which Kroetz carefully constructs his dialogues, rather than simply copying the speech of rural people, and his considered addition of pauses indicate the importance of the form of the text in conveying the message. These elements compose the core of his negative dramatics and are closely connected to his simultaneous employment and negation of the genre *Volksstück*. His texts are aesthetic negations in Adorno's sense and thoroughly condemn through their form the inadequacies in the situation of the characters.

Kroetz's early plays thus seem almost merciless in the overwhelmingly negative effect of their language. In the plays of Brecht, characters could talk about problems and potentially achieve insight, but in Kroetz the very medium is lacking, and insight is impossible (Burger and von Matt 291). Yet language provides a slight opening for utopian hope, even though it is incapable of giving it content. Donna Hoffmeister points out that in the later play *Oberösterreich*, which deals with petit-bourgeois rather than lower-class characters, "much of the talk aims to achieve a harmony, to give mutual reassurance, and to quiet discontent, which is often lurking below the surface of the dialogue" (*Theater* 116). She calls such verbal and gestural responses "reassurance displays," and whereas they are much less frequent in the earlier *Stallerhof*, they are present there as well. At the beer garden Beppi nods in response to Sepp's remark that eating would be too expensive and thereby indicates that agreement is more important to her than satisfying her hunger. Yet Sepp also shows that he does not want to force such an agreement at the expense of her appetite and says that she can order a sausage if she wishes. The dialogue continues, with each paying attention to the other's expectations, even though the topic changes sporadically and they achieve little insight into their situation (17–18). In this scene language "contains" very little meaning, yet it does not fail as in so many other instances, where violence serves as the only alternative. Walther finds that "the communicative intentions behind the often empty phrases" and "even the first beginnings on the part of the characters" are apparent to the audience; these openings let us see a possibility for overcoming the reality that is portrayed so negatively (54-56).

Kurzenberger is correct in stating that it is absurd "to celebrate the utopia of the human, which is based on debility. Beppi's limited capacities rule this out." Yet he claims that this apparently disconsolate play repeatedly shows "actual moments of happiness, of mutual joy" ("Negativ-Dramatik" 11). They seem all the more intense as a result of Kroetz's dramatic method: "they have been won by spite from a threatening environment, whose pressure never relents" (11). Utopia cannot be shown, though the same language which so intensively portrays this gruesome present opens to provide a hint of something better, as well as the overwhelming need for it.

Kroetz's attention to form is also evident in the arrangement of the 21 short scenes, which are set in fourteen different locations. The brevity and stark contrast of the juxtapositions (for example, Sepp's masturbation in the outhouse between scenes with Beppi in the barn and the family in the kitchen) achieve an economy of force similar to that of the dialogue. Selection is at work, rather than simple mimesis. The intensification of excerpts from the lives of a limited number of characters through "the techniques of reduction and concentration" is what prompts Hoffmeister to call this drama the "theater of confinement" and what gives it its uncompromising force (*Theater* 77). Although there are outbursts, such as the expulsion of Sepp or the planned abortion, they do not represent the dramatic turning points. As Motekat says, the everyday returns after such eruptions, and the closing scene reveals the same state as found at the beginning (122).

The play more or less breaks off; what can occur after the open ending would be more of the same, and thus the ending is negative.[17] Even though Sepp and Beppi become a couple, the ending here can be neither tragic nor that of a happy love story. And though it is a command from above that separates them, they lack the necessary prerequisites for mastering their difficulties and achieving contentment (Carl, *Kroetz* 61–62). The ending contrasts sharply with the happy resolution of a Western movie whose plot Sepp relates to Beppi: the Indians offer a white doctor (and thus an outsider) the choice of one of their number as a wife, but to their chagrin he chooses a maiden whom they have cast out. His example shows, however, that their belief that harm will come from touching the outcast is groundless superstition, and he manages to achieve a cease-fire between the whites and the Indians (11–12).

The outcasts Sepp and Beppi will never be able to experience such a personal triumph, however. As *Stallerhof* ends, Beppi's labor pains begin and she utters the single word "Papamama" (35). A very traditional symbol of hope for the future is given expression in the impending birth of Beppi's child, yet it here has an ironic function, serving as a negative comment on the condition into which Beppi has been forced and as a reminder of the repetition of these circumstances that the child of this child is certainly doomed to repeat. Yet just as Nestroy was unable to let the ending to *Der Unbedeutende* remain unadulterated in its happiness, Kroetz cannot allow *Stallerhof* to close in complete negation. In the penultimate scene, the pregnant Beppi and her mother pick berries on a hillside. In childlike simplicity Beppi expresses her delight at finding so many, and her mother is able to smile with her (35). The audience knows that this picture of idyllic harmony is cruel in its deceptiveness, but like the impending childbirth, it dialectically conveys both the inadequacy of the present and the image of what should be.

Kroetz cannot give a positive ending that portrays the attainment of such a utopia, and moreover such an ending would be less effective. A positive conclusion that provides dogmatic answers in the manner of socialist realism would hinder comprehension in its exclusion of other possibilities (Kroetz, "Zu Brechts 20. Todestag" 254). Because his stories are multi-levelled they are more dialectical and in the end, he feels, more positive (Arnold 57). The structural complexity that contains these faint signs of hope within such stark rejections of the status quo makes them more convincing, while the open ending refains from offering a pat solution.

The question of reception is important to any play that claims to be social-critical, just as it has been for the *Volksstück* in general. Involved in a play's reception are the complex relationships between Kroetz's intentions as expressed in his essays, the actual form and content of his dramatic texts, the reaction to his dramas by literary and theater critics, and the response of audiences. All of Kroetz's plays through 1978 with one exception were premiered at small theaters or the studio stages of major houses (Schregel 127). *Stallerhof* was first performed in the Malersaal of the Deutsches Schauspielhaus in Hamburg, and the production ran for two years, including guest performances at five other European cities (Heising 210). In the next six years it received eleven additional stagings at other theaters and was instrumental in making Kroetz the most frequently performed German playwright (Schregel 54). *Stallerhof* continues to hold theatrical interest: in June 1988 the composer Gerd Kühr's musical version, based on Kroetz's text, was performed at the first Münchner Biennale für Musiktheater.[18]

The overall performance record indicates, however, that *Stallerhof* was not reaching the *Volk* that it portrayed, but rather the upper-middle class audiences of the subsidized houses. Herbert Gamper attributes the origins of this failure to Horváth's portrayal of the "Dummheit," or stupidity of his characters. He says that Horváth and followers such as Kroetz portrayed the condition of a certain segment of the people as they perceived it to be, rather than through their eyes, a procedure that resulted in a form of theater that was about the *Volk*, rather than of or for them (74). There is a danger that spectators, including those from the lower classes, might share this perception, but it is important to note that Kroetz made a distinction between denouncing the people and condemning the situation that keeps them in a state of "Dummheit," and he felt that a more positive portrayal would be both inaccurate and less effective.

In an essay from this period Kroetz expressed the dilemma of the *Volkstheater*, which "sits between two chairs:" either it has a mass audience, like the television farces of Hamburg's Ohnsorg-Theater, and works against the true interests of the people, or it loses that audience in attempting to take the right path, in which case it becomes an inside joke for intellectuals ("Soll der Kumpel" 543). When asked if he thought that his plays would ever be performed at Bauerntheater, he replied that they are too difficult for that to occur at present; he felt he would have to work for at least five years as a manager at a rural theater in order to change the composition and expectations of such an audience (Calandra 104-5). He was pleased that *Stallerhof* has played in respected subsidized houses, but also had a guilty conscience, because such theaters are in the end used to preserve society as it is ("Lust" 593).

The widespread acclaim for Kroetz's plays and his winning of numerous prizes helped his message reach an audience, although rejection might have represented stronger confirmation of his left political views.[19] The ability and even need of the prevailing culture to incorporate a certain amount of criticism has a negative effect on his negation, though one that tends to result in affirmation rather than in progress toward utopia. Kroetz later found naive his statement from 1971 that said, "If people go to one of my plays, they'll have to end up reaching for a gun." He pointed out that he is read today by pupils in schools, but that little has changed, and consumerism goes on ("Ich habe immer" 83). The reception of a work of art is complicated by too many factors to expect a simple relationship between it and its effect; the negative or utopian impact of *Stallerhof* can only be small, rather than massive and unambiguous.[20]

Yet the play is extremely intense and unrelenting in its refusal to provide the possibility of escape for the audience. This comes not solely from the content, consisting of characters and behavior that most people would prefer to ignore, but content mediated by form, which is here quite different from farcical *Volksstücke* that showed farmers whose individual folly could be denounced through laughter. To seek a thematic incorporation of social causes is to overlook the necessity and power of formal mediation, and to expect a clear-cut indication of perspective is to overestimate the didactic power of the authorial authority. Any change in attitude or awareness can only be gained through a dialectical process that involves the participation of the spectators (cf. Hoffmeister, "Zamhalten" 448-49). Walther finds that even though Kroetz manages to convey the illusion of reality, his form and language are abstract enough to spur analysis on the part of the audience. In *Stallerhof* the impetus for this process is provoked by the form, which combines utter negativity with compassion in order to jolt the audience into seeking a better alternative. This is what makes the play more effective than one with an overtly tendentious message would have been and what brings it closer to the truly committed literature as defined by Adorno in "Engagement."

The effect of this negativity may be softened by too strong an emphasis on the compassion within the play or on the characters as individuals, yet it is a mistake to assume that Kroetz flees from important political themes simply because he does not state them. The necessity for change is to be found in the extreme distance between the desire for harmony that these characters possess and the overwhelmingly negative quality of their situation.[21] Töteberg points out that Kroetz's later attempts to give his plays a more positive turn use the child as a symbol of hope for the future ("Ein konservativer Autor" 290), yet the baby serves that function in *Stallerhof* as well, even though the hope is cruelly dashed at the same time.

Such a longing, however, does not represent a regressive attempt to return to a more innocent world. The play in no way implies that such a world ever existed, and for these characters to raise a child in the proper way, society would have to be changed radically. As Bloch states, our images of a harmonious *Heimat* have been present from the first years of our lives, even though we were never actually there (*Das Prinzip Hoffnung* 1628). Spectators have an awareness of utopia from their own experience and from previous literature, although they lack a precisely delineated notion of that utopia. The impending childbirth in *Stallerhof* is a glimpse of utopia that condemns existing society without pretending that utopia is possible under existing conditions.

Nicht Fisch nicht Fleisch

The problem of trying to avoid repetition and the tendency of audiences and critics to view his portrayals as fatalistic rather than social-critical led Kroetz to search for new methods that offer a more positive perspective on the future. One attempt resulted in plays such as *Globales Interesse* (1972) and *Münchner Kindl* (1973) that incorporated the techniques of agitprop theater; another spawned dramas such as *Oberösterreich* [Upper Austria, 1972] that portrayed characters from a slightly higher rung on the social ladder who are somewhat more articulate about their problems and less likely to resort to violent extremes. In *Oberösterreich* Heinz and Anni seek fulfillment in the offerings of the consumer society, a dream that is revealed as illusory. The form is not substantially different from that of the early plays, though it is less intense and enclosing, and the language is a more obvious collection of second-hand clichés and phrases that demonstrate the emptiness of the characters' desires and consciousness (cf. Kafitz 100). Yet Heinz and Anni do discuss problems and strive to maintain a state of agreement with one another (see Hoffmeister, "'Zamhalten'"), and they decide in the end to keep the child of an initially unwanted pregnancy, even though it will mean financial hardship and an end to their dream of a swimming pool.[22]

The direction that Kroetz began with *Oberösterreich* culminated in *Das Nest* (1974), which he labelled *Volksstück*. In *Das Nest* Kurt is a loyal and unquestioning employee who works overtime in order to provide the best for his infant son. One of his jobs involves the illegal dumping of toxic chemicals into a remote lake, in which his son is later seriously injured. Perceiving the consequences of his actions, Kurt realizes that the only chance for resisting such dangerous practices lies in solidarity with the union. In contrast to *Stallerhof*, *Das Nest* points to a possible solution. As Carl indicates, the situation of pregnancy and the arrival of a newborn child is repeated, but with different consequences. In *Heimarbeit* (1971) the result was violence; in *Oberösterreich* the parents kept the child in the hope that it would have a better life than they do, but they fail to achieve any insight into their situation. In *Das Nest*, the characters are prepared to act personally for change (*Kroetz* 108).

There is disagreement among critics as to whether this positive dramatics represents a step forward.[23] Although the form of the play is less stark and severe than that of *Stallerhof* and therefore more conventional, the main vehicles for the message are the plot and content, which are most likely to be positively received by those who already have similar opinions. The danger with *Stallerhof* was that the message of social causes and their changeability would not be perceived; in *Das Nest*, the message is more obvious, but not necessarily more likely to evoke a change in the spectator.

Deciding whether or not to offer a model through positive heroes is a problem with which Kroetz has had to deal continually, but just as important is the finding of a satisfactory form. In his recent attempts he has searched for more varied means to portray lower middle-class people and their problems; his *Nicht Fisch nicht Fleisch* [Neither Fish nor Fowl] represented a breakthrough and was named "Play of the Year" in 1981 by the journal *Theater heute*.[24] One reviewer called it a "topical *Volksstück* about living, loving, and working in the Federal Republic of Germany at the beginning of the 1980's (Michaelis, "Phantastisches Zeitstück").

The main characters, two print shop workers and their wives, come from the same industrial lower middle-class background that was found in *Oberösterreich* and *Das Nest*, but the characters have more insight into their lives than in the former play, and the optimistic, clear-cut solution of the latter is lacking here. In an article written before the appearance of *Nicht Fisch nicht Fleisch* Cocalis claimed that critical *Volksstücke* have to contain an atmosphere of provincialism and therefore exclude conflicts at the workplace ("Politics" 299). Such a view restricts itself to surface content and tends to fossilize the genre definition; even though the *Volksstück* has its roots in the regional play and can still deal with a non-synchronous provincialism, there is no reason why such plays cannot portray industrial workers and their situation, which is what Kroetz attempts here. see p. 280

Edgar, who enjoys his job and avoids controversy with his employer, is contrasted with Hermann, who is more critical of workplace relations and has already lost one job because of his unwillingness to put up with adverse treatment. Edgar's wife Emmi works in a supermarket and has the prospect of becoming a branch manager; Hermann's wife Helga stays at home to take care of their children. The meaning of work, the problems of the workplace, the relations between management and workers, the effects of the increasing use of technology, the relation between work and private life, the increasing commodification of all aspects of life, the role of women, and the decision about whether or not to have children are all themes of the play.

The dramatic conflicts intensify as Hermann and Edgar have to learn new computer technology in order to keep their jobs after a larger company has bought out their firm and as Helga finds out that she is pregnant with a third child. The negative criticism of society is carried out by presenting the effects that social contradictions have on the characters. Edgar's inability and unwillingness to master the computer spoil his sense of pride and accomplishment in his work, and the firm becomes impatient with this formerly loyal worker. Although the union has enough power to prevent existing employees from being fired, they would be kept on only through featherbedding, and Edgar quits rather than suffer the indignity of made-up work. His decision also has consequences at home, since he is unable to face up to his wife's becoming the breadwinner. In Hermann's case, the cost of a third child would put quite a strain on his small income. As in earlier plays, abortion is a proposed solution; Hermann wants to get rid of the child (129–31). Helga, who at first resists, later agrees, since it seems pointless to restrict their expenditures so much that they deny everything to the first two children in order to have a third (52–54). In the end, however, she decides to keep the baby.

The search for alternatives to the present situation often takes the form of escape or regression, or, in the case of the considered abortion, in negative solutions to problems that should not be problems in the first place. Edgar's initial stance is to fit in and to separate work from private life; when someone insults him at work he lets it pass, because he knows that he is king at home (18–20). This idea is an illusion, and Helga later realizes that it was wrong to think "daß mir in der Familie frei sind" [that we're free within the family] (33). Economic conditions affect their private lives, and the family cannot represent a self-contained idyll.

Frustrated with the changes in the profession, Edgar pictures the world as an airless dystopia beneath a giant dome in which the workers are held captive to produce commodities for those outside. To escape, he creates a "Robinsonade" in his imagination in which he, alone with his family in the wilderness, produces all that he needs (41–52). Like Raimund's misanthrope Rappelkopf, he dreams of a solitary utopia. For Edgar, work is what distinguishes humans from apes, and he is determined not to surrender his humanity. Despite Hermann's poking holes in his argument, Edgar holds fast to his regressive illusion of the completely independent individual. The "Sehnsucht" [longing, 50] and "Heimweh" [homesickness, 48] that he so strongly feels are valid, as are their objects in non-alienated work and the family. The utopian forms of these objects do not exist at present, however, and the question remains open as to how they might be attained.[25] In *Das Nest* the labor union represented a first step in the right direction. Here, the union is already present and can prevent Hermann and Edgar from being fired, though it cannot solve the problem of maintaining qualitatively meaningful work.[26]

Rather than providing an answer, the play starts a process through its juxtaposition of opposing points of view, a process that is highlighted by the design of the set ("two apartments of the same size, above one another," 8) and the alternating configurations of characters on stage. In *Das Nest* the actual antagonist, the boss of the firm, did not appear on stage, and though Kurt represented his point of view at first by being a loyal employee, the boss's absence facilitated the presentation of a solution (the union) that could improve things. The structure of *Nicht Fisch nicht Fleisch* is more clearly dialogical: the various partners in conversation represent points of view that appear equally strong. Hoffmeister feels that a balance is retained here that was lacking in *Das Nest*: "The audience is called upon to judge how inadequately each of the four characters responds to this crisis" (*Theater* 76).

In the first scene Edgar and Emmi talk in bed about their jobs; the fact that Emmi faces a demanding workday leads her to resist her husband's sexual advances. Although they are able to laugh and reassure one another, it is clear that Edgar is not entirely comfortable with the emancipation that takes his wife into the world of work. She says, "Erst die Arbeit macht den Menschen, ob Mann oder Frau" [Only work makes you human, whether man or woman] (10), and even though Edgar later expresses this same idea (44), the contradictions that prevent fulfillment in both employment and family relationships are continually revealed throughout the play. The first scene also indicates that Emmi finds Edgar and his colleagues too docile, in contrast to the more militant workers in England.

A parallel situation is presented in the play's second scene, where Helga and Hermann are also preparing to go to sleep. Here, however, it is the wife who would like to make love, but Hermann is too excited about workplace politics. Helga is worried that he might again go too far in stirring things up, since he already lost one job on account of his agitation. The outlooks within the couples are reversed: Edgar and Helga represent traditional male-female roles, whereas Emmi and Hermann expect fulfillment from work, whose relations they believe they can alter (Kässens 278).

The proper attitudes of workers to their jobs and their employers and the place of women in the home and the workplace are treated from another angle in the dialogue between the two men in the third scene. Though they are friends and colleagues, their positions on opposing sides of the discussion are emphasized visually through their practicing karate at a sports

club. Hermann is driven by a resentment toward those who earn more than
he does; Edgar attributes Hermann's feelings to the individual psychological
motivation of an inferiority complex and possession of a job that does not
suit him, rather than to social and economic reasons. The next scene
presents a dialogue between the two women, and the play continues with
repetitions and variations of these character arrangements. Splitting the play
into such scenes both unifies and separates: because the scenes match up and
provide mirror images of one another, we see that women's problems are
also men's problems and vice versa, and that the meaning of work has
implications for home life.

Yet the contradictions that arise from present social relations, according
to which employment and families are structured, is expressed by the
fragmentation into various groups of characters. In the final scene of the
first act all four are together at the Oktoberfest, but just as in *Kasimir und
Karoline*, the festive atmosphere is spoiled, this time by the fear of the
effect that technological rationalization will have on jobs at the printing
firm. The unities between husband and wife, work and home, and groups
of friends that appear to prevail at the beginning of this interlude actually
represent an illusion. The separation becomes clearest when the fourth and
fifth scenes of the third act are staged simultaneously: Hermann no longer
considers Edgar his friend, and Helga considers her husband unwelcome
after he rejects Edgar. Edgar is unable to cope with his new situation of
unemployment and the resulting financial dependence on Emmi. He
performs a symbolic castration on a teddy bear as Hermann packs a suitcase,
and both walk out of their respective apartments (73–74).

That the discussion cannot simply be divided into two sides, one of which
is right and the other wrong, becomes clear after the change in the situation
at the workplace. It is now Edgar who does not enjoy his work, whereas
Hermann is excited about the computer, whose capabilities he admires.
Edgar is unable to follow his own earlier advice to Hermann to be flexible
and adapt (26), and he eventually quits. This casts doubt on his original
position, and Hermann, ironically, becomes the one to defend the status quo:
not the employer's position of course, but the possibility of improvement
through an existing institution, the union. Edgar strikes out blindly at the
new technology, but like Marx, who felt that contradictions in the use of
machinery lay in the capitalist employment of machinery rather than
machinery itself (*Das Kapital*, MEW 23: 465), Hermann thinks progress
should serve the worker rather than the owner (41).

However, the problem of sitting in a non-functional job is a real one for which Hermann's position fails to provide an adequate solution. His answers are too theoretical and his attempts to force them on his basically conservative fellow workers, who lack his degree of consciousness, result in their cruel inflating of his intestines with an air pump. Helga too accuses him of wanting to create a better world for the workers of tomorrow while at the same time thinking of aborting his own child and rejecting his best friend (69). The desire of both Edgar and Hermann to live in a non-alienated world evokes sympathy, as do both their positions, even when these positions sometimes lead to illusory goals. The dialogues delineate the problems more clearly than the display techniques of *Stallerhof,* and the dialectical complexity, which is in part conveyed by the structural arrangement of the scenes, prevents an overly-simplistic positive conclusion, as in *Das Nest.*

In *Stallerhof* the characters were unable to articulate their problems or to discuss them in any depth; in *Oberösterreich* they were capable of discussion but failed to reach any insights. In *Nicht Fisch nicht Fleisch* they achieve a certain amount of insight without finding a solution. Hoffmeister points out that in *Oberösterreich* Heinz and Anni, in reaching the decision to have a child even though it will involve financial sacrifice, never mention the idea "that every couple has a right to children regardless of income level" (*Theater* 131). In the later play, however, Hermann is very much aware that the industrialist Siemens can afford to have both children and a non-working wife because he has 100,000 people working for him (17). This is expressed in a language capable of putting problems into words and demonstrates a major difference between this play and *Stallerhof.*

Rolf Michaelis says that this position is new for Kroetz, since two intelligent workers fight here with words, rather than their fists. One of Edgar's hobbies is in fact the Duden dictionary ("Traumspiel"). The characters of course are not completely in control of their own language, and some of the communication that does occur is achieved, as in *Oberöster-reich,* through "inarticulation, talking past one another, insinuations, implications, the use of ready-made phrases and clichés, and subtle undercurrents of feeling and thought" (Hoffmeister, Theater 4). The characters frequently employ the proverbs and jargon of others in order to justify and master their situation, but such uses are convincing only to the speakers themselves, and the conversation partner is for the most part not taken in by the supposed arguments. Edgar defends his ability to separate work from home by quoting "My home is my castle," but Hermann is not satisfied with the explanation and points out the impossibility of splitting oneself into two people (20).

Emmi's description of the ideal store, which would be a cross between a supermarket and a mom-and-pop operation, is obviously jargon from the world of management and advertising, rather than a genuine, individual expression of the desire to provide the best for the customer. When she speaks of "das Wohlgefühl einer nicht repressiven Einkaufsumwelt" [the feeling of well-being found in a non-repressive shopping environment], the stage directions indicate that Edgar looks up at the mention of the word "repressive," and the attention of audience is directed to the artificiality of her language (54). The scene is a monologue, since Edgar is unable to reply for two reasons: not only is it almost impossible to respond to this type of jargon, but unbeknownst to Emmi, he has quit his job, and the misery of his situation contrasts too strongly with the satisfaction she finds in her work.

Yet his silence should make evident the inadequacy of her situation as well, which conceives of itself in consumerist terminology. Her speech here is High German, which contrasts with the dialect she usually employs when talking with Edgar. Her integration into the business world changes her language and hinders her communication with her husband. In the play's first scene the two communicated and managed to reassure one another, even though they disagreed on a number of issues. In the later scene, there is no communication at all, and the inability to achieve it seems more clearly to result from the power that the social and economic substructure has taken over their lives. Yet the unrelenting conversations between various pairs and groups of characters is the expression of a search for a better alternative, though the search at times leads to breakdowns and disagreement and at times to consensus.

Hoffmeister says that in *Oberösterreich*, where Heinz and Anni reach an unsatisfactory agreement, the closure of consensus actually is received as openness by the audience: "After sensing the limitations, the falseness of so much earlier conflict-avoidance, the audience cannot suddenly accept a happy ending: it is compelled to imagine an alternative society in which the language systems governing human communication would provoke ... the possibility of ongoing mutual progress" (*Theater* 131). Though the quality of the ending is different in *Nicht Fisch nicht Fleisch*, the same dialectic process is at work, and it is one whose completion the audience will have to imagine.

As in earlier plays, the use of dialect is also important here. The stage directions indicate, "Dialekte sind nicht Ausdruck von Arbeit, Landschaft und Gesellschaft. Dialekte sind Verhaltensweisen in der Sprache" [Dialects are not an expression of work, region, and society. Dialects are behaviors in language]. Kroetz feels that the performers have to reflect on this and work at it carefully to avoid both the superficiality of an imitative naturalism and an aesthetic dilettantism (8).

The same problems of avoiding affirmation through identification or of making irrelevant through the portrayal of exotics exist here as they did in *Stallerhof*, though the former problem is greater since these characters are closer to the mainstream of society. In the contrast mentioned above between Emmi's customary way of talking to her husband and her imitation of business jargon, dialect appears to be a natural, adequate type of speech, yet it is never completely successful in providing insights or solutions. It is still not the expression of a utopian idyll, but neither does it serve so strongly as a negative indicator of social expropriation.

But because some of the language in the play appears to be able to further communication and to articulate problems, there is a possibility that the audience will perceive an adequate relationship between signifier and signified and assume that progress toward a solution through the existing verbal medium is simpler than is actually the case. The same danger could result from the perception of a mimetic realism, which is the style that dominates in the play. In order to call attention to and to question language and to make this drama more autonomous, Kroetz adds a metalinguistic feature to *Nicht Fisch nicht Fleisch* with elements of a type and magnitude new to him, though not of course to literature: metaphors and imagery, both verbal and visual. The extended use of these throughout the play takes on symbolic and surrealistic functions.[27]

The play's title is a suggested answer to the question, "What is a human being?," that constantly occupies the characters. It is, however, a negative answer, defining humans by what they are not, rather than what they are. This question, which was also central to Brecht's *Herr Puntila und sein Knecht Matti*, is treated dialectically in *Nicht Fisch nicht Fleisch* as well, though less from the perspective of master and servant as from that of the individual and society. The imagery of the title becomes visual and metaphorical in the scene where the two men are standing in front of Edgar's aquarium. Edgar says that one has to understand fish in order to keep them from eating one another up, but even so they often confuse a member of their own species with an edible variety (23). It is clear that a comparison is being made to the cannibal-like behavior of humans that occurs later: Edgar's betrayal of the union by quitting his job, Hermann's subsequent rejection of Edgar, and the mistreatment of Hermann by his colleagues, not to mention the treatment of the workers at the hands of industry. Edgar is probably unaware of the comparison at the time he is speaking, but the relation between the topic of fish and the play's title and thematics allows another commenting voice to be heard. *Stallerhof* also used animal metaphors, but they were more a mimetic representation of the language of a certain type of rural character. Though they may function as commentary, they can do so only implicitly. On certain occasions in *Nicht Fisch nicht Fleisch*, however, Edgar makes such comparisons explicit: he says he is not going to allow himself to be treated like an animal, since he is a human being (34), and later insists that he is no ape, because he can perform work (44). The threat to his job seems to be a threat to humanity; thus in his dystopian vision he is submerged like a fish in an airless glass dome (43–44).

The description of the dome is purely verbal, but in the penultimate scene the imagery becomes visual through the staging: Edgar stands naked at the water's edge, prepared to swim away to a new life. In Berlin, the director Peter Stein used real water and technical effects to portray this dream of a flight into the wilderness, whereas in Düsseldorf Volker Hesse created grey clouds over a dismal sewage canal to emphasize this urge as the crazy notion of a man blinded by fear (Michaelis, "Traumspiel"). The former production thus emphasizes the utopian drive behind Edgar's dream, and the latter the negative state in which he finds himself and the regressive solution that he is attempting. Rather than physical reality, the surrealistic vision conveys the psychological pressure that Edgar feels (Rischbieter 3–4), yet it also attempts to go beyond language in exploring human beings and their possibilities, as well as exposing their illusions. Hermann also thought that he had a solution, yet he was unable to convey it to Edgar or the other workers.

In the same scene slang expressions are taken literally in a grotesquely comical way in order to indicate that Hermann's ideas cannot simply be accepted at face value. He too appears on the shore, farting painfully from the air that his co-workers have forced into him. Edgar asks, "Bist ihnen mit dem Arsch ins Gesicht, bis dich *bläst sich in die Faust* [You stuck your ass in their faces, until you got *blows into his fist*], using the idiom that means to address someone brusquely, and he continues with similar puns, including "Jetzt ham sie dir den Marsch geblasen" [now they've blown the march for you], meaning that they have reprimanded him (75–76).[28] Having always disagreed with Hermann's ideas, he employs this same line of imagery to express his opinion of their emptiness: "Der Teufel fährt aus. *Lacht*. Karl Marx persönlich, der durch das Arschloch des Herrn Hermann Zwiebel ausfährt" [The devil departs. *Laughs*. Karl Marx in person, who is departing through the asshole of Mr. Hermann Zwiebel] (76).

In Edgar's case language becomes figurative through metaphors and visual images; in Hermann's, figurative uses are made literal. In both cases their respective points of view are called into question, and neither can be considered victorious, since at the end of the scene neither character has changed his mind: Edgar is determined to swim off into the "wilderness of oceans," and Hermann, who does not think his colleagues really meant anything by their prank, crawls back to the world of humanity (76–78). He calls out "Mensch!," but a definition of a human being has not been provided, and both characters still seem lost, neither fish nor fowl. But through language and around language the contemporary situation has been revealed as inadequate, and the same means have simultaneously indicated the strength of the characters' utopian desires.

For Raimund, the possibility of writing a comedy with a harmonious conclusion represented a difficult generic problem, and his humorous plays could exist only with serious and potentially tragic overtones. Kroetz does not even attempt so strong a degree of harmony as Raimund did, yet in *Nicht Fisch nicht Fleisch* the comic and the serious are also interwoven, interestingly enough, with phantastically staged dream-worlds that are somewhat reminiscent of Raimund. In a review entitled "Phantastisches Zeitstück" Michaelis also calls this work a "tragic, comic didactic play." In the first scene the humor is still light: both Emmi and Edgar are able to joke and laugh about his unsuccessful erotic overtures and go to sleep without any bad feelings.

However, the lack of unity that stems from an inability to reach a consensus on Emmi's role as wife and member of the workforce has a potentially threatening quality that manifests itself when Edgar no longer has a job. Edgar and Hermann both laugh at the puns in the surrealistic scene just mentioned, but the joviality is punctured by Hermann's screams of pain, since his plight is by no means merely a laughing matter. We laugh with the protagonists when they laugh at themselves and experience in the process a hint of what harmonious agreement might be, yet this feeling is not unadulterated: we cannot laugh at their pain, and the serious undercurrents prevent us from affirming the present situation, either by believing that the characters can achieve real harmony with things as they are or from experiencing the theatrical performance as a sublimation of our own desire for harmony.

The conclusion is also ambiguous and open-ended. Like many other recent German plays, *Nicht Fisch nicht Fleisch* rejects monocausal explanations. In the final scene, the pregnant Helga is cooking, while Emmi and Hermann are seated at the kitchen table. Hermann drinks tea for his condition. Edgar appears at the door, naked, wet, and shivering. Helga gives him a bowl of soup with the command to "eat," which he does, and, according to the final stage direction, "Alle sind beschäftigt" [All are occupied] (78–79). Kässens states that Kroetz has put all the possible historically optimistic and pessimistic arguments into the mouths of the two male protagonists but leaves the question open for the public to take home (280–81). Like the title, the ending refrains from taking sides and offering a simple truth (Riewoldt, "Der ganze Kroetz" 15). Yet some find the play's ending an affirmation of the traditional family: Michaelis reported that the Düsseldorf production showed the final togetherness of the sexes as a utopian idyll ("Traumspiel") and Rischbieter calls the final scene an "unnatural, glowing yet poisonous idyll" in which the women seem like kitsch-madonnas (4). Töteberg thinks that the characters' tendency to remain within traditional roles (including Helga's pregnancy) as well as extra-textual remarks by Kroetz ("Ich ... beschütze immer die Einheit der Familie" [I ... always protect the unity of the family]) provide such an affirmation, and he also finds the conclusion unsatisfactory ("Ein konservativer Autor" 287–94). Such a conclusion, however, is actually an extension of the dialectical relation between play and audience that contemporary critical plays must maintain in order to achieve any degree of effectiveness.

Several years before this play was written, Kroetz expressed skepticism about an ending that contained a positive utopia and about the simple relationship between stage event and later effect (Reinhold, "Interview" 52), and it is no doubt correct that plays which offer a positive model are less likely to be effective than ones which raise questions. The dialogue must go on, rather than come to theatrical closure. More recently, in a response to a question from Monika Sperr, Kroetz said that his ideological perspective is one of the "changeability of history," a "utopia of a better world [that] every artist should have." When Sperr protested that Kroetz's plays lack such a utopia, he replied that he himself has one, even if his dramas do not portray it. "In *Nicht Fisch nicht Fleisch* my own perplexity is conspicuously present: the failure of all participants." He thinks that the purpose of the theater is not to answer questions, but to make it possible to experience questions. He is opposed to taking a superior position that is smarter than society's (qtd. in Hein 92). Hermann and Edgar return to the family because see p. 288 nothing else is available, and pessimism results from the doubt as to whether the characters' situation will improve.

Yet pessimism is not synonymous with inevitability, and like the battle between the points of view of Hermann and Edgar, the struggle over presenting a negative or a positive conclusion ends in a draw. The characters are together at the end, but no one speaks. They are all "occupied," but not integrally "employed." The women are not winners in the sexual struggle, as Rischbieter claims (4), since there can be no winners until the situation is improved for all. His description of a "poisonous idyll" is more accurate: a truly harmonious togetherness would indeed be idyllic, but it has not yet been achieved here. The scene, including Kroetz's oft-repeated use of pregnancy as a sign of hope for the future, represents a reminder of what utopia could be without actually portraying it as such. As in Raimund and Nestroy, the ending contains both the negative and the utopian, though the balance between them is different here. In the earlier authors, the negative strains persisted despite the harmony in the foreground; in Kroetz, the expression of hope is to be glimpsed amidst the dominating negativism.

Cocalis claims the contemporary *Volksstück* does not travel well because of provincialism, "its reliance on a subtle use of language, and its dependence on certain audience expectations" ("Politics" 306). Though *Nicht Fisch nicht Fleisch* is very precisely set in Munich in 1980 and the characters speak the local dialect, provincialism is less an issue here than in *Stallerhof*. The characters are no longer bound by provincial social and economic structures that are out of sync with industrial development, but beset by problems common to workers in the rest of Germany and the other developed Western countries. The inclusion of the surrealistic-expressionistic water scene shows a greater similarity to mainstream theatrical tradition than to the traditional *Volksstück*, though the latter genre has always incorporated elements from other sources, and Raimund's plays are anything but purely realistic. The form of *Nicht Fisch nicht Fleisch* should make it acceptable to both upper-middle class audiences at the major theaters, where it has been performed to great acclaim, and to *Volkstheater*, should it reach them. The division of the public into various theater-going and non-theater-going groups, which is a result of the organization of society and the institution of the theater and which had an ambiguous effect on the reception of *Stallerhof*, continues to manifest itself in the reception of *Nicht Fisch nicht Fleisch*. The force of its negativity is mitigated by its widespread acceptance in certain circles, and any possible impetus toward social change that it may provoke is hampered by its failure to reach beyond the narrow group that actually attends the theater.

In his essay "Über die Maßnahme" Kroetz criticizes the character in Brecht's play "The Measures Taken" who agrees with the "erasure of his face," since the main characteristic of the proletariat cannot be "the obliterated." Separating a person from his biography "disregards the dialectic between individual and society." Kroetz refuses moreover to condone the use of unethical means to reach a just end (573–74). In *Nicht Fisch nicht Fleisch* Edgar has developed an individual means of coping with unpleasantness at work and, when the nature of his profession changes, he seeks a solution in individual escape.

Hermann, on the other hand, seeks socially induced change, not only at the beginning, but also after the introduction of computerization. Although his methods are not unethical, his manner of going at his goal threatens to destroy his individual home life and fails to convince the specific colleagues with whom he must deal. In the latter case the gap between theory and practice is too great for him to overcome. Both characters thus disregard the dialectic between the individual and society, and that is the reason that neither position alone can be taken as the solution.

In his "Offener Brief an Rolf Hochhuth" Theodor Adorno disagrees with the Lukács sentence quoted by Hochhuth which claims that the concrete, particular human being is the starting and concluding point of artistic formation, since Lukács apparently forgot that Hegel and Marx considered the individual as a historical category, emerging from labor (179). Regarding the individual as an invariant of world literature petrifies the dialectic into a *Weltanschauung*. Although Adorno finds it disgusting that humans are modelled according to the methods of production, he believes this has long been the case. It is contradictory and absurd that the methods of production that are supposed to serve and free the individual actually result in the loss of individuality (180). But it is only individuals who are able to represent the concerns of collectivity in the face of the collective forces that liquidate this individuality (181).

Adorno finds that Brecht had the right instinct in *Furcht und Elend des dritten Reichs* [*The Private Life of the Master Race*] to portray the effects on the people, rather than to attempt to portray the actions of the rulers as Hochhuth had proposed to do in his intended drama about Truman and Stalin. Adorno finds, however, that Brecht did not go far enough in showing to what extent these people had become objects. For him Beckett's

"Menschenstümpfe" [human stumps] are more realistic than "die Abbilder einer Realität, welche diese durch ihre Abbildlichkeit bereits sänftigen" [the representations of a reality which they already soften by their representation] (182). The absurdity of reality demands "a form that destroys the realistic façade" (183).

Although *Stallerhof* presented a realistic façade, it was so stark and confining and the language so restricted and sparse that the effect of the absurdity of reality was nonetheless conveyed. But Kroetz was criticized for what Adorno also regards as a danger: that in showing victims who lack insight into the relations of power, one portrays their situation as the result of unavoidable fate (183). In *Nicht Fisch nicht Fleisch* no successful action is depicted, despite the determination shown by the protagonists in their respective forms of resistance. *Volksstücke* make the little people a fit subject for drama in a manner similar to that in which bourgeois tragedy discovered the middle classes. But to say that they can represent humanity just as well as kings is a bourgeois idea, dependent on the belief that such subjects are capable of individual action (Burger and von Matt 294-95). Though Kroetz's figures have a certain amount of individual distinguishability, they cannot take their fate into their own hands or become the heroes of tragedy because of their victimization and objectification.

The representations of the characters in *Nicht Fisch nicht Fleisch* are probably too closely situated to median life to satisfy Adorno's demands for a form that destroys the façade of reality, but the surrealistic and expressionistic elements give it an artistic autonomy that is lacking in *Das Nest* and criticize existing conditions more forcefully than would a more consistently "realistic" portrayal. Although the characters themselves cannot display the proper regard for the dialectic between individual and society, the play attempts to convey this dialectic through the juxtaposition of their points of view and the open-ended conclusion. The possibility of the freedom of the subject is problematized (Kafitz 95), even though that freedom is never achieved because of the extent to which the characters are victims of the relations of production. They are viewed as individuals, with limitations, of course; yet their situation can be generalized because of their quest to become "Menschen" in an industrial society in the 1980's. They can thus be viewed as a synthesis between a dramatics of the parable and a dramatics of identification, and their longed-for actualization as human beings will be achieved only when the proper synthesis between the individual and the social becomes possible. That synthesis is the utopian, and the distance between it and present reality is the negation; in his *Volksstücke* Kroetz has searched for forms that would prove adequate to both.

CONCLUSION

DURING THE PAST CENTURY AND a half quite a number of German and Austrian authors have sought a form of drama that would be suitable for addressing the lower classes, as opposed to the ruling or cultural elite. Many of these writers have succeeded in creating literarily demanding and theatrically effective plays, even though others, who addressed similar audiences, contented themselves with providing farcical amusement. The precise composition of this *Volk* has varied with the changing economic structure of society and has ranged from the craftsmen and tradesmen of the early nineteenth century to industrial workers and farmers of the past hundred years, as well as to lower middle-class civil servants and employees of the Weimar years and the current era. In the early period there was a close relationship among the institution of the *Volkstheater*, its actors and authors, and its public, but in more recent years plays dealing with such types of people have become more detached from their institutional and public base. Changes in society and the theater have been accompanied by changes in literary form, but even though the types of plays that can be considered *Volksstücke* are quite varied, there is validity in approaching them as part of a common genre.

The word *Volk* within the genre's name implies that the designation is sociological as well as literary, and in fact its origins within the suburban *Volkstheater* and its inclusion of the "people," both as audience and as material for portrayal, make the *Volk* a starting point for classification. Because these connections are so important, any study must consider the relation between a given *Volksstück* and the social reality from which it emerges. But more important to a literary analysis than either reception or thematics is the form employed by such a text as well as the relationship between that form and the play's content, the external situation, the literary tradition, and the public response. Art is a central aspect of the life of the people, arising out of a given situation, although not solely determined by it. Art gives expression to reality, yet it also counters it imaginatively and transforms it, embodying the present while containing the seeds for the future. The set of interrelationships involved in a literary text must be examined in all its complexity. Only through such an analysis can one come to an understanding of what these plays represent as literature and also what connection they have with reality, since that connection does not always take the form of attempted verisimilitude.

Authors who were principally interested in success could employ comedy, stunning visual effects, catchy melodies, sentimentality, or melodrama in order to achieve popular acclaim. Plays that stressed one or more of these effects could prove entertaining, but they ran the danger of providing nothing more than a forgettable evening's escape or a vehicle that made the audience feel good about their own existence. In fulfilling these functions and in failing to go beyond audience expectations, such plays affirmed the status quo and provided little impetus for change either in society or in literary expectations. Even the critical remarks that such plays occasionally contained failed to have much effect, because the overall message was one of affirmation. Comedies of this kind still abound on provincial stages and on national television, as for example in the offerings of Hamburg's Ohnsorg Theater.

But other authors were more profoundly affected by the reality in which they found themselves, and they attempted to come to terms with it in a different way through the form of their literary texts. Their great respect for the *Volk* whom they were addressing prevented them from either making fun of the people or idealizing them, even when honest portrayals meant exposing illusions that some would rather maintain. Characters in these plays, even in comedies, are neither laughingstocks as a result of their lower-class station nor idealized kitsch-figures representing some eternal, mythical quality inherent in the ethnic group. And in most cases they do not represent political idealizations either, such as a fully conscious proletariat that is capable of immediately carrying out a triumphant revolution. Successful political portrayals depict the members of the *Volk* and the shortcomings of their current state without implying that the present condition need be permanent.

The *Volk* that is being addressed and portrayed has never led an intact existence, largely as a result of its exclusion from full participation in society, the economy, and politics. Increasing commodification in the present era has also brought increasing alienation. Individual members of this group are often limited in their comprehension of their own plight and in their ability to act with full humanity. And although individual characters are portrayed, a complete and balanced individuality cannot be achieved as long as contradictions persist within society. The plays discussed in this study demonstrate an awareness of such inadequacies and, either explicitly or implicitly, take a negative stance toward the status quo. But because the *Volk* is so important, and because the necessity of overcoming the limitations of the present situation is so great, these plays are also inspired by a utopian impulse that is equally important in determining the shape they take.

These impulses coexist in a dialectical relationship, and they exert different degrees and types of formal influences in different historical periods. Raimund's plays carry the overt message that harmony can be achieved by overcoming a flaw within the individual. Anzengruber thought community education based on reason could bring the necessary improvement, and Brecht believed that the proper class consciousness could lead to action and change for the proletariat. Kroetz shows workers who have attained such a level of awareness, though he is skeptical of their ability to institute change. But negation cannot be expressed simply through criticism or overt didacticism, and the plays, as we have seen, are more than their explicit messages: Raimund's harmony is achieved at great cost, and the negation expressed by the form continues to disrupt the unity of Rappelkopf's personal improvement. And at the other end of the chronological spectrum, Kroetz's refusal to provide a concrete utopian ending cannot suppress the movement his plays make in the direction toward such a conclusion beyond the ending of the text itself.

The need to address a mass audience and the intent to promote change, whether within the individual or society as a whole, has led to the frequent description of the *Volksstück* as a combination of entertainment and didacticism. Useful and valid though this framework may be, it involves concepts that too often lead to a separation of form and content or to an unwarranted assignment of superiority to one function over the other. Moreover, the overtly didactic message may in the end be less strong than an unconscious, ultimately political one. The negative and utopian, in relation to the current and eventual status of the *Volk* that is addressed, maintain the implications of *prodesse* and *delectare* but do more as well. An adequate embodiment of these two impulses results in a literarily valid text that provides a genuine voice for the *Volk*. An honest treatment is more than merely entertaining, and it is also unable to impose an artificial unity. The negative and the utopian prevent a generic definition from being based on superficial characteristics: the specifics of form become less important to the definition, though they remain a matter of utmost importance to each playwright. Both negation and the utopian find expression in the content of these *Volksstücke*, but content alone is not very effective in conveying the urgency of these impulses: few of these authors have believed that the mere statement of a polemical message could have much effect outside the theater.

Because of the problematics involving explicit messages, the aesthetic and philosophical thought of Adorno has provided a useful basis for an examination of the plays' overall effect. Rather than serving as a decorative vehicle, the form of all of these plays contains the most effective resistance to existing reality. Form and content are of course closely linked, even though this study has on occasion artificially separated them for heuristic purposes. Although popular success is an important formative criterion for most of the *Volksstücke* considered here, these plays are also autonomous to the extent that they resist both the clichés of the genre and an affirmation of existing society. They hardly seem to resemble the difficult and more obviously autonomous texts of Beckett and Kafka that were favored by Adorno, but similar processes are at work within these *Volksstücke* as well. The refusal to assume a formal response that accepts society as it is and the differences between any one of these plays and previous *Volksstücke* are what most profoundly express negation.

But these differences also provide an opening for a new awareness on the part of the spectator, an awareness that can spur the hope for something qualitatively better. Because the *Volksstücke* discussed in this study are formed from both impulses, the thought of Ernst Bloch has been employed to offer insight into an understanding of the truly utopian that is the goal of hope. Most of the plays under discussion contain positive elements, which, although typical of the genre, cannot be regarded as utopia itself. Their manner of inclusion within the text shows that they are actually limited affects, which only appear to provide satisfactory alternatives for the characters. Such false utopias are presented to serve as contrasts to a genuine utopia, which cannot be portrayed directly as content because it has never before been experienced. The content offers hints as to the qualities of the truly different, but again, it is in the form of these *Volksstücke* that the drive toward this utopia is best expressed. Although utopia cannot be attained within the play itself or in reality as it currently exists, these plays should not be regarded as mere presentations of illusions.

They represent for the most part a genuine expression of and for the *Volk*: their self-exertion carves out a place in the theater, in literature, and in society and thus increases the momentum for genuine improvement, however slight the plays' measurable effect may be and whether or not they propagate an explicit formula for change. They are not to be considered vocalizations of a pre-formed political ideology, whose institution they hope to encourage. Political ideologies, rather, cannot be formed apart from valid, concrete expressions of the people. Theory alone cannot provide a path to the future: praxis within society is also necessary. And as a type of creation and production that both emerges from changes in consciousness and society and works to bring these about, art relates to both theory and praxis. The study of these dramas is important for this reason, since they can negate and express hope in ways that theory cannot: in order to obtain a better comprehension of them, one must analyze and attempt to understand their form and their art. In this way one can observe how they stand in opposition, and in what direction they point.

These plays are products of history, as they take a form and employ content that attempts to provide adequate expression for a people in a particular situation. In responding to changes in reality and in the group whom they address, they also modify the inherited elements of the literary and theatrical tradition. The *Volksstück* cannot be understood simply in terms of sociological categories, fixed genre definitions, or the dual function of instructing and entertaining. All these components in all their dialectical complexity must be taken into account in order to comprehend how *Volksstücke* provide voices in the dialogue of history: voices that obstinately resist appropriation through their negation of the idea that an adequate unity is attainable within the current order, and voices that proclaim the hope for a utopia in which all members of the entire *Volk* will find a home.

NOTES

Chapter I: Introduction

1 "Only for the sake of the hopeless is hope given to us." "Goethes Wahlverwandt-schaften," *Gesammelte Schriften* 1.1: 201. All translations in this work are mine, unless otherwise noted.

2 Walter Benjamin, "Urspung des deutschen Trauerspiels," *Gesammelte Schriften* 1.1: 224–25.

3 See Jauß, esp. pp. 173–77.

4 Wolfgang Kayser names Croce and Voßler as two examples (332).

5 Fredric Jameson, *The Political Unconscious*, 144. Subsequent references to this work will be indicated in the text with the abbreviation PU and the page number.

6 For discussions of different uses of the term *Volksstück* see Bauer, "Volksstück" 32–34; Baur 28–30; and Lengauer, "Läuterung" 153–56. Jürgen Hein, in "Volks-stück als didaktisches Drama," gives a useful survey of how the terms *Volksstück* and *Volkstheater* were understood in the nineteenth century. For discussions of *Volk* see Aust, Haida, and Hein 17–18; Bauer, "Wiener Volksstück" 29.

7 Aust, Haida, and Hein trace the different uses of the term since 1774 (21–31).

8 A famous turning point was reached with Karl Kraus's praise of Nestroy in 1912 ("Nestroy und die Nachwelt"). Kraus criticized the posterity that had ignored Nestroy in the fifty years since his death, for he correctly realized that the strength of Nestroy's dramas lay in the uncompromising verbal wit of their satire, rather than in the entertainment that they provided or the Viennese material that they portrayed. Most of the scholarly attention paid to the *Volksstück* has been recent, however: Aust, Haida, and Hein call it a "neglected" genre in their opening sentence (17).

9 "Anmerkungen zum Volksstück," in *Gesammelte Werke in 20 Bänden* 17: 1162. For a fuller discussion see my Chapter VIII.

10 Rommel, *Alt-Wiener Volkskomödie* 15–17. Aust, Haida, and Hein also stress in their introduction that the text alone is not sufficient to provide an understanding of the genre (17). Their study provides the most recent as well as one of the most comprehensive overviews of the *Volksstück*. The authors discuss the problematics of defining the genre and refrain from offering a traditional "Gattungsgeschichte," providing instead a throrough review of the the scholarship. Pointing to gaps in the latter as well as accomplishments, their study is an essential reference work on the *Volksstück*.

11 See Hüttner, "Parodie" 102–103, 112, 114. The function of the *Volkstheater* was fulfilled to varying degrees by these *Vorstadttheater*. Like the concept *Volksstück*, that of *Volkstheater* changes over time. Roger Bauer compares the early use of the term *Volkstheater* with the rise of the *Nationaltheater*: both wanted to provide a theater for "all," but from different perspectives ("Volkstheater" 9–11). Two complementary activities occurred within drama: tragedy became more middle-class, and comedy was ennobled (13). The improvisational character of the suburban theater also became more literary (9). Bauer finds that a *Volkstheater* for all was achieved

in the *Theater in der Leopoldstadt* in 1819, though it was gone by 1833 (20). For a good overview of the theater during this period see Aust, Haida, and Hein 114–81.

12 See Rommel, *Alt-Wiener Volkskomödie* 975; Crößmann 48, 54–63; and Lengauer, "Läuterung" 150–51.

13 In the German Democratic Republic Peter Hacks often adopted what he calls a "plebeian position," introducing elements from the *Volksstück* tradition into some of his plays. Other writers attempted more purely functional plays in this vein, but these attempts to harness literature to immediate topical ends rarely went beyond the trivial (Hintze 37–40). In attempting to employ this type of play as a positive didactic model, authors gave language and comedy a different function from that of the contemporary *Volksstück* in the West, and the frequently encountered happy ending also served to differentiate them (Hein, "Volksstück: Entwicklung" 24). There also existed the opinion that the term "Volksstück" had become superfluous in the "new" society of the GDR (Hoffmann 394–95; Hintze 38). See also Aust, Haida, and Hein 345–49.

14 Yates claims that Gerd Müller's study confirms that there was "no real continuity between the popular drama of mid-nineteenth-century Vienna and the *Volksstücke* of the 1920s and 1930s ("Idea" 470). While Yates is technically correct in claiming that there were no unbroken links, the inability to trace a genealogy does not mean that there is no such thing as a history of something called the *Volksstück*. In addition, Yates tends to maintain the narrow definition of the term as it was understood in the earlier period. Even though Müller's definition runs the danger of circularity — he says the limits of the term *Volksstück* will emerge from its history and then chooses examples by authors who have used the term — he is aware of the the importance of historical context in his study (10). Although I disagree with Hein that the didactic provides the principal continuing element within these plays, he too accurately recognizes that transgressions against the norm can also represent continuity ("Volksstück als didaktisches Drama" 102).

15 Michael Holquist, "Introduction" in Bakhtin, *The Dialogic Imagination*, xviii–xix. The quotations from Bakhtin that follow are from the final essay in this volume, "Discourse in the Novel," 259–422.

16 Jameson says that New Criticism is ideological despite its claims to the contrary (PU 58–59), as does Eagleton (*Literary Theory*, 22, 50). Because of its stress on immanence, this school devoted most of its attention to lyric poetry.

17 Grossberg and Nelson discuss this problem in their "Introduction," esp. pp. 2–7. They correctly state, for example, "The overdetermination of a social practice by all levels of the social formation meant that culture could not be reduced to the effects of economic relations, even if mediated through ideology" (7). Eagleton points out that even sophisticated varieties of this type of approach, such as Lucien Goldmann's attempt to show homologies, or common structural patterns in literary texts and the thought of the social classes that produced them, run the danger of becoming too deterministic (*Marxism and Literary Criticism* 34).

18 In Althusser's view the economy does not mechanistically bring about changes in literature, nor does it find homologous expression in social practice and literary texts, but rather the economy and elements of the superstructure are effects of the same

structure, which exists through them and their relationship, rather than outside them. It is difficult in an introduction of this type to go into sufficient detail concerning the theories discussed. The reader is advised to consult Althusser and Jameson directly, or, for a clear introduction to both, see William C. Dowling, *"Jameson, Althusser, Marx: An Introduction to The Political Unconscious.*

19 Althusser had considered history an absent cause without a subject or a telos, but Jameson argues that although history is not a text itself, it is accessible only in textual form and approachable through its having been turned into narrative in the political unconscious. See PU 34–35. On p. 81 Jameson offers further elaboration on the relation of the text to the real, of history not as 'context' but as 'prior subtext' that can only be reconstructed after the fact. He gives a more recent response to criticisms of Althusser and the concept of totality in "Cognitive Mapping," esp. pp. 354–56.

20 PU 56. Jameson claims that in the subsequent chapters of his book he has been able to respect both methodological imperatives without any great inconsistency. In the rest of his initial chapter "On Interpretation" he then builds his own theoretical framework, starting with a historicized version of Freud's notion of the unconscious as a basis for his own concept of the political unconscious and continuing with a discussion of Northrop Frye's archetypal system as a variation of the medieval system of the four levels of scripture (PU 58–74). This latter system is important for Jameson because it opens up a text to multiple meanings without reducing any of the levels to inferiority through its insistence on maintaining the literality of the original text (PU 29–33).

21 Nineteenth-century theater critics demanded edifying dramas, such as Kaiser's *Lebensbilder*, which had a wholesome, didactic function. Critics tended to feel threatened by satires and "realistic" portrayals. See Yates, "Idea," esp. pp. 462–85, and Lengauer, "Läuterung," 156–60.

22 Hein lists some of these considerations in "Volksstück: Entwicklung" 9–10.

23 In "Volkstheater als Geschäft" Johann Hüttner argues that the Viennese *Vorstadttheater* did not have the character of "Gegentheater" [oppositional theaters] as found in London and Paris at the time. He claims that since they became "Volkstheater" only on Sundays and holidays, when the cheapest performances were held, the "Volk" did not have a stage for itself alone and no "public counterculture" developed (132). Yet as his own "Literarische Parodie" points out, certain plays were written principally for uneducated, lower-class audiences (see pp. 103–107, 112–14). And even though members of other classes often attended the *Vorstadttheater*, the *Possen* and many of the other plays that were offered there did not have to follow the aesthetic restrictions of the elitist high culture centered in the Burgtheater. The alternative presented was not only an aesthetic one: political implications are also present in its anti-aristocratic, egalitarian character (Decker 44–45). For additional views on the *Volkstheater* as opposing institution see Hein, "Volksstück als Didaktisches Drama" 98–102, Bauer "Wiener Volksstück" 29–32, and G. Müller 144.

24 Critical theory, the general method employed by the Frankfurt School as a whole, is of course not to be considered interchangeable with Adorno's own negative dialectics (see Buck-Morss 65).

25 In the process of demythologizing, the Enlightenment succumbed to a new mythology of its own by equating ideas with the quantifiable (*die Zahlen*; 10). The Enlightenment put formulas in the place of concepts, which are dialectical in their retention of both the negative and the positive: "The concept ... was rather from the beginning the product of dialectical thinking, in which everything is always that which it is only in its becoming that which it is not" (17). All authors who write on Adorno comment on the presumption and impossibility of summarizing his intentionally difficult thought and style. See for example Martin Jay, *Adorno* 11–14. Jay's book provides an excellent introduction to the thought of this difficult thinker, as do David Held's *Introduction to Critical Theory* and Susan Buck-Morss's *The Origin of Negative Dialectics*.

26 Theodor W. Adorno, *Negative Dialektik* 19–20. Subsequent references will be made in the text with the abbreviation ND and the page number.

27 Theodor W. Adorno, *Ästhetische Theorie* 12. Subsequent references will be made in the text with the abbreviation AT and the page number.

28 Theodor W. Adorno, "Engagement" in *Noten zur Literatur* III: 113. Susbsequent references will be made in the text with the abbreviation En and the page number.

29 Ernst Bloch, *Das Prinzip Hoffnung* 2. Subsequent references will be made in the text with the abbreviation PH and the page number. The same same pagination can be found in Ernst Bloch, *Gesamtausgabe*, vol. 5.

30 Buck-Morss 76. In his *Adorno* Jay continually returns to the faint but ever-present existence of the utopian in Adorno's thought. See pp. 20, 78, 87, 105, and 154–55.

31 Adorno in fact felt in 1935 that he and Benjamin could develop a common philosophy based on the method proposed in Benjamin's study of the German *Trauerspiel*, or tragic drama. (Wolin 173. Wolin discusses the Adorno-Benjamin dispute in detail on pp. 163–212.) However, he soon realized from Benjamin's Arcades Exposé and his "The Work of Art in the Age of Mechanical Reproduction" that there were significant differences in their thinking, which he elaborated in his correspondence with Benjamin. In contrasting the novelty of the commodity-dominated nineteenth century with its *Urgeschichte* in a classless society as represented by remnants in art and architecture, Benjamin says that the latter engender utopia as a collective dream of a following, better epoch ("Paris, die Hauptstadt des XIX. Jahrhunderts" in *Gesammelte Schriften* 5.1: 45–59). To Adorno, this was undialectical because the idea of classlessness became mythologized and linked to the present age in timeless fashion, rather than serving to expose both the present and the past as catastrophes. He feels that Benjamin mistakenly holds the *Urgeschichte* to be a Golden Age, rather than a category of Hell (Letter to Benjamin, in Taylor, *Aesthetics and Politics* 110–20).

32 Walter Benjamin, "Das Kunstwerk im Zeitalter seiner technischen Reproduzierbarkeit," in *Gesammelte Schriften*, I.ii: 431 ff; Theodor W. Adorno, letter to Walter Benjamin in Taylor, *Aesthetics and Politics*, 120–126.

33 His criticism of jazz as a commodity like any other produced by the culture industry, which only seems to liberate while maintaining the status quo, has not been widely accepted as an accurate analysis, despite its many acute perceptions. It ignores, for example, the oppositional elements in this music that derive its creative origins

among an excluded class. See "Über Jazz," *Zeitschrift für Sozialforschung* 5.2 (1936) and "Perennial Fashion— Jazz," in *Prisms* 119-32.

34 "Zerstörung, Rettung des Mythos durchs Licht" in *Literarische Aufsätze*, 344.

35 The authors chosen here have also been discussed by other scholars in connection with the *Volksstück*. I do not intend to repeat or establish a restrictive canon, however. Most of the authors mentioned throughout this introduction and even others, such as Hochwälder, Morre, or Valentin could have been included. It would also be worthwhile to examine a trivial *Volksstück* in detail to examine the reasons for its failure more precisely, or to analyze the incorporation of *Volksstück*-elements by writers such as Kaiser, Lasker-Schüler, Hofmannsthal, or Canetti. (Aust, Haida, and Hein should be consulted for treatment of a variety of authors such as these). Yet because of space limitations I have decided to include only full-length plays from successive periods that fulfill the criteria of addressing the *Volk* while providing genuine and adequate expression to the negative and the utopian. Gerd Müller gives useful and insightful analyses into plays by many of the same authors, yet his study is not guided by a precise definition of the genre or an overall concept, other than the application of the term itself (see note 14 above). *Volksstück*, by Aust, Haida, and Hein, is comprehensive, but its breadth allows it to devote only one or two pages to individual plays. In addition to the discussion of Thoma's *Magdalena*, which they base on my previous work, they treat four of the dramas I analyze here.

Chapter II: Raimund

1 "He is a poet; he believes that he is one, and yet does not know how much a poet he is. Above all, he is this — a child of the people. For this reason he is an individual, and at the same time, a world."

2 Claude David says that even though they are so tied to their Austrian tradition that export is impossible, they possess literary merit ("Raimund" 120). Sengle claims for several of Raimund's plays a solid place in the canon of German literature (*Biedermeierzeit* 3: 41) and Schmidt-Dengler ("Alpenkönig" 160) go so far as to say that their repeated performance into the present enables them to be classified as "Weltliteratur." Prohaska's book *Raimund and Vienna* discusses the relationship to the *Volkstheater* (see esp. pp. 2, 53, and 135). *Der Alpenkönig und der Menschenfeind* was the second offering in the 1989-90 season of the Schauspiel Bonn, a season that included many plays specifically chosen to counter the successes of parties of the radical right (*Deutschland Nachrichten* [German Information Center, New York], 21 June 1989: 6).

3 See Klotz, *Dramaturgie* 51. Hein says that these plays attempted to criticize the folly of wishing for the unattainable and provided a comedy of reconciliation. Instead of exposing contradictions in the manner of satire, these plays covered them up ("Volksstück: Entwicklung" 15). In criticizing the shortcomings of these three writers Urbach says that Gleich's magical spectacles suppressed the everyday misery of the public through the illusion of a transformation, that Bäuerle's local-color comedies resulted in a transfiguration of Vienna, and that Meisl's mythological caricatures both ridiculed and reconciled (*Wiener Komödie*, 100-101).

4 "Ferdinand Raimund" 121. Klotz's _Dramaturgie des Publikums_ also discusses the reciprocal relationship between public and author and devotes an entire chapter to Raimund (26–88).

5 Rommel, _Alt-Wiener Volkskomödie_ 42; Harding 169.

6 Schaumann, "Theater" 81; Hein, _Ferdinand Raimund_ 45. Though one need not go as far as Grillparzer, who stated that the public's role in writing the play was as important as Raimund's (95), one should not underestimate that role.

7 In addition to act and scene number, page numbers referring to Raimund's _Sämtliche Werke_ (1966) are given in parentheses. This edition follows the text of the 1924 _Säkularausgabe_.

8 In _Biedermeierzeit_, his three-volume treatment of the era of the Metternich restoration, Sengle stresses that a number of political and literary currents existed simultaneously. He sees the following, however, as characterizing the basic mood of the era: _Weltschmerz_, renewal and extension of empiricism, predilection for the smaller political and social forms (_Heimat_-state, the family, the home), and a general love of order (I: 1–82).

9 This word is a descriptive term applied by later scholarship. Although the term is useful, my study will indicate that it is only partially applicable to this play.

10 See Hein, _Raimund_ 46. This comes across clearly, and Sengle is correct in saying that it is hard to doubt the sincerity of the morality expressed in the play, or, unhistorically, to say that Raimund's didactic intentions were not serious (_Biedermeierzeit_ 3: 13).

11 Schmidt-Dengler disagrees with Hein's opinion (_Raimund_ 46) that the title is misleading and designed to attract the public into believing that the magical plays an even more important role than it actually does, since the dual configuration continues through the entire work (164). The play does, however, dispense with the frame plot in the spirit world and the dualistic principle of opposing good with evil spirits. (Schaumann, _Gestalt_ 65).

12 According to Rommel, this is what happened when Baroque dramatists presented a theodicy: there can be no dynamic plot when an outcome is preordained as the result of divine providence (_Alt-Wiener Volkskomödie_ 128–29).

13 Quoted in Raimund, _Säkularausgabe_ 5.1: 450 and 484. Other reviewers who praised the mixture and the unity of the play quoted on pp. 436, 438–40, 444–46, 477, 482, and 484, and those who criticized it on pp. 471 and 485.

14 Hein mentions these three functions in _Wiener Volkstheater_ (108), though he cautions elsewhere that it is wrong to reduce the function of Raimund's comedy to either the "affirmative-conciliatory" or the "socially-critically aggressive" ("Gefesselte Komik" 74–75). See also Rommel, _Alt-Wiener Volkskomödie_ 156–57.

15 This is what Wiltschko claims (14), though Harding asserts the opposite, that "Viennese is the norm, and deviations from it are exploited comically" (131).

16 Cf. Greiner 30. As Hein says, the harmony becomes problematic, because it is only achieved through the power of money (Hein, _Ferdinand Raimund_ 77–78).

17 Martin Greiner also emphasizes the extreme realism in this scene (qtd. in Hein, _Ferdinand Raimund_ 49). Prohaska says that this scene is the only one in all of

Raimund's plays to show the ugliness of real poverty. Yet she also points to its sentimental aspects (*Raimund and Vienna* 171-73).

18 Gerd Müller points out, for example, especially in plays like *Der Bauer als Millionär* that the earthly hierarchy is uncritically repeated in the fairy realm (22-25). Astragalus is still a monarch, though an ideal one, in that he is an enlightened servant of his people (Schmidt-Dengler 172).

19 Sengle says that this mixture accomplishes in "niedere[m] Stil" [vulgar style] what great poets had also accomplished (20).

20 Gerd Müller says, for example, that the "utopia of another world" is lacking in Raimund's plays, since they mainly seem to try to carve out a niche in the present one (23).

21 The position of women might be added to the list of problems that the play touches on without resolving, though its explicit mention is restricted to a song that is not fully integrated into the plot.

22 It might be noted here that in contrast to other authors of his time, who used islands as settings for utopias, Raimund in four of his other plays employed them as places of decadence. (See Schaumann, "Das Theater Ferdinand Raimunds" 88).

23 Urbach claims: "Es ist Raimund nicht um Akklamation des Bestehenden oder pseudopatriotische Verherrlichung eines 'Austria as it is' zu tun. Raimund versucht vielmehr in seinen Stücken eine harmonische Ordnung zu schaffen, die durch ihre unwahrscheinliche, märchenhafte Form kritisch wirkt" (*Wiener Komödie* 102). Hein says that Raimund "hält das *Volkstheater* offen für neue und leisere Formen, die nicht kritische Zeitbilder, sondern Gegenbilder der Wirklichkeit sein wollen" ("Gefesselte Komik" 86).

24 See Hein, *Raimund* 75-79 for a summary of these views.

Chapter III: Nestroy

1 "Frau von Erbsenstein: Truth is what I want, truth from your lips, I already have an inkling. Schnoferl: Then you also have everything, for the greatest scholars have never had anything more than an inkling of the truth." Text references are to Johann Nestroy, *Sämtliche Werke*, ed. Fritz Brukner and Otto Rommel. *Der Unbedeutende* is in volume 7: page references are included in parentheses in this discussion, preceded by act and scene number. Other references to the *Sämtliche Werke* will include the abbreviation SW and the volume number. A new, improved edition of Nestroy's plays is presently being published: Johann Nestroy, *Sämtliche Werke. Historisch-kritische Ausgabe*, ed. Jürgen Hein and Johann Hüttner, 1977 ff. Instead of grouping the plays by genres, it orders them chronologically. See Yates, "Nestroy und die Rezensenten;" 39-40.

2 Franz Mautner has summed up the commonly accepted dissimilarities between the two as follows: Raimund's comedies, just as his serious dramas, are dominated to a greater extent by the spiritual and the visual, Nestroy's by the intellectual and the verbal. Raimund's mirth consists of jest, Nestroy's of wit (without disdaining the burlesque). Raimund is inspired by nature and precisely formulated morality, Nestroy by the antithesis between essence and appearance, by the tension between reality and

language, in fact, by the individual word. ("Wiener Volkskomödie" 209). In addition, Nestroy was more prolific than Raimund and completed at least 83 plays.

3 See Jansen 275–76. Jürgen Hein, in *Das Wiener Volkstheater* (118–33) and in "Nestroyforschung" and "Neue Nestroyforschung," provides excellent summaries of the stages of Nestroy reception by critics and scholars from the 1840's through the present.

4 Yates, "Das Werden eines Nestroystücks" 65–66. See also Hüttner, "Nestroy im Theaterbetrieb" 233.

5 Recent editions of Nestroy texts have overcome earlier weaknesses of Nestroy scholarship that resulted from emendations by the editors of the first collection of his plays (Chiavacci/Ganghofer 1890–91) and the early attempts to render Nestroy harmless. Although the confused state of manuscripts and theater documents still makes a final evaluation of Nestroy texts difficult (see Hein, *Wiener Volkstheater* 119–20), the new edition (see note 1) attempts to address this problem.

6 Qtd. in May 90. See also Hüttner, "Literarische Parodie," for a discussion of different segments of the public.

7 Rommel, who is critical of Carl's exploitation of actors in order to make a profit for himself, says that "he bore the stamp of the entrepreneurial type of early capitalism in its purest form" ("Johann Nestroy, Ein Beitrag" 46). Hüttner points out that all the theaters were dependent on the sale of tickets and says that Carl was probably typical of theater managers of the time ("Volkstheater als Geschäft" 139–40).

8 SW 8:322, 337. See Yates, "Nestroy und die Rezensenten," "Kriterien der Nestroyrezeption," and "The Idea of the 'Volksstück' in Nestroy's Vienna" for analyses of critics' demands and Nestroy's reactions to them. Jürgen Hein writes that the critics considered *Die Unbedeutende* the beginning of a new phase as a "serious, realistic *Volksstück*" and that in this play "entfaltet Nestroys Emanzipations- und soziale Abgrenzungsbemühungen des Bürgertums" (*Johann Nestroy* 87). Hein also discusses the problems of genre and reception in Aust, Haida, Hein 144–49. See also Aust 185.

9 The former view is taken by Mautner (*Nestroy* 63–64) and the latter by Hein (*Spiel und Satire*) and Rommel ("Johann Nestroy, der Satiriker" 57). Yates correctly recognizes that his plays "betray from the early 1830's on an aggressive dissatisfaction with existing society" (*Nestroy* 152).

10 See Hein, *Spiel und Satire* 161; May 121.

11 The more Nestroy simplifies his sources, the more political they become, according to Preisner ("Johann Nestroy. Der Schöpfer" 106).

12 Brill makes important observations on Nestroy's use of language, though he is too one-sided in regarding it as the only effective element in his comedies (see 12–13, 91–91, 171, 181).

13 Sengle starts with the conventions of literary rather than social language and suggests that the assumption of important roles in Nestroy plays by lower class characters derives from the fact that the language of literature had been used up by *Empfindsamkeit* and Idealism. In order to rejuvenate what would have sounded hollow and pathetic, Nestroy employed dialect (*Biedermeierzeit* 3: 202–03). But an explanation of this type at the level of the superstructure is probably not without structural

parallel at the level of the base. And in any case the effect is the same: the creation of a privileged forum for spokespeople from the lower classes. This is another example of a resemblance between the *Volksstück* and Bakhtin's view of the novel, which incorporates a multiplicity of dialogical voices.

14 An even more clearly stated positive alternative might be expected in *Freiheit in Krähwinkel*, a play written two years later when the revolution brought a temporary end to censorship. Some spectators greeted it as a call to revolution, but others thought it was a vulgar trivialization of a serious political movement (Jones, "Authorial Intent" 22–25). This results from a satirical attack that condemns both the dominant government and the inadequacies of the revolutionaries (Seeba 136–43). Although Eberhard Ultra's revolt is successful (cf. Decker 55, 59), he is more effective in revealing the limitations of the current government and how it maintains control through language than in providing an adequate replacement.

15 The very structure that requires such an ending, like almost everything else, is also a target for Nestroy's mockery (Mautner, "Wiener Volkskomödie" 209). Sengle admits that the endings of Nestroy's plays are often less than convincing in their abruptness, but he argues that we should not assume for that reason that Nestroy failed to believe them or that he is modern. He thinks that Nestroy was simply unable to employ a *Seelensprache* except through parody (3: 202–03, 221–22, 263).

16 Although Nestroy took critics' views into account when developing his "classical" *Posse* in the years 1838–1844, his "predilection for the sharpness of wit as opposed to edifying and facetious effects was unalterable" (Yates, "Nestroy und die Rezensenten" 31–32). Thus the form of his *Possen* tended to go more against the tide of critical opinion (Yates, "Kriterien" 11). This contradictory attitude with relation to the central milieu of the play and to the public is described by Volker Klotz as centripetal in its striving toward and thus affirming of that milieu, and centrifugal as it strives away, and thus negates it (*Bürgerliches Lachtheater* 114).

17 Hannemann says that Nestroy's theater cannot be called 'critical' because it is so completely negative and offers no alternatives; negation, in fact, may be considered the basic characteristic of his very being (123, also 30–31). Preisendanz even doubts whether one can say that this type of comedy results from the discrepancy between utopia and reality, since he fails to find traces of the utopian in Nestroy's 83 plays (21). Sengle, on the other hand, finds this element in an underlying adherence to moral norms. However, he does not sufficiently recognize that such an interpretation overlooks the skeptical direction of the plays themselves, even though these norms may have played a role in Nestroy's own life. As mentioned above, Hein's "Der utopische Nestroy" represents a stimulus toward a counter-trend. Jansen's "Nestroys skeptische Utopie" also illustrates how the form of the fairy tale, when employed in *Der Talisman*, responds to the very basic human need for an alternative world (279). This play does not portray a solution in reality "but as a utopia, which shames reality" (280). The outcast redheads Titus and Salome point to the hope for justice that is lacking in this life, in which the last shall be made first.

18 Other critics also see something positive in the negative. The act of creation itself is what leads Hannemann to admit begrudgingly that Nestroy is not completely negative: "by aestheticizing nihilism in the *Posse*, Nestroy created, perhaps against

his will, something positive" (156). Corriher finds that "in negating the world, the skeptic implicitly affirms his own negating faculty, or in Nestroy's case, the rational mind" (29). Bauer observes that "the sarcasm that judges reality goes hand in hand with the exaltation of that reality, and vice versa. This explains that the cynicism of Nestroy, in spite of its exaggeration, is never absolute. Condemnation never excludes a last recourse in grace, if only in that of redeeming laughter" (*Realité* 253).

Chapter IV: Anzengruber

1 "Yes, everything speaks in favor of glorifying life, and only one thing speaks against it: the truth." References to *Ludwig Anzengrubers Sämtliche Werke* will be included in the text with the abbreviation SW and the volume and page number.
2 Cf. Schmidt-Dengler 134 and May 63–87. Klotz also convincingly points out how the operetta provides a collective dramatic voice for the people ("Vox Populi").
3 See e.g. Frenzel 105, Martini, *Deutsche Literaturgeschichte* 446, Cowen 71, Koessler 451. In an early study Fritz Weber found Anzengruber naturalistic in his belief that all of life was suitable for artistic representation, his scientific manner of observation, his use of dialect, and his method of portraying contemporary matters and empirical reality (106–09). Weber sees differences between Anzengruber and Zola, however, in the latter's more studious observation of the environment and willingness to place the unpleasant in the foreground.
4 Howe summarizes this as follows: "to bring social awareness into the theater, to enlighten and free humanity from literal-minded and hence narrow-minded beliefs, its pious inertia and unthinking acceptance of traditional authority.... The specific issues of his time, such as industrialization, religious tolerance, poverty, and loss of community, serve as impetus for such enlightenment" (141).
5 *Die Kreuzelschreiber* is found in *Ludwig Anzengrubers Sämtliche Werke*, vol. 4. References included in the text will omit the volume number but will indicate act, scene, and page number.
6 Cf. G. Müller 54–56, Rossbacher 233, Lengauer, "Anzengruber's Kunst" 388.
7 See Hein, "Volksstück: Entwicklung" 19; Howe 150; and G. Müller 54–56. In the 1880's, however, Anzengruber had attained the status of a sort of classic, and his plays represented the model for what was to be performed at the newly established Deutsches Volkstheater. But the type of edifying dramas that the directors had in mind was already perceived by Anzengruber as being practically impossible to attain, and the audience envisioned was the educated bourgeoisie, rather than the broader mass of the public that he had tried to reach. See also Bauer "Wiener Volkstheater" 31.

Chapter V: Thoma

1 "Oh, the picture-pretty Bavarian maids with their modestly bashful, occasionally naughty, but always so affecting charm, who smile in the paintings of Defregger and coo in the plays of Ganghofer — why did you, O Ludwig Thoma, eliminate them from the world of the peasants in your newest *Volksstück*?" These ironic comments

are contained in a review of the first Munich performance of *Magdalena* ["Residenz-theater: 'Magdalena' von Ludwig Thoma." *Münchner Post* (22 Oct. 1912) 3–4.

2 References to Ludwig Thoma, *Ein Leben in Briefen*, will be indicated with the abbreviation LB.

3 References to Ludwig Thoma, *Gesammelte Werke*, will be given in the text with the abbreviation GW and the volume and page numbers. Thoma's criticisms of the vast majority of *Volksstücke* resemble the objections that Brecht would later voice.

4 For additional discussions of *Magdalena*, see Jones, "Tradition and Innovation: The *Volksstücke* of Ludwig Thoma" and "Ludwig Thoma's *Magdalena*: A Transitional *Volksstück*." The former also treats Thoma's other plays in their relation to the *Volksstück* as genre.

5 In his article "Wunschbild Land und Schreckbild Stadt," Sengle gives a detailed survey of the tradition in literature that contrasts city and country.

6 Act, scene, and page numbers included within the text refer to Thoma, *Gesammelte Werke*, vol. 2. The same pagination is found in Thoma, *Theater*.

7 A literary history published in the GDR says, for example, that Thoma's accomplishment lies in confronting two spheres of society in the person of Leni: the intolerance of the outmoded patriarchal farm society becomes evident when its members instinctively attempt to stamp out the destructive capitalist element that the young woman as prostitute introduces (Kaufmann and Schlenstedt 264). While it is true that Leni treats love as a commodity like any other as a result of her situation, it is simplistic to view her as a representative of capitalism, and the motivations of the villagers are more complex than this. More important perhaps is the mayor's subordination of human relations to property relations, which further reifies community values.

8 He writes for example "Leut" instead of "Leit," "Alte" instead of "Oide," and "Deuter" instead of "Deida" (Gerd Müller 67).

Chapter VI: Fleißer

1 "He was and became an outsider in a village. The boy does not get to know love, but does without it; this need for love occupies him his whole life long, drives him to strange decisions." Marieluise Fleißer, "Foundling and Rebel: On Jean Genet." *Gesammelte Werke* 2: 325.

2 Many scholars, however, stress that the roots of the twentieth century *Volksstücke* lie in the old Viennese comedy tradition. (Cf. Dimter 219–20, Hoffmeister, *Theater* 2. Hoffmeister rejects the term *Volksstück* for most twentieth-century examples, however, because this category "must be so stretched and differentiated that its perimeters lose the power of signification" (11). She prefers the term "milieu play" for this type of drama.

3 Hein summarizes the other three major authors of this type of drama in the Weimar period as follows: "Horváth attempts a renewal with the destruction of the 'old' *Volksstück*, Zuckmayer discovers the sensuously vital components, Brecht experiments with the forms of expressionist dramaturgy and the farce (*Die Kleinbürger-hochzeit*, [1926]) ("Formen des Volkstheaters" 502).

4　*Materialien zum Leben und Schreiben der Marieluise Fleißer*, ed. Günther Rühle, contains numerous reviews of performances, essays by and about Fleißer, and other pertinent materials. References will be included in the text with the abbreviation *Mat.* and the page number.

5　For a discussion of different approaches to the notion of *Heimat* in lyric poetry, see Jones, "Past Idyll or Future Utopia: *Heimat* in German Lyric Poetry of the 1930s and 1940s."

6　Mannheim pointed out four intellectual groups that opposed the loss of the utopian: (1) those who sought it in the past or in Nature, (2) those who looked for a romantic revival of myths and symbols, (3) those who identified with the proletariat, e.g. Brecht and Friedrich Wolf, and (4) those who sought it outside history in the chiliastic or ecstatic, e.g. Ernst Toller (in Rotermund 20).

7　According to Gerd Müller, "the unspoiled nature of this intact world along the Rhine" seems like a fairy tale when compared to the reality of a generation that had lost its hopes in the world war and its belief in a better future as a result of the failed revolution and the economic crises that followed (75); "closeness to the *Heimat* means strength, security, and vitality for Zuckmayer" (78). Müller, who retains the traditional definition of *Volksstück* as a play that both entertains and instructs, goes so far as to say that Zuckmayer's plays are not *Volksstücke*, since they fail to perform the latter function at all. My study stresses the utopian and the negative, and I would contend that *Der fröhliche Weinberg* displays little of either.

8　The negative reaction to the second play stemmed largely from prudish middle-class offense at the treatment of sexuality, which had been exaggerated in Brecht's staging. Fleißer's lawsuit against the mayor brought her additional unwelcome attention, and local appreciation for her work did not come until shortly before her death. The first play actually offers a bleaker picture of Ingolstadt than does *Pioniere*, but since it had had only one experimental matinee performance in Berlin, it received less attention in the provinces (cf. Rühle, "Leben" 24–25).

9　Dieter Bachmann claims that the title is misleading because this purgatory does not purify (*Mat.* 316). Purification does not need to occur within the play itself, however, in order for this hope to be expressed. McGowan quotes Fleißer as saying that the play could also have been called "Die Eingeschloßenen" (*Fleißer* 25).

10　The original version of this play (written in 1924) has been lost. The stage version for the performance by the Junge Bühne Berlin (in the Deutsches Theater, 25 April 1926) still exists, but the text that will be discussed here is the one that the author revised for the performance in Wuppertal in 1971 and that is contained in *Gesammelte Werke* 1: 61–125. Subsequent references will be indicated in the text by the page number. Other references to the *Gesammelte Werke* will include the abbreviation GW and the volume number.

11　Kässens and Töteberg say that Olga's attempt to find a moment of freedom in sexuality fails because this sexuality turns out to be only the freedom of a male society, which assigns certain places to women and refuses to tolerate any behavior on their part that deviates from the roles of "capital, labor, and sex object" (*Fleißer* 52).

12 Gerd Müller observes a similar phenomenon in the next play, *Pioniere*. Hoffmeister points out that the plots of drama are usually driven forward by conflict: "In this play, however, a certain stasis prevails, despite all the commotion. It is a tug of war where no one goes anywhere" (*Theater* 40). Buck thinks that the plot of all three of Fleißer's *Volksstücke* always takes the form of a circle. This epic method grants an x-ray view into social conditions and justifies Fleißer's claim, "Fürs Theater schreiben heißt für mich Gesellschaftskritik" [to me, writing for the theater is social criticism] (qtd. in Buck, "Kleinbürger" 49–50).

13 Ursula Roumois-Hasler says the ambivalence resluting from the text's "singular hermeticism and self-refusal" make the dialogue the only means for approaching this "puzzling play" (9). She analyzes the dialogues with linguistic criteria devised to investigate everyday speech and, finding significant differences between the aesthetic language of the drama and actual conversation, achieves important insights. This, in her opinion, leads to a literary evaluation that was impossible in the 1920s without such linguistic tools (37).

14 See McGowan, "Kette" 30–31. Fleißer's later *Volksstück*, *Der starke Stamm* (1944–45), uses much stonger dialect. Cf. *Mat.* 345, Betten 205–207.

15 Hoffmeister finds that the dialogue's tendency to work against the smooth development of plot is an innovative feature, since plot usually develops from dialogue (*Theater* 23). She states that "aggressive maneuvering, not development of thought or action, provides the dynamism" in the play's opening scene (30).

16 Susan Cocalis takes at face value Fleißer's later statements that she merely reported her observations and thus developed a new synthetic form of drama in contrast to the analytic, male type. To Cocalis, Fleißer's success as a realist results from her unwillingness to add commentary or offer a solution. Though this observation has important implications for the play's effect, it does not offer a valid criterion for determining realism ("Weib ist Weib" 208–09).

17 In an article on Roland Barthes's *S/Z* Sandy Petrey uses J.L. Austin's theory of speech acts to argue that mimesis may remain a useful concept if one separates it from the referential fallacy by observing that "realism enacts a constative vision of the world by simultaneously denying language's connection to objective truth and affirming its expression of social truth" (153–55). The combination of the verb "enact" with "constative" shows that the latter word is here to be taken not just in its usual meaning of describing something outside itself but as a sub-category of the performative aspect of language. Furthermore, reference does in fact take place, but to a socially agreed upon meaning, rather than to an objective truth. "*Sarrasine* authenticates, signs, signifies the 'real' as just that, the reality that is what people say it is. Its authentification comes not in opposition to but in collusion with the coded operations through which a community's members effect and ratify their ontology" (165).

18 Cocalis, for example, concludes that Fleißer offers neither a feminist alternative nor utopian illusions ("Weib ist Weib" 209). Kässens and Töteberg state, "Another world is unimaginable for the spectators, the utopia of a better future is not visible in any of the plays" (*Fleißer* 41). Wendt says that Fleißer's perspective is characterized by "hopelessness, immobility, and the only way out of these: the no-man's-land of

deluded amorality" (*Mat.* 288). McGowan says that Fleißer differs from Brecht in her lack of all utopian and forward-looking tendencies ("Kette" 30).

19 Gerd Müller comments on this same aspect in *Pioniere*: trying to divorce herself from the falseness of a belief in the purity of timeless myths, Fleißer nonetheless created what may be called *Volksstücke* because of the exactitude and intensity with which she portrayed the current lives of the people, even when such portrayals were not the most flattering. Her plays are "volkstümlich" [appropriate to the people], he says, because she represents complicated processes unpretentiously and graphically (90–92).

Chapter VII: Horváth

1 "That the interest in the theater has declined among the broad mass of the people probably results from the fact that we do not have a real *Volkstheater* any more — but we are headed toward it." References in my study to Ödön von Horváth, *Gesammelte Werke in acht Bänden* (1978), contain the abbreviation GW, volume number, and page number. The various reasons for the unreliabilty of this text and the four-volume clothbound edition that preceded it are elaborated by Hillach in his review in *Germanistik*. Suhrkamp is issuing a new edition of the *Gesammelte Werke* in 15 individual volumes that attempts to correct the insufficiencies of the earlier collected works. See note 8.

2 Cf. Fritz 9–12, 261; Reich-Ranicki 88; and Dimter 228–29.

3 See Hein, "Ödön von Horváth — Kasimir und Karoline" 50, and Klotz, *Dramaturgie des Publikums* 187. All references to Hein and Klotz in this chapter are to these texts.

4 The "tradition" of course, is a broad one and by no means follows a unilinear path; Horváth stressed some components while rejecting others. Horváth's plays are similar in many respects to Fleißer's, and both were seeking to solve similar dramatic problems. Fleißer's plays were not widely performed at this time, however, and it is not likely that she had much influence on him.

5 Hein is correct in observing that the most useful studies do not try to categorize Horváth too rapidly but instead attempt to reveal his social-critical intentions through subtle formal analyses (43–44).

6 *Materialien zu Ödön von Horváths "Kasimir und Karoline,"* ed. Traugott Krischke, contains essays and comments by Horváth, reviews of performances, and other materials. References will be indicated in the text with the abbreviation *Mat.* and the page number.

7 Bartsch feels that Horváth's refusal to give monocausal explanations is an important part of his realism: in the conflicts that he portrays there is always a collision of at least two elements, (economic, social, or political) that hinders communication between persons. Horváth was rediscovered in the 1960's partly because his perceptive analysis of lower middle-class behavior contributes to an understanding of the rise of fascism (Bruns 109). His cultural analyses have been compared to those of Wilhelm Reich (Bance 251–52; Schulte 78) and to the critical theory of the Frankfurt School (Rotermund 40–45; Schulte 71). Meinrad Pichler's study compares Horváth's portrayals with those of sociologists and finds them valid, both as a

demographic analysis and as a pathogenesis of "the psychological decline in character of the members of an entire class," who had no unified ideology of their own but patched one together from slogans, *ressentiments*, and influences from the culture industry (63–66; see also Dimter 223). The connection to external reality makes Horváth's *Volksstücke* historical, but, perhaps paradoxically, it is these plays, rather than the ones dealing with more timeless themes and subjects, that have proved more lasting and received more critical esteem (Wapnewski 17; Jenny, "Horváth's Größe" 71).

8   *Kasimir und Karoline*, issued separately by Suhrkamp, forms volume 5 of the new *Gesammelte Werke* (1986). This volume contains Horváth's first typewritten version in seven "Bilder" as well as the printed theater version of 1932. Page references in my study are to the second of the versions in this volume. Since the play consists of 117 short scenes, the scene number will also be given when appropriate. (*Kasimir und Karoline* is in volume 1 of the 1978 *Gesammelte Werke*.)

9   This is the assessment of Neikirk, who sees a progression in the role of women throughout Horváth's work. In the early political plays, she says that they "expose the brutal stupidity of men devoted almost solely to poltical ideals." The *Volksstücke* represent the second group. In the third group, the later comedies, the women are able to act and triumph over adversity. The women in the last plays are similar, in her opinion, but in addition come to terms with metaphysical forces greater than themselves. Here the timelessness of the human condition is expressed. See also Reich-Ranicki 90.

10 Hajo Kurzenberger's excellent study, *Horváths Volksstücke. Beschreibung eines poetischen Verfahrens*, is basically formalist, and he admits that its most difficult part is its attempt to define the exact relation between the aesthetic and the social in the verbal work of art (123). He praises Fritz's book, but faults it for tending to confuse the social with the content (124). All references to Kurzenberger in this chapter are to this book.

11 According to Hein, Horváth's criticism of the old *Volksstück* results from its inability to perceive the changes that had taken place in the populace that it depicts, its holding fast to the notion of unchangeable, eternal problems, its sovereign treatment of verbal means, and its suggestion of the "little person's" capability for effective action through the creation of a positive hero (50).

12 Hein 53; Hummel 24; Klotz 197; Kurzenberger 9; Schaarschmidt 202; Buck, "Stille" 180. Klotz says that the old *Volksstück*, which is less than 200 years old, broke with the classical dramatic canon and its *Standesregel* [rule of class standing] in order to portray the problems of the *Volk* seriously. In employing comedy the *Volksstück* could not make laughingstocks of the *Volk*, and thus it abandoned the inherited two-class dramaturgy. It incorporated elements from subliterary areas, such as dialect, proverbs, folksongs, and dances in a style that often mixed the comic and the tragic. Klotz finds nonetheless that the *Volksstück* did not break completely with the classical dramaturgical form, retaining, for example, a consistently motivated plot, a clearly visible theme, a distinction between individual actors and individual foils, and carefully balanced acts and scenes (183–85). Horváth completes the task of emancipating the *Volksstück* from the classical tradition (197), not merely by

incorporating the appropriate sociological level as content, but through the creation of character through the *Bildungsjargon* that had replaced dialect (188–89), the use of an epic structure (192), and the abandonment of a single, visible theme and single individual hero with whom the public was supposed to identify (197–98). Klotz refers to Horváth's method as "Reagenz-Dramatik," meaning that he reacts against the old form of the *Volksstück* (182), whose prefabricated parts he experimentally puts together in order to disassemble later (187).

13 Horváth, who also wrote novels, chose to make *Kasimir und Karoline* a play and thus ran up against what Szondi called the basic problem of modern social drama: how to convert the "entfremdete Zuständlichkeit" [alienated conditionality] of human relations in our times into "zwischenmenschliche Aktualität" [interpersonal actuality] (qtd. in Joas 55). But since alienation prevents the portrayal of a dramatic collision in the Hegelian sense through individual relationships and through dialogue (as had been the case in classical drama), a loose structure results (55). Chance, which had been omitted in classical drama, plays an important role here in the construction: the linking together of newly made acquaintanceships is carried out in the chain of individual scenes (57). For Hegel, the dialogue was the most perfect dramatic form, but in Horváth, the spoken word no longer produces results (Kurzenberger 34–36).

14 Only in accentuating the thematics of language, says Hein, does *Kasimir und Karoline* become "a play that gives a glimpse into the socio-economic and political relations of the Weimar Republic" (61). In earlier drafts of the play the situation becomes an object of conversation, but the final version omits such speeches, since the characters cannot communicate, and their language becomes a symptom of the effect that conditions have on them, rather than as bearers of ideas (see also Kurzenberger 142). To Franz Xaver Kroetz, who modelled his own early works on the plays of Horváth, the degree of reality that these plays convey marks the conscious birth of a new *Volkstheater*. Though Kroetz naively establishes a contrast between realism and subjective artistry, he observes the former in Horváth's recognition of "Sprachlosigkeit" [loss of speech], which is found not in absolute silence but in truisms, clichés, proverbs, and expressions of politeness or discomfort (91–92).

15 To Horváth, the term *Bildungsjargon* describes the language that was shared by the more educated bourgeoisie, whose material position had sunk in the years of inflation and depression, and the strata immediately below, who aspired to a position that reflected education and achievement. Characters use it to give the impression of a higher status than they actually have or to hide a social decline that they do not want to admit (Bartsch 39–40). *Bildungsjargon* only superficially resembles educated speech, though it must be understood that Horváth was not using it to condemn a sort of limited education or the characters themselves (Erken, "Horváth" 141).

16 Bartsch (39) correctly criticizes Hildebrandt (237) for calling language a "corrupt medium;" it is rather the characters' use of language that is condemned, according to Bartsch.

17 Horváth strives not for an "Entlarvung des Kleinbürgers" [unmasking of the petit-bourgeois] but "Entlarvung der Kleinbürgerlichkeit des modernen Bewußtseins" [unmasking of the petit-bourgeois character of modern consciousness] (Jarka 584).

Annoyed that audiences at the Berlin premiere thought that he was trying to unmask Munich and the Oktoberfest through parody, Horváth wrote in the "Gebrauchsanweisung": "Keine Demaskierung eines Menschen, einer Stadt — das wäre ja furchtbar billig!" [No unmasking of a human being, of a city — that would be terribly cheap!] (GW 8: 660).

18 In Reich-Ranicki's words, Horváth's plays make "mit volkstümlichen Kunstmitteln die Fragwürdigkeit des Volkstümlichen augenscheinlich" [use folksy means to reveal the dubiousness of the commonly held idea of the distinctiveness of folk traits] (84).

19 Yates says that the greatest similarities between Nestroy and Horváth lie in the "satire of the linguistic cliché" ("Idea" 471).

20 Kienzle refers to the play as a "dialektisches Spannungsfeld aus komischen Ursachen und tragischen Auswirkungen, lustspielhaften Situationen und beklemmenden Erfahrungen" (19).

21 The disappointed reaction of Berlin audiences to a 1967 performance of *Geschichten aus dem Wiener Wald* is described in a *Bild-Zeitung* article with its typically exaggerated headline: "Publikum ahnungslos — fast ein Skandal: Viele waren dem verlockenden Operettentitel auf den Leim gegangen ... Nichts da von Wiener Charme und Gemütlichkeit" (qtd. in Hummel 131; see Schulte 80–88). A similar response occurred after a 1952 Munich performance of *Kasimir und Karoline* in which the audience booed at what they perceived to be an insult to their beloved Oktoberfest (*Mat.* 142–56). A collection of 200 reviews of performances, including all premieres, can be found in Krischke, *Horváth auf der Bühne 1926–1938.*

22 Schulte 89. Schulte documents the phases in Horváth's reception since the 1930', from oblivion, through hesitant recognition, to the Horváth-boom of the 1960s, followed by his establishment as a "classic" with a standard place in the repertoires of German theaters (108–109).

23 Since the social totality cannot be pressed into a dramatic construction, it is made visible through the medium of socially determined verbal forms, rather than through conflict-schemata or plot (Kurzenberger 143). This situation results in characters who no longer display a self-determining integral personality (Kurzenberger 44, Hein 55), even though most scholars agree that Horváth sided strongly with the individual (von Wiese, "Horváth" 40–41, Hillach, "Das Volksstück" 242–43).

24 Gerhard Jörder criticized the 1986 production in Freiburg for showing too little of this hope, "von dieser immerwährenden Suche nach dem kleinen, großen Glück; von den echten Gefühlen, die ihnen so leicht zur falschen Phrase, zur kitschigen Pose verrutschen." This critic is more aware that the dialectic in which this play exists has been overlooked, for the director "zeigt Endstadien — keine Progresse, keine Entwicklungen, kein Auf und Ab zwischen Himmel und Erde."

25 And even in the last works, according to Hillach, his outlook does not deteriorate into a middle-class inwardness, but remains grounded in a material ethics ("Volksstück" 242–43).

26 In response to a question from a member of the audience after a reading from *Die Rättin*, Freiburg im Breisgau, 13 April 1986.

Chapter VIII: Brecht

1 "The poor need courage.... The fact that they bring children into the world already shows that they have courage, for they don't have any prospects" (*Gesammelte Werke* 4: 1404).

2 *Herr Puntila und sein Knecht Matti* is found in volume 4 of Brecht's *Gesammelte Werke*. References to this play will be indicated in the text by page numbers in parentheses. "Anmerkungen zu dem Volksstück" is in volume 17. References to this and other writings by Brecht will be indicated in parentheses by the abbreviation GW together with the volume and page number.

3 For discussions of the similarities between Nestroy and Brecht see Slobodkin, "Nestroy und die Tradition des *Volksstücks* im Schaffen Brechts," and Hein, *Spiel und Satire in der Komödie Johann Nestroys* (127–31). McGowan treats Brecht and his contemporaries in "Comedy and the Volksstück" (73).

4 The contract that they drew up indicates that they considered themselves collaborators and were to share equally in the royalties; each was to retain the rights for his or her native country while acknowledging the other's role (Deschner 125). As Knopf points out, however, Brecht did not abide by the terms of the contract, and failed to list Wuolijoki at first as co-author (216). In the present text, the play is introduced with the phrase "Geschrieben nach den Erzählungen und einem Stückentwurf von Hella Wuolijoki" [written after the stories and the draft of a play by Hella Wuolijoki] (1610). For discussions of the play's genesis see Knopf 213–16, Deschner, Mews 17–21, and Neureuter 9–113; see also Semrau 11–12. Most also list these additional influences: Charlie Chaplin's film *City Lights*, Denis Diderot's novel *Jacques le fataliste*, and Jaroslav Hasek's novel *The Adventures of the Good Soldier Schweik*.

5 See Hermand, "Herr Puntila" for a summary of these reactions (11–19). Also see Mews 48–51.

6 White summarizes these views at the beginning of his article but finds himself that the play does indeed have a plot (880–82).

7 Knopf discusses the Hegelian model in more detail (217–18) as does Hans Mayer in "Herrschaft und Knechtschaft" (quoted to a large extent in Mews 9–17).

8 Hoffmeister finds that plays like *Puntila* and the later socialist *Volksstücke* of Peter Hacks are different from the milieu plays of Fleißer and Kroetz because of their "ontological commitment to an explicit a priori ideology rather than to the imperatives of mimesis" (*Theater* 11). Similarly, Hinck finds that the typology used to illustrate these classes results in the omission of realistic details of everyday reality (*Dramaturgie* 33).

9 Butzlaff adds, however, that terms of Marxist vocabulary hidden within the play add to a clarification of *Mensch* in the Brechtian sense. As an example, he quotes Matti's remark that it does not matter whether Puntila gives him a recommendation as a "red" or as a "Mensch," since either one would disqualify him from future employment. Butzlaff claims this equates the two terms and thus indicates that the exemplary human is a communist. Certainly Brecht's play attempts to correspond to a Marxist historical vision, but for reasons explained later, it would be an oversimpli-

fication to look for an understanding of the concept *Mensch* in an equivalency with "communist," especially in its contemporary manifestation.

10 Martini says that in the formation of the dramatic characters and in the structuring of the scenes and the language of dialogue Brecht made the dialectic the ruling structural principle of the *Volksstück* (*Lustspiele* 240). Hermand says that the dramatic dialectics involved here make the play an equal to the more famous *Mutter Courage* and *Leben des Galilei* ("Herr Puntila" 127).

11 Hermand, "*Herr Puntila und sein Knecht Matti*," 124–26. See my p. 131 above for additional comments on Zuckmayer's play. Berckman is perhaps more correct in saying that Brecht's play is written against a type of comedy, rather than a specific play (in Neureuter 284).

12 Reinhold Grimm lists detailed examples and analyzes their function in *Bertolt Brecht. Die Struktur seines Werkes* (Nürnberg: Hans Carl, 1968). A summary of the remarks that pertain to *Herr Puntila und sein Knecht Matti* can be found in Mews 51–55.

13 Hinck points out the importance of the epic to Brecht's "open dramaturgy," in which the parts fail to conform to strict laws of causality or temporality such an arrangement enables the introduction of several perspectives as opposed to one (*Dramaturgie* 25–27). In his essay "Was ist das epische Theater?" Walter Benjamin recognized that interruptions to the plot, such as the songs, the narrative insertions, and the plays within the play provided the function of leading the viewer to new discoveries (*Gesammelte Schriften* 2.2: 519–31).

14 Cf. Knopf 221 and Fritz Martini, *Soziale Thematik und Formwandlungen des Dramas*, 273–74, qtd. in Mews 64–65. Slobodkin contrasts this master-servant relationship with the one in Nestroy's *Frühere Verhältnisse* in "Nestroy und die Tradition" 104–107.

15 Hinck says that the play itself cannot resolve the contradictions within society, but only point them out (*Dramaturgie* 22). It would have been dishonest to try to clear up complicated social relations with a simplified conclusion like that of the *Besserungsstück*, which brought characters to a moral improvement in the end. In Hinck's opinion, an important intended effect of the critical *Volksstück* was to convey an uneasiness that extends beyond the play's finish ("Mutter Courage" 174). To Martini, a happy conclusion is not necessary in order to consider the play a comedy: the other aspects of the form, the *Volksstück*-style, and the possibility of "comic play" put it into that genre (*Lustspiele* 256).

16 Translations of the important essays by Bloch, Lukács, Brecht, Benjamin, and Adorno that make up this debate are collected in *Aesthetics and Politics*, ed. Ronald Taylor, which also includes useful explanatory introductions by the editors and a conclusion by Fredric Jameson. The following are quoted in the remainder of this essay, and the page numbers from the translations in *Aesthetics and Politics* will follow references to the original German, when the latter is included: Bloch, "Discussing Expressionism" (16–27); Lukács, "Realism in the Balance" (28–59); Brecht, "The Essays of Georg Lukács" (68–69), "On the Formalistic Character of the Theory of Realism" (70–76), and "Popularity and Realism" (79–85); and Adorno, "Commitment" (177–95). Since an entire book could be devoted to this issue alone,

only a brief mention of the important issues can be included in my chapter. In addition to *Aesthetics and Politics* one should see Friedrich Gaede, "Realismus von Brant bis Brecht" 52–68), Eugene Lunn (especially pp. 71–127) and Susan Buck-Morss (especially pp. 24–62).

17 In Jameson's words, Brecht's aesthetics "restores to 'realistic' art that principle of play and genuine aesthetic gratification which the relatively more passive and cognitive aesthetic of Lukács had seemed to replace with the grim duty of a proper reflection of the world" ("Reflections in Conclusion" in Ronald Taylor, 205).

18 Reviews of the first two are quoted in Mews 93–95, 97–98. For the third, see Rolf Michaelis, "Sternhagelnüchtern," in *Die Zeit*, North American edition, 16 August 1985: 18.

19 Tatlow says that Stalinism explains Adorno's attitude towards Brecht and that he missed "completely the Chinese reverberations in Brecht's thought which presuppose the potentiality, the essentially relative condition of qualities." Tatlow also claims that Adorno's demand for autonomous works separated "from any intervention in process" run a greater danger of affirming that which is (24).

20 According to Volckmann the dialectic principle of construction relates each part to the dramatic whole, yet allows each part to retain its own independence, "for only where utopia already occurs to the extent possible within existing reality and is able to be disclosed negatively from this reality can the playwright record it without unconsciously transfiguring the present" (451). She continues: "Brecht's plays do not limit themselves to the aesthetic reproduction of extra-aesthetic reality; they do not imitate it without simultaneously surpassing it. That, not abstract doctrine, constitutes the plays' subversiveness but also their enjoyment in the theater" (452).

Chapter IX: Kroetz

1 "The surprising quality surprised me too: in a decade in which the theater mainly appears to be provided with the lamentation and scorn of a crew of authors, there is one who is loving and concrete almost without interruption. He has as little prospect and change to offer as anyone else." — Martin Walser, "Report of a Performance" [of *Nicht Fisch nicht Fleisch*].

2 Hein summarizes the similarities among these playwrights as follows: "Proceeding from conventional listening and viewing habits of the public, from the apparently serene atmosphere of dialect, from the background of the regionally limited and socially determined *Heimat*, simple problems and conflicts, and a manageable cast of characters in the microcosm of the everyday, [these plays] alienate the viewer by turning the familiar into an uncanny idyll, an oppressive narrowness" (*F.X. Kroetz* 10; also see 5–6). In an interview in 1973 Kroetz said that he perceives his plays consciously to be in the tradition of Anzengruber and Thoma (qtd. in Hein 23). In addition to providing a good introduction to Kroetz and two of his plays, Hein's volume also includes the most important of Kroetz's theoretical essays. All references to Hein in this chapter are to this text. Betten also links him to the tradition by pointing out similarities in language use to Thoma (186), Fleißer (238–43), and Horváth (229–38). Ingeborg C. Walther's excellent and comprehensive study of *The*

Theater of Franz Xaver Kroetz, published after my initial manuscript was completed, discusses his relation to the New *Volksstück* in her introductory chapter. She views him in terms of the larger context of contemporary German theater, however, an approach that is of course necessary for a fuller understanding. She gives a close reading of several plays, including the two I discuss here.

3 Several scholars have commented on these discrepancies. Cf. Carl, *Kroetz* 13, 45; Carl, "Theatertheorie" 7; Buddecke and Fuhrmann 149; Töteberg, "Ein konservativer Autor" 284.

4 Included in *Weitere Aussichten* 375–425. But Hein points out that this experience shows little influence on his later plays (21).

5 References to *Stallerhof* and *Nicht Fisch nicht Fleisch* will be indicated by page numbers in parentheses within the text.

6 See Fleißer's account of the opening night in "Kroetz."

7 *Franz Xaver Kroetz,* edited by Otto Riewoldt, contains numerous essays, reviews of performances, and useful background material. Abbreviated FXK in the text.

8 In the sequel *Geisterbahn* Beppi takes her child to the city, where the now retired Sepp lives in a rented room; when he dies shortly thereafter, she kills the infant rather than allowing it to be taken from her and placed in a home.

9 See Cocalis, "Mitleid" 203. Petersen characterizes Kroetz's first phase as "Mitleids-poesie." He finds that the crippled nature of the characters cannot be viewed as socially caused and that they can only evoke emotion from the spectator, rather than social action (291–303). Although Cocalis finds that the brutality of Kroetz's early plays gives them an emancipatory potential and enables them to stand in autonomous opposition to prevailing conditions, she says that this force can be neutralized through too strong an element of compassion ("Politics" 303–04). In a later essay on Brecht's play "Die Maßnahme" ["The Measures Taken"] Kroetz seems to agree that compassion directed toward an individual is an act of charity that cannot result in the liberation of an entire class, but he adds that it may provide a motivation for moving in that direction ("Über die Maßnahme" 574–75). Walther views the presence of compassion in *Stallerhof* as positive, since it overcomes what was easily misunder-stood as denunciation of the characters in the earlier play *Männersache* (55–56). Although he did not label any plays *Volksstück* until he had achieved a synthesis of compassion and commitment (Cocalis, "Mitleid" 209), both elements have been perceived to be present in *Stallerhof,* as the varied descriptions of the reception indicate.

10 Kässens and Töteberg, for example, find *Stallerhof* unhistorical because it fails to deal with contemporary contradictions in the situation of farmers that result from the non-synchronous development of rural areas under capitalism. General forms of community in the village predominate over problems such as the proletarianization of farmers and capitalization of large farms ("Fortschritt" 45–47). It is unfair, however, to fault Kroetz for not including particular areas of subject matter, though one might indeed question his effectiveness in making certain connections apparent.

11 Kroetz says that realism for him means "aus erster Hand kommend" [experienced first-hand], and that viewing realistically portrayed events is enough to change a spectator (*Weitere Aussichten* 601). In "Die Schwierigkeiten des einfachen Mannes"

he finds his dramatic means superior to the "Urschleimtaucherei" [diving into the primeval mud] of Beckett and Ionesco, because he considers it to portray real people (606).

12 Though Kroetz labelled *Stallerhof* and most of his other early plays simply "Stück" [play], he accepted the critics' and public's use of the term and later designated *Das Nest* as a *Volksstück*. Cocalis summarizes the contradictions in Kroetz's use of the *Volksstück* as an anti-genre: it attempts to bring about political change while avoiding an explicit political message, to promote the humanitarian by portraying bestial behavior, and to appeal to compassion in order to awaken a critical attitude ("Mitleid" 206).

13 But opinions vary as to what this type of language means. Kroetz himself claimed that his dialogue was true to reality, rather than the theater. Wendt ("Eine neue Heimatkunst," qtd. in Evalouise Panzer 84) and Reinhold (65) also stress the realism of the speech. For additional discussions of the language of Kroetz's early plays see especially Carl, *Kroetz* 37–39, 49–51; Schaarschmidt 212; Kässens 263; Burger and von Matt; Schmid 250; Betten 221–28; Walther 52–56; Kroetz, "Liegt die Dummheit" 524–25, "Die Sprache meiner Figuren" 63–65, and "Horváth von heute."

14 For a discussion of the connection between violence and the inability to speak, see Wendt, "Bürgerseelen" 96; Kässens 269–71; Evalouise Panzer 14–15).

15 This has often been pointed out: see Burger and von Matt 270–72; Kässens and Töteberg 43; Hoffmeister, *Theater* 79; and G. Müller 121.

16 He says on the one hand that human qualities can be expressed only in dialect (qtd. in E. Panzer 25), and on the other, that Bavarian conveys the "oppressed, used-up quality of humanity" (qtd. in Blevins 242). Carl finds that the illusionistic quality promotes sympathy (*Kroetz* 42), whereas Reinhold finds that it has a distancing effect (66). See also Walther 8–10.

17 The sequel to *Stallerhof* in fact shows that life continues as before, though with certain intensifications.

18 The reviewer for *Die Zeit* found fault, however, with this version's attempt to provide interpretation, which endangered "the essential burden of the word-pauses" (Herbort).

19 Carl, for example, notes this dilemma (*Kroetz* 14). Kroetz was not interested in politics in the late 1960's, but became politicized shortly thereafter and joined the German Communist Party (DKP) in 1972. He resigned in 1980 as a result of his lack of effectiveness within the party and differences of opinion concerning political tactics. He claims his views have not changed significantly, though politics no longer plays so central a role in his life. Cf. "Ich habe immer nur von mir geschrieben."

20 There is a divergence of views concerning the ability of Kroetz's dramas to effect political change. Kroetz thinks the play should reveal the difference between the reality that the spectator believes in and the "unbelievable" reality that the author wants to communicate ("Form" 89); it should make transparent power relationships and the manner in which they operate ("Lust" 599). Carl (*Kroetz* 70) and Wendt ("Dramen" 36) agree that the depiction and its shock effect make the social causes obvious enough, though others find that the exhibition quality of the early plays fails

tó achieve these ends: see Kässens and Töteberg ("Fortschritt" 39–40), Sauerland (35), and Blevins (182). In May 1992 Kroetz himself expressed skepticism concerning drama's ability to effect change: "Man kann mit Kunst nichts verändern... Van Gogh hat nichts verändert... Man kann mit Kunst weh tun." He said that he wrote political plays at a time when it was difficult to be political in the theater. Now that this tendency has become inflationary, he writes in a different way ("Auf der Couch").

21 Though one might dispute Kroetz's later evaluation of a scene from *Stallerhof* in the following quotation, the play's expression of a need for harmony can hardly be denied: "I have a need for harmony. And this need for harmony is found of course in very extreme situations; in *Stallerhof*, for example, in the scene where Sepp sits on the toilet and masturbates: those are the most harmonious scenes that I have ever succeeded in portraying; that is poetic, that is wonderful. That is harmony in the form of a poetic transmission." ("Ich habe immer nur" 84).

22 During this period Kroetz stressed the influence of Brecht on his work, yet this theoretical kinship did not necessarily mean a similar result in praxis (Carl, *Kroetz* 27). As Carl points out, his plays still seem to resemble more closely the identification drama of Friedrich Wolf than the *Verfremdungseffekte* of Brecht. Kroetz was attracted to the effects that socialist realism was supposed to bring about through the presentation of a positive hero, while he at the same time remained skeptical of the efficacy of such dramatic means (26–27).

23 Töteberg, for example, calls *Das Nest* Kroetz's most convincing work ("Kleinbürger" 170) and explains that the audience knows why Kurt changes because they made the development with him (Kässens and Töteberg 42). Walther also finds the characters' behavior plausible and seems to think that the audience can learn vicariously from this on-stage learning process (130, 138–39). Carl, on the other hand, finds that the plot is too improbable to be effective (*Kroetz* 111). I tend to agree with Hoffmeister that "giving the message" does not work here, since it "is a betrayal of the dialectical rhythm" (*Theater* 75–76).

24 Plays that Kroetz has written since 1981 are less representative as attempts to find an adequate form for the *Volksstück*. His *Furcht und Hoffnung der BRD* [Fear and Hope in the FRG, 1984], which deals with contemporary unemployment, is actually a series of one-act plays that consist largely of monologues (Hein 19–20). *Bauern sterben* [Farmers die], which received its premiere in 1985 and its publication in late 1986, is labelled a "fragment" by Kroetz because Munich's Kammerspiele performed it even though he had not given it final form. Kroetz claims he lost interest before the play's completion because it had no concrete status and was too unpolitical ("Ich habe nur immer" 84). It is deserving of further attention, however, because its combination of material from farm life with an extremely expressionistic-surrealistic style shows the attempt to find a new approach. *Der Nusser* (1986) is essentially a reworking of Ernst Toller's expressionistic *Der deutsche Hinkemann*; about one-third of the text represents additions by Kroetz. It was given mixed reviews, partially as a result of the awkward combination of original and source materials (Merschmeier 38–41). In *Der Weihnachtstod* [Christmas Death], which premiered in December 1986, there is no room in the inn for a homeless Turkish guestworker and his wife,

who gives birth in the apartment of an unemployed Munich couple (cf. Schödel). Walther finds that the last plays, including *Zeitweh* (1988) show the increasing difficulties Kroetz has had in integrating the central aesthetic impulses that she discusses in her study (273).

25 Töteberg argues in "Ein konservativer Autor" that the portrayal of traditional women's roles and the men's return to the family in the final scene show that Kroetz embraces conservative values. Yet this critic makes the mistake of equating characters' opinions with the author's and of assuming that a portrayal of the negative effects of technology and social conditions on the family is a flight from concrete measures that would change things. Similarly, it is hard to agree with his view of Kroetz as a conservative defender of traditional values simply because the desire for children on the part of his characters represents a positive moment in his plays (see pp. 284–85 and 290–92).

26 Walther points out the technological change that causes changes in the workplace and says: "The conflicts and contradictions that surface in *Nicht Fisch nicht Fleisch* reflect the complexities of a socio-economic reality which is less easily analyzed in terms of class struggle and economic exploitation." Kroetz continues to portray the effects of socio-economic reality, "but his recognition that there are no simple solutions to the problems confronting these individuals necessitated a re-thinking of his artistic intentions and of the formal means through which they are conveyed" (157–58).

27 Walther finds that all of Kroetz's plays, including this one, move "within the parameters of naturalism and abstraction" (175). But the "'fantastic' realism of *Nicht Fisch nicht Fleisch* represents a radical extension of Kroetz's dramaturgical technique: the transparent machinery provides a distancing framework in which critical analysis can take place" (179).

28 Definitions from *Illustriertes Lexikon der deutschen Umgangssprache.*

BIBLIOGRAPHY

I. General Works

A. The *Volksstück* in General and Works Dealing with More than one Author

Arnold, Heinz Ludwig and Theo Buck. *Positionen des Dramas: Analysen und Theorien zur deutschen Gegenwartsliteratur*. Munich: Beck, 1977.

Arnold, Heinz-Ludwig and Volker Sinemus. *Literaturwissenschaft*. Vol. I of *Grundzüge der Literatur- und Sprachwissenschaft*. Munich: Deutscher Taschenbuch Verlag, 1974. 2 vols.

Aust, Hugo, Peter Haida and Jürgen Hein. *Volksstück. Vom Hanswurstspiel zum sozialen Drama der Gegenwart*. Munich: Beck, 1989.

Bauer, Roger. "Das Wiener Volkstheater zu Beginn des 19. Jahrhunderts: Noch nicht und (oder) doch schon Literatur?" *Theater und Gesellschaft*. Ed. Jürgen Hein. 29–43.

_____. *La Réalité. Royaume de Dieu. Etudes sur l'originalité du théâtre viennois dans la première moitié du XIXe siècle*. Munich: Max Hueber, 1965.

_____. "'Volkstheater' et 'Nationaltheater': Deux variants du 'Théâtre pour tous.'" *Volk — Volksstück — Volkstheater*. Ed. Jean-Marie Valentin. 9–24.

Betten, Anne. *Sprachrealismus im deutschen Drama der siebziger Jahre*. Heidelberg: Carl Winter Universitätsverlag, 1985.

Bosch, Manfred. "Heimat und Dialekt." *Kürbiskern* 3 (1975): 102–109.

Dimter, Walter. "Die ausgestellte Gesellschaft. Zum Volksstück Horváths, der Fleißer und ihrer Nachfolger." *Theater und Gesellschaft*. Ed. Jürgen Hein. 219–45.

Fülleborn, Ulrich. "Offenes Geschehen in geschlossener Form: Grillparzers Dramenkonzept: Mit einem Ausblick auf Raimund und Nestroy." *Deutsche Dramentheorien* II. Ed. Reinhold Grimm. Wiesbaden: Athenaion, 1981. 1–24.

Hein, Jürgen. "Formen des Volkstheaters im 19. und 20. Jahrhundert." *Handbuch des deutschen Dramas*. Ed. Walter Hinck. Düsseldorf: Bagel, 1980. 489–505.

_____, ed. *Theater und Gesellschaft: Das Volksstück im 19. und 20. Jahrhundert*. Literatur in der Gesellschaft 12. Düsseldorf: Bertelsmann Universitätsverlag, 1973.

_____. "Volksstück als didaktisches Drama." *Literatur und Medien in Wissenschaft und Unterricht*. Ed. Walter Seifert et al. Köln: Böhlau, 1987. 98–103.

√ _____. "Das Volksstück: Entwicklung und Tendenzen." *Theater und Gesellschaft*. 9–28.

_____. *Das Wiener Volkstheater*. Erträge der Forschung 100. Darmstadt: Wissenschaftliche Buchgesellschaft, 1978.

Hintze, Joachim. "Volkstümliche Elemente im modernen deutschen Drama. Ein Beitrag zur Theorie und Praxis des Volksstücks im 20. Jahrhundert." *Hessische Blätter für Volkskunde* 61 (1970): 11–43.

Hoffmann, Ludwig, ed. *Volksstücke*. Berlin (GDR): Henschelverlag, 1968.

Hoffmeister, Donna L. *The Theater of Confinement. Language and Survival in the Milieu Plays of Marieluise Fleißer and Franz Xaver Kroetz*. Columbia, SC: Camden House, 1983.

Hüttner, Johann. "Volkstheater als Geschäft: Theaterbetrieb und Publikum im 19. Jahrhundert." *Volk — Volksstück — Volkstheater*. Ed. Jean-Marie Valentin. 127–49.

Jones, Calvin N. "Ferdinand Raimund and Ödön von Horváth: The *Volksstück* as Negation and Utopia." *The German Quarterly* 64 (1991): 325–38.

Koppensteiner, Jürgen. "Anti-Heimatliteratur: Ein Unterrichtsversuch mit Franz Innerhofer's Roman Schöne Tage." *Die Unterrichtspraxis* 14 (Spring 1981), 9–19.

Lengauer, Hubert. "Läuterung der Besitzlosen." *Volk — Volksstück — Volkstheater*. Ed. Jean-Marie Valentin. 150–72.

√ Mennemeier, Franz Norbert. "Volkstheater gegen den Strich." *Modernes deutsches Drama*. Vol. 2. Munich: UTB/ W. Finck, 1977. 291–306. 2 vols.

√ Müller, Gerd. *Das Volksstück von Raimund bis Kroetz*. Munich: Oldenbourg, 1979.

Rommel, Otto. *Die Alt-Wiener Volkskomödie. Ihre Geschichte vom barocken Welt-Theater bis zum Tode Nestroys*. Vienna: Anton Schroll, 1952.

Sengle, Friedrich. *Biedermeierzeit. Deutsche Literatur im Spannungsfeld zwischen Revolution und Restauration*. Stuttgart: Metzler. 3 vols. 1971–80.

Valentin, Jean-Marie, ed. *Volk — Volksstück — Volkstheater im deutschen Sprachraum des 18.- 20. Jahrhunderts*. Bern: Peter Lang, 1986.

Wormbs, Brigitta. "Wie herrlich leuchtet uns die Natur?" *Kürbiskern* 3 (1975): 110–21.

Yates, W. Edgar. "The Idea of the 'Volksstück' in Nestroy's Vienna." *German Life and Letters* (New Series) 38 (1984–85): 462–73.

Yates, W. Edgar and John R.P. McKenzie, ed. *Viennese Popular Theatre. A Symposium.* Exeter: Department of German, University of Exeter, 1985.

Zuckmayer, Carl. *Der fröhliche Weinberg. Meisterdramen.* New York and Frankfurt/Main: Fischer, 1966.

B. Literary Theory and Other Secondary Literature

Adorno, Theodor W. *Ästhetische Theorie.* Frankfurt/Main: Suhrkamp Verlag, 1973.

——————. *Einleitung in die Musiksoziologie.* Reinbek: Rowohlt, 1968.

——————. "Engagement." *Noten zur Literatur.* Vol. 3. 109–35.

——————. *Gesammelte Schriften.* 23 vols. Frankfurt/Main: Suhrkamp Verlag, 1970– .

——————. *Jargon der Eigentlichkeit.* Frankfurt/Main: Suhrkamp, 1964.

——————. *Negative Dialektik.* Frankfurt/Main: Suhrkamp Verlag, 1982.

——————. *Noten zur Literatur.* 4 vols. Frankfurt/Main: Suhrkamp Verlag, 1980.

——————. "Offener Brief an Rolf Hochhuth." *Zur Dialektik des Engagements.* 179–86.

——————. *Prisms.* Trans. Samuel and Shierry Weber. Cambridge, Mass.: MIT, 1981.

——————. "Resumé über Kulturindustrie." *Ohne Leitbild. Parva Aesthetica.* Frankfurt/Main: Suhrkamp, 1967. 60–70.

——————. "Transparencies on Film." Trans. Thomas Y. Levin. *New German Critique* 24–25 (1981–82): 199–205.

——————. *Zur Dialektik des Engagements.* Frankfurt: Suhrkamp Verlag, 1973.

Althusser, Louis and Etienne Balibar. *Reading Capital*. Trans. Ben Brewster. London: Verso, 1983.

Bakhtin, M.M. *The Dialogic Imagination. Four Essays*. Trans. Caryl Emerson and Michael Holquist. Austin: U Texas P, 1983.

Benjamin, Walter. *Gesammelte Schriften*. 6 vols. Ed. Rolf Tiedemann and Hermann Schweppenhäuser. Frankfurt: Suhrkamp Verlag, 1972– .

Bloch, Ernst. *Literarische Aufsätze*. Frankfurt/Main: Suhrkamp Taschenbuch Wissenschaft, 1984.

_____. *Gesamtausgabe*. 16 vols. Frankfurt/Main: Suhrkamp Verlag, 1967–76.

_____. *Das Prinzip Hoffnung*. Frankfurt/Main: Suhrkamp Taschenbuch Wissenschaft, 1980.

Buck-Morss, Susan. *The Origin of Negative Dialectics. Theodor W. Adorno, Walter Benjamin, and the Frankfurt Institute*. New York: Free Press, 1977.

Derrida, Jacques. "The Law of Genre." *Critical Inquiry* 7.1 (Autumn 1980): 55-81.

Dowling, William C. *Jameson, Althusser, Marx. An Introduction to The Political Unconscious*. Ithaca, N.Y.: Cornell UP, 1984.

Eagleton, Terry. *Literary Theory: An Introduction*. Minneapolis: U Minnesota P, 1983.

_____. *Marxism and Literary Criticism*. Berkeley, U California P, 1976.

Grossberg, Lawrence and Cary Nelson. "Introduction: The Territory of Marxism." *Marxism and the Interpretation of Culture*. Ed. Cary Nelson and Lawrence Grossberg. 1-13.

Habermas, Jürgen. *Strukturwandel der Öffentlichkeit*. Neuwied: Luchterhand, 1984.

Hegel, G.W.F. *Phänomenologie des Geistes*. Hamburg: Felix Meiner, 1952.

Held, David. *Introduction to Critical Theory: Horkheimer to Habermas*. Berkeley: U California P, 1980.

Horkheimer, Max. "Art and Mass Culture." *Studies in Philosophy and Social Science* 9 (1941).

Horkheimer, Max and Theodor W. Adorno. *Dialektik der Aufklärung.* Frankfurt/Main: Fischer Taschenbuch Verlag, 1984.

Hudson, Wayne. *The Marxist Philosophy of Ernst Bloch.* New York: St. Martin's Press, 1982.

Jameson, Fredric. "Cognitive Mapping." *Marxism and the Interpretation of Culture.* Ed. Cary Nelson and Lawrence Grossberg. 347-57.

_____. *Marxism and Form: Twentieth Century Dialectical Theories of Literature.* Princeton: Princeton UP, 1974.

_____. *The Political Unconscious: Narrative as a Socially Symbolic Act.* Ithaca, N.Y.: Cornell UP, 1981.

Jauß, Hans Robert. "Literaturgeschichte als Provokation der Literaturwissenschaft." *Literaturgeschichte als Provokation.* Frankfurt/ Main: Suhrkamp: 1974. 144–207.

Jay, Martin. *Adorno.* Cambridge, Mass.: Harvard UP, 1984.

_____. *The Dialectical Imagination: A History of the Frankfurt School and the Institute of Social Research, 1923–1950.* Boston: Little, Brown, 1973.

Kayser, Wolfgang. *Das sprachliche Kunstwerk: Eine Einführung in die Literaturwissenschaft.* Bern: Francke, 1973.

Löwenthal, Leo. *Literature, Popular Culture, and Society.* Palo Alto, California: Pacific Books, 1968.

_____. *Mitmachen wollte ich nie.* Ein autobiographisches Gespräch mit Helmut Dubiel. Frankfurt/Main: Suhrkamp, 1980.

Lukács, Georg. "Erzählen oder Beschreiben?" *Begriffsbestimmung des literarischen Realismus.* Ed. Richard Brinkmann. Darmstadt: Wissenschaftliche Buchgesellschaft, 1974. 33–85.

_____. *Schriften zur Literatursoziologie.* Neuwied: Luchterhand, 1972.

Lunn, Eugene. *Marxism and Modernism: An Historical Study of Lukács, Brecht, Benjamin and Adorno.* Berkeley: U of California P, 1984.

Marx, Karl and Friedrich Engels. *Werke.* [MEW]. 42 vols. Berlin (GDR): Dietz, 1975-83.

Marx, Karl. *The Portable Karl Marx*. Ed. Eugene Kamenka. New York: Penguin, 1983.

Nelson, Cary and Lawrence Grossberg, eds. *Marxism and the Interpretation of Culture*. Urbana and Chicago: U Illinois P, 1988.

Taylor, Ronald, ed. *Aesthetics and Politics*. London: NLB, 1979.

Vietor, Karl. "Probleme der literarischen Gattungsgeschichte." *Deutsche Vierteljahrsschrift* 9 (1931): 425–47.

Wilpert, Gero von. *Sachwörterbuch der Literatur*. Stuttgart: Kröner, 1969.

Wolin, Richard. *Walter Benjamin: An Aesthetic of Redemption*. New York: Columbia University Press, 1982.

II. Raimund

Crockett, Roger. "Raimund's Der Verschwender: The Illusion of Freedom." *German Quarterly* 58 (1985): 184–93.

David, Claude. "Ferdinand Raimund: Moisasurs Zauberfluch." *Das deutsche Lustspiel* Vol. 1. Ed. Hans Steffen. Göttingen: Vandenhoeck & Ruprecht, 1968. 120–143. 2 vols.

Erken, Günther. "Ferdinand Raimund." *Deutsche Dichter des 19. Jahrhunderts*. Ed. Benno von Wiese. Berlin: Erich Schmidt, 1969.

Geißler, Rolf. "Lehrspiel von den bürgerlichen Erkenntnis: Raimunds 'Der Alpenkönig und der Menschenfeind.'" *Literatur für Leser* (1980): 157–66.

Greiner, Martin. *Zwischen Biedermeier und Bourgeoisie*. Göttingen: Vandenhoeck & Ruprecht, 1953.

Grillparzer, Franz. *Sämtliche Werke*. Abt.1, Vol.14. Vienna: Schroll, 1925. 92–95.

Harding, Laurence V. *The Dramatic Art of Ferdinand Raimund and Johann Nestroy. A Critical Study*. The Hague: Mouton, 1974.

Hein, Jürgen. *Ferdinand Raimund*. Stuttgart: Metzler, 1970.

_____. "'Gefesselte Komik' — Der Spielraum des Komischen in Ferdinand Raimunds Volkstheater." *Austriaca: Cahiers Universitaires d'Information sur l'Autriche* 14 (1982): 73–86.

Hofmannsthal, Hugo von. "Ferdinand Raimund: Einleitung zu einer Sammlung seiner Lebensdokumente." *Gesammelte Werke. Prosa.* Vol. 3. Frankfurt/Main: Fischer, 1952. 471–78. 14 vols.

Klotz, Volker. *Dramaturgie des Publikums: Wie Bühne und Publikum aufeinander eingehen, insbesondere bei Raimund, Büchner, Wedekind, Horváth, Gatti und im politischen Agitationstheater.* Munich: Hanser, 1976.

Mühlher, Robert. "Ferdinand Raimund." *Das österreichische Volksstück.* Ed. Alfred Doppler. Vienna: Ferdinand Hirth, 1971. 17–35.

Politzer, Heinz. "Der Alpenkönig und der Menschenfeind." In *Das deutsche Drama.* Vol. 2 *Vom Realismus bis zur Gegenwart.* Ed. Benno von Wiese. Düsseldorf: Bagel, 1964. 9–22.

Prohaska, Dorothy. *Raimund and Vienna. A Critical Study of Raimund's Plays in their Viennese Setting.* Cambridge: UP, 1970.

————————. "Raimund's Contribution to Viennese Popular Comedy." *German Quarterly* 42 (1969): 352–67.

Raimund, Ferdinand. *Sämtliche Werke.* Munich: Winkler, 1966.

————————. *Sämtliche Werke: Historisch–kritische Säkularausgabe.* Ed. Fritz Brukner and Eduard Castle. 6 vols. Vienna: Anton Schroll, 1924.

Rommel, Otto. *Ferdinand Raimund und die Vollendung des Alt-Wiener Zauberstückes.* Vienna: 1947.

Schaumann, Frank. *Gestalt und Funktion des Mythos in Ferdinand Raimunds Bühnenwerken.* Vienna: Bergland, 1970.

————————. "Das Theater Ferdinand Raimunds zwischen Originalitätsanspruch und Tradition." *Theater und Gesellschaft.* Ed. Jürgen Hein. 81–93.

Schmidt-Dengler, Wendelin. "Der Alpenkönig und der Menschenfeind." *Die deutsche Komödie: Vom Mittelalter biz zur Gegenwart.* Ed. Walter Hinck. Düsseldorf: Bagel, 1977. 160–74.

Urbach, Reinhard. *Die Wiener Komödie und ihr Publikum: Stranitzky und die Folgen.* Vienna: Jugend und Volk, 1973.

_____. "Zufriedenheit bei Ferdinand Raimund." *Austriaca: Beiträge zur österreichischen Literatur.* Ed. Winfried Kudszus und Hinrich C. Seeba. Tübingen: Max Niemeyer, 1975. 107–26.

Wagner, Renate. *Ferdinand Raimund. Eine Biographie.* Vienna: Kreymayr & Scheriau, 1985.

Wiltschko, Günther. *Raimunds Dramaturgie.* Munich: Fink, 1973.

Zeman, Herbert. "Das Märchen vom realen Leben: Zur Dramatik Franz Grillparzers und Ferdinand Raimunds." *Die österreichische Literatur: Ihr Profil im 19. Jahrhundert (1830–1880).* Ed. Herbert Zeman. Graz: Akad. Druck- und Verlagsanstalt, 1982. 297–322.

III. Nestroy

Aust, Hugo. "Nestroy's Kampl. Aspekte der klassischen Form." *Wirkendes Wort* 37 (1987): 181–90.

Baur, Uwe. "Nestroy und die oppositionelle Literatur seiner Zeit. Zum Verhältnis von 'Volk' und Literatur in der Restaurationsepoche." *Studien zur Literatur des 19. und 20. Jahrhunderts in Österreich.* Ed. Johann Holzner and Wolfgang Wiesmüller. Innsbruck: Innsbrucker Beiträge zur Kulturwissenschaft, 1981. 25–34.

Berghaus, G. "Nestroys Revolutionspossen im Rahmen des Gesamtwerks." *DAI* 42.3 (1983): 3070C. Freie Universität Berlin.

Brill, Siegfried. *Die Komödie der Sprache. Untersuchungen zum Werke Johann Nestroys.* Nürnberg: Hans Carl, 1967.

Charue-Ferrucci, Jeanine. "Du roman populaire au 'Volksstück.' L'adaptation par Nestroy de la nouvelle de Michel Raymond: 'Le grain du sable.'" *Volk — Volksstück — Volkstheater.* Ed. Jean-Marie Valentin. 62–78.

Conrad, Günter. *Johann Nepomuk Nestroy 1801–1862: Bibliographie zur Nestroyforschung und -rezeption: Forschungsbericht, biographische Zeittafel, Verzeichnis der Stücke, Bibliographie.* Berlin: Schmidt, 1980.

Corriher, Kurt. "The Conflict between Dignity and Hope in the Works of Johann Nestroy." *South Atlantic Review* 46.2 (1981): 28–42.

Decker, Craig Joseph. "Towards a Critical *Volksstück*: Nestroy and the Politics of Language." *Monatshefte* 79 (1987): 44–61.

Dürrenmatt, Friedrich. "Anmerkung zum 'Besuch der alten Dame.'" *Theater- Schriften und Reden.* Zürich: Arche, 1966. 180–83.

Eder, Alois. "'Die geistige Kraft der Gemeinheit.' Zur Sozialgeschichte der Rezeption Nestroys." *Theater und Gesellschaft.* Ed. Jürgen Hein. 133–54.

Fischer, Ernst. *Von Grillparzer zu Kafka.* Vienna: Globus, 1962.

Hannemann, Bruno. *Johann Nestroy. Nihilistisches Welttheater und verflixter Kerl. Zum Ende der Wiener Komödie.* Bonn: Bouvier, 1977.

Hein, Jürgen. *Johann Nestroy.* Stuttgart: Metzler, 1990.

——————. "Nestroyforschung 1901–66." *Wirkendes Wort* 18 (1968): 323–45.

——————. "Neue Nestroyforschungen (1967–73)." *Wirkendes Wort* 25 (1975): 140–50.

——————. "Possen- und Volksstück-Dramaturgie im Vormärz Volkstheater: Zu Johann Nestroys *Zu ebener Erde und erster Stock* und *Der Unbedeutende.*" *Der Deutschunterricht* 31.2 (1979): 122–37.

——————. *Spiel und Satire in der Komödie Johann Nestroys.* Bad Homburg: Gehlen, 1970.

——————. "Der utopische Nestroy." *Nestroyana* 6. 1–2 (1984–85): 13–23.

Hillach, Ansgar. *Die Dramatisierung des komischen Dialogs. Figur und Rolle bei Nestroy.* München: Fink, 1967.

Hinck, Walter. "Komödie zwischen Satire und Utopie." Reinhold Grimm and Walter Hinck. *Zwischen Satire und Utopie.* Frankfurt/Main: Suhrkamp, 1982. 7–19.

Höllerer, Walter. *Zwischen Klassik und Moderne. Lachen und Weinen in der Dichtung einer Übergangszeit.* Stuttgart: Klett, 1958.

Hüttner, Johann. "Johann Nestroy im Theaterbetrieb seiner Zeit." *Maske und Kothurn* 23 (1977): 233–43.

——————. "Literarische Parodie und Wiener Vorstadtpublikum vor Nestroy." *Maske und Kothurn* 18 (1972): 99–139.

Jansen, Peter K. "Johann Nepomuk Nestroys skeptische Utopie in 'Der Talisman.'" *Jahrbuch der deutschen Schillergesellschaft* 24 (1980): 246–82.

Jones, Calvin N. "Authorial Intent and Public Response to *Uriel Acosta* and *Freiheit in Krähwinkel.*" *South Atlantic Review* 47.4 (1982): 17–26.

Keller, Gottfried. *Gesammelte Briefe.* Vol. 1. Bern: Benteli, 1950. 4 vols. 1950–54.

Klotz, Volker. *Bürgerliches Lachtheater. Komödie. Posse. Schwank. Operette.* Darmstadt: Wissenschaftliche Buchgesellschaft, 1984.

Kraus, Karl. "Nestroy und die Nachwelt." *Grimassen.* Munich: Langen Müller, 1971. Vol. 1 of *Ausgewählte Werke.* 422–39. 3 vols.

Mautner, Franz H. *Nestroy.* 1974. Frankfurt/Main: Suhrkamp, 1978.

——————. "Nestroy. Der Talisman." *Das deutsche Drama.* Ed. Benno von Wiese. Düsseldorf: Bagel, 1958. 23–42.

——————. "Die Wiener Volkskomödie: Raimund und Nestroy." *Handbuch des deutschen Dramas.* Ed. Walter Hinck. Düsseldorf: Bagel, 1980. 200–15.

May, Erich Joachim. *Wiener Volkskomödie und Vormärz.* Berlin (GDR): Henschelverlag, 1975.

McKenzie, John R. P. "Political Satire in Nestroy's Freiheit in Krähwinkel." *Modern Language Review* 75 (1980): 322–32.

Nestroy, Johann. *Gesammelte Werke.* 6 vols. Vienna: Anton Schroll, 1948.

——————. *Komödien. Ausgabe in sechs Bänden.* Ed. Franz H. Mautner. Frankfurt a.M.: Insel, 1979.

——————. *Sämtliche Werke,* ed. Fritz Brukner and Otto Rommel. 15 Vols. Vienna: Anton Schroll, 1924–30.

——————. *Sämtliche Werke. Historisch-kritische Ausgabe,* ed. Jürgen Hein and Johann Hüttner. Vienna: Jugend und Volk, 1977– .

Preisendanz, Wolfgang. "Nestroys komisches Theater." *Das deutsche Lustspiel* Vol. 2. Ed. Hans Steffen. Göttingen: Vandenhoek und Rupprecht, 1969. 7–24. 2 vols.

Preisner, Rio. "Der konservative Nestroy: Aspekte der zukünftigen Nestroyforschung." *Maske und Kothurn* 18 (1972): 23–37.

——————. *Johann Nepomuk Nestroy. Der Schöpfer der tragischen Posse.* Munich: Hanser, 1968.

Rommel, Otto. "Johann Nestroy. Ein Beitrag zur Geschichte der Wiener Volkskomik."
Johann Nestroy. *Sämtliche Werke*. Vol. 15. 3–357.

_____. "Johann Nestroy, der Satiriker auf der Altwiener Komödienbühne."
Johann Nestroy. *Gesammelte Werke* Vol 1. Vienna: Anton Schroll, 1948. 5–193.

Seeba, Hinrich. "Die Sprache der Freiheit in Krähwinkel." *Austriaca: Beiträge zur
österreichischen Literatur — Festschrift für Heinz Politzer*. Ed. Winfried Kudszus and
Hinrich Seeba. Tübingen: Niemeyer, 1975. 127–47.

Slobodkin, G.S. "Das Wesen des Komischen in Nestroys Volkskomödien." *Weimarer
Beiträge* 26.12 (1980): 49–64.

Yates, W, Edgar. "Kriterien der Nestroyrezeption 1837–1838." *Nestroyana* 5 (1983–84):
3–11.

_____. "Nestroy und die Rezensenten." *Nestroyana* 7 (1987): 28–40.

_____. *Nestroy. Satire and Parody in Viennese Popular Comedy*. Cambridge:
UP, 1972.

_____. "An Object of Nestroy's Satire. Friedrich Kaiser and the *Lebens-
bild*." *Renaissance and Modern Studies* 22 (1978): 45–62.

_____. "Nestroy's Weg zur klassischen Posse." *Nestroyana* 7 (1987):
93–109.

_____. "Das Werden eines Nestroystücks." *Viennese Popular Theatre*. Ed.
W. Edgar Yates and John R.P. McKenzie. 55–66.

IV. Anzengruber

Anzengruber, Ludwig. *Ludwig Anzengrubers Sämtliche Werke*, ed. Rudolf Latzke and
Otto Rommel. 15 vols. Vienna: Anton Schroll, 1920–22.

Böttcher, Kurt, ed. *Geschichte der deutschen Literatur*. Vol. 8.2. *Von 1830 bis zum
Ausgang des 19. Jahrhunderts*. Berlin (GDR): Volk und Wissen, 1975. 12 vols.
1963–83.

Cowen, Roy C. *Der Naturalismus*. Munich: Winkler, 1973.

Crößmann, Helga. "Zum sogenannten Niedergang des Wiener Volkstheaters." *Zeitschrift
für Volkskunde* 71 (1975): 48–63.

David, Claude. *Von Richard Wagner zu Bertolt Brecht.* Frankfurt/Main: Fischer Bücherei, 1959.

Frenzel, Herbert A. and Elisabeth Frenzel. *Daten deutscher Dichtung.* Vol. 2. Munich: dtv, 1966. 2 vols.

Howe, Patricia. "End of a Line: Anzengruber and the Viennese Stage." *Viennese Popular Theatre: A Symposium.* Ed. W.E. Yates and John R.P. McKenzie. 139-52.

Jones, Calvin N. "Variations on a Stereotype: The Farmer in the Nineteenth Century *Volkskomödie.*" *Maske und Kothurn* 27 (1981): 155-62.

Klotz, Volker. "Vox populi in der Operette. Was ist das, Volkstheater, und wie steht die Operette dazu?" *Volk — Volksstück — Volkstheater.* Ed. Jean-Marie Valentin. 209-29.

Koessler, Louis. *Louis Anzengruber, auteur dramatique.* Diss. Strasbourg 1943.

Lengauer, Hubert. "Anzengrubers realistische Kunst." *Österreich in Geschichte und Literatur* 21 (1977): 386-404.

Martin, Werner. "Anzengruber und das Volksstück." *Neue Deutsche Literatur* 9.2 (1961): 110-21.

Martini, Fritz. *Deutsche Literaturgeschichte.* Stuttgart: Kröner, 1968.

McInnes, Edward. "Ludwig Anzengruber and the Popular Dramatic Tradition." *Maske und Kothurn* 21 (1975): 131-52.

Rommel, Otto. "Ludwig Anzengruber als Dramatiker." *Ludwig Anzengrubers Sämtliche Werke.* Vol. 2. 335-594.

Rossbacher, Karlheinz. "Ludwig Anzengruber: Die Märchen des Steinklopferhanns (1875-79): Poesie der Dissonanz als Weg zur Volksaufklärung." *Romane und Erzählungen des bürgerlichen Realismus.* Ed. Horst Denkler. Stuttgart: Reclam, 1980. 231-45.

Schmidt-Dengler, Wendelin. "Die Unbedeutenden werden bedeutend. Anmerkungen zum Volksstück nach Nestroy's Tod: Kaiser, Anzengruber und Morre." *Die andere Welt: Aspekte der Österreichischen Literatur des 19. und 20. Jahrhunderts. Festschrift für Hellmuth Himmel.* Ed. Kurt Barsch et al. Bonn: Francke Verlag, 1979. 133-46.

Weber, Fritz. *Anzengrubers Naturalismus.* Berlin: Ebering, 1929.

Yates,W. Edgar. "Nestroysche Stilelemente bei Anzengruber: Ein Beitrag zur Wirkungsgeschichte der Possen Nestroys." *Maske und Kothurn* 14 (1968): 287–96.

V. Thoma

Dewitz, Jean. *Ludwig Thoma et le théâtre populaire.* Bern/ Frankfurt/M./ New York: Peter Lang, 1985.

Fenzel, Fritz. "Ludwig Thoma: Ein bayrischer Dichter der Jahrhundertwende." Diss. Munich 1983.

Gierl, Irmgard. *Raritäten aus Schmellers Bayrischem Wörterbuch.* Rosenheim: Rosenheimer Verlagshaus, 1974.

Jones, Calvin N. "Ludwig Thoma's *Magdalena*: A Transitional Volksstück." *Seminar* 16 (1980): 83–95.

——————. "Tradition and Innovation: The *Volksstücke* of Ludwig Thoma." Diss. U of North Carolina at Chapel Hill, 1976.

Kaiser, Joachim. "Leni hatte keine Chance." *Süddeutsche Zeitung* 15/16 July 1978: 16.

Kaufmann, Hans and Silvia Schlenstedt, ed. *Geschichte der deutschen Literatur: Vom Anfang des 19. Jahrhunderts bis 1917.* Vol. 9 of *Geschichte der deutschen Literatur: Vom Anfang bis zur Gegenwart.* Berlin (GDR): Volk und Wissen, 1974. 12 vols. 1963–83.

Kerr, Alfred. *Gesammelte Schriften.* 3 vols. Berlin: Fischer, 1917.

Kluge, Manfred and Rudolf Radler, ed. *Hauptwerke der deutschen Literatur.* Munich: Kindler, 1974.

Ronde, Gertrud. "Die Mundart im Werke Ludwig Thomas." *Schöne Heimat: Erbe und Gegenwart* 56 (1967): 61–67.

Schultes, Bertl. *Ein Komödiant blickt zurück: Erinnerungen an Ludwig Thoma, das Bauerntheater und deren Freunde.* Munich: Feder, 1963.

Sengle, Friedrich. "Wunschbild Land und Schreckbild Stadt: Zu einem zentralen Thema der neueren deutschen Literatur." *Studium Generale* 16 (1963): 619–31.

Stark, Anna. "Die Bauern bei Ludwig Thoma mit besonderer Berücksichtigung der Dachauer Bauern." Diss. Munich 1938.

Thoma, Ludwig. *Ausgewählte Briefe.* Ed. Josef Hofmiller and Michael Hochgesang. Munich: Albert Langen, 1927.

_____. *Gesammelte Werke.* 8 vols. Munich: Piper, 1956.

_____. *Ein Leben in Briefen: 1875–1921.* Ed. Anton Keller. Munich: Piper, 1963.

_____. *Theater.* Sämtliche Bühnenstücke. Munich: Piper, 1964.

_____. "Theater- und Literaturbrief II." *Der Sammler: Belletristische Beilage zur Augsburger Abendzeitung.* 6 Sept. 1900: 6–7.

VI. Fleißer

Benjamin, Walter. "Echt Ingolstädter Originalnovellen." *Gesammelte Schriften.* Vol. 3. 189–91.

Buck, Theo. "Dem Kleinbürger aufs Maul geschaut: Zur gestischen Sprache der Marieluise Fleißer." *Text + Kritik* 64 (1979): 35–53.

Cocalis, Susan L. "The Politics of Brutality: Toward a Definition of the Volksstück." *Modern Drama* 24 (1981): 292–313.

_____. "'Weib ist Weib': Mimetische Darstellungen contra emanzipatorische Tendenz in den Dramen Marieluise Fleißers." *Die Frau als Heldin und Autorin: Neue kritische Ansätze zur deutschen Literatur.* 10. Amherster Kolloquium zur deutschen Literatur, 1977. Ed. Wolfgang Paulsen. Bern: Francke, 1977. 201–10.

_____. "Weib ohne Wirklichkeit, Welt ohne Weiblichkeit: zum Selbst-, Frauen- und Gesellschaftsbild im Frühwerk Marieluise Fleißers." *Entwürfe von Frauen in der Literatur des 20. Jahrhunderts.* Ed. Irmela von der Lühe. Berlin: Argument, 1982. 64–85.

Fleißer, Marieluise. *Gesammelte Werke.* 3 vols. Frankfurt/Main: Suhrkamp, 1983.

Jones, Calvin N. "Past Idyll or Future Utopia: *Heimat* in German Lyric Poetry of the 1930s and 1940s." *German Studies Review* 8 (1985): 281–98.

Kässens, Wend and Michael Töteberg. *Marieluise Fleißer.* Munich: Deutscher Taschenbuch Verlag, 1979.

Kraft, Friedrich, ed. *Marieluise Fleißer. Anmerkungen, Texte, Dokumente.* Mit Beitr. von Eva Pfister und Günther Rühle. Ingolstadt: Donau Kurier, 1981.

Kroetz, Franz Xaver. "Liegt die Dummheit auf der Hand?" *Pioniere in Ingolstadt —
Überlegungen zu einem Stück von Marieluise Fleißer." Weitere Aussichten.* 523-28.

Lutz, Günther. *Marieluise Fleißer. Verdichtetes Leben.* Dachau: Obalski & Astor, 1989.

——————. *Die Stellung Marieluise Fleißers in der bayerischen Literatur des 20.
Jahrhunderts.* Frankfurt/Bern/Cirencester: Peter Lang, 1979.

McGowan, Moray. "Kette und Schuß: Zur Dramatik der Marieluise Fleißer." *Text +
Kritik* 64 (1979): 11-34.

——————. *Marieluise Fleißer.* Munich: Beck, 1987.

Petrey, Sandy. "Castration, Speech Acts, and the Realist Difference: *S/Z* versus
Sarrasine. PMLA 102 (1987): 153-65.

Rotermund, Erwin. "Zur Erneuerung des Volksstückes in der Weimarer Republik." *Über
Ödön von Horváth*, ed. Dieter Hildebrandt and Traugott Krischke. 18-45.

Roumois-Hasler, Ursula. *Dramatischer Dialog und Alltagsdialog im wissenschaftlichen
Vergleich. Die Struktur der dialogishen Rede bei den Dramatikerinnen Marieluise
Fleißer ("Fegefeuer in Ingolstadt") und Else Lasker-Schüler ("Die Wupper").*
Bern/Frankfurt a.M.: Peter Lang, 1982.

Rühle, Günther. "Die andere Seite von Ingolstadt. Wirkung und Umfang des Fleißerschen Werks." *Marieluise Fleißer. Anmerkungen, Texte, Dokumente.* Ed. Friedrich
Kraft. 53-68.

——————. "Leben und Schreiben der Marieluise Fleißer aus Ingolstadt."
Marieluise Fleißer, *Gesammelte Werke.* Vol. 1. 5-60.

——————, ed. *Materialien zum Leben und Schreiben der Marieluise Fleißer.*
Frankfurt: Suhrkamp, 1973.

VII. Horváth

Arntzen, Helmut. "Ödön von Horváth, Geschichten aus dem Wiener Wald." *Die
deutsche Komödie.* Ed. Walter Hinck. Düsseldorf: Bagel, 1977. 246-68.

Bance, Alan. "Ödön von Horváth: *Kasimir und Karoline. Austrian Life and Letters
1780–1938.* Ed. Peter Branscombe. Edinburgh: Scottish Academic Press, 1978.
81-93.

_____. "Ödön von Horváth: Sex, Politics and Sexual Politics." *German Life and Letters* 38 (1984–85): 249–59.

Bartsch, Kurt. "Scheitern im Gespräch." *Horváth Diskussion*. Ed. Kurt Bartsch et al. 38–54.

Bartsch, Kurt, Uwe Baur and Dietmar Goltschnigg, ed. *Horváth Diskussion*. Kronberg/-Ts.: Scriptor, 1976.

Best, Alan. "Ödön von Horváth: The Volksstück Revived." *Modern Austrian Writing: Literature and Society after 1945*. Ed. Alan Best and Hans Wolfschütz. London: Oswald Wolff, 1980. 108–27.

Bruns, Dirk. "Horváth's Renewal of the Folk Play and the Decline of the Weimar Republic." *New German Critique* 18 (1979): 136–50.

Buck, Theo. "Die Stille auf der Bühne: Zum dramaturgischen Verfahren in den Volksstücken Ödön von Horváths." *Recherches Germaniques* 9 (1979): 174–85.

Carl, Rolf-Peter. "Theatertheorie und Volksstück bei Ödön von Horváth." *Theater und Gesellschaft*. Ed. Jürgen Hein. 175–85.

Doppler, Alfred. "Bemerkungen zur dramatischen Form der Volksstücke Horváths." *Horváth Diskussion*. Ed. Kurt Bartsch et al. 11–21.

_____. "Ödön von Horváth: 'Geschichten aus dem Wiener Wald.'" *Das österreichische Volksstück*. Institut für Österreichkunde. Vienna: Ferdinand Hirth, 1971. 77–92.

Erken, Günther. "Ödön von Horváth: Geschichten aus dem Wiener Wald." *Von Lessing bis Kroetz. Einführung in die Dramenanalyse*. Ed. Jan Berg et al. Kronberg/TS: Scriptor: 1975. 138–79.

François, Jean-Claude. *Histoire et fiction dans le théâtre d'Ödön von Horváth*. Grenoble: Presses Universitaires, 1978.

Fritz, Axel. *Ödön von Horváth als Kritiker seiner Zeit. Studien zum Werk und seinem Verhalten zum politischen, sozialen, und kulturellen Zeitgeschehen*. Munich: List, 1973.

Gamper, Herbert. "Horváth und die Folgen — Das Volksstück?" *Theater heute* (1971): 73–77.

Handke, Peter. "Persönliches Postscriptum." *Materialien zu Ödön von Horváth*. Ed. Traugott Krischke. 179–80.

Hein, Jürgen. "Ödön von Horváth: Kasimir und Karoline." *Deutsche Dramen: Interpretationen zu Werken von der Aufklärung bis zur Gegenwart*. Ed. Harro Müller-Michaels. Vol. 2. Königstein: Athenäum, 1981. 42–67. 2 vols.

Hildebrandt, Dieter. "Der Jargon der Uneigentlichkeit. Notizen zur Sprachstruktur Horváths 'Geschichten aus dem Wiener Wald.'" *Materialien zu Ödön von Horváth*. Ed. Traugott Krischke. 231–45.

Hildebrandt, Dieter und Traugott Krischke, ed. *Über Ödön von Horváth*. Frankfurt: Suhrkamp, 1972.

Hillach, Ansgar. Review of Ödön von Horváth, *Gesammelte Werke* (Frankfurt/Main: Suhrkamp, 1970–71). *Germanistik* 12 (1971): 620–21.

——————————. "Das Volksstück als Kosmologie der Gewalt. Psychologie und Marxismus in Ödön von Horváth's 'Revolte auf Cote 3015.'" *Germanisch-Romanische Monatsschrift* N.F. 24 (1974): 223–43.

Himmel, Hellmuth. "Ödön von Horváth und die Volksstücktradition." *Ödön von Horváth*. Ed. Traugott Krischke. 46–56.

Hinck, Walter. *Das moderne Drama in Deutschland*. Göttingen: Vandenhoek & Rupprecht, 1973.

Horváth, Ödön von. *Kasimir und Karoline. Gesammelte Werke*. Vol. 5. Frankfurt/Main: Suhrkamp, 1986. 15 vols. 1986– .

——————————. *Gesammelte Werke*. werkausgabe edition suhrkamp. 8 vols. Frankfurt/Main: Suhrkamp, 1978.

Huder, Walther. *Inflation und Lebensform. Ödön von Horváths Kritik am Spießertum. Ein Querschnitt durch das Gesamtwerk*. Gütersloh: Sonderdruck, 1972.

Hummel, Reinhard. *Die Volksstücke Ödön von Horváths*. Baden-Baden: Hertel, 1970.

Jarka, Horst. "Ödön von Horváth und das Kitschige." *Zeitschrift für deutsche Philologie* 91 (1972): 558–85.

Jenny, Urs. "Horváth realistisch, Horváth metaphysisch." *Akzente* 18 (1971): 289–95.

_____. "Ödön von Horváths Größe und Grenzen." *Über Ödön von Horváth*. Ed. Dieter Hildebrandt and Traugott Krischke. 71–78.

Joas, Hans. "Kasimir und Karoline." *Österreich in Geschichte und Literatur* 15 (1971): 337–46.

Jörder, Gerhard. "Partnerwechsel auf dem Oktoberfest." *Badische Zeitung* 17 February 1986: 14.

Karasek, Hellmuth. "Die Erneuerung des Volksstücks: Auf den Spuren Marieluise Fleißers und Ödön von Horváths." *Positionen des Dramas*. Ed. Heinz Ludwig Arnold and Theo Buck. 137–69.

_____. "Kasimir und Karoline." *Materialien zu Ödön von Horváths "Kasimir und Karoline"*. Ed. Traugott Krischke. 63–76.

Kienzle, Siegfried. *Ödön von Horváth*. Berlin: Colloquium Verlag, 1977.

Krischke, Traugott, ed. *Horváth auf der Bühne 1926–1938. Dokumentation*. Vienna: Edition S, Verlag der Österreichischen Staatsdrückerei, 1991.

_____. *Materialien zu Ödön von Horváth*. Frankfurt/Main: Suhrkamp, 1970.

_____. *Materialien zu Ödön von Horváth's "Geschichten aus dem Wiener Wald"*. Frankfurt/Main: Suhrkamp, 1972.

_____. *Materialien zu Ödön von Horváths "Kasimir und Karoline"*. Frankfurt/Main: Suhrkamp, 1973.

_____. *Ödön von Horváth*. Frankfurt/Main: Suhrkamp, 1981.

Kroetz, Franz Xaver. "Horváth von heute für heute." *Über Ödön von Horváth*. Ed. Dieter Hildebrandt and Traugott Krischke. 91–95.

Kurzenberger, Hajo. *Horváths Volksstücke. Beschreibung eines poetischen Verfahrens*. Munich: Fink, 1974.

_____. "Negativ-Dramatik, Positiv-Dramatik." *Text + Kritik* 57 (1978): 8–19.

Mayer, Hans. "Beethoven und das Prinzip der Hoffnung." *Versuche über die Oper*. Frankfurt/Main: Suhrkamp, 1981. 71–89.

Neikirk, Joan Cantwell. "The Role of the Woman in the Works of Ödön von Horváth."
DAI (31.12) 1971, 6622-A.

Nolting, Winfried. *Der totale Jargon. Die dramatischen Beispiele Ödön von Horváths.*
Munich: Fink, 1976.

Pichler, Meinrad. "Von Aufsteigern und Deklassierten: Ödön von Horváths literarischen
Analyse des Kleinbürgertums und ihr Verhältnis zu den Aussagen der historischen
Sozialwissenschaften." *Österreichischer Literatur seit den 20er Jahren: Beiträge zu
ihrer historisch- politischen Lokalisierung.* Schriften des Instituts für Österreichkunde.
Ed. Friedbert Aspetsberger. Vienna: Österreichischer Bundesverlag, 1979. 55–67.

Reich-Ranicki, Marcel. "Horváth, Gott und die Frauen. Die Etablierung eines neuen
Klassikers der Moderne." *Über Ödön von Horváth.* Ed. Dieter Hildebrandt and
Traugott Krischke. 83–90.

Reinhardt, Hartmut. "Die Lüge des 'Prinzipiellen.' Zur Begrenzung der Kompetenz von
Kritik in Horváth's Stücken." *Deutsche Vierteljahrsschrift für Literaturwissenschaft
und Geistesgeschichte* 49 (1975): 332–55.

Schmid, Christof. "Neue 'Geschichten aus dem Wiener Wald'— oder: Was ist ein neuer
Horváth?" *Materialien zu Ödön von Horváths "Geschichten aus dem Wiener Wald."*
Ed. Traugott Krischke. 246–54.

Schneider, Hansjörg. "Der Kampf zwischen Individuum und Gesellschaft." *Über Ödön
von Horváth.* Ed. Dieter Hildebrandt and Traugott Krischke. 59–70.

Schulte, Birgit. *Ödön von Horváth, verschwiegen - gefeiert - glattgelobt: Analyse eines
ungewöhnlichen Rezeptionsverlaufs.* Bonn: Bouvier, 1980.

Wapnewski, Peter. "Ödön von Horváth und seine 'Geschichten aus dem Wiener Wald.'"
Materialien zu Ödön von Horváths "Geschichten aus dem Wiener Wald". Ed.
Traugott Krischke. 10–43.

Wiese, Benno von. "Ödön von Horváth." *Ödön von Horváth.* Ed. Traugott Krischke.
7–45.

VIII. Brecht

Brecht, Bertolt. *Arbeitsjournal.* Ed. Werner Hecht. Frankfurt/Main: Suhrkamp, 1973.
2 vols.

_____. *Gesammelte Werke.* 20 vols. Frankfurt/Main: Suhrkamp, 1967.

Deschner, Margareta N. "Wuolijoki's and Brecht's Politicization of the Volksstück."
Bertolt Brecht: Political Theory and Literary Practice. Ed. Betty Nance Weber and
Hubert Heinen. 115–28.

Dickson, Keith. *Towards Utopia. A Study of Brecht.* Oxford: Clarendon Press, 1978.

Fetscher, Iring. "Bertolt Brecht and Politics." Trans. Betty Nance Weber. Foreword.
Bertolt Brecht: Political Theory and Literary Practice. Ed. Betty Nance Weber and
Hubert Heinen. 11–17.

Gaede, Friedrich. *Realismus von Brant bis Brecht.* Uni- Taschenbücher 171. Munich:
Francke, 1972.

Hermand, Jost. "Herr Puntila und sein Knecht Matti. Brechts Volksstück." *Brecht heute.
Brecht Today* 1 (1971): 117–36.

_____. "Zwischen Tuismus und Tümlichkeit. Brechts Konzept eines
'klassischen' Stils." *Brecht Jahrbuch* (1975): 9–34.

Hinck, Walter. *Dramaturgie des späten Brecht.* Göttingen: Vandenhoek & Rupprecht,
1971.

_____. "'Mutter Courage und ihre Kinder:" ein kritisches Volksstück." *Brechts
Dramen. Neue Interpretationen.* Ed. Walter Hinderer. Stuttgart: Reclam, 1984.
162–77.

Knopf, Jan. *Brecht Handbuch. Theater.* Stuttgart: Metzler, 1980.

Ley, Ralph. *Brecht as Thinker.* Normal, Ill.: Applied Literature Press, 1979.

Martini, Fritz. *Lustspiele und das Lustspiel.* Stuttgart: Klett, 1974.

McGowan, Moray. "Comedy and the Volksstück." *Brecht in Perspective.* Ed. Graham
Bartram and Anthony Waine. London and New York: Longman, 1982. 63–82.

Mews, Siegfried. *Bertolt Brecht. Herr Puntila und sein Knecht Matti. Grundlagen und
Gedanken zum Verständnis des Dramas.* Frankfurt/Main: Diesterweg, 1985.

Müller, Klaus-Detlef. *Bertolt Brecht. Epoche—Werk—Wirkung.* Munich: Beck, 1985.
Nägele, Rainer. "Brecht und das politische Theater." Literatur nach 1945. Ed. Jost
Hermand. Vol. 1. Wiesbaden: Athenaion, 1979. 117–56. 2 vols.

Neureuter, Hans-Peter, ed. *Brechts "Herr Puntila und sein Knecht Matti."* Frankfurt
a.M.: Suhrkamp, 1987.

Poser, Hans. "Brechts Herr Puntila und sein Knecht Matti: Dialektik zwischen Volksstück und Lehrstück." *Theater und Gesellschaft*. Ed. Jürgen Hein. 187–200.

Ralinofsky, Dagmar. "Theater und Kritik — Theaterkritik?" *Die Horen* 18.4 (1973): 69–74.

Schumacher, Ernst. *Die dramatischen Versuche Bertolt Brechts 1918–33*. Berlin: Rütten & Loening, 1955.

Semrau, Richard. *Die Komik des Puntila*. Berlin (GDR): Brecht Zentrum der DDR, 1981.

Slobodkin, G. S. "Nestroy und die Tradition des Volkstheaters im Schaffen Brechts." *Weimarer Beiträge* 24 (1978): 99–117.

Sokel, Walter. "Brecht's Split Characters and His Sense of the Tragic." *Brecht. A Collection of Essays*. Ed. Peter Demetz. Englewood Cliffs: Prentice Hall, 1962. 127–37.

Speidel, Erich. "Brecht's 'Puntila': A Marxist Comedy." *Modern Language Review* 65 (1970): 19–32.

Tatlow, Anthony. "Critical Dialectics." *Bertolt Brecht: Political Theory and Literary Practice*. Ed. Betty Nance Weber and Hubert Heinen. 21–28.

Volckmann, Silvia. "Brechts Theater zwischen Abbild und Utopie." *Handbuch des deutschen Dramas*. Ed. Walter Hinck. Düsseldorf: Bagel, 1980. 440–52.

Weber, Betty Nance and Hubert Heinen, eds. *Bertolt Brecht: Political Theory and Literary Practice*. Athens, GA: U of Georgia P, 1980.

White, Alfred D. "Plot and Narrative Elements in Brecht's Herr Puntila und sein Knecht Matti." *Modern Language Review* 76.4 (1981): 880–88.

Wiese, Benno von. *Zwischen Utopie und Wirklichkeit*. Düsseldorf: Bagel, 1963.

IX. Kroetz

Arnold, Heinz Ludwig. "'Der lebende Mensch ist der Mittelpunkt': Gespräch mit Franz Xaver Kroetz." *Als Schriftsteller leben: Gespräche mit Peter Handke, Franz Xaver Kroetz, Gerhard Zwerenz, Walter Jens, Peter Ruhmkorf, Günter Grass*. Hamburg: Rowohlt, 1979.

"Auf der Couch." [Television program featuring Franz Xaver Kroetz.] ARD. Broadcast 21 May 1992.

Blevins, Richard Wayne. *Franz Xaver Kroetz: The Emergence of a Political Playwright*. New York, Bern, Frankfurt/Main: Peter Lang, 1983.

Buddecke, Wolfram and Helmut Fuhrmann. *Das deutschsprachige Drama seit 1945*. Munich: Winkler, 1981.

Burger, Harald und Peter von Matt. "Dramatischer Dialog und restringiertes Sprechen. F.X. Kroetz in linguistischer und wissenschaftlicher Sicht." *Zeitschrift für germanistische Linguistik* (1974): 269–98.

Calandra, Denis. *New German Dramatists*. New York: Grove, 1983.

Carl, Rolf-Peter. *Franz Xaver Kroetz*. Munich: Beck, 1978.

───────────. "Zur Theatertheorie des Stückeschreibers Franz Xaver Kroetz." *Text + Kritik* 57 (1978): 1–7.

Cocalis, Susan L. "'Mitleid' and 'Engagement': Compassion and/or Political Commitment in the Works of Franz Xaver Kroetz." *Colloquia Germanica* 14.3 (1981): 203–19.

Fleißer, Marieluise. "Franz Xaver Kroetz." *Franz Xaver Kroetz*. Ed. Otto Riewoldt. 85–86.

Hein, Jürgen. *Franz Xaver Kroetz: "Oberösterreich" — "Mensch Meier"*. Frankfurt/Main: Diesterweg, 1986.

Heising, Ulrich. "Der radikale Realismus von Kroetz." *Franz Xaver Kroetz*. Ed. Otto Riewoldt. 201–12.

Herbort, Heinz Josef. "Utopie von einer anderen Oper." *Die Zeit*, North American edition (17 June 1988): 18.

Hess-Lüttich, Ernst W.B. "Neo-Realismus und sprachliche Wirklichkeit. Zur Kommunikationskritik bei Franz Xaver Kroetz." *Franz Xaver Kroetz*. Ed. Otto Riewoldt. 297–318.

Hoffmeister, Donna L. "'Zamhalten muss man dann': Reassurance Displays in Franz Xaver Kroetz' *Oberösterreich*." *German Quarterly* 54 (1981): 447–60.

Illustriertes Lexikon der deutschen Umgangssprache. Stuttgart: Klett, 1982. 8 vols.

Kafitz, Dieter. "Die Problematisierung des individualistischen Menschenbildes im deutschsprachigen Drama der Gegenwart (Franz Xaver Kroetz, Thomas Bernhard,

Botho Strauss)." *Basis: Jahrbuch für deutsche Gegenwartsliteratur* 10 (1980): 93–126.

Karasek, Hellmuth. "Die Sprache der Sprachlosen. Über das Volksstück, insbesondere die Stücke von Kroetz." *Franz Xaver Kroetz.* Ed. Otto Riewoldt. 76–82.

Kässens, Wend. "Wer durchs Laub geht, kommt darin um. Zur Sprachbehandlung und zu einigen Motiven in den Dramen von Franz Xaver Kroetz." *Franz Xaver Kroetz.* Ed. Otto Riewoldt. 262–83.

Kässens, Wend and Michael Toteberg. "Fortschritt im Realismus? Zur Erneuerung des kritischen Volksstücks seit 1966." *Basis: Jahrbuch für deutsche Gegenwartsliteratur* 6 (1976): 30–47.

Kroetz, Franz Xaver. "Dramatiker Umfrage." [Replies to questionnaire]. *Theater heute* Sonderheft (1972): 64–65.

——————————. "Form ist der Teller, von dem man ißt." *Franz Xaver Kroetz.* Ed. Otto Riewoldt. 88–92.

——————————. "Ich habe immer nur von mir geschrieben. Dem Volk hab' ich nie aufs Maul geschaut." Interview. *Theater 1985. Jahrbuch der Zeitschrift Theater heute* (1985): 72–87.

——————————. "Die Lust am Lebendigen." Discussion with the editors of *kürbiskern. Weitere Aussichten.* 324-35.

——————————. *Nicht Fisch nicht Fleisch. Verfassungsfeinde. Jumbo-Track.* Frankfurt/Main: Suhrkamp, 1981.

——————————. "Die Schwierigkeiten des einfachen Mannes." *Weitere Aussichten.* 605–608.

——————————. "Soll der Kumpel Abonnent werden?" *Weitere Aussichten.* 541–47.

——————————. "Die Sprache meiner Figuren." *Franz Xaver Kroetz.* Ed. Otto Riewoldt. 63–65.

——————————. *Stallerhof. Geisterbahn. Lieber Fritz. Wunschkonzert.* Frankfurt/Main: Suhrkamp, 1973.

——————————. "Über die Maßnahme von Bertolt Brecht." *Weitere Aussichten.* 570–82.

_____. *Weitere Aussichten. Ein Lesebuch.* Köln: Kiepenheuer & Witsch, 1976.

_____. "Wenn das Theater Machtverhältnisse zeigt, ohne Menschen zu zeigen, ist es für mich uninteressant." Interview with Manfred Bosch. *Die Horen* 18.4 (1973): 75–79.

_____. "Zu Bertolt Brechts 20. Todestag." *Positionen des Dramas.* Ed. Heinz Ludwig Arnold and Theo Buck. 245–58.

Merschmeier, Michael. "Deutsches Leben — kein Leben. Franz Xaver Kroetz inszeniert sein neues Stück 'Der Nusser' am Münchner Residenztheater. *Theater heute* 5 (1986): 38–41.

Michaelis, Rolf. "Phantastisches Zeitstück. Der neue Kroetz in Düsseldorf." *Die Zeit,* North American edition (12 June 1981).

_____. "Traumspiel und Wirklichkeit. Peter Stein und Volker Hesse inszenieren *Nicht Fisch nicht Fleisch.*" *Die Zeit,* North American edition (19 June 1981): 17.

Motekat, Helmut. "Das 'neue Volksstück'." *Das zeitgenössische deutsche Drama.* Stuttgart: Kohlhammer, 1977. 106–28.

Panzer, Evalouise. *Franz Xaver Kroetz und seine Rezeption: Die Intentionen eines Stückeschreibers und seine Aufnahme durch die Kritik.* Stuttgart: Klett, 1976.

Panzer, Volker. "Franz Xaver Kroetz und die Kritiker." *Text + Kritik* 57 (1978): 49–56.

Petersen, Jürgen H. "Franz Xaver Kroetz: Von der Tragödie der Unfreiheit zum Lehrstück für Werktätige." *Amsterdamer Beiträge zur Neueren Germanistik* 16 (1983): 291–312.

Reinhold, Ursula. "Franz Xaver Kroetz: Dramenaufbau und Wirkungsabsicht." *Weimarer Beiträge* 22.5 (1976): 60–79. (Also in *Franz Xaver Kroetz.* Ed. Otto F. Riewoldt, 229–51).

_____. "Interview mit Franz Xaver Kroetz." *Weimarer Beiträge* 22.5 (1976): 46–59.

Riewoldt, Otto, ed. *Franz Xaver Kroetz.* [FXK]. Frankfurt/Main: Suhrkamp, 1985.

_____. "Der ganze Kroetz." *Franz Xaver Kroetz.* 9–19.

Rischbieter, Henning. "Vom Druck auf den Durchschnitt und vom Drang, auszubrechen. *Nicht Fisch nicht Fleisch* von Franz Xaver Kroetz in Berlin und Düsseldorf." *Theater heute* 7 (1981): 1–5.

Sauerland, Karol. "Kroetz und Brecht." *Text + Kritik* 57 (1978): 35–36.

Schaarschmidt, Peter. "Das moderne Volksstück. Sprache und Figuren." *Theater und Gesellschaft.* Ed. Jürgen Hein. 201–18.

Schödel, Hellmut. "Bethlehem in Bayern." *Die Zeit,* North American edition (2 January 1987): 18.

Schregel, Ursula. *Neue deutsche Stücke im Spielplan am Beispiel von Franz Xaver Kroetz.* Berlin: Volker Spiess, 1980.

Töteberg, Michael. "Der Kleinbürger auf der Bühne: Die Entwicklung des Dramatikers Franz Xaver Kroetz und das realistische Volksstück." *Akzente* 23 (1976): 165–73.

——————————. "Ein konservativer Autor. Familie, Kind, Technikfeindlichkeit, Heimat: traditionsgebundene Werte in den Dramen von Franz Xaver Kroetz." *Franz Xaver Kroetz.* Ed. Otto Riewoldt. 284–96.

Walser, Martin. "Bericht über eine Aufführung." *Franz Xaver Kroetz.* Ed. Otto Riewoldt. 224–26.

Walther, Ingeborg C. *The Theater of Franz Xaver Kroetz.* New York/San Francisco: Peter Lang, 1990.

Wendt, Ernst. "Bürgerseelen und Randexistenzen. Über die Dramatiker Harold Pinter und Franz Xaver Kroetz." *Moderne Dramaturgie.* Frankfurt/Main: Suhrkamp, 1974. 91–117.

——————————. "Dramen über Zerstörung, Leiden, Sprachlosigkeiten im Alltag — auf der Flucht vor den großen politischen Stoffen?" *Theater heute* 5 (1971): 32–40.

INDEX